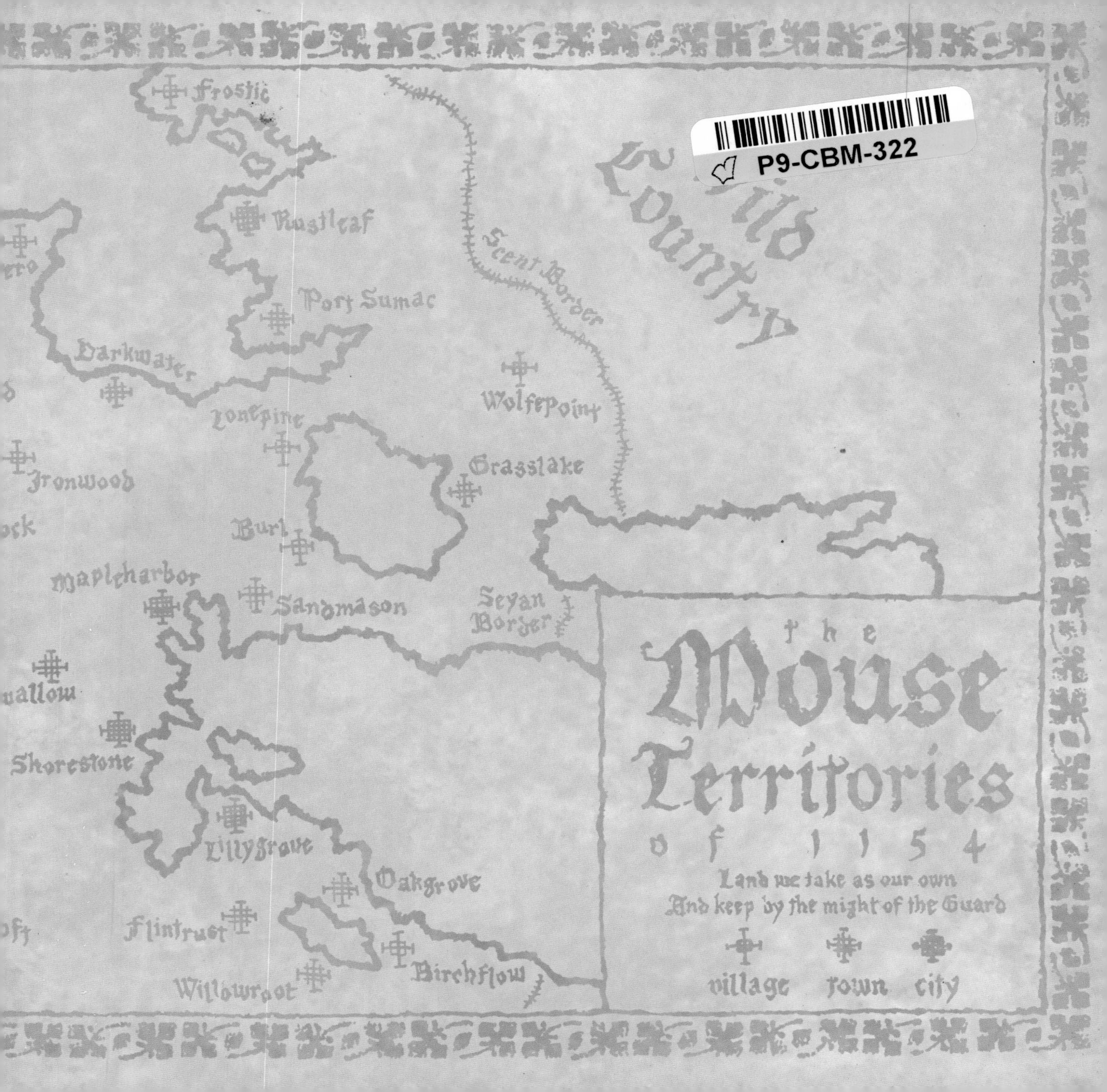
Frostic
Rustleaf
Port Sumac
Darkwater
Lonepine
Ironwood
Burl
Grasslake
Wolfepoint
Scent Border
Country
Mapleharbor
Sandmason
Seyan Border
Shorestone
Lillygrove
Oakgrove
Flintrust
Birchflow
Willowroot
the Mouse Territories of 1154
Land we take as our own
And keep by the might of the Guard
village
town
city

MOUSE GUARD:
LEGENDS
OF THE
GUARD™
VOLUME THREE

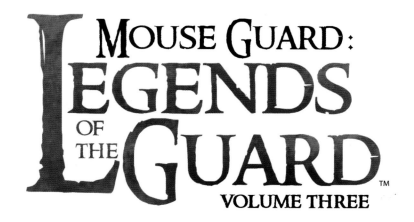

Published by
ARCHAIA™

FOR THE FANS OF MOUSE GUARD

SPECIAL THANKS TO:
MARK BUCKINGHAM, SKOTTIE YOUNG, HANNAH CHRISTENSON,
NICOLE GUSTAFSSON, C.M. GALDRE, DUSTIN NGUYEN, KYLA VANDERKLUGT,
MARK A. NELSON, JAKE PARKER, RAMÓN K. PÉREZ, BECKY CLOONAN, RYAN LANG,
FABIAN RANGEL JR., AARON CONLEY, LAUREN PETTAPIECE

Mouse Guard: Legends of the Guard

of the

Guard

VOLUME THREE

SCOTT NEWMAN, *DESIGNER*

CAMERON CHITTOCK, *ASSISTANT EDITOR*

REBECCA TAYLOR, *EDITOR*

BRYCE CARLSON, *EDITOR*

DAVID PETERSEN, *EDITOR*

MOUSE GUARD: LEGENDS OF THE GUARD Volume Three, November 2015. Published by Archaia, a division of Boom Entertainment, Inc., registered in various countries and categories. Mouse Guard is ™ & © 2015 David Petersen. Originally published in single magazine form as MOUSE GUARD: LEGENDS OF THE GUARD Volume Three No. 1-4. ™ and © 2015 David Petersen. All Rights Reserved. Archaia™ and the Archaia logo are trademarks of Boom Entertainment, Inc., registered in various countries and categories. All characters, events, and institutions depicted herein are fictional. Any similarity between any of the names, characters, persons, events, and/or institutions in this publication to actual names, characters, and persons, whether living or dead, events, and/or institutions is unintended and purely coincidental.

BOOM! Studios, 5670 Wilshire Boulevard, Suite 450, Los Angeles, CA 90036-5679. Printed in China. First Printing.

ISBN: 978-1-60886-767-7, eISBN: 978-1-61398-438-3

FOREWORD

WELCOME BACK TO THE JUNE ALLEY INN. THIS VOLUME MARKS THE THIRD TIME JUNE THE INNKEEP HAS WELCOMED PATRONS TO TELL TALL TALES IN AN ATTEMPT TO CLEAR THEIR PAST DUE BAR TAB. IN REALITY, THIS TAVERN SETUP IS REALLY JUST A FORMAT FOR ME TO ASK SOME OF THE FINEST VISUAL STORYTELLERS I KNOW TO CREATE A MOUSE GUARD FABLE. LIKE EVERY VOLUME OF LEGENDS OF THE GUARD SO FAR, I TRY TO MIX TOGETHER TALENTS WHOSE NAMES ARE WELL KNOWN WITH CREATORS I FEEL ARE UNDER APPRECIATED, AND THEN A FEW FOLKS WHO, WHILE SKILLED ARTISTS IN OTHER ARENAS, ARE DOING THEIR FIRST SEQUENTIAL WORK HERE IN THESE PAGES.

VOLUME THREE ALSO MARKED THE FIRST TIME ANY MOUSE GUARD ISSUES HAD VARIANT COVERS. LIKE WITH ALL MY PAST COVERS FOR LEGENDS OF THE GUARD, I WROTE ONE PARAGRAPH TALES TO ACCOMPANY THE VARIANT WORKS OF RAMÓN K. PÉREZ, ERIC MULLER, AND HUMBERTO RAMOS. FOR FANS UNABLE TO COLLECT ALL THE HARD TO FIND ISSUES, THOSE COVERS AND TALES, ALONG WITH MY OWN, ARE COLLECTED HERE IN THIS VOLUME.

SO, PULL UP A CHAIR TO THE HEARTH, POUR A TANKARD OF YOUR FAVORITE BEVERAGE, AND ENJOY WHAT ALL OF THESE WONDERFULLY TALENTED CONTRIBUTORS HAVE ADDED TO THE MOUSE GUARD TAPESTRY OF MYTH AND LEGEND. I AM THANKFUL TO ALL OF THEM FOR SHARING THEIR TIME AND SKILL. AND I AM THANKFUL FOR THE READERS AND FANS OF MOUSE GUARD WHO ENJOY THESE LEGENDS AS MUCH AS I DO.

DAVID PETERSEN
MICHIGAN 2015

Story and Contributor Index:

LEGEND COVER GALLERY & EXTRAS

On the Cover:

When clearing the territory surrounding the town of Cloverdale, a guardmouse came upon a clutch of snake eggs. All but one had been broken. The mouse carefully hatched the egg itself, with a plan to raise the offspring as his own mount for patrolling the cloverfields and ridding them of predators. And while this was famed to have briefly worked, somebeast's nature is rumored not to be swayed, and the guardmouse and town all fell victim to the scaled predator's fang.

Alley Inn

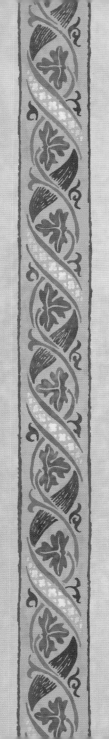

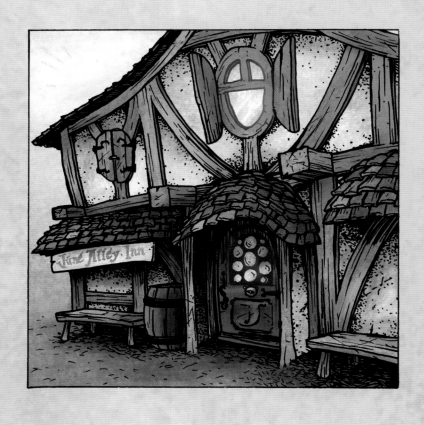

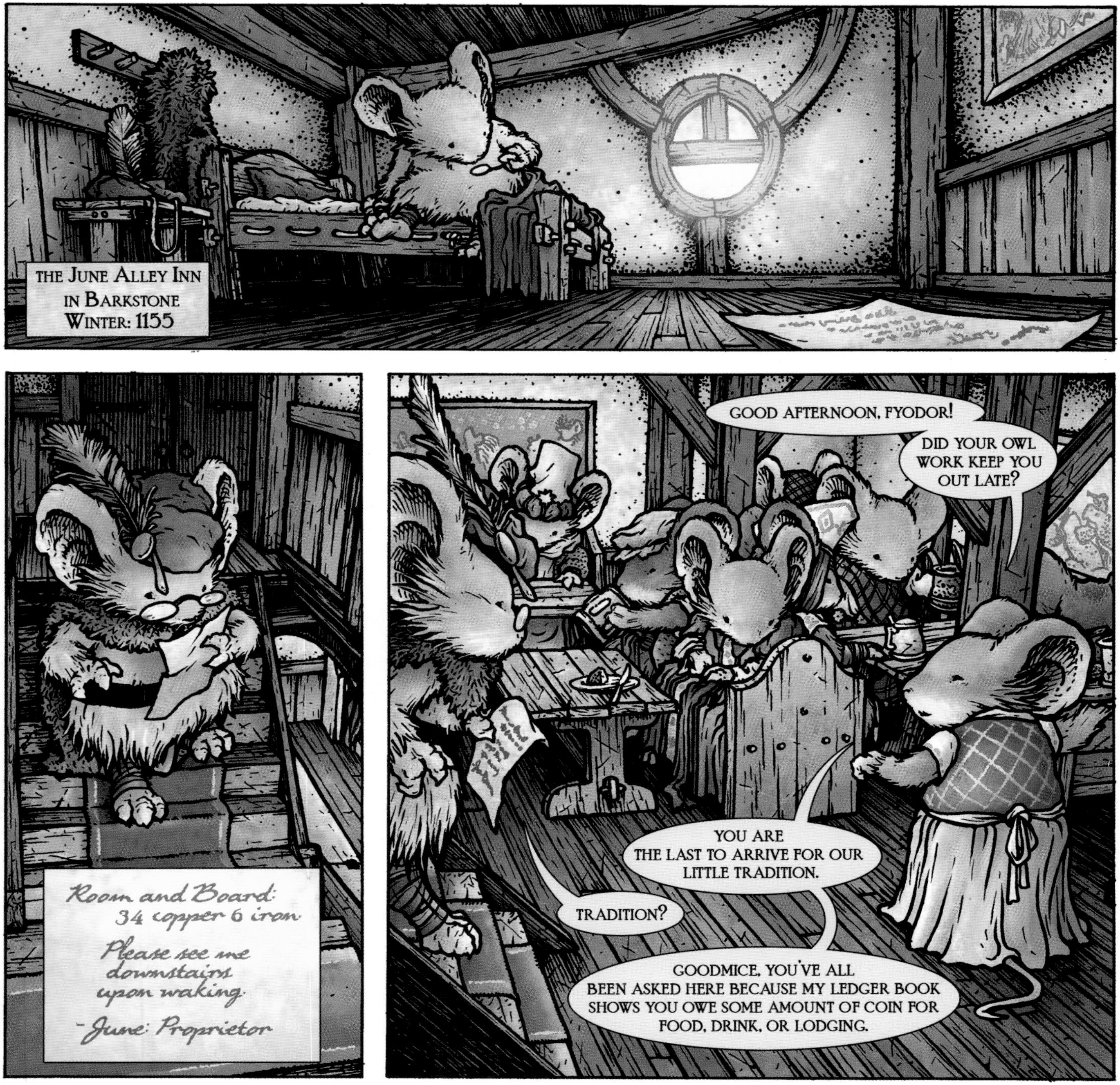

THE JUNE ALLEY INN IN BARKSTONE WINTER: 1155
Room and Board: 34 copper 6 iron
Please see me downstairs upon waking.
-June: Proprietor
GOOD AFTERNOON, FYODOR!
DID YOUR OWL WORK KEEP YOU OUT LATE?
YOU ARE THE LAST TO ARRIVE FOR OUR LITTLE TRADITION.
TRADITION?
GOODMICE, YOU'VE ALL BEEN ASKED HERE BECAUSE MY LEDGER BOOK SHOWS YOU OWE SOME AMOUNT OF COIN FOR FOOD, DRINK, OR LODGING.

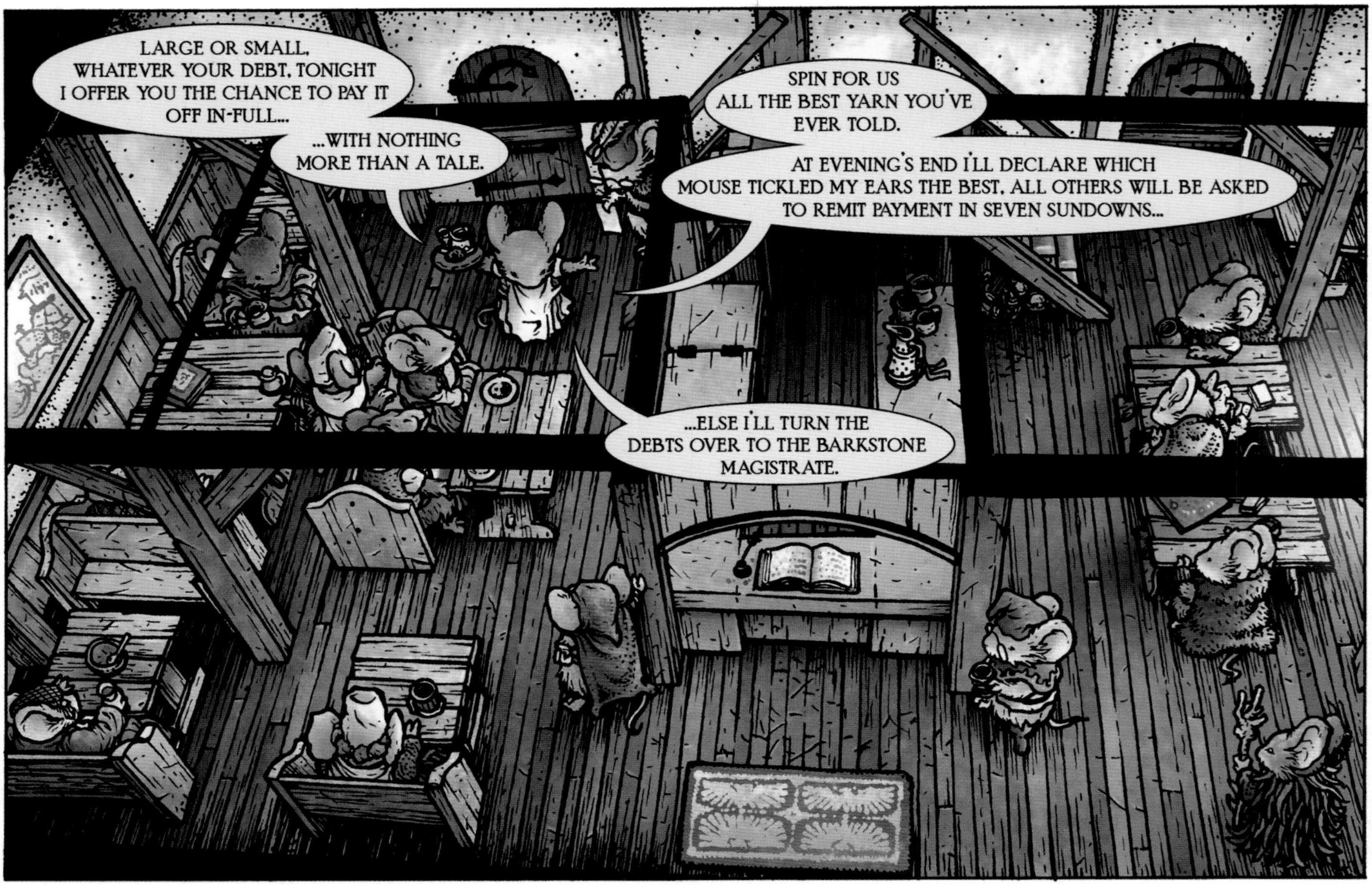
LARGE OR SMALL, WHATEVER YOUR DEBT, TONIGHT I OFFER YOU THE CHANCE TO PAY IT OFF IN-FULL...
...WITH NOTHING MORE THAN A TALE.
SPIN FOR US ALL THE BEST YARN YOU'VE EVER TOLD.
AT EVENING'S END I'LL DECLARE WHICH MOUSE TICKLED MY EARS THE BEST, ALL OTHERS WILL BE ASKED TO REMIT PAYMENT IN SEVEN SUNDOWNS...
...ELSE I'LL TURN THE DEBTS OVER TO THE BARKSTONE MAGISTRATE.

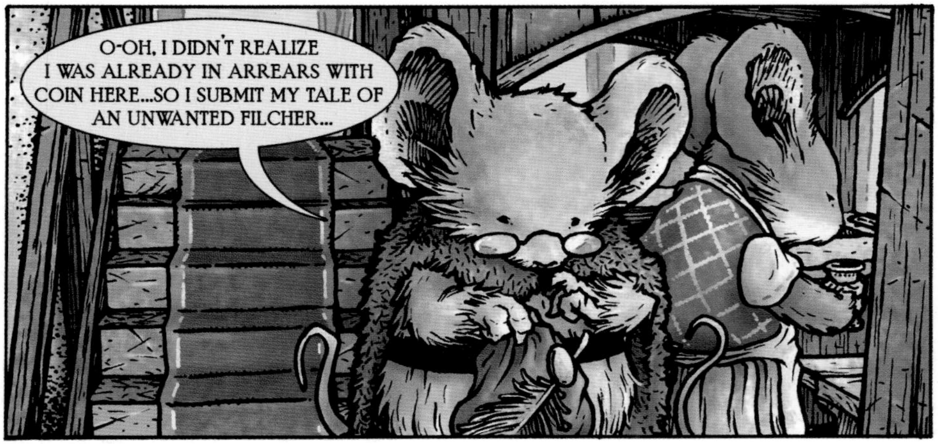
O-OH, I DIDN'T REALIZE I WAS ALREADY IN ARREARS WITH COIN HERE...SO I SUBMIT MY TALE OF AN UNWANTED FILCHER...

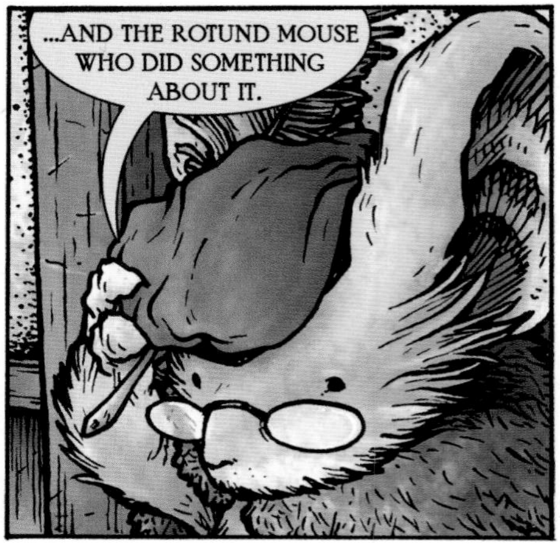
...AND THE ROTUND MOUSE WHO DID SOMETHING ABOUT IT.

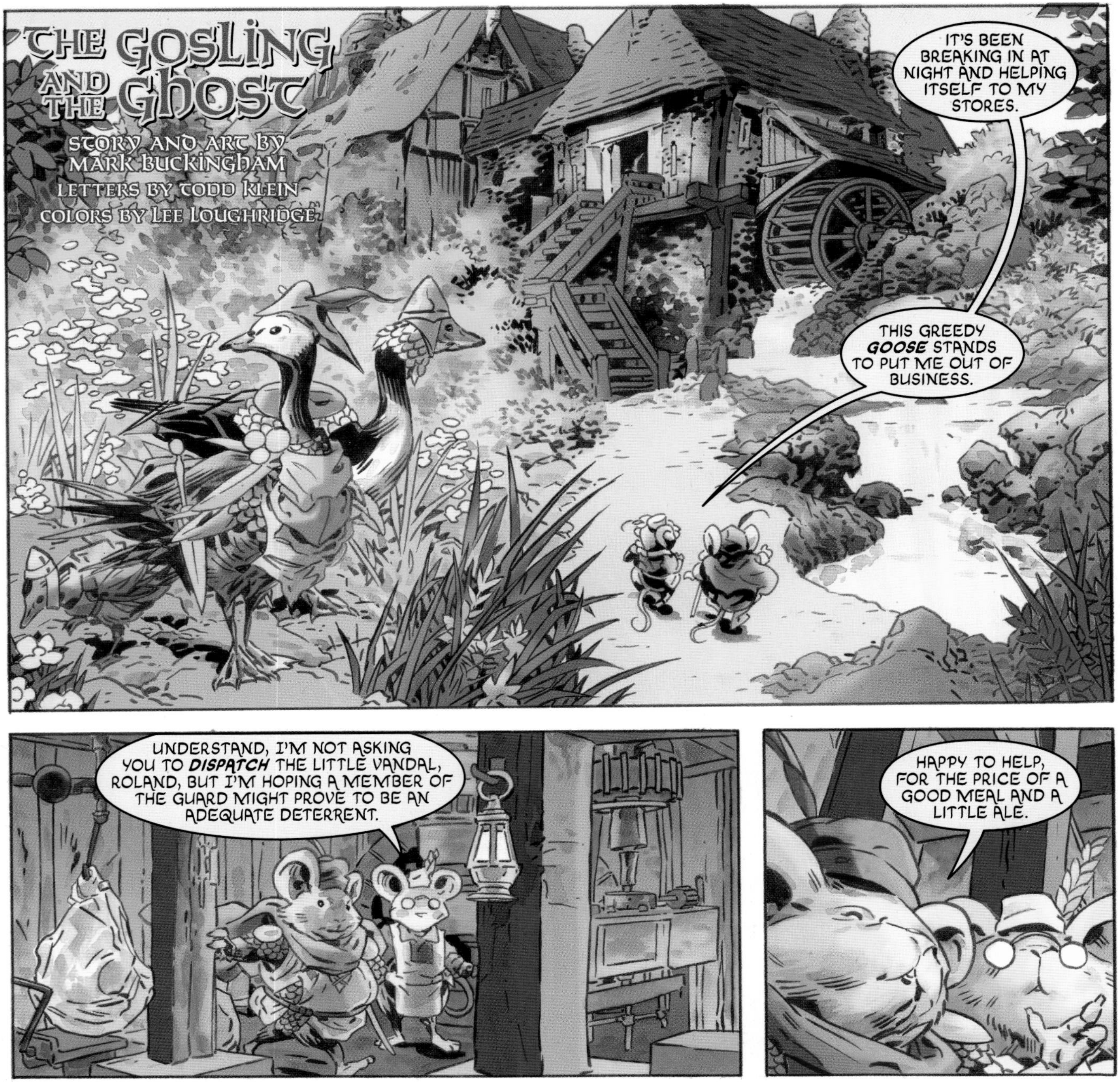
THE GOSLING AND THE GHOST
STORY AND ART BY MARK BUCKINGHAM
LETTERS BY TODD KLEIN
COLORS BY LEE LOUGHRIDGE
IT'S BEEN BREAKING IN AT NIGHT AND HELPING ITSELF TO MY STORES.
THIS GREEDY GOOSE STANDS TO PUT ME OUT OF BUSINESS.
UNDERSTAND, I'M NOT ASKING YOU TO DISPATCH THE LITTLE VANDAL, ROLAND, BUT I'M HOPING A MEMBER OF THE GUARD MIGHT PROVE TO BE AN ADEQUATE DETERRENT.
HAPPY TO HELP, FOR THE PRICE OF A GOOD MEAL AND A LITTLE ALE.

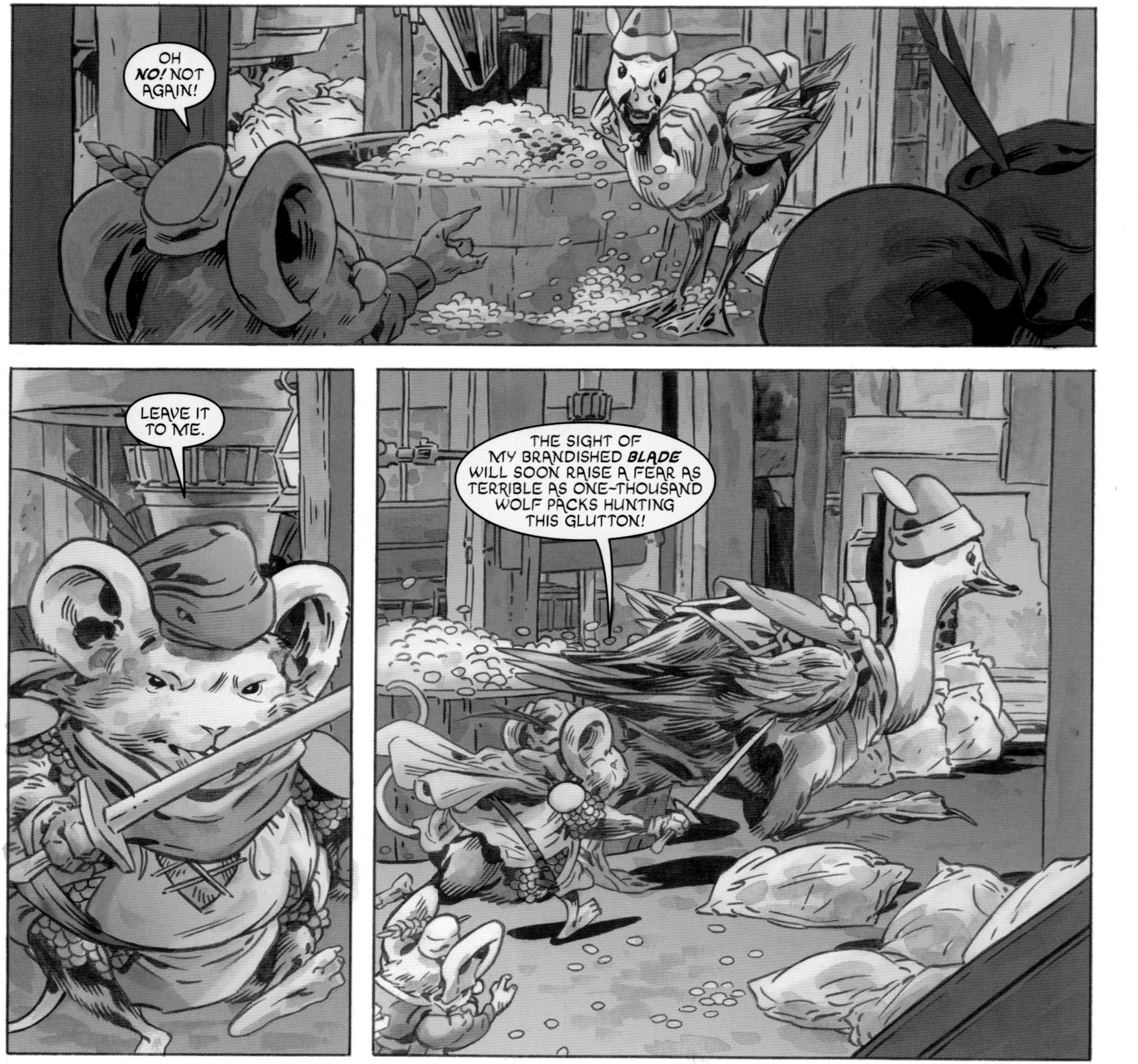
OH NO! NOT AGAIN!
LEAVE IT TO ME.
THE SIGHT OF MY BRANDISHED BLADE WILL SOON RAISE A FEAR AS TERRIBLE AS ONE-THOUSAND WOLF PACKS HUNTING THIS GLUTTON!

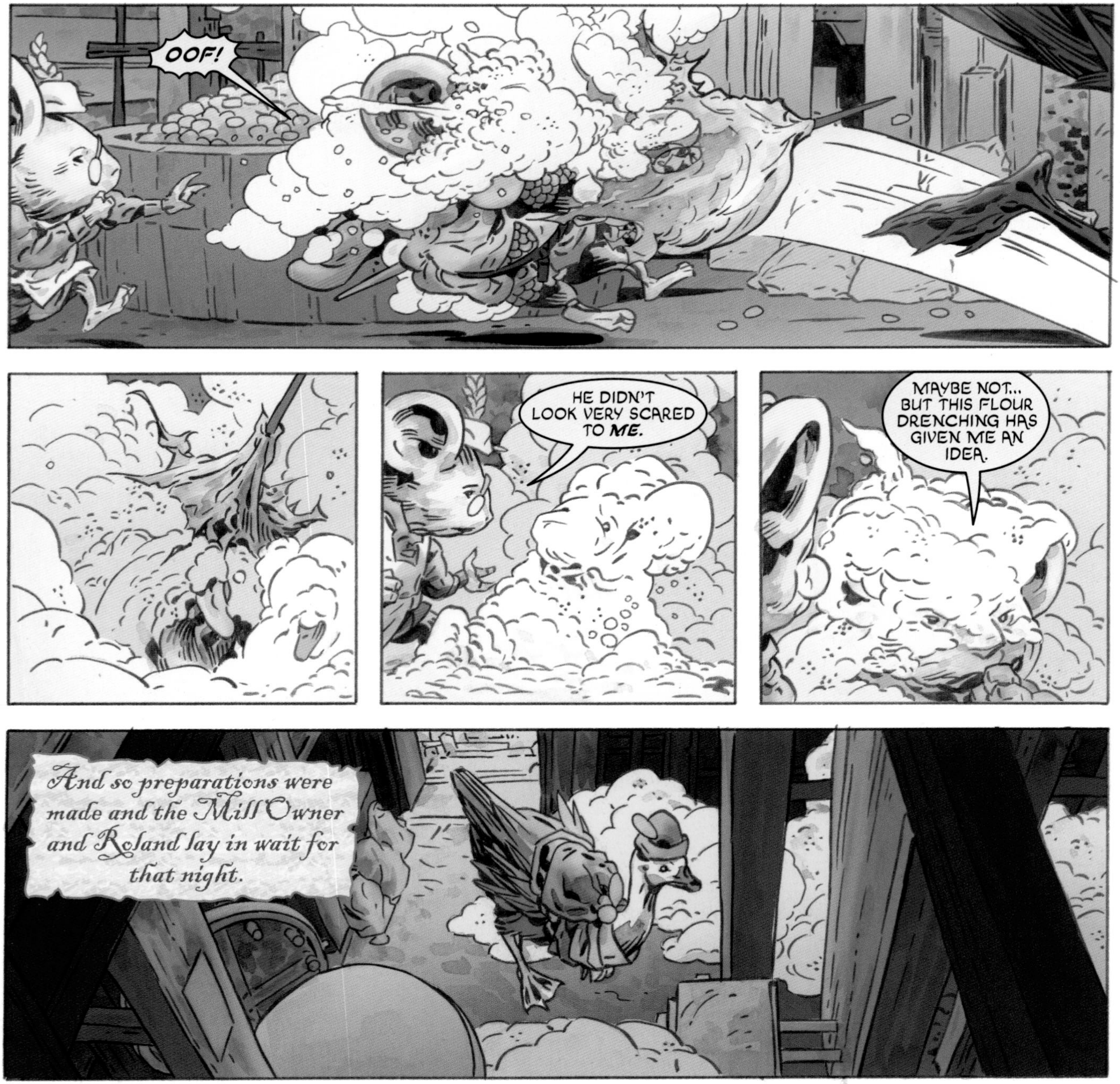
OOF!
HE DIDN'T LOOK VERY SCARED TO ME.
MAYBE NOT... BUT THIS FLOUR DRENCHING HAS GIVEN ME AN IDEA.
And so preparations were made and the Mill Owner and Roland lay in wait for that night.

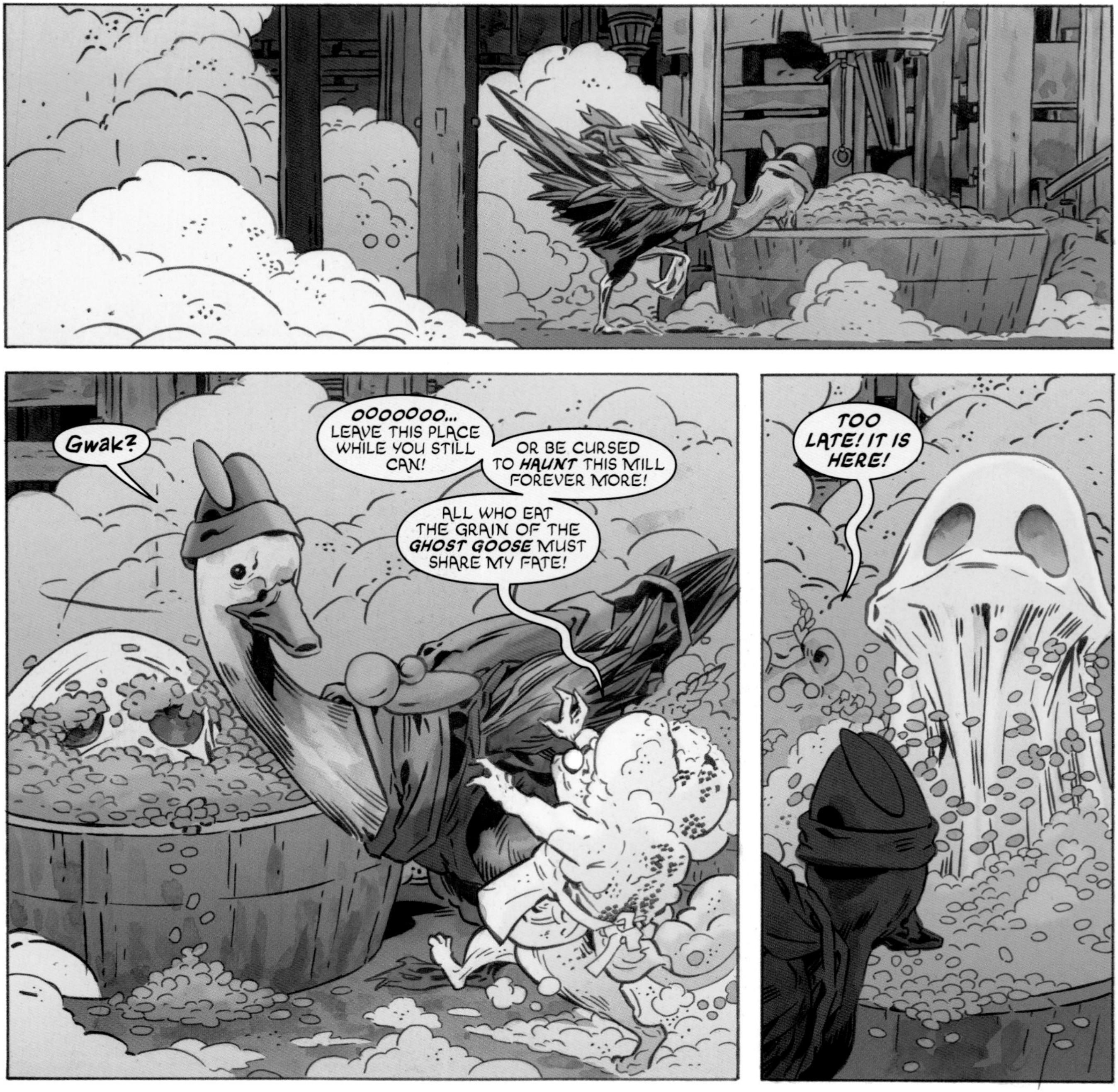
Gwak?
OOOOOOO... LEAVE THIS PLACE WHILE YOU STILL CAN!
OR BE CURSED TO HAUNT THIS MILL FOREVER MORE!
ALL WHO EAT THE GRAIN OF THE GHOST GOOSE MUST SHARE MY FATE!
TOO LATE! IT IS HERE!

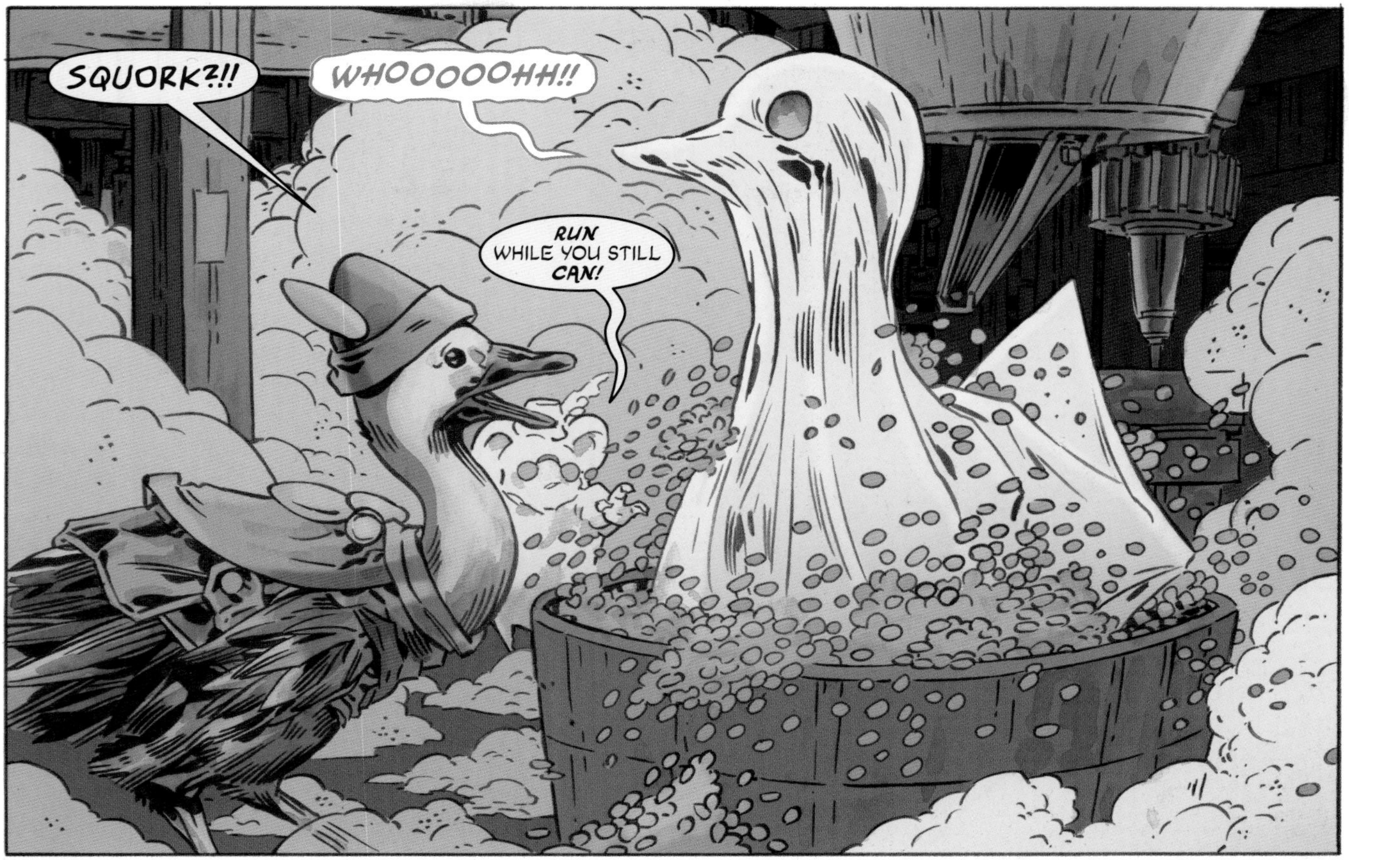
SQUORK?!!
WHOOOOOOHH!!
RUN WHILE YOU STILL CAN!

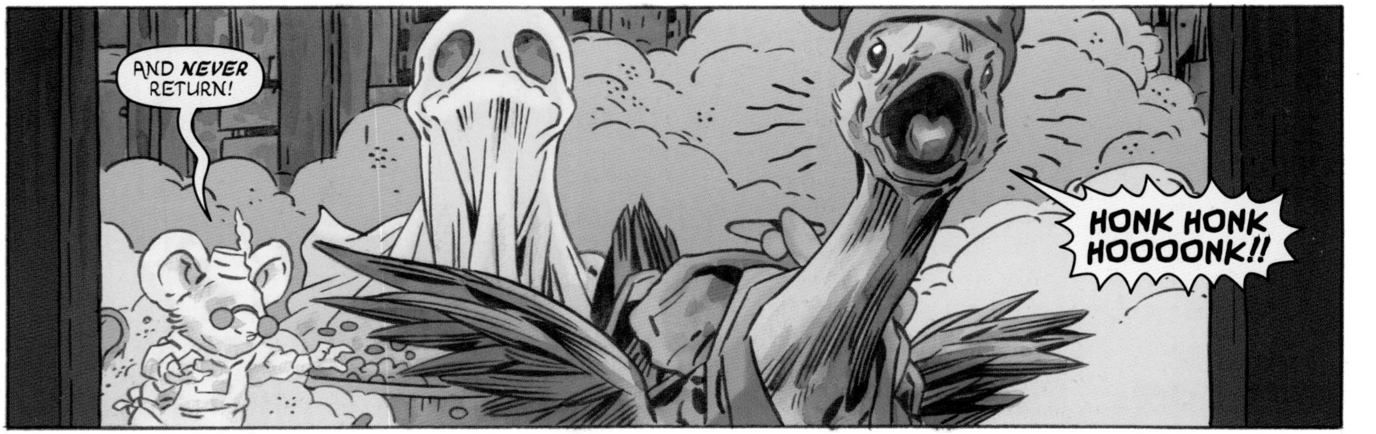
AND NEVER RETURN!
HONK HONK HOOOONK!!

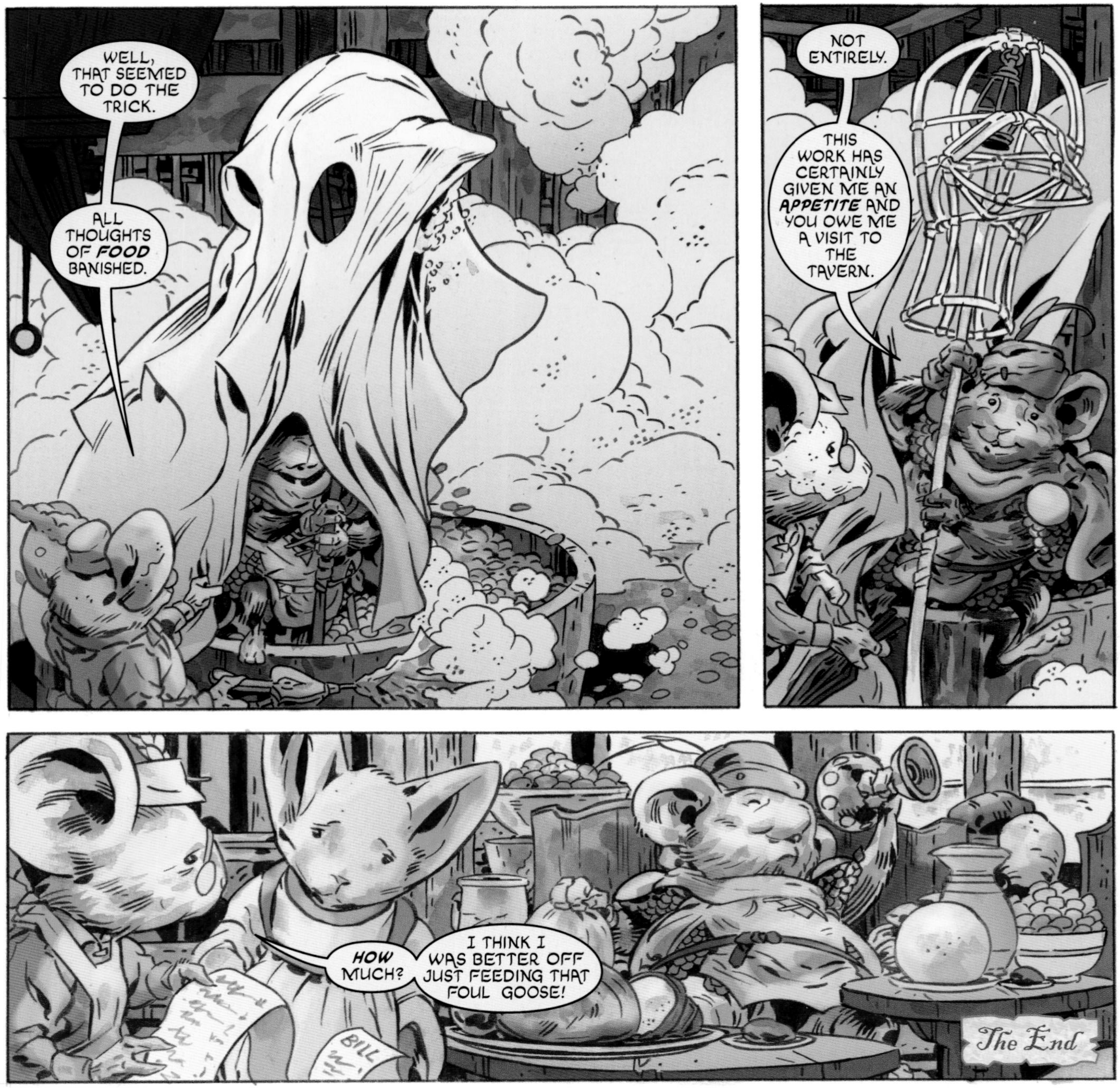
WELL, THAT SEEMED TO DO THE TRICK.
ALL THOUGHTS OF *FOOD* BANISHED.
NOT ENTIRELY.
THIS WORK HAS CERTAINLY GIVEN ME AN *APPETITE* AND YOU OWE ME A VISIT TO THE TAVERN.
HOW MUCH?
I THINK I WAS BETTER OFF JUST FEEDING THAT FOUL GOOSE!
BILL
The End

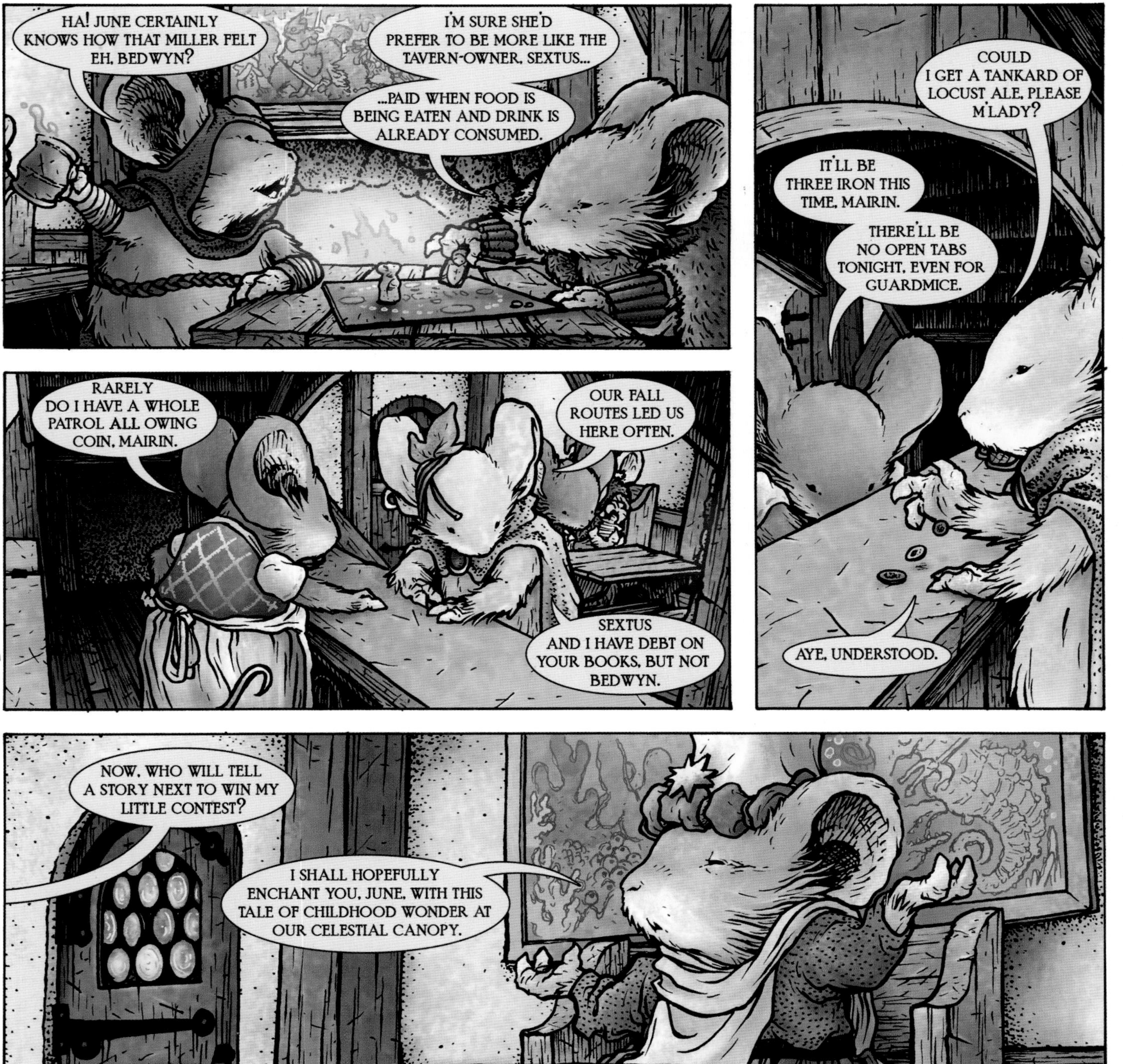
HA! JUNE CERTAINLY KNOWS HOW THAT MILLER FELT EH, BEDWYN?
I'M SURE SHE'D PREFER TO BE MORE LIKE THE TAVERN-OWNER, SEXTUS...
...PAID WHEN FOOD IS BEING EATEN AND DRINK IS ALREADY CONSUMED.
COULD I GET A TANKARD OF LOCUST ALE, PLEASE M'LADY?
IT'LL BE THREE IRON THIS TIME, MAIRIN.
THERE'LL BE NO OPEN TABS TONIGHT, EVEN FOR GUARDMICE.
AYE, UNDERSTOOD.
RARELY DO I HAVE A WHOLE PATROL ALL OWING COIN, MAIRIN.
OUR FALL ROUTES LED US HERE OFTEN.
SEXTUS AND I HAVE DEBT ON YOUR BOOKS, BUT NOT BEDWYN.
NOW, WHO WILL TELL A STORY NEXT TO WIN MY LITTLE CONTEST?
I SHALL HOPEFULLY ENCHANT YOU, JUNE, WITH THIS TALE OF CHILDHOOD WONDER AT OUR CELESTIAL CANOPY.

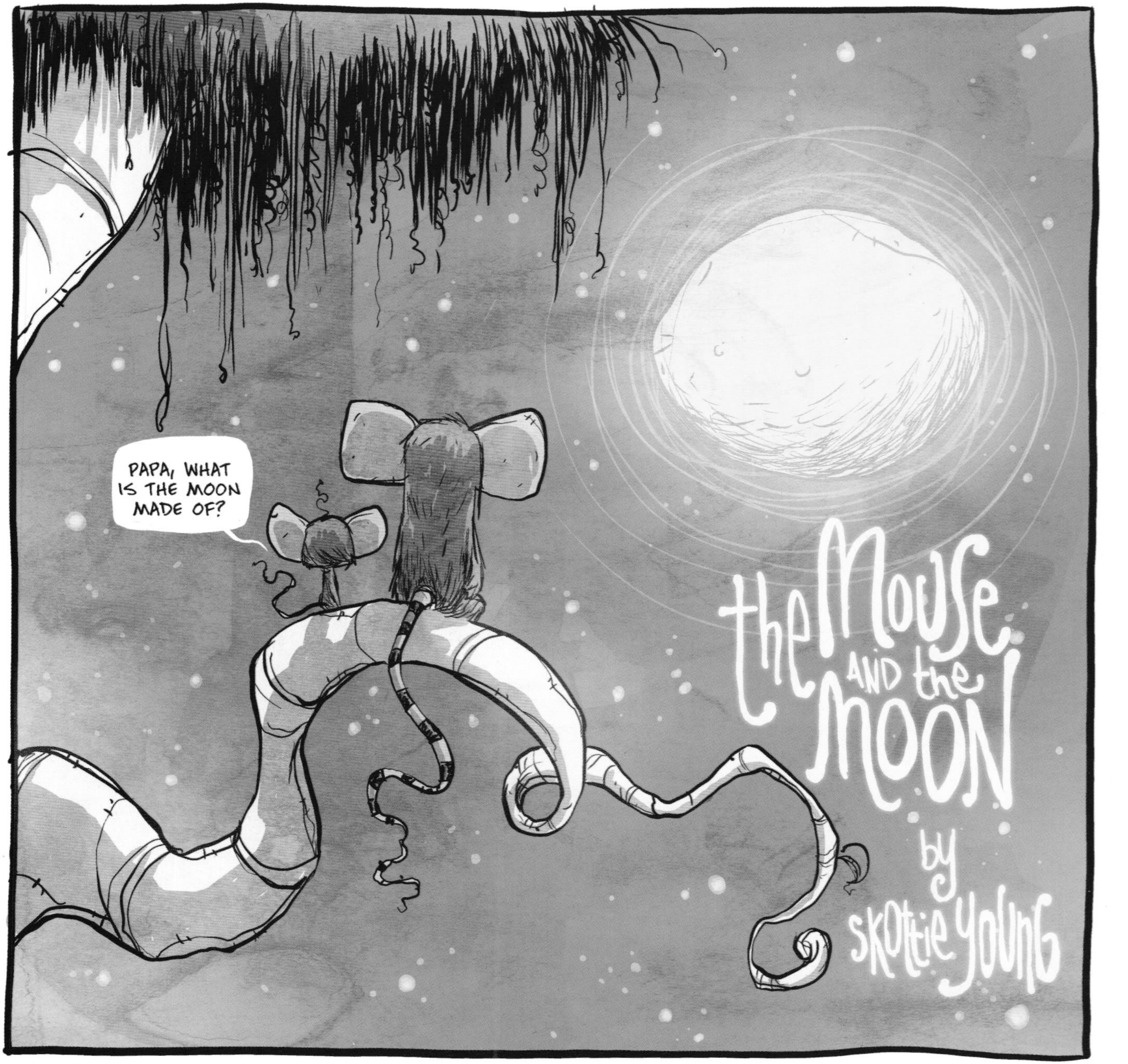
PAPA, WHAT IS THE MOON MADE OF?
the Mouse AND the MOON
by Skottie Young

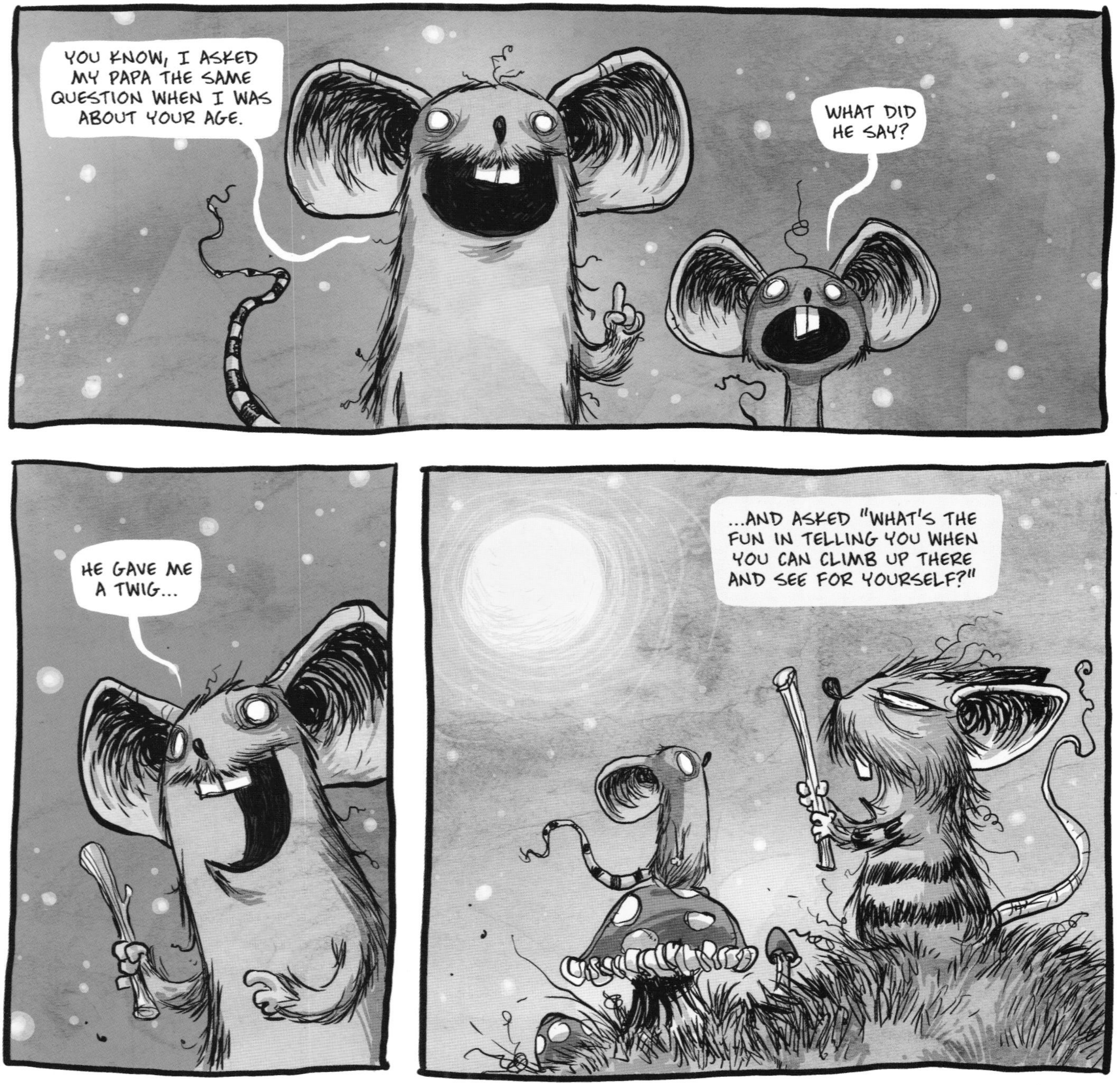
YOU KNOW, I ASKED MY PAPA THE SAME QUESTION WHEN I WAS ABOUT YOUR AGE.
WHAT DID HE SAY?
HE GAVE ME A TWIG...
...AND ASKED "WHAT'S THE FUN IN TELLING YOU WHEN YOU CAN CLIMB UP THERE AND SEE FOR YOURSELF?"

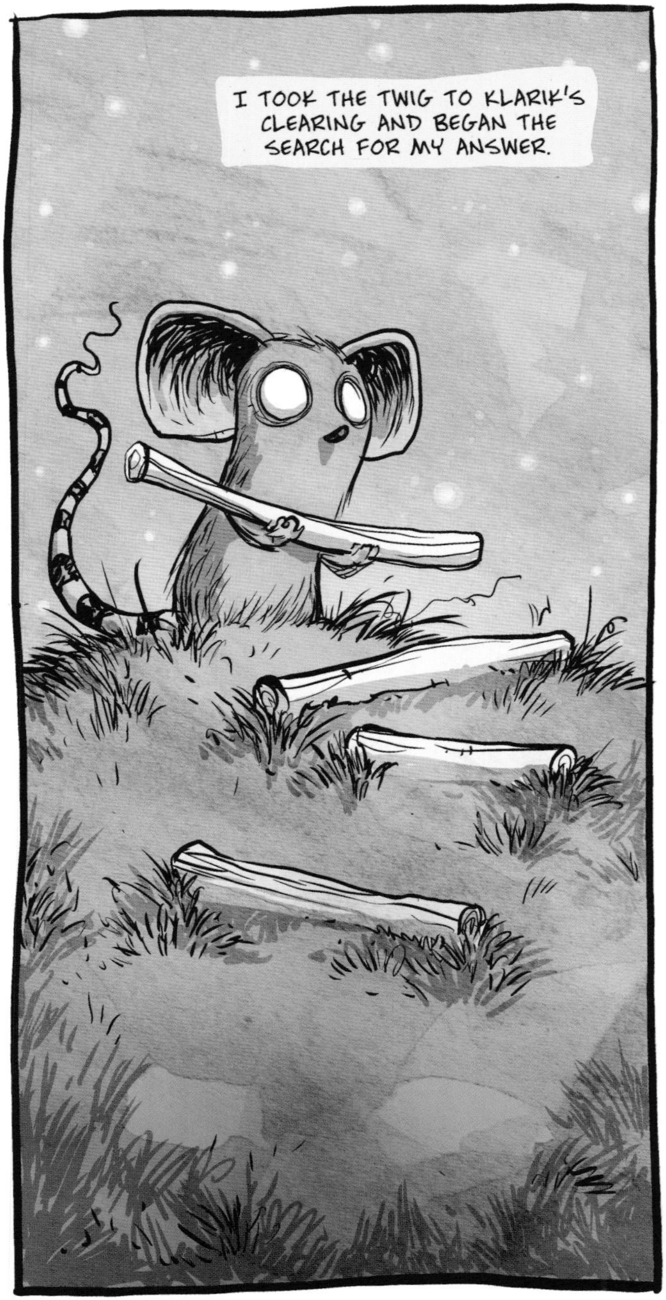
I TOOK THE TWIG TO KLARIK'S CLEARING AND BEGAN THE SEARCH FOR MY ANSWER.

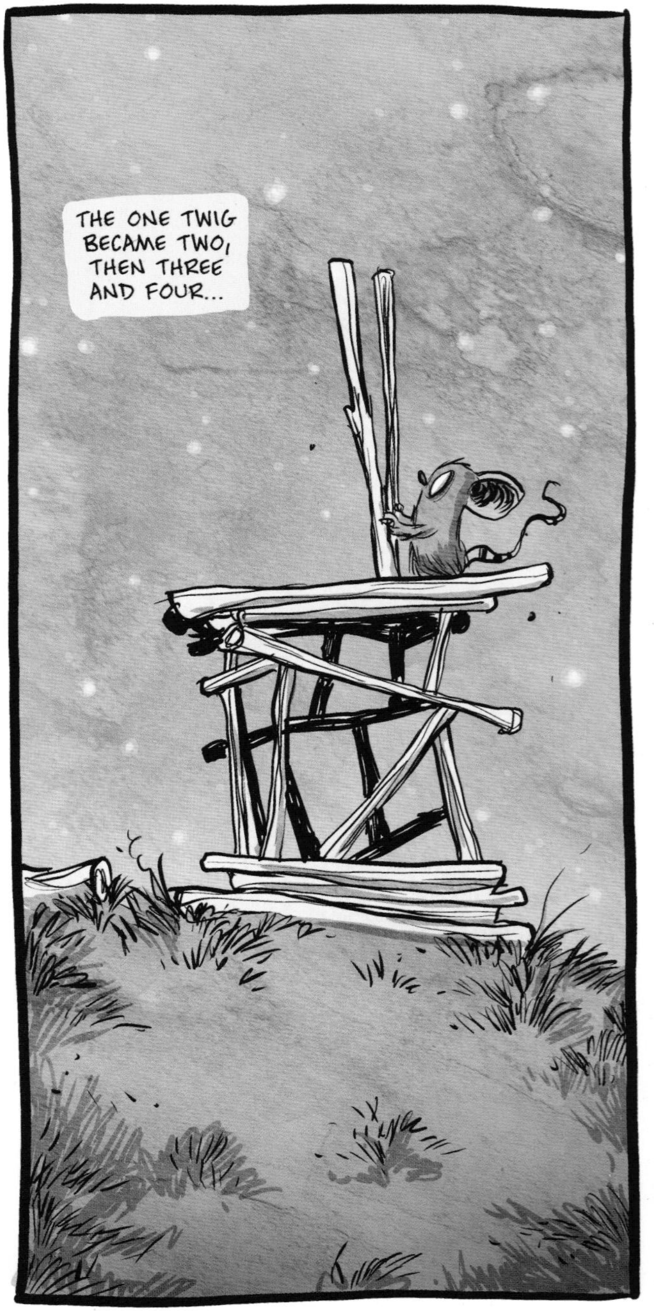
THE ONE TWIG BECAME TWO, THEN THREE AND FOUR...

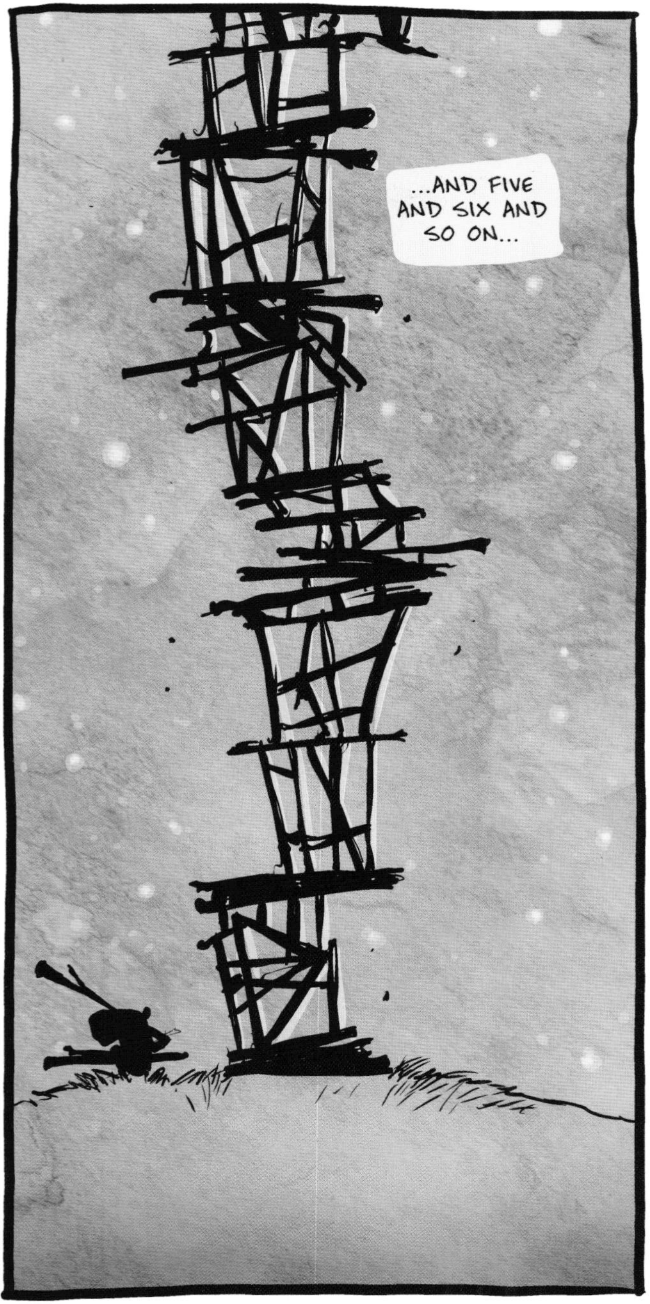
...AND FIVE
AND SIX AND
SO ON...

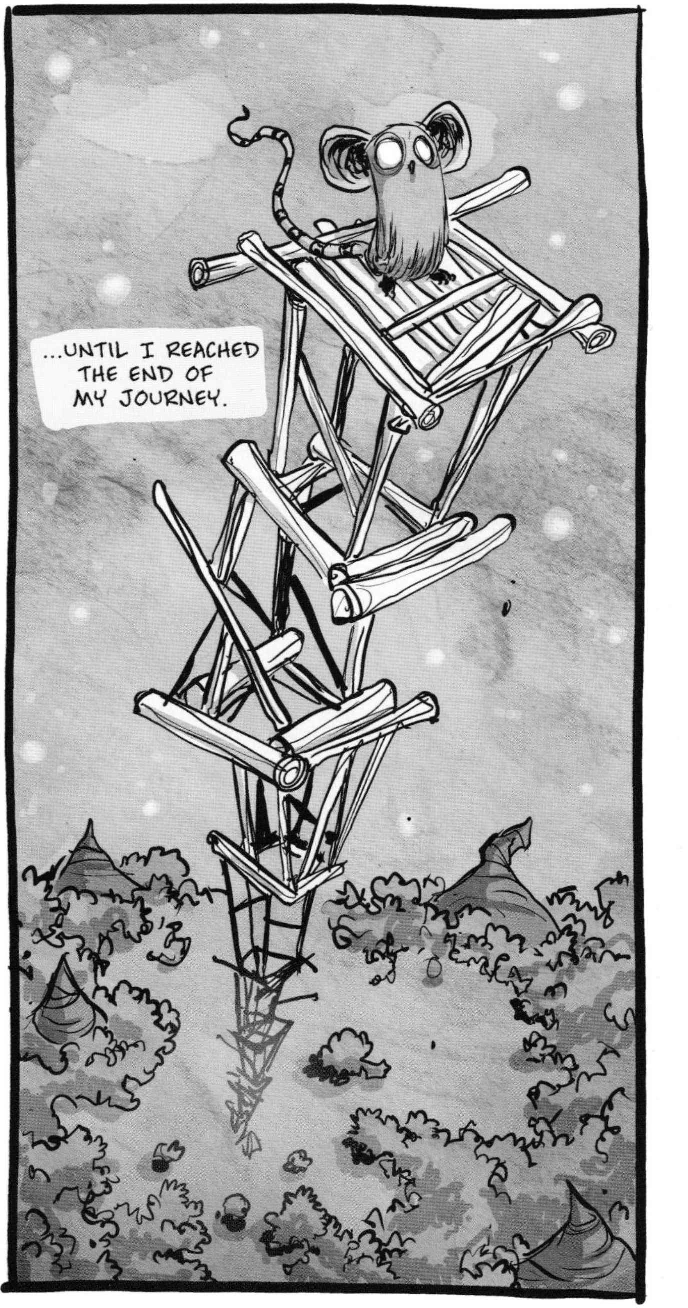
...UNTIL I REACHED
THE END OF
MY JOURNEY.

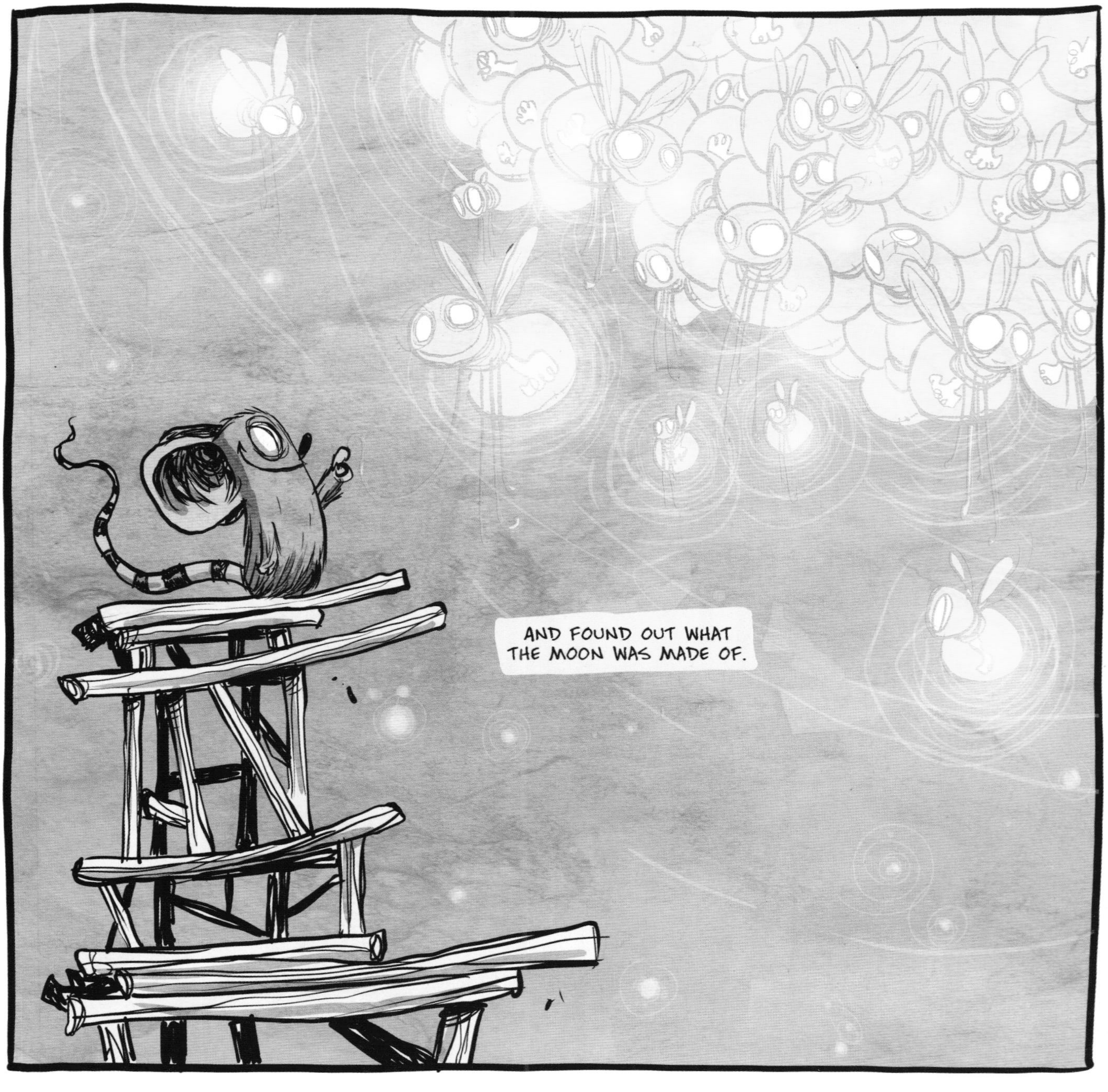
AND FOUND OUT WHAT THE MOON WAS MADE OF.

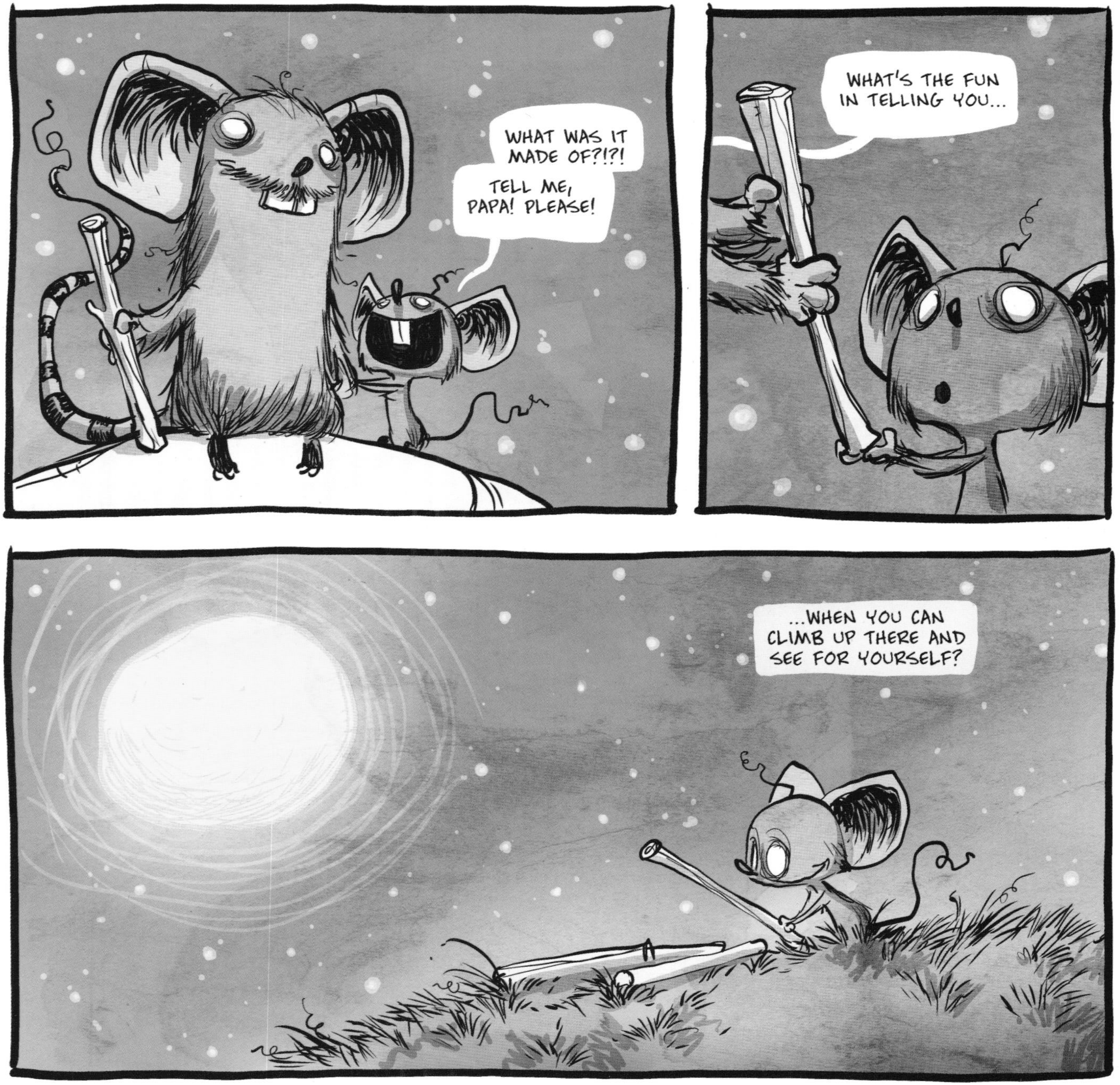
WHAT WAS IT MADE OF?!?!
TELL ME, PAPA! PLEASE!
WHAT'S THE FUN IN TELLING YOU...
...WHEN YOU CAN CLIMB UP THERE AND SEE FOR YOURSELF?

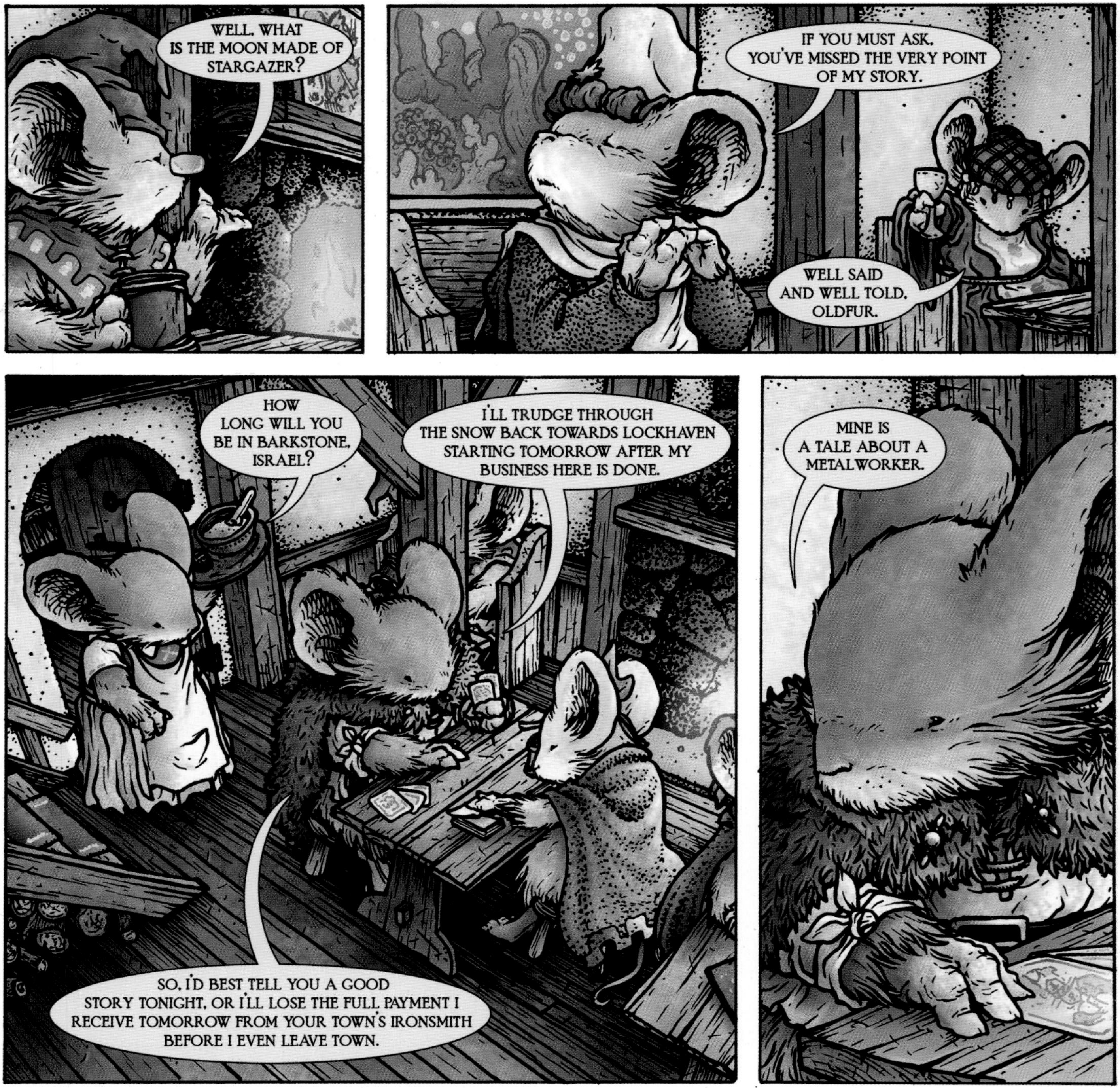
WELL, WHAT IS THE MOON MADE OF STARGAZER?
IF YOU MUST ASK, YOU'VE MISSED THE VERY POINT OF MY STORY.
WELL SAID AND WELL TOLD, OLDFUR.
HOW LONG WILL YOU BE IN BARKSTONE, ISRAEL?
I'LL TRUDGE THROUGH THE SNOW BACK TOWARDS LOCKHAVEN STARTING TOMORROW AFTER MY BUSINESS HERE IS DONE.
SO, I'D BEST TELL YOU A GOOD STORY TONIGHT, OR I'LL LOSE THE FULL PAYMENT I RECEIVE TOMORROW FROM YOUR TOWN'S IRONSMITH BEFORE I EVEN LEAVE TOWN.
MINE IS A TALE ABOUT A METALWORKER.

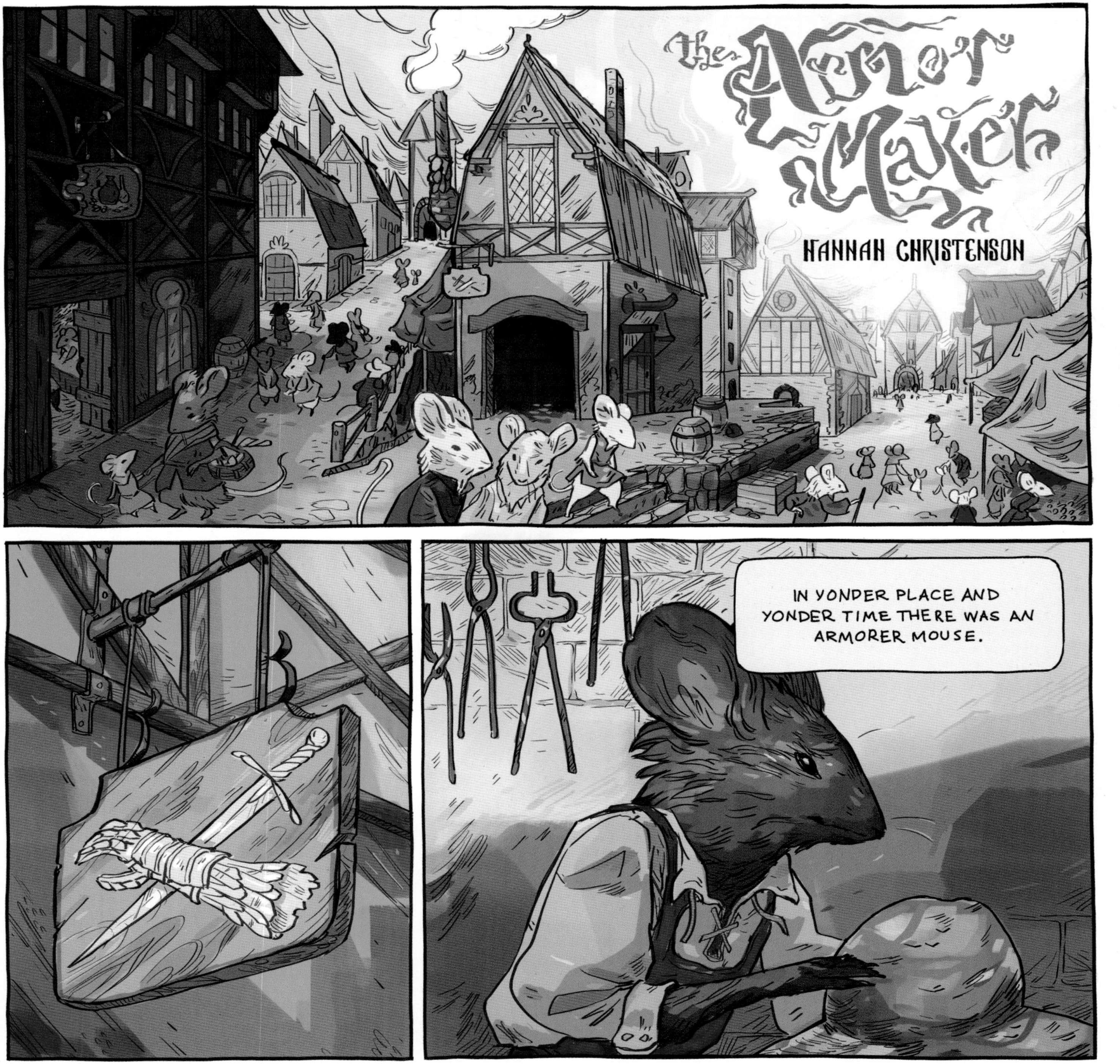
The Armor Maker
HANNAH CHRISTENSON
IN YONDER PLACE AND YONDER TIME THERE WAS AN ARMORER MOUSE.

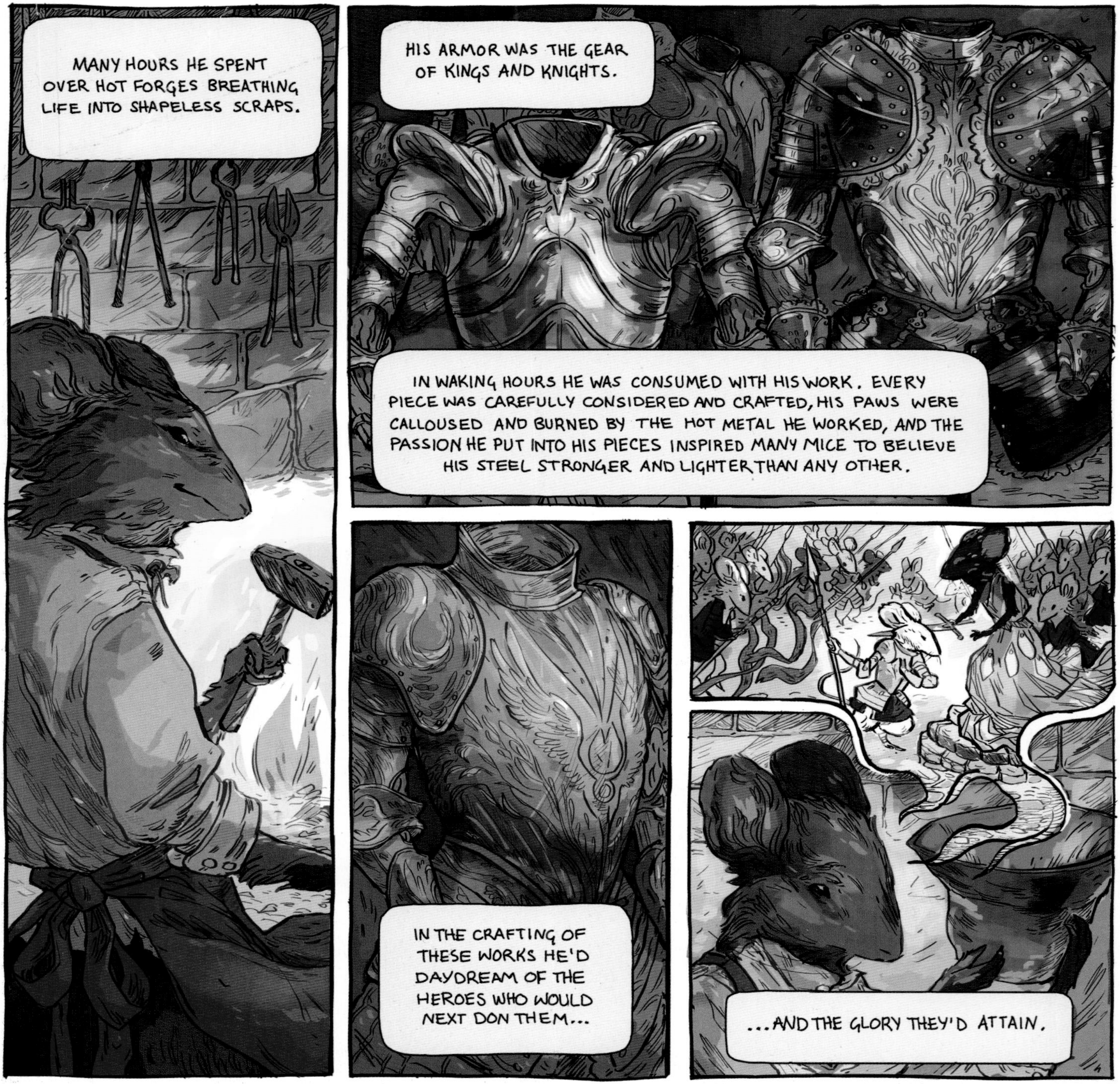
MANY HOURS HE SPENT OVER HOT FORGES BREATHING LIFE INTO SHAPELESS SCRAPS.
HIS ARMOR WAS THE GEAR OF KINGS AND KNIGHTS.
IN WAKING HOURS HE WAS CONSUMED WITH HIS WORK. EVERY PIECE WAS CAREFULLY CONSIDERED AND CRAFTED, HIS PAWS WERE CALLOUSED AND BURNED BY THE HOT METAL HE WORKED, AND THE PASSION HE PUT INTO HIS PIECES INSPIRED MANY MICE TO BELIEVE HIS STEEL STRONGER AND LIGHTER THAN ANY OTHER.
IN THE CRAFTING OF THESE WORKS HE'D DAYDREAM OF THE HEROES WHO WOULD NEXT DON THEM...
...AND THE GLORY THEY'D ATTAIN.

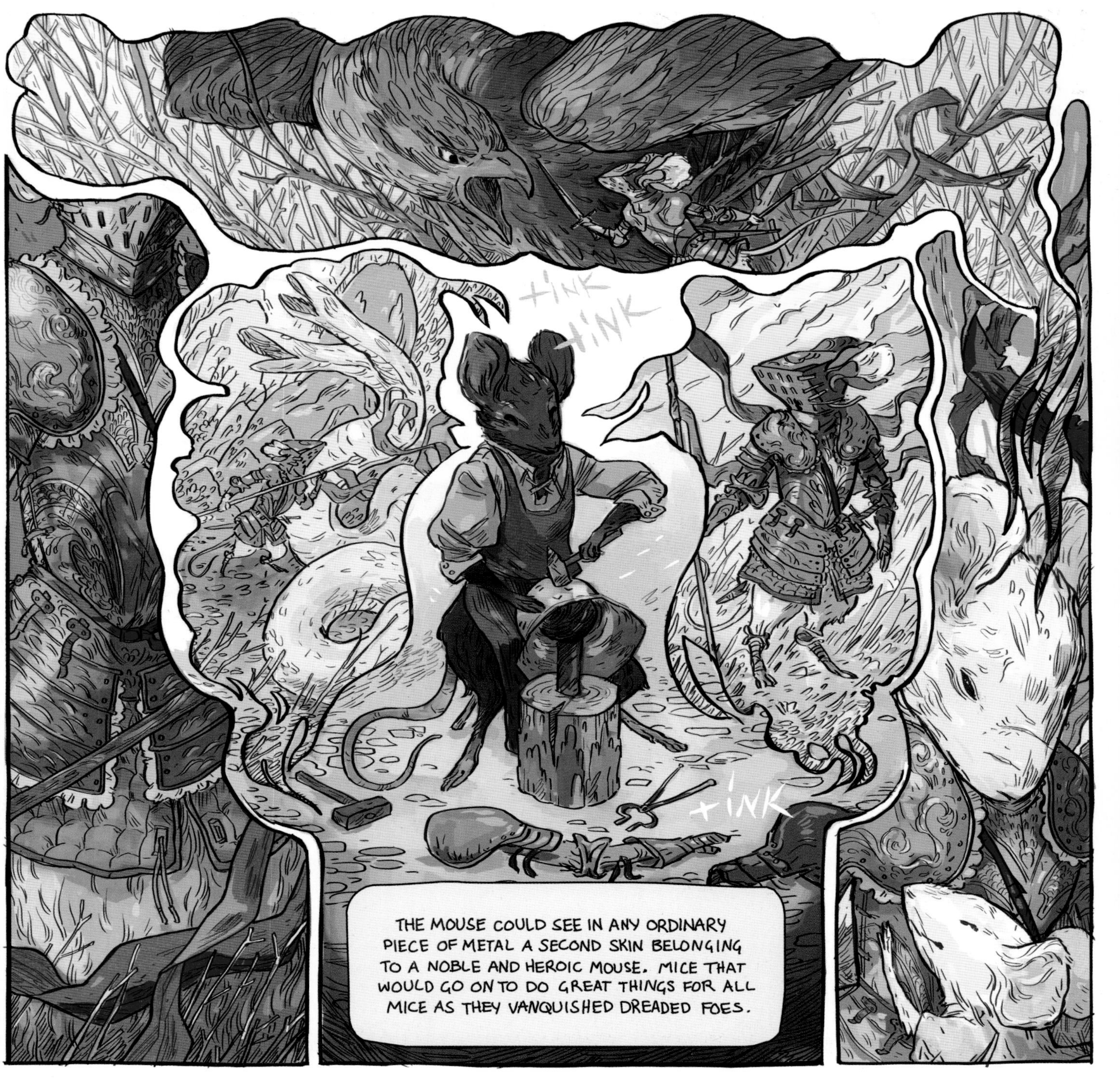
TINK
TINK
TINK
THE MOUSE COULD SEE IN ANY ORDINARY PIECE OF METAL A SECOND SKIN BELONGING TO A NOBLE AND HEROIC MOUSE. MICE THAT WOULD GO ON TO DO GREAT THINGS FOR ALL MICE AS THEY VANQUISHED DREADED FOES.

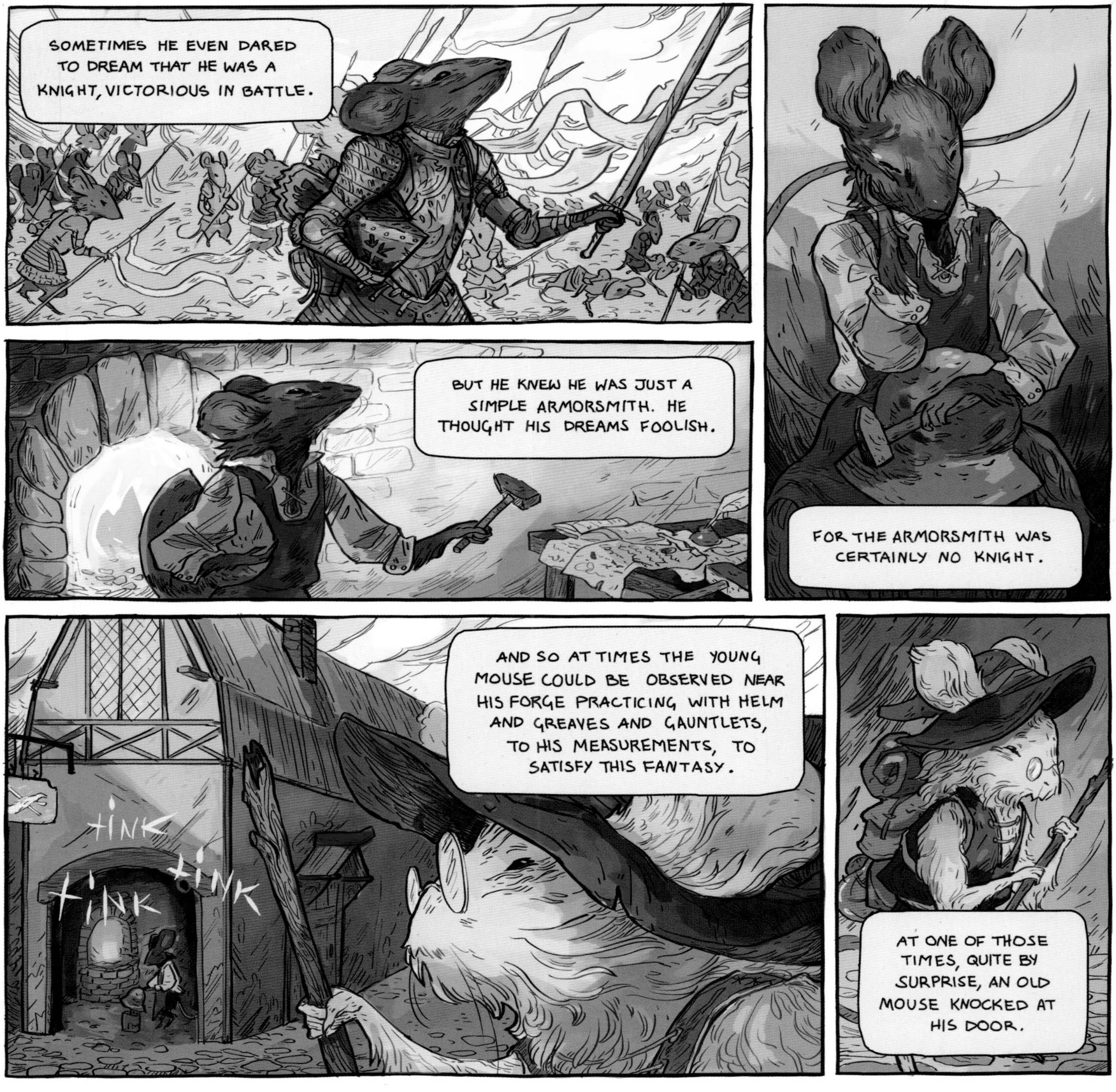
SOMETIMES HE EVEN DARED TO DREAM THAT HE WAS A KNIGHT, VICTORIOUS IN BATTLE.
BUT HE KNEW HE WAS JUST A SIMPLE ARMORSMITH. HE THOUGHT HIS DREAMS FOOLISH.
FOR THE ARMORSMITH WAS CERTAINLY NO KNIGHT.
AND SO AT TIMES THE YOUNG MOUSE COULD BE OBSERVED NEAR HIS FORGE PRACTICING WITH HELM AND GREAVES AND GAUNTLETS, TO HIS MEASUREMENTS, TO SATISFY THIS FANTASY.
TINK
TINK
TINK
AT ONE OF THOSE TIMES, QUITE BY SURPRISE, AN OLD MOUSE KNOCKED AT HIS DOOR.

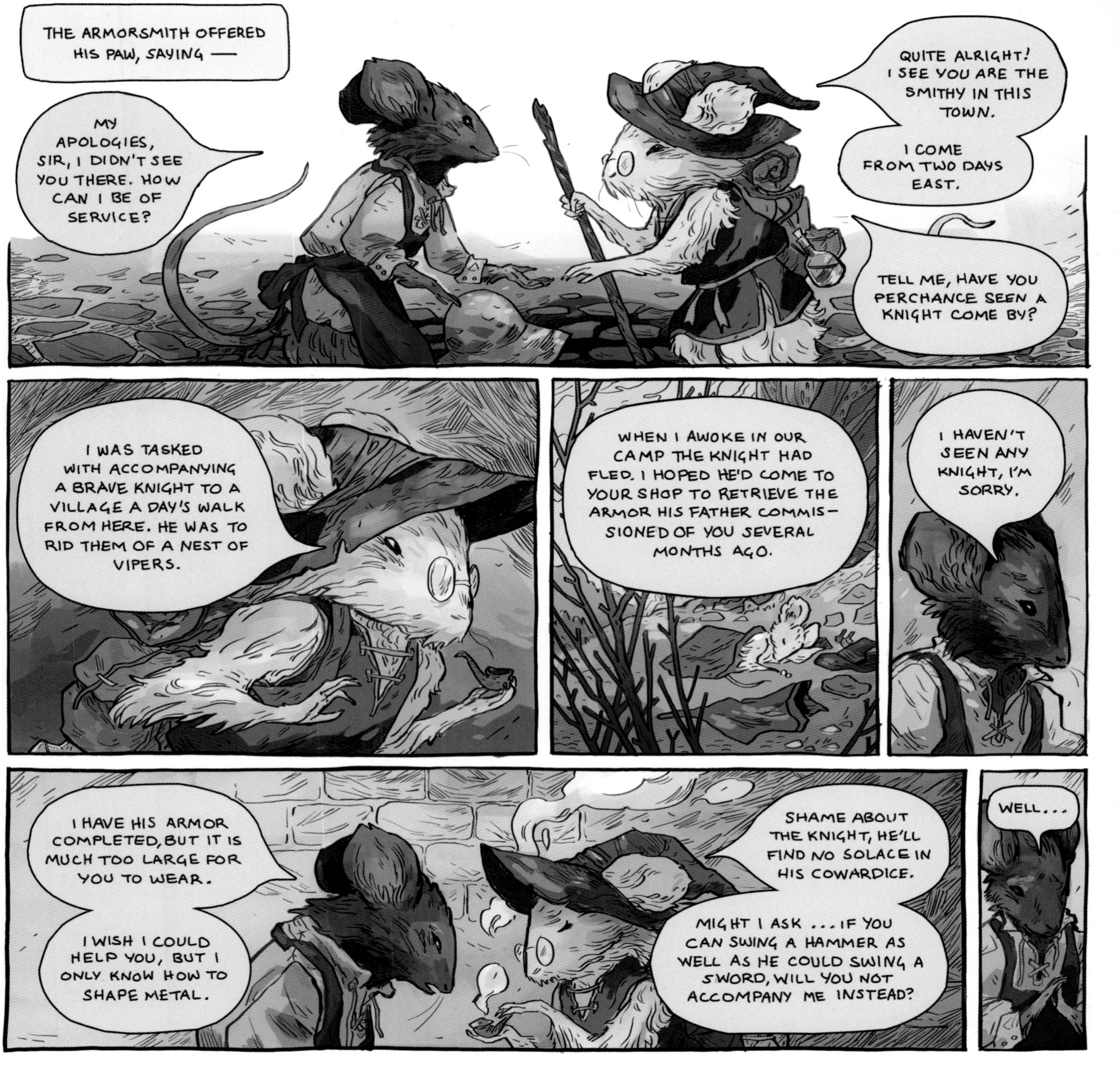
THE ARMORSMITH OFFERED HIS PAW, SAYING —
MY APOLOGIES, SIR, I DIDN'T SEE YOU THERE. HOW CAN I BE OF SERVICE?
QUITE ALRIGHT! I SEE YOU ARE THE SMITHY IN THIS TOWN.
I COME FROM TWO DAYS EAST.
TELL ME, HAVE YOU PERCHANCE SEEN A KNIGHT COME BY?
I WAS TASKED WITH ACCOMPANYING A BRAVE KNIGHT TO A VILLAGE A DAY'S WALK FROM HERE. HE WAS TO RID THEM OF A NEST OF VIPERS.
WHEN I AWOKE IN OUR CAMP THE KNIGHT HAD FLED. I HOPED HE'D COME TO YOUR SHOP TO RETRIEVE THE ARMOR HIS FATHER COMMISSIONED OF YOU SEVERAL MONTHS AGO.
I HAVEN'T SEEN ANY KNIGHT, I'M SORRY.
I HAVE HIS ARMOR COMPLETED, BUT IT IS MUCH TOO LARGE FOR YOU TO WEAR.
I WISH I COULD HELP YOU, BUT I ONLY KNOW HOW TO SHAPE METAL.
SHAME ABOUT THE KNIGHT, HE'LL FIND NO SOLACE IN HIS COWARDICE.
MIGHT I ASK ... IF YOU CAN SWING A HAMMER AS WELL AS HE COULD SWING A SWORD, WILL YOU NOT ACCOMPANY ME INSTEAD?
WELL...

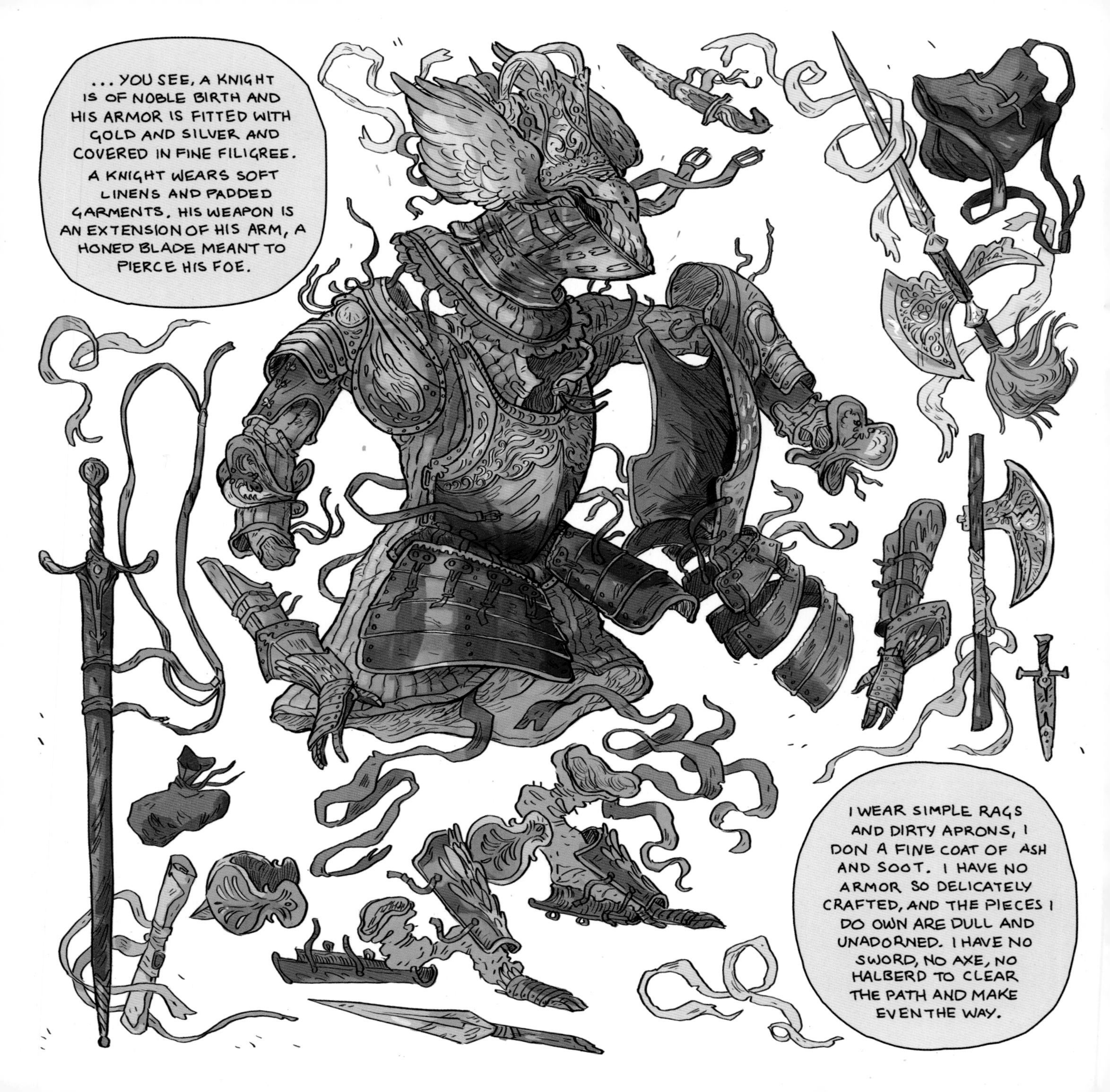

... YOU SEE, A KNIGHT IS OF NOBLE BIRTH AND HIS ARMOR IS FITTED WITH GOLD AND SILVER AND COVERED IN FINE FILIGREE. A KNIGHT WEARS SOFT LINENS AND PADDED GARMENTS. HIS WEAPON IS AN EXTENSION OF HIS ARM, A HONED BLADE MEANT TO PIERCE HIS FOE.
I WEAR SIMPLE RAGS AND DIRTY APRONS, I DON A FINE COAT OF ASH AND SOOT. I HAVE NO ARMOR SO DELICATELY CRAFTED, AND THE PIECES I DO OWN ARE DULL AND UNADORNED. I HAVE NO SWORD, NO AXE, NO HALBERD TO CLEAR THE PATH AND MAKE EVEN THE WAY.

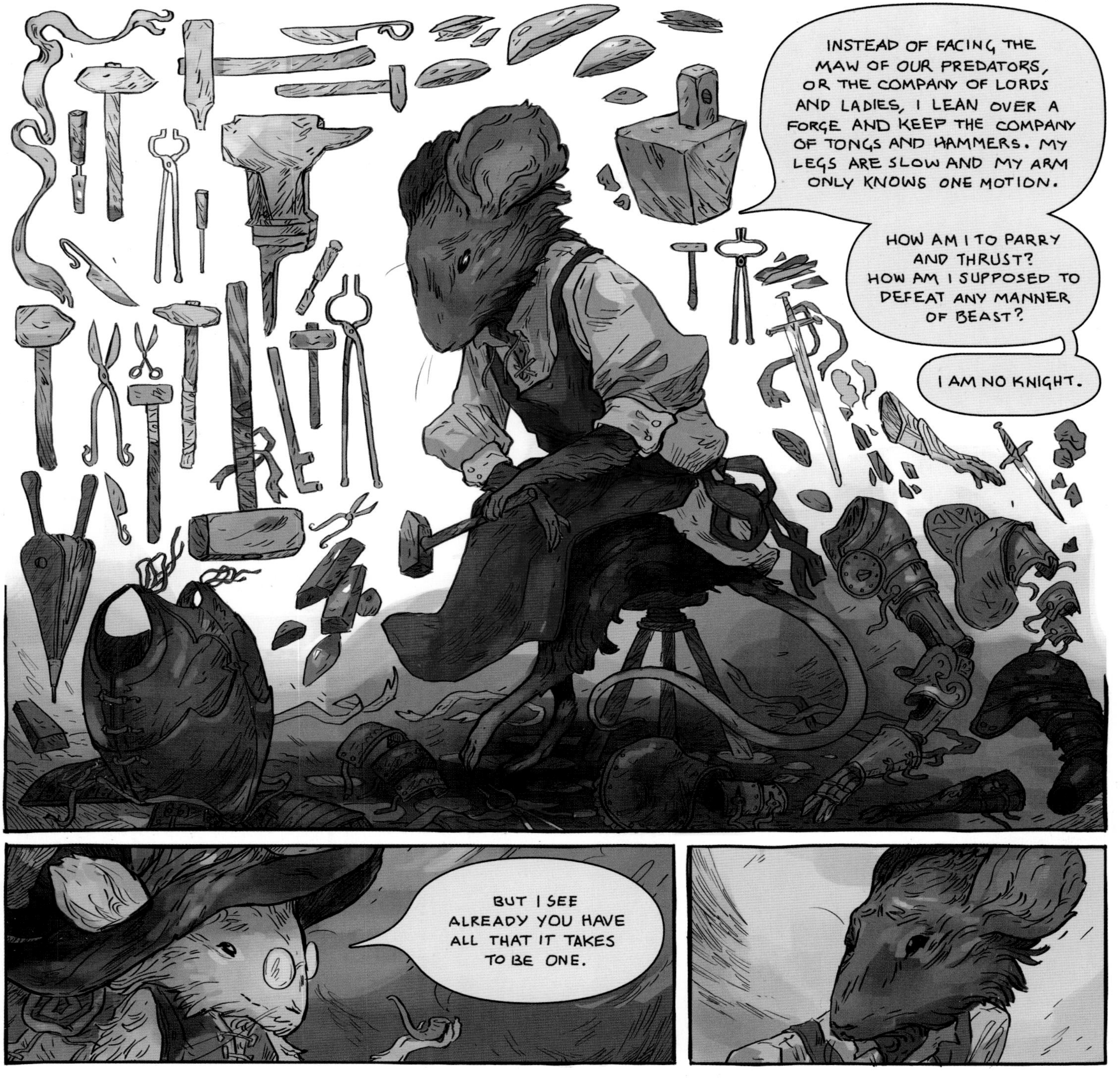
INSTEAD OF FACING THE MAW OF OUR PREDATORS, OR THE COMPANY OF LORDS AND LADIES, I LEAN OVER A FORGE AND KEEP THE COMPANY OF TONGS AND HAMMERS. MY LEGS ARE SLOW AND MY ARM ONLY KNOWS ONE MOTION.
HOW AM I TO PARRY AND THRUST? HOW AM I SUPPOSED TO DEFEAT ANY MANNER OF BEAST?
I AM NO KNIGHT.
BUT I SEE ALREADY YOU HAVE ALL THAT IT TAKES TO BE ONE.

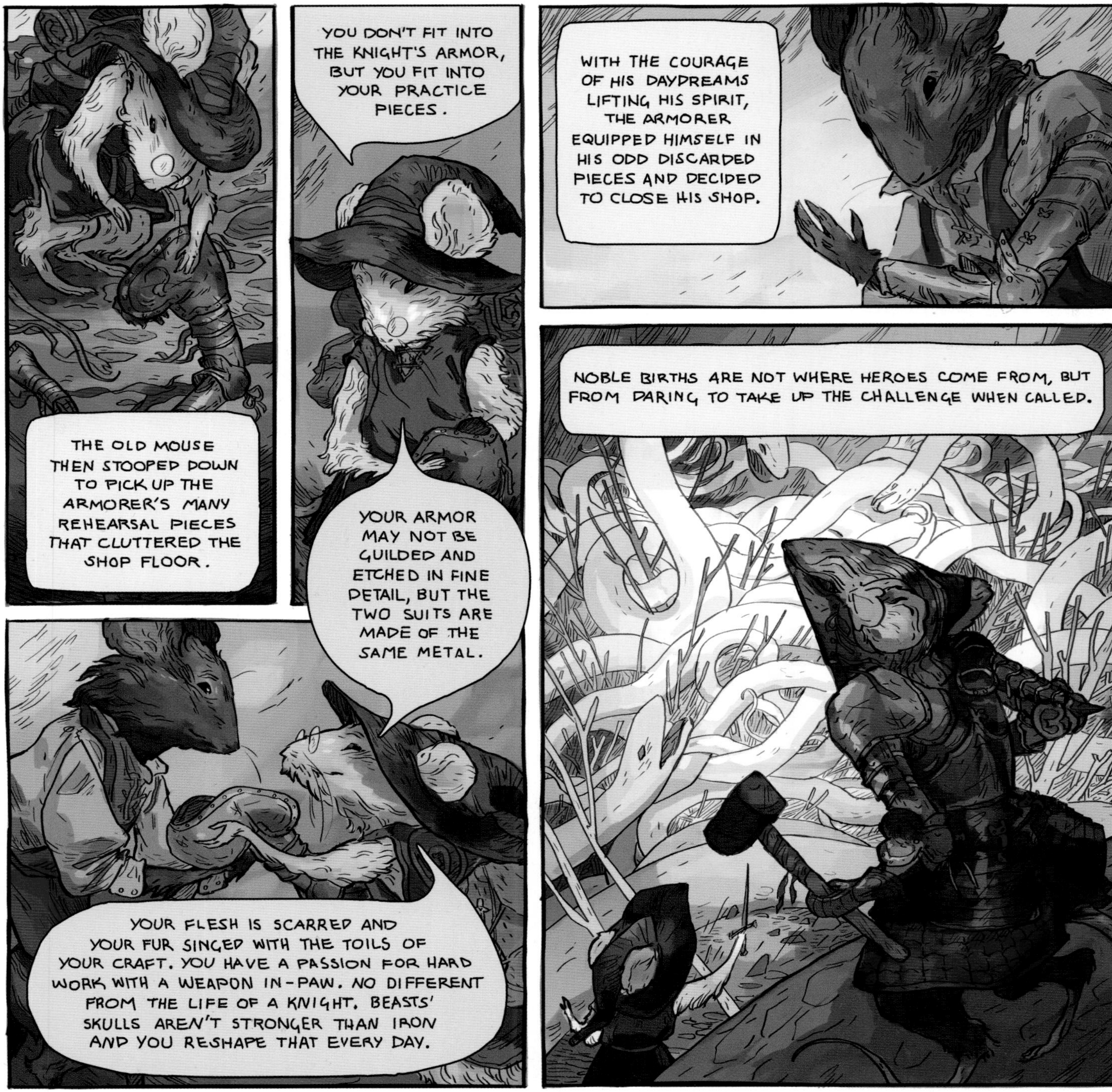
THE OLD MOUSE THEN STOOPED DOWN TO PICK UP THE ARMORER'S MANY REHEARSAL PIECES THAT CLUTTERED THE SHOP FLOOR.
YOU DON'T FIT INTO THE KNIGHT'S ARMOR, BUT YOU FIT INTO YOUR PRACTICE PIECES.
YOUR ARMOR MAY NOT BE GUILDED AND ETCHED IN FINE DETAIL, BUT THE TWO SUITS ARE MADE OF THE SAME METAL.
YOUR FLESH IS SCARRED AND YOUR FUR SINGED WITH THE TOILS OF YOUR CRAFT. YOU HAVE A PASSION FOR HARD WORK WITH A WEAPON IN-PAW. NO DIFFERENT FROM THE LIFE OF A KNIGHT. BEASTS' SKULLS AREN'T STRONGER THAN IRON AND YOU RESHAPE THAT EVERY DAY.
WITH THE COURAGE OF HIS DAYDREAMS LIFTING HIS SPIRIT, THE ARMORER EQUIPPED HIMSELF IN HIS ODD DISCARDED PIECES AND DECIDED TO CLOSE HIS SHOP.
NOBLE BIRTHS ARE NOT WHERE HEROES COME FROM, BUT FROM DARING TO TAKE UP THE CHALLENGE WHEN CALLED.

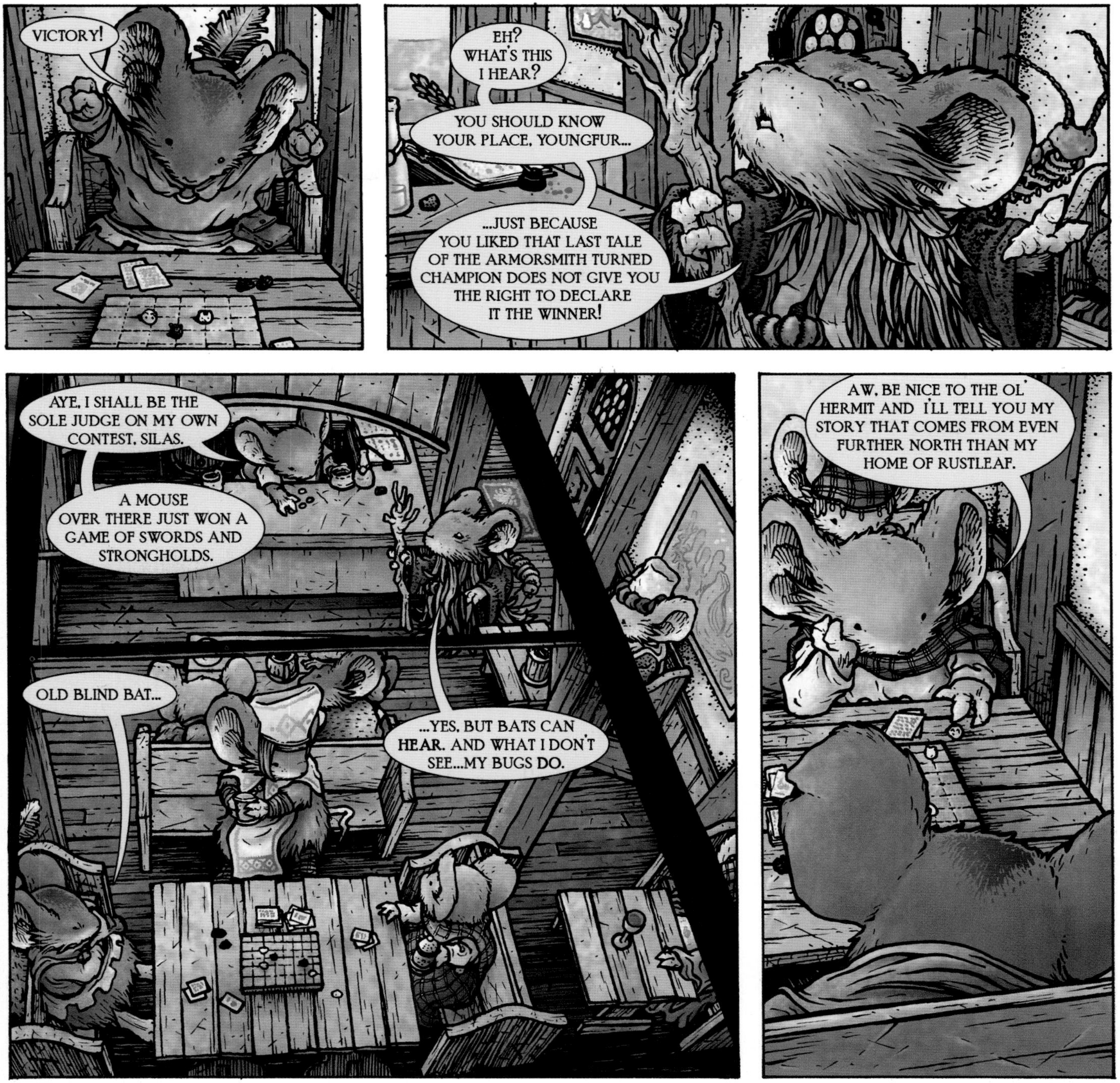
VICTORY!
EH? WHAT'S THIS I HEAR?
YOU SHOULD KNOW YOUR PLACE, YOUNGFUR...
...JUST BECAUSE YOU LIKED THAT LAST TALE OF THE ARMORSMITH TURNED CHAMPION DOES NOT GIVE YOU THE RIGHT TO DECLARE IT THE WINNER!
AYE, I SHALL BE THE SOLE JUDGE ON MY OWN CONTEST, SILAS.
A MOUSE OVER THERE JUST WON A GAME OF SWORDS AND STRONGHOLDS.
OLD BLIND BAT...
...YES, BUT BATS CAN HEAR. AND WHAT I DON'T SEE...MY BUGS DO.
AW, BE NICE TO THE OL' HERMIT AND I'LL TELL YOU MY STORY THAT COMES FROM EVEN FURTHER NORTH THAN MY HOME OF RUSTLEAF.

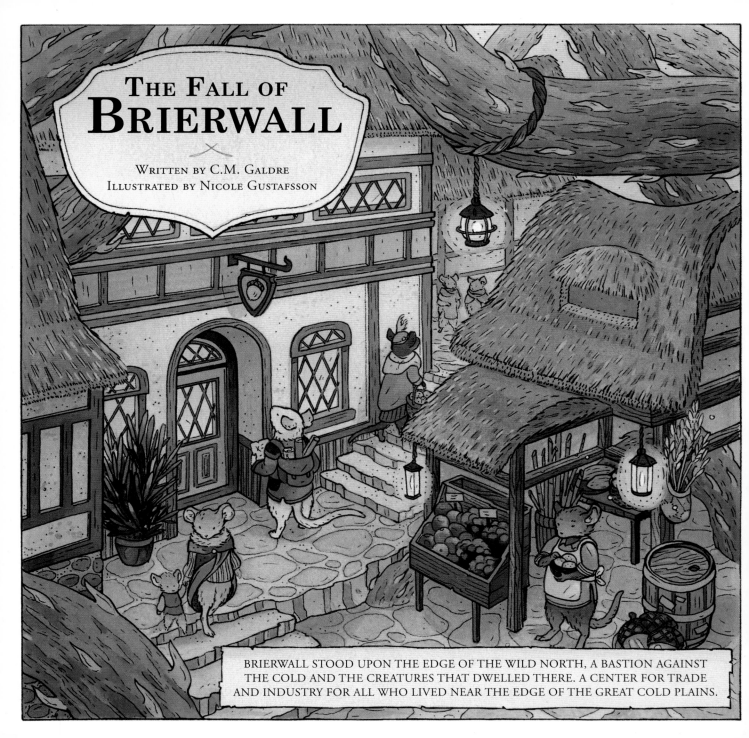

THE FALL OF
BRIERWALL

Written by C.M. Galdre
Illustrated by Nicole Gustafsson

BRIERWALL STOOD UPON THE EDGE OF THE WILD NORTH, A BASTION AGAINST THE COLD AND THE CREATURES THAT DWELLED THERE. A CENTER FOR TRADE AND INDUSTRY FOR ALL WHO LIVED NEAR THE EDGE OF THE GREAT COLD PLAINS.

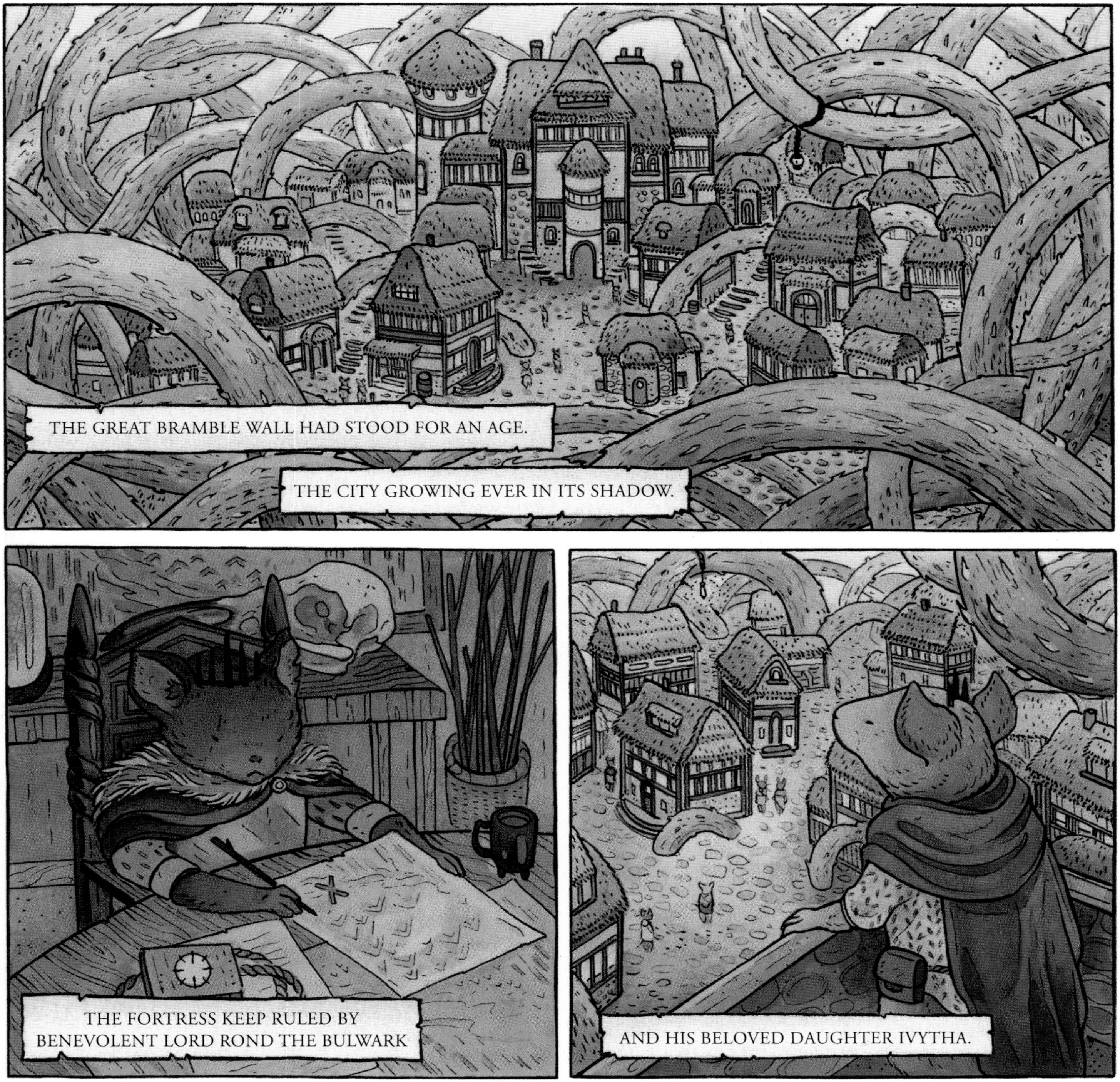
THE GREAT BRAMBLE WALL HAD STOOD FOR AN AGE.
THE CITY GROWING EVER IN ITS SHADOW.
THE FORTRESS KEEP RULED BY BENEVOLENT LORD ROND THE BULWARK
AND HIS BELOVED DAUGHTER IVYTHA.

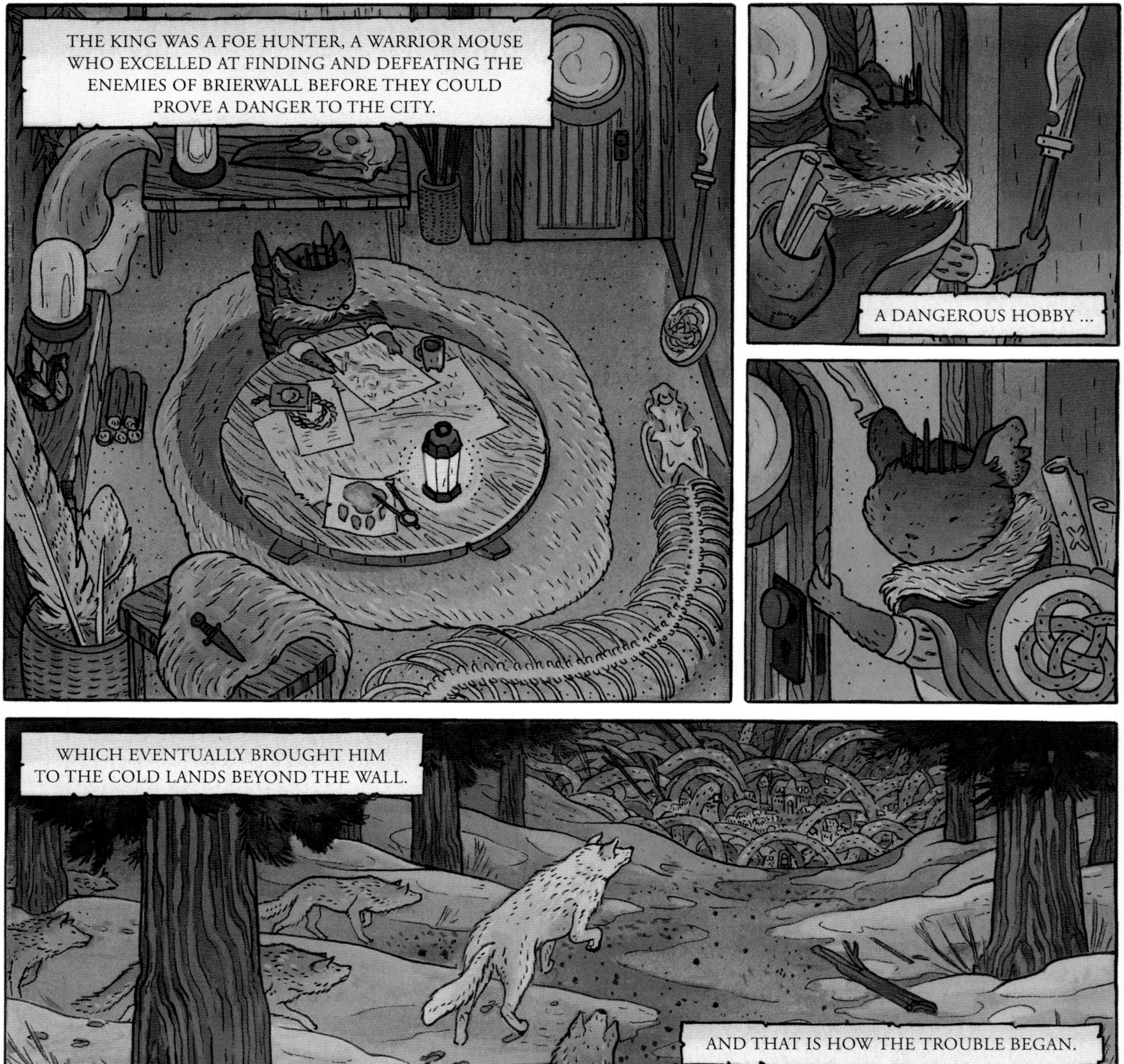
THE KING WAS A FOE HUNTER, A WARRIOR MOUSE WHO EXCELLED AT FINDING AND DEFEATING THE ENEMIES OF BRIERWALL BEFORE THEY COULD PROVE A DANGER TO THE CITY.
A DANGEROUS HOBBY ...
WHICH EVENTUALLY BROUGHT HIM TO THE COLD LANDS BEYOND THE WALL.
AND THAT IS HOW THE TROUBLE BEGAN.

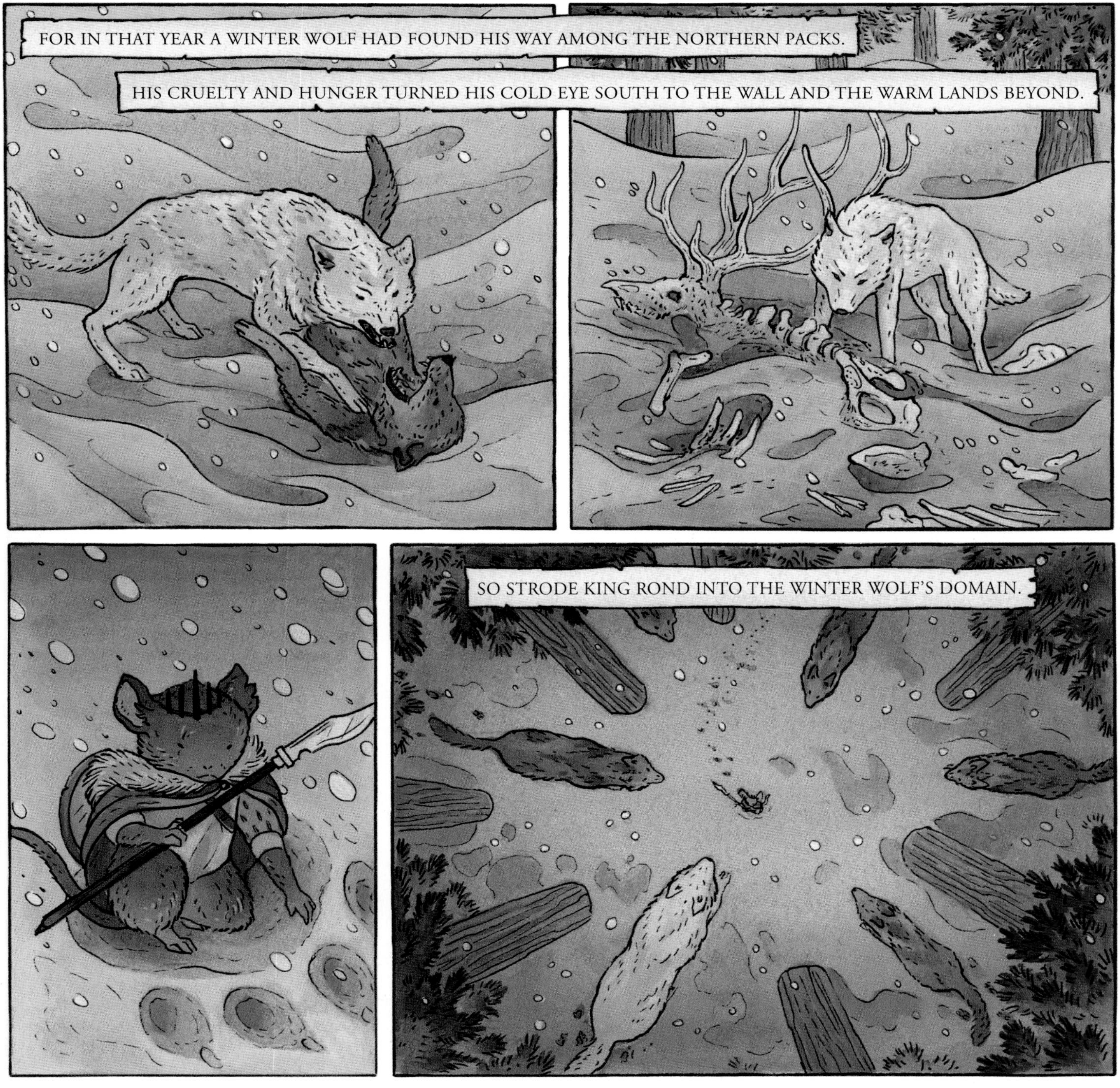
FOR IN THAT YEAR A WINTER WOLF HAD FOUND HIS WAY AMONG THE NORTHERN PACKS.
HIS CRUELTY AND HUNGER TURNED HIS COLD EYE SOUTH TO THE WALL AND THE WARM LANDS BEYOND.
SO STRODE KING ROND INTO THE WINTER WOLF'S DOMAIN.

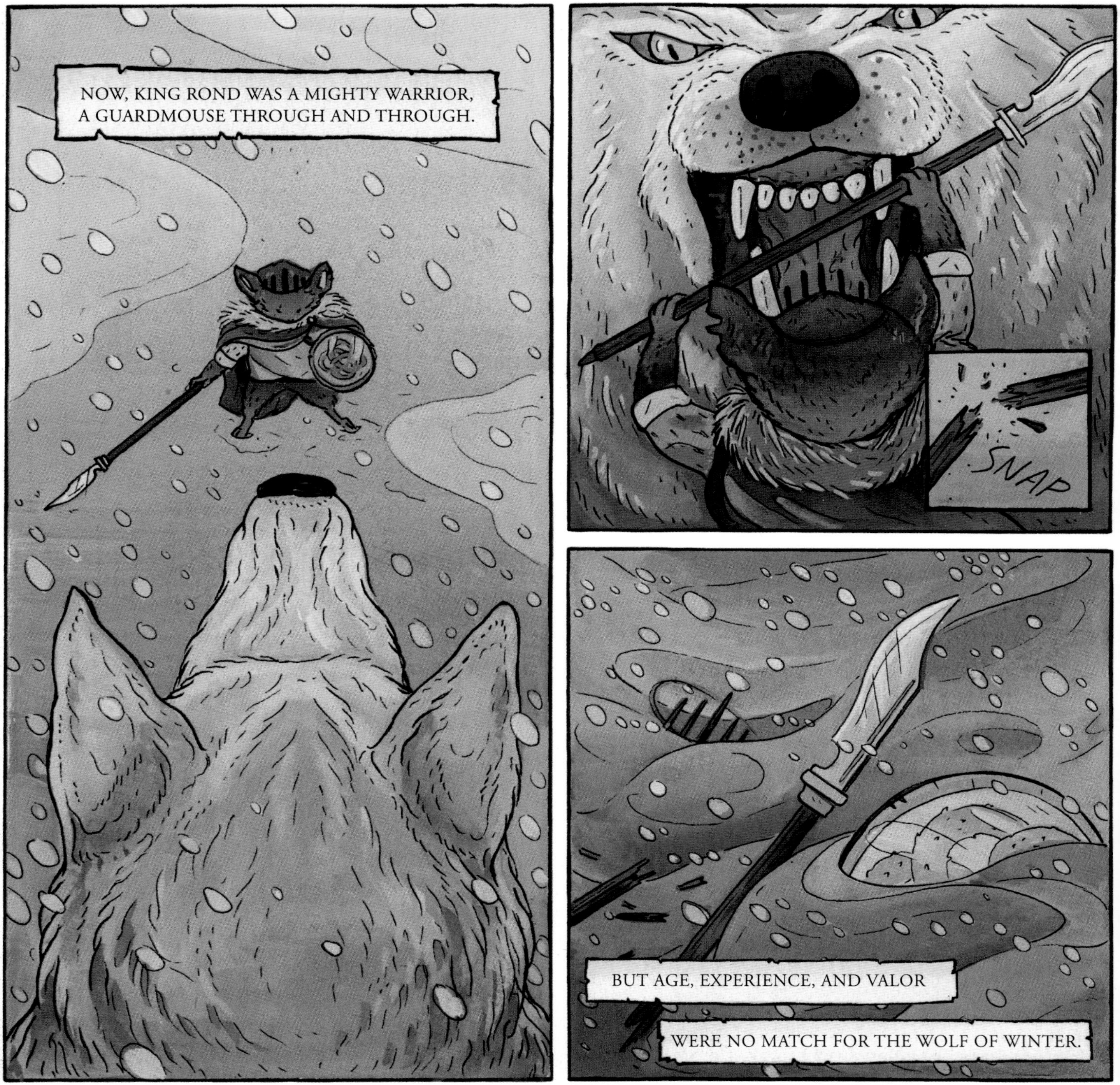
NOW, KING ROND WAS A MIGHTY WARRIOR, A GUARDMOUSE THROUGH AND THROUGH.
SNAP
BUT AGE, EXPERIENCE, AND VALOR
WERE NO MATCH FOR THE WOLF OF WINTER.

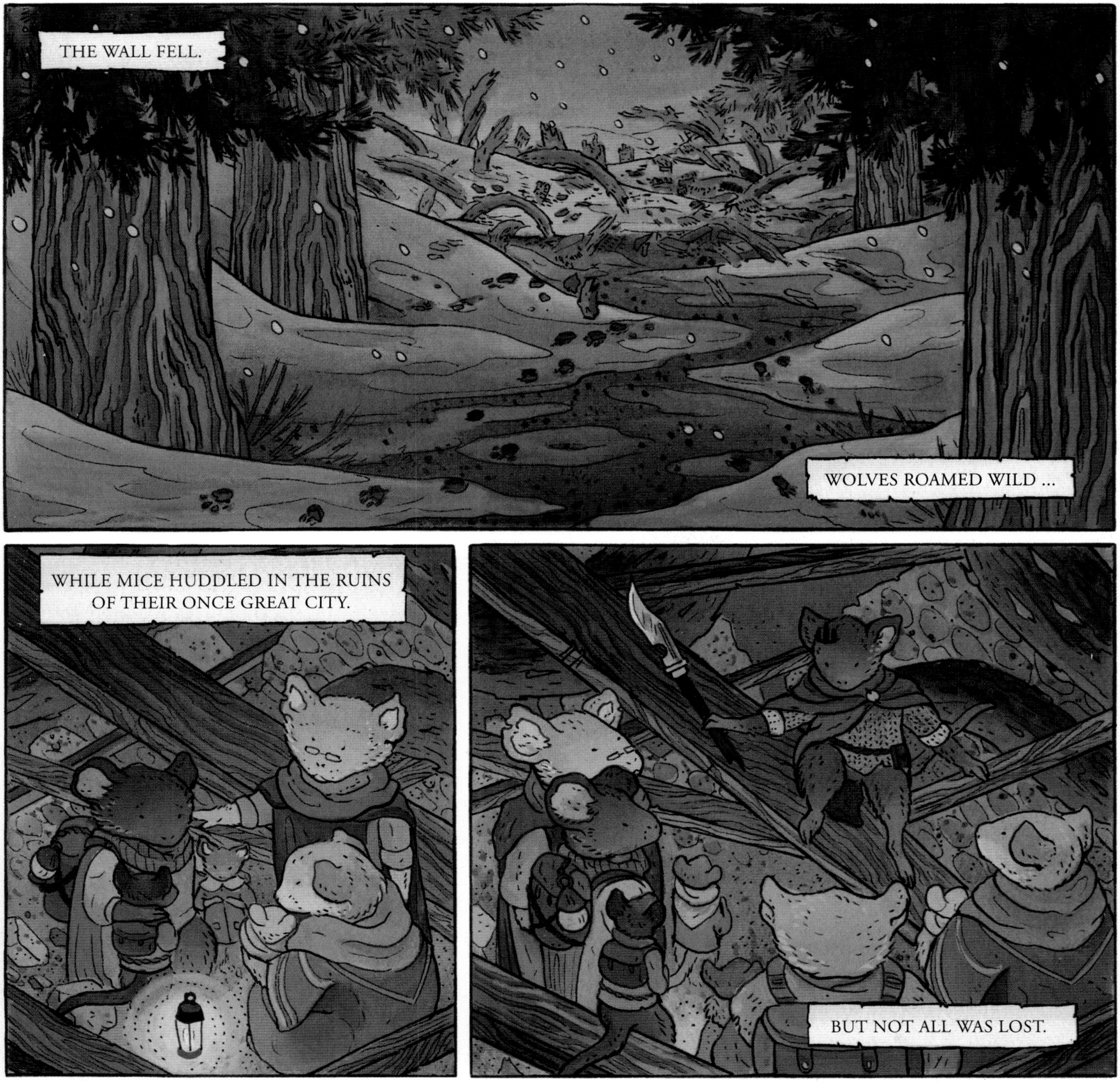
THE WALL FELL.
WOLVES ROAMED WILD ...
WHILE MICE HUDDLED IN THE RUINS OF THEIR ONCE GREAT CITY.
BUT NOT ALL WAS LOST.

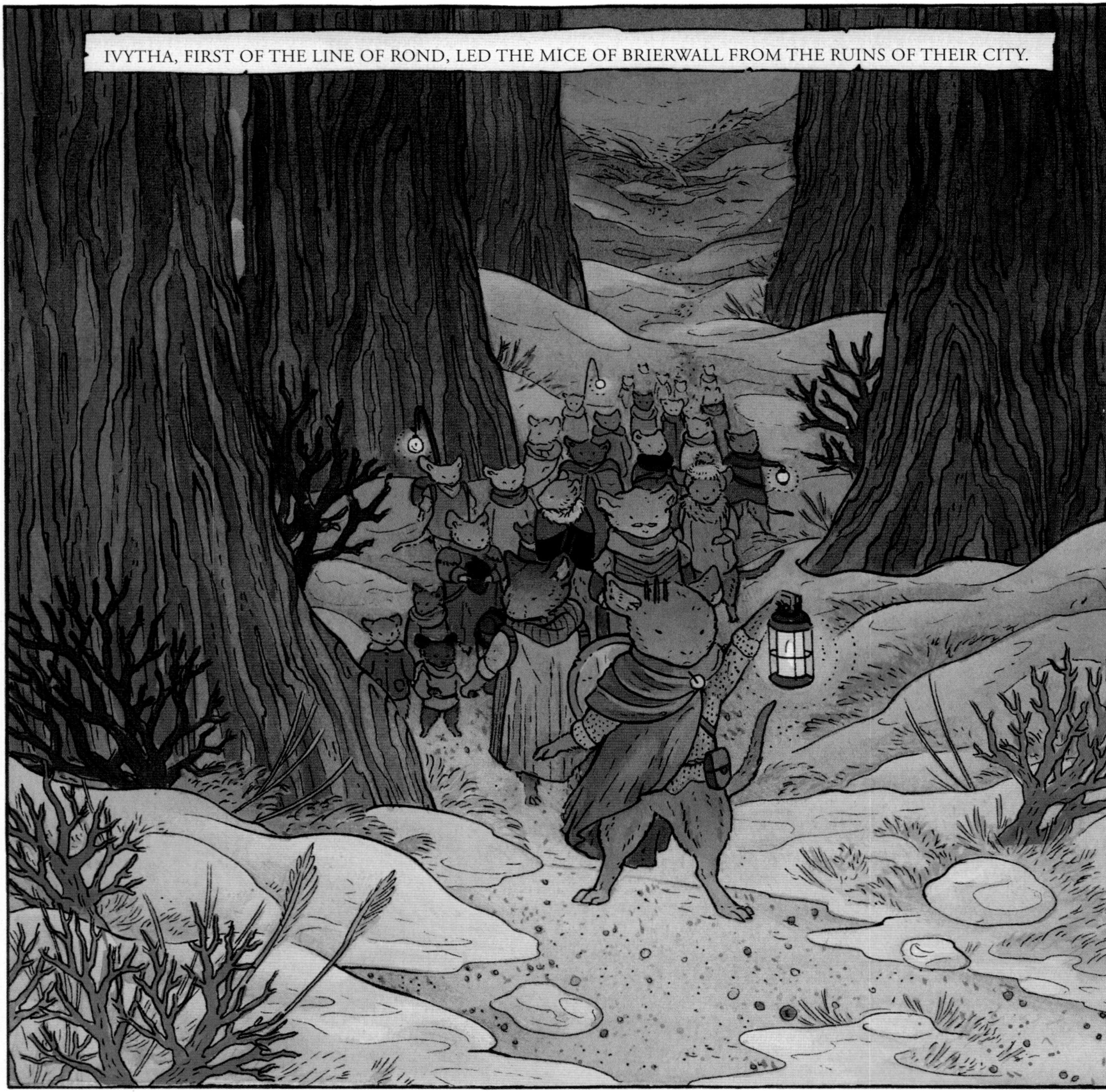
IVYTHA, FIRST OF THE LINE OF ROND, LED THE MICE OF BRIERWALL FROM THE RUINS OF THEIR CITY.

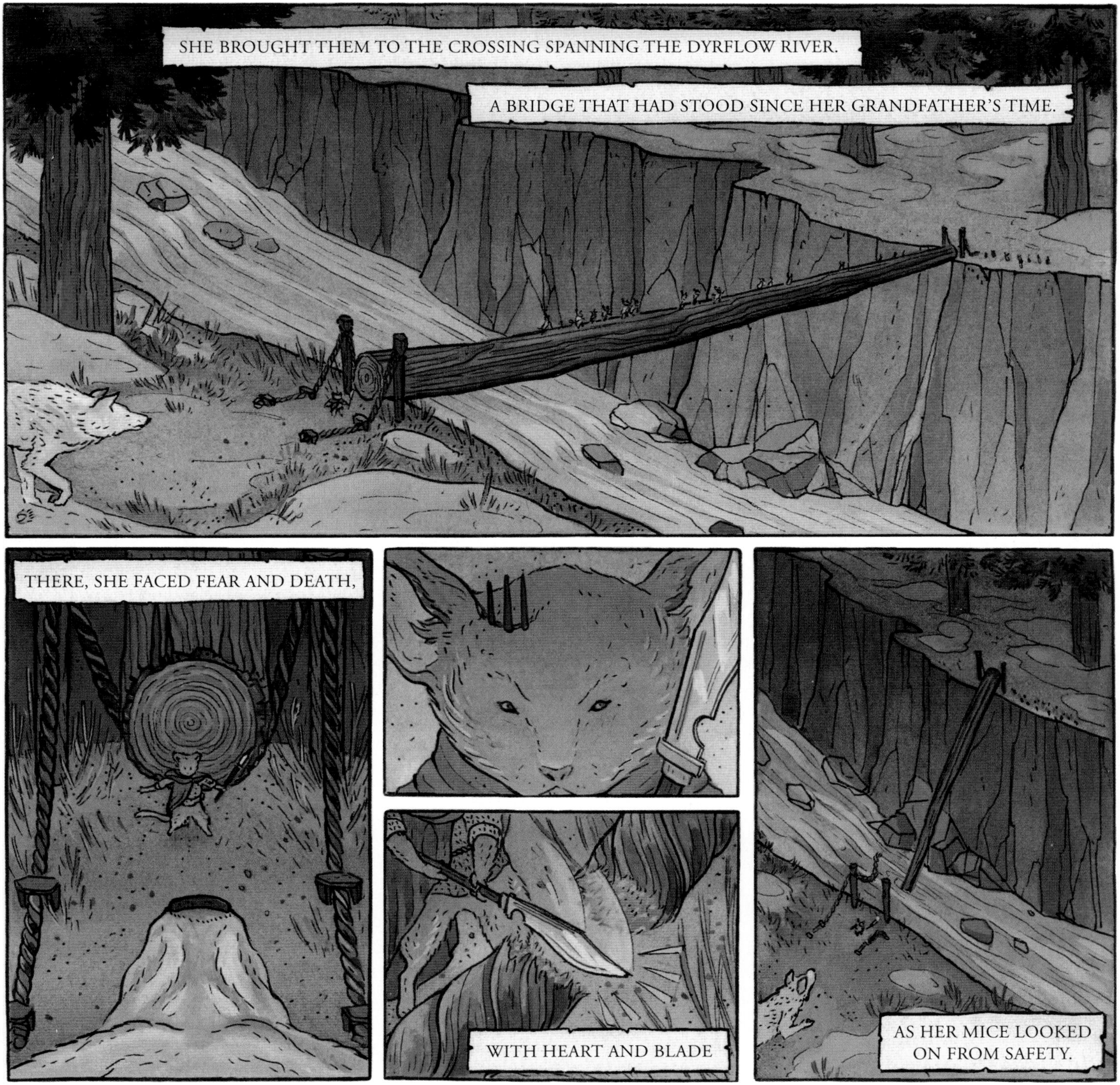
SHE BROUGHT THEM TO THE CROSSING SPANNING THE DYRFLOW RIVER.
A BRIDGE THAT HAD STOOD SINCE HER GRANDFATHER'S TIME.
THERE, SHE FACED FEAR AND DEATH,
WITH HEART AND BLADE
AS HER MICE LOOKED ON FROM SAFETY.

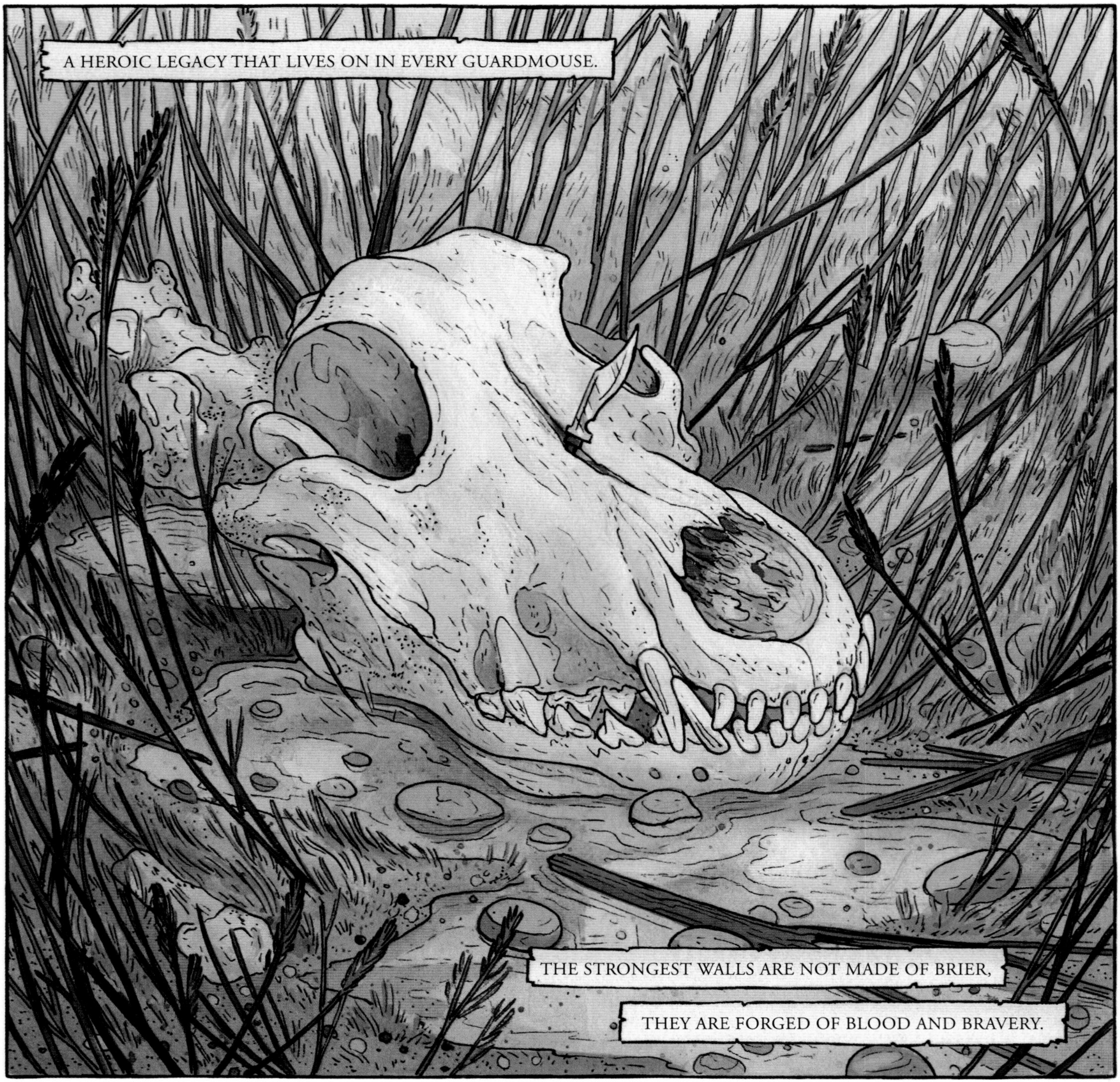
A HEROIC LEGACY THAT LIVES ON IN EVERY GUARDMOUSE.
THE STRONGEST WALLS ARE NOT MADE OF BRIER,
THEY ARE FORGED OF BLOOD AND BRAVERY.

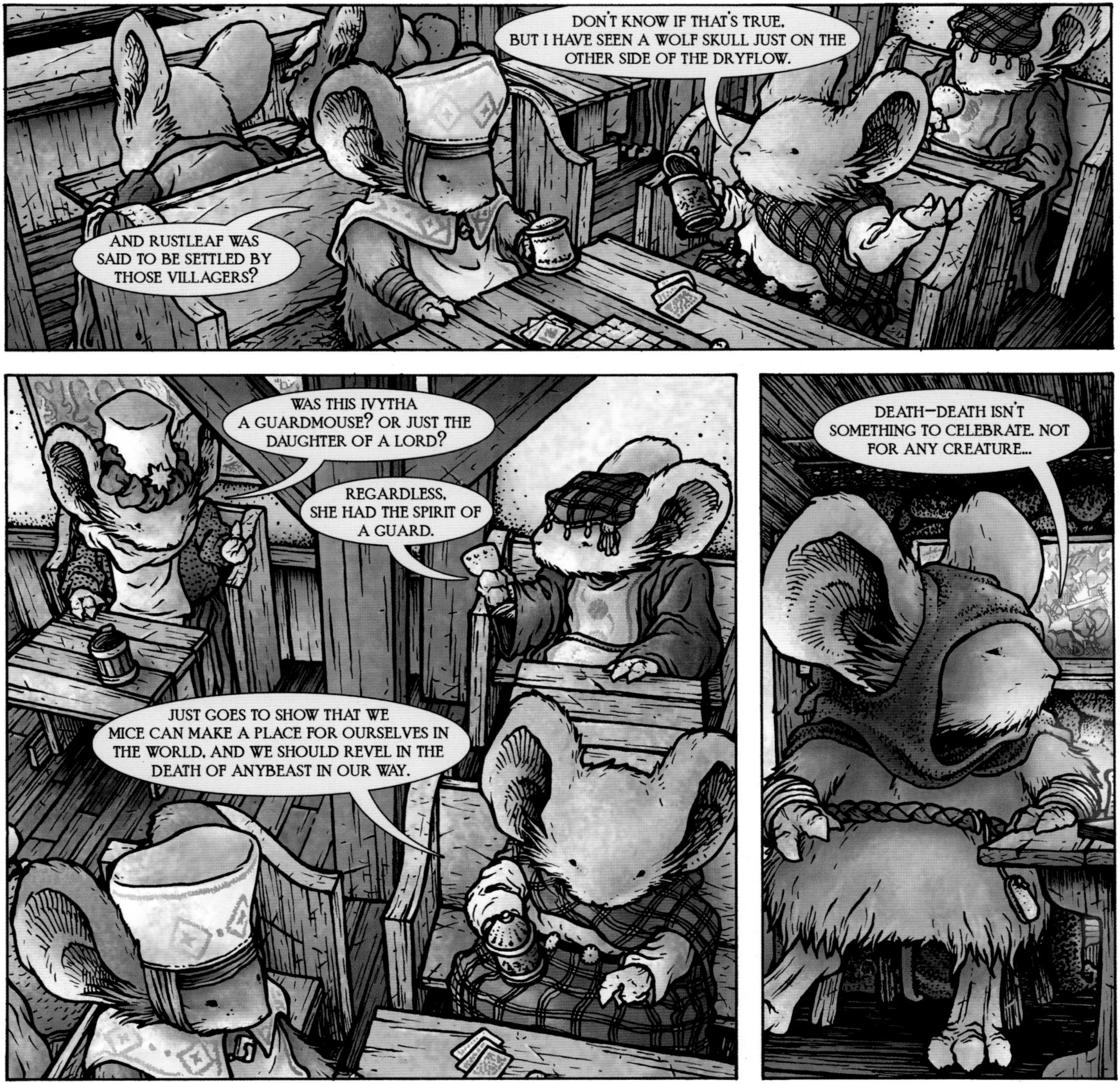

AND RUSTLEAF WAS SAID TO BE SETTLED BY THOSE VILLAGERS?
DON'T KNOW IF THAT'S TRUE, BUT I HAVE SEEN A WOLF SKULL JUST ON THE OTHER SIDE OF THE DRYFLOW.
WAS THIS IVYTHA A GUARDMOUSE? OR JUST THE DAUGHTER OF A LORD?
REGARDLESS, SHE HAD THE SPIRIT OF A GUARD.
JUST GOES TO SHOW THAT WE MICE CAN MAKE A PLACE FOR OURSELVES IN THE WORLD, AND WE SHOULD REVEL IN THE DEATH OF ANYBEAST IN OUR WAY.
DEATH—DEATH ISN'T SOMETHING TO CELEBRATE. NOT FOR ANY CREATURE...

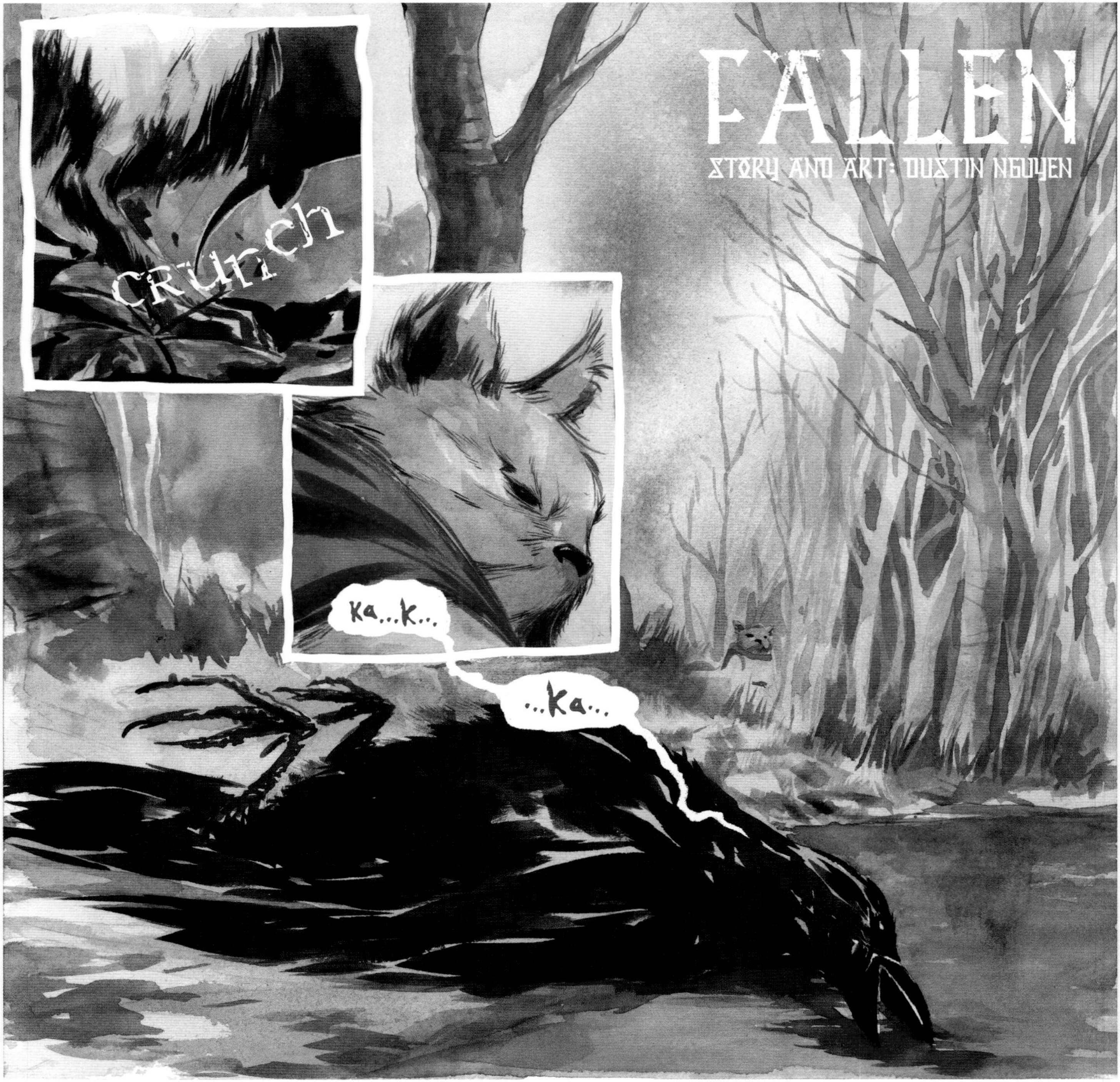
FALLEN
STORY AND ART: DUSTIN NGUYEN
crunch
Ka...k...
...Ka...

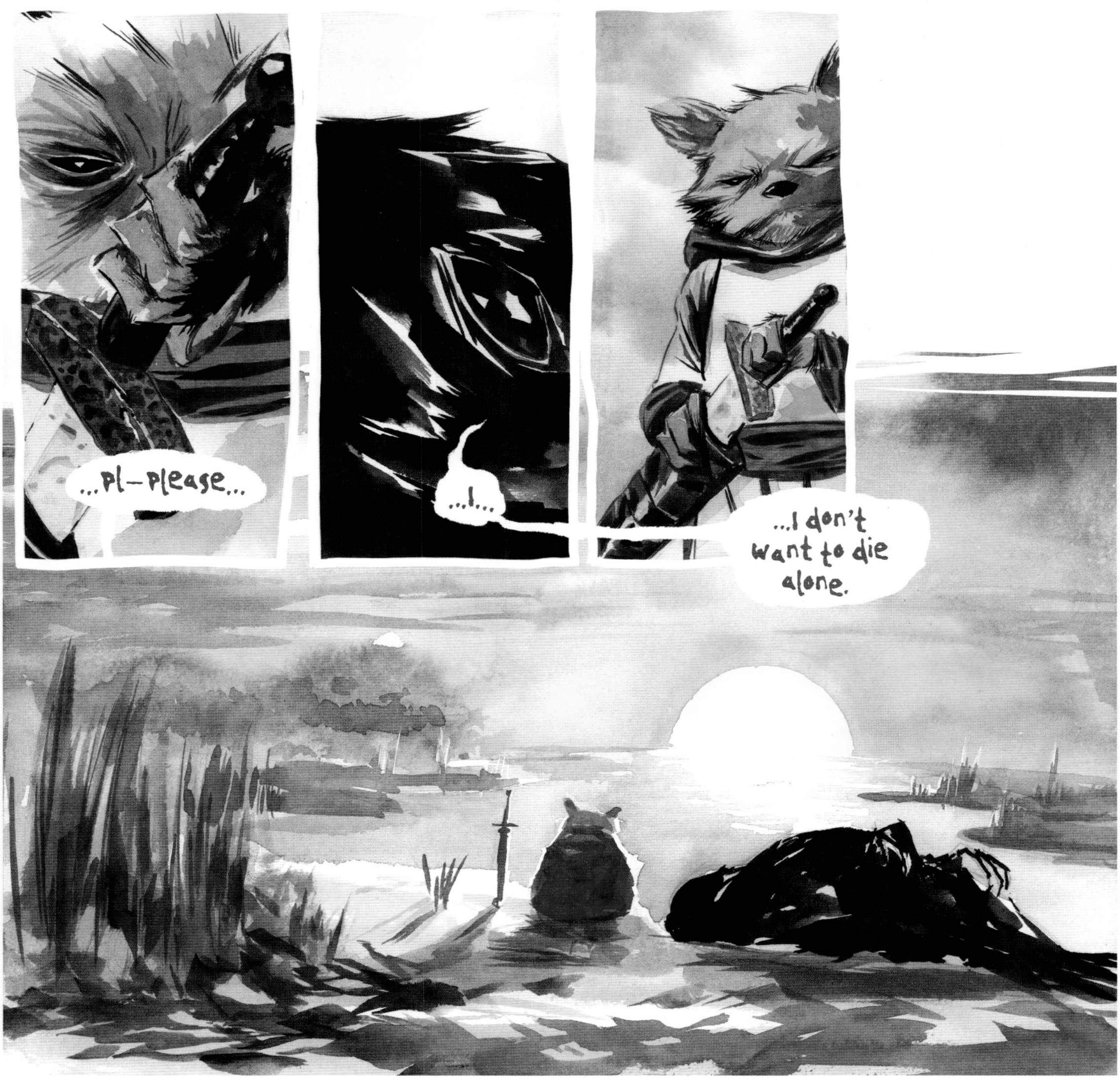
...Pl-Please...
...I...
...I don't want to die alone.

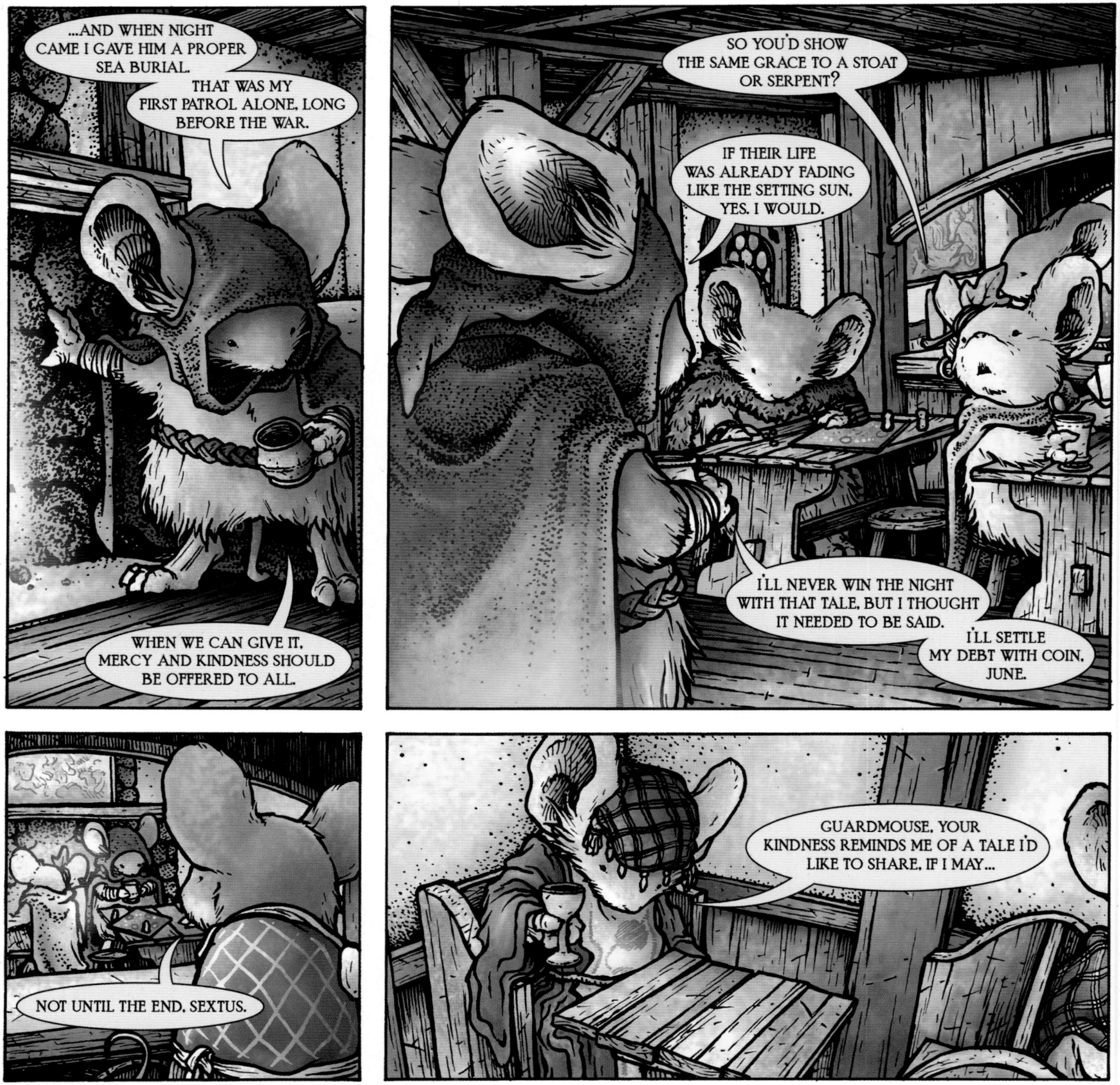
...AND WHEN NIGHT CAME I GAVE HIM A PROPER SEA BURIAL.
THAT WAS MY FIRST PATROL ALONE, LONG BEFORE THE WAR.
WHEN WE CAN GIVE IT, MERCY AND KINDNESS SHOULD BE OFFERED TO ALL.
SO YOU'D SHOW THE SAME GRACE TO A STOAT OR SERPENT?
IF THEIR LIFE WAS ALREADY FADING LIKE THE SETTING SUN, YES. I WOULD.
I'LL NEVER WIN THE NIGHT WITH THAT TALE, BUT I THOUGHT IT NEEDED TO BE SAID.
I'LL SETTLE MY DEBT WITH COIN, JUNE.
NOT UNTIL THE END, SEXTUS.
GUARDMOUSE, YOUR KINDNESS REMINDS ME OF A TALE I'D LIKE TO SHARE, IF I MAY...

THE DANCERS

A Tale of the Mouse Guard
as told by Kyla Vanderklugt

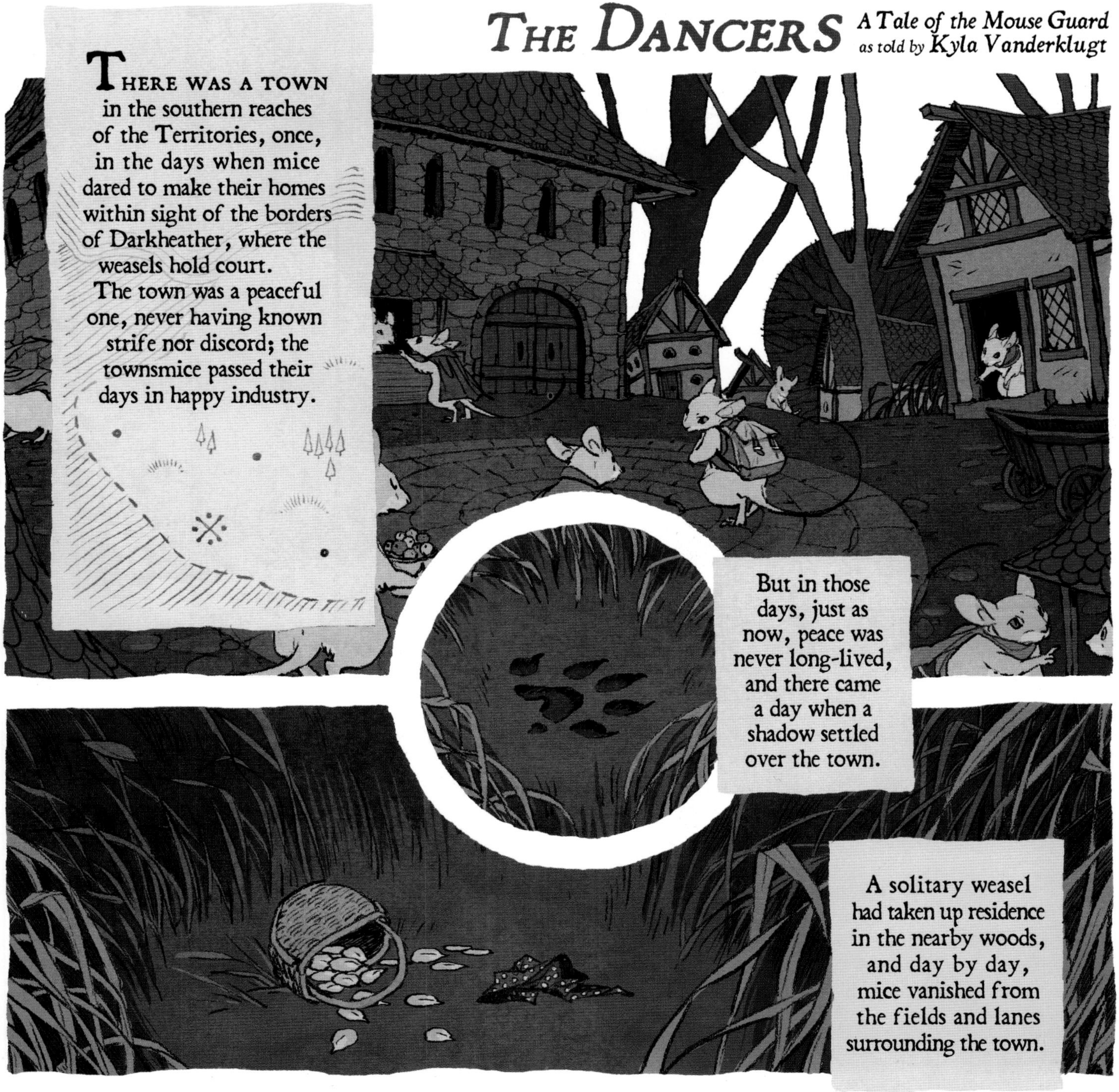
THERE WAS A TOWN in the southern reaches of the Territories, once, in the days when mice dared to make their homes within sight of the borders of Darkheather, where the weasels hold court.
The town was a peaceful one, never having known strife nor discord; the townsmice passed their days in happy industry.
But in those days, just as now, peace was never long-lived, and there came a day when a shadow settled over the town.
A solitary weasel had taken up residence in the nearby woods, and day by day, mice vanished from the fields and lanes surrounding the town.

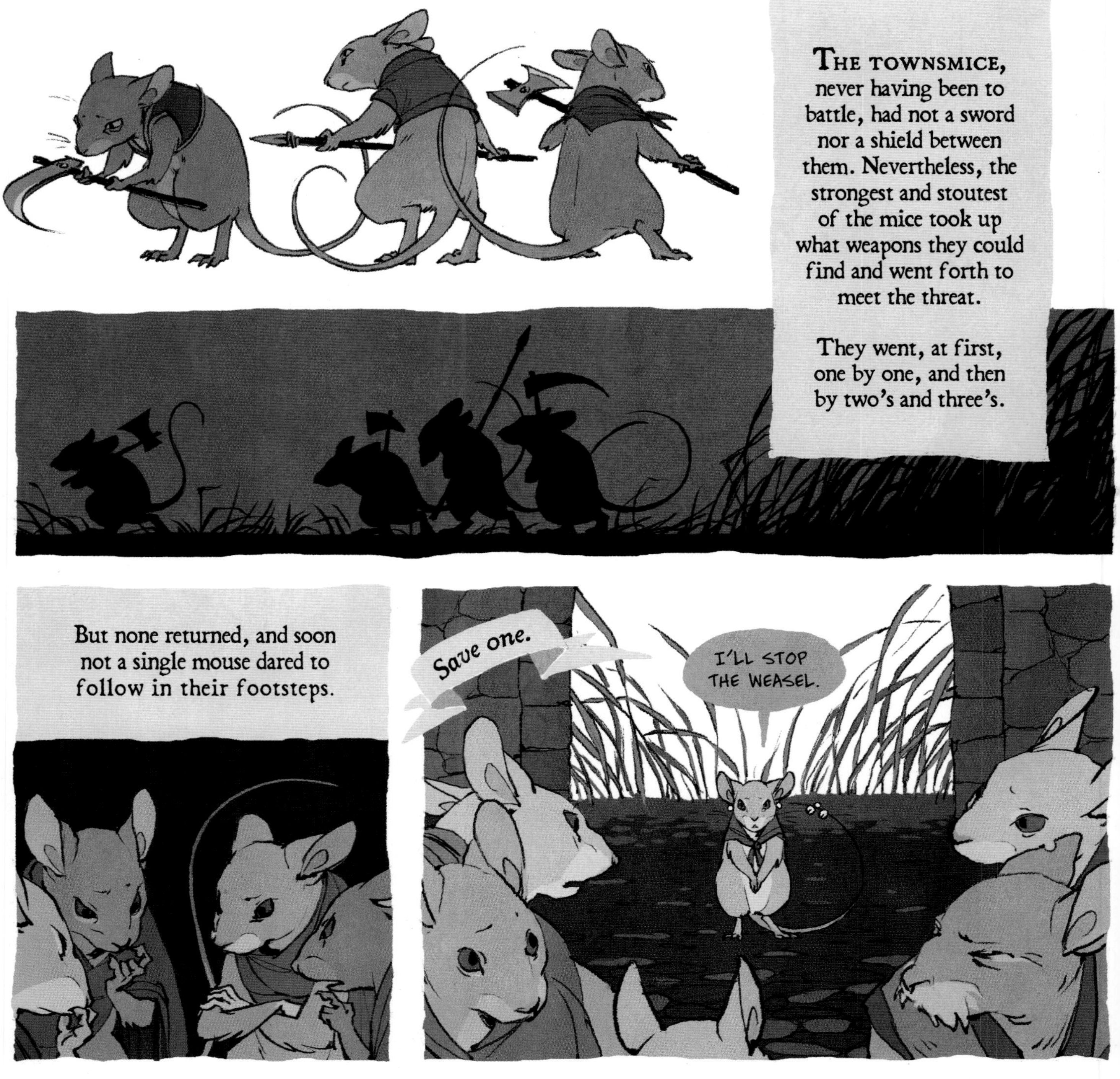

The townsmice, never having been to battle, had not a sword nor a shield between them. Nevertheless, the strongest and stoutest of the mice took up what weapons they could find and went forth to meet the threat.
They went, at first, one by one, and then by two's and three's.
But none returned, and soon not a single mouse dared to follow in their footsteps.
Save one.
I'LL STOP THE WEASEL.

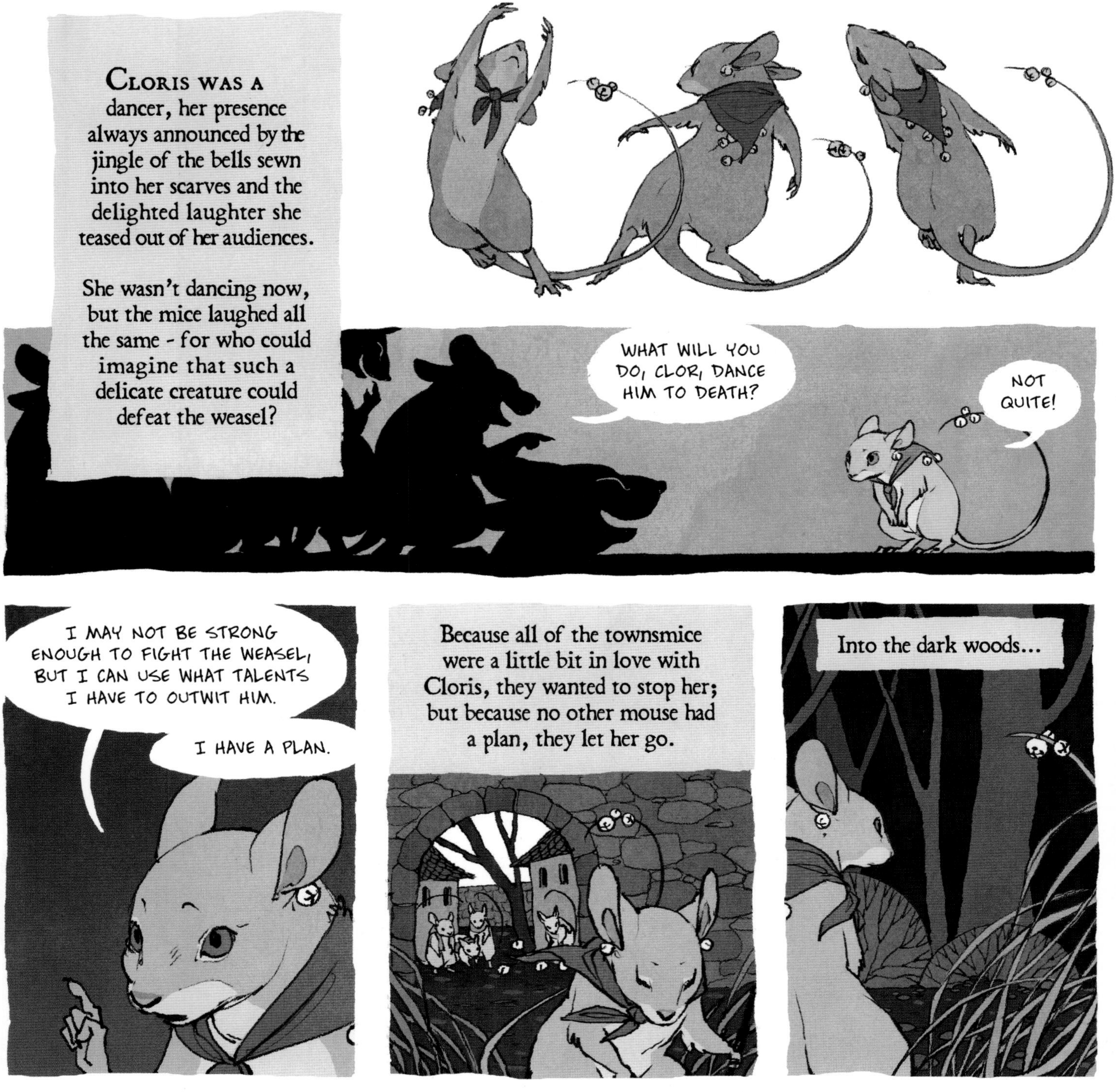

Cloris was a dancer, her presence always announced by the jingle of the bells sewn into her scarves and the delighted laughter she teased out of her audiences.
She wasn't dancing now, but the mice laughed all the same - for who could imagine that such a delicate creature could defeat the weasel?
WHAT WILL YOU DO, CLOR, DANCE HIM TO DEATH?
NOT QUITE!
I MAY NOT BE STRONG ENOUGH TO FIGHT THE WEASEL, BUT I CAN USE WHAT TALENTS I HAVE TO OUTWIT HIM.
I HAVE A PLAN.
Because all of the townsmice were a little bit in love with Cloris, they wanted to stop her; but because no other mouse had a plan, they let her go.
Into the dark woods...

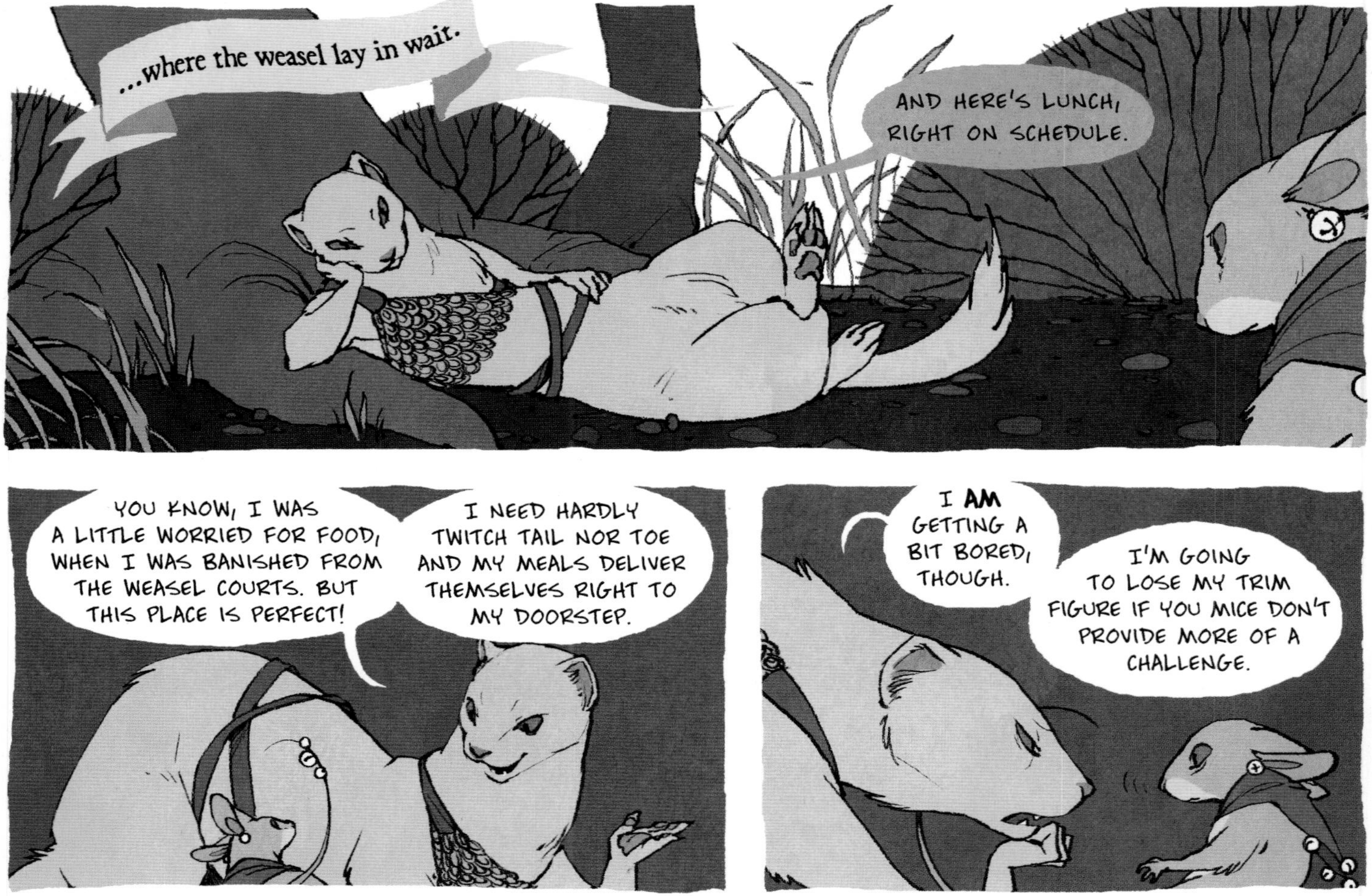
...where the weasel lay in wait.
AND HERE'S LUNCH, RIGHT ON SCHEDULE.
YOU KNOW, I WAS A LITTLE WORRIED FOR FOOD, WHEN I WAS BANISHED FROM THE WEASEL COURTS. BUT THIS PLACE IS PERFECT!
I NEED HARDLY TWITCH TAIL NOR TOE AND MY MEALS DELIVER THEMSELVES RIGHT TO MY DOORSTEP.
I **AM** GETTING A BIT BORED, THOUGH.
I'M GOING TO LOSE MY TRIM FIGURE IF YOU MICE DON'T PROVIDE MORE OF A CHALLENGE.

Cloris quaked at the sight of the weasel's gleaming eyes and glinting teeth. But she was accustomed to putting on a show, and so she stilled the trembling of her paws and said:

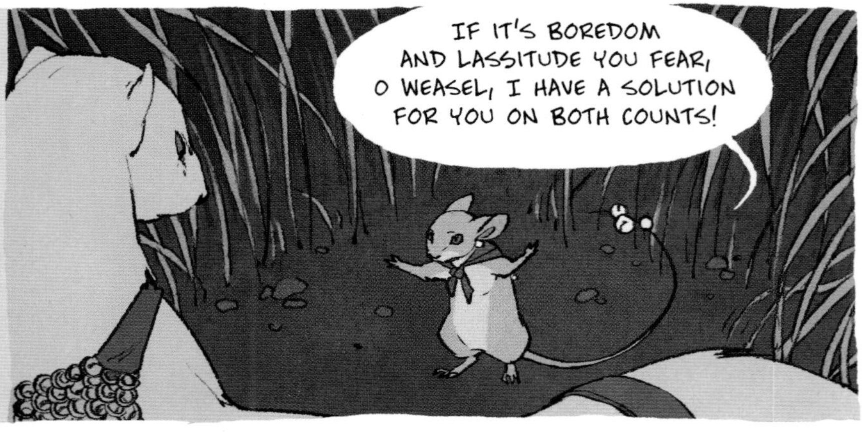
IF IT'S BOREDOM AND LASSITUDE YOU FEAR, O WEASEL, I HAVE A SOLUTION FOR YOU ON BOTH COUNTS!

And she began to dance.

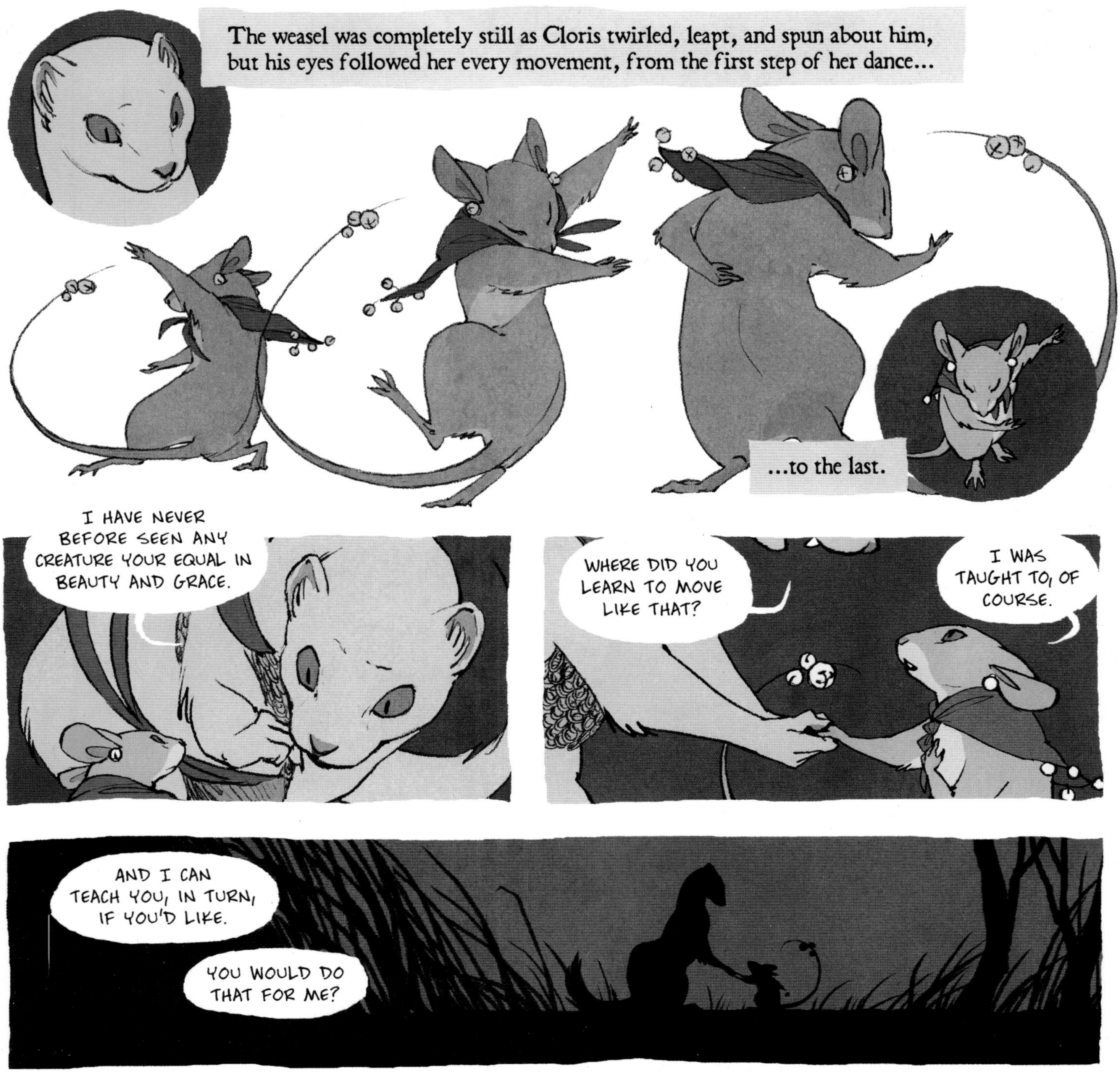
The weasel was completely still as Cloris twirled, leapt, and spun about him, but his eyes followed her every movement, from the first step of her dance...
...to the last.
I HAVE NEVER BEFORE SEEN ANY CREATURE YOUR EQUAL IN BEAUTY AND GRACE.
WHERE DID YOU LEARN TO MOVE LIKE THAT?
I WAS TAUGHT TO, OF COURSE.
AND I CAN TEACH YOU, IN TURN, IF YOU'D LIKE.
YOU WOULD DO THAT FOR ME?

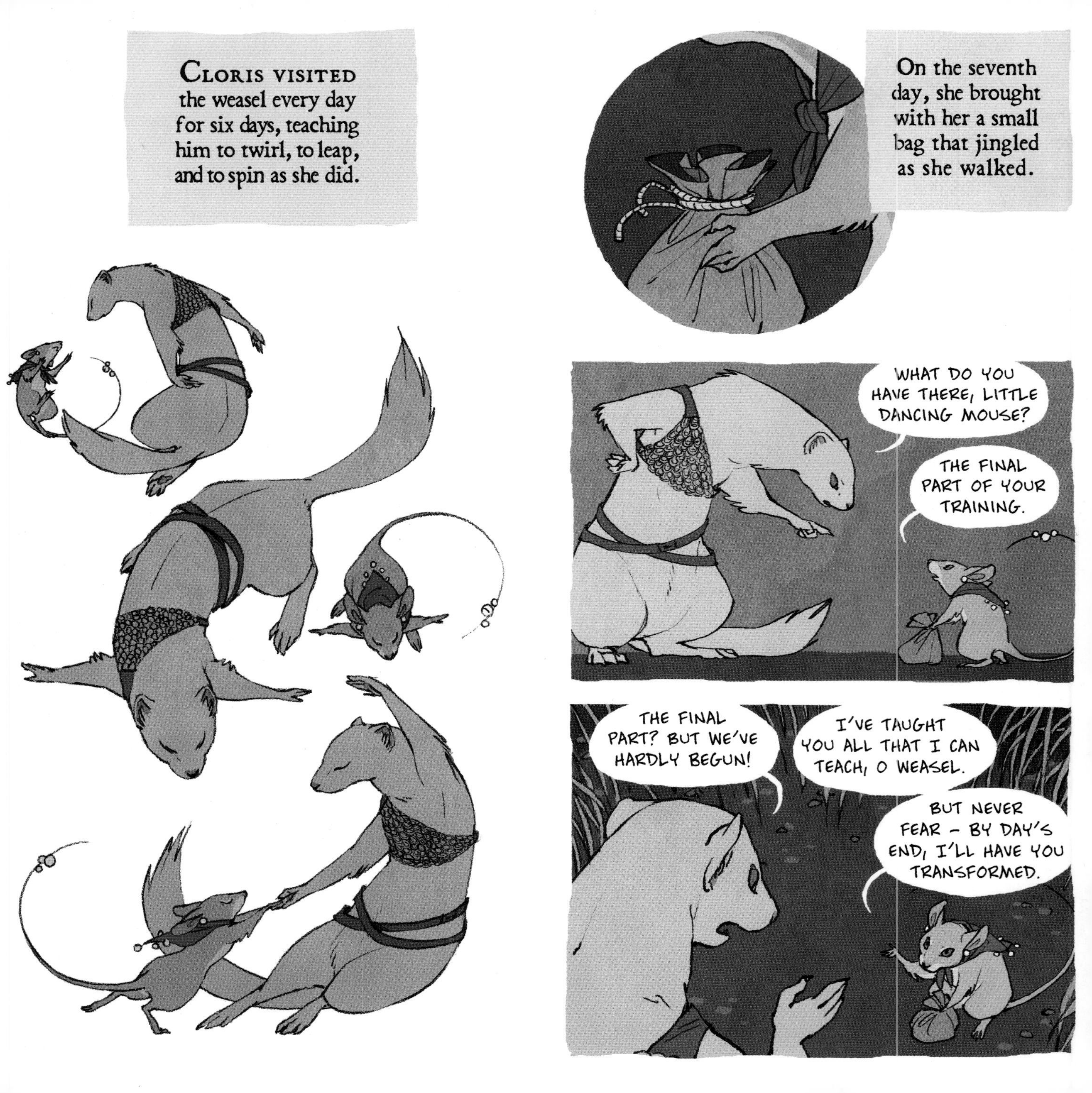
Cloris visited the weasel every day for six days, teaching him to twirl, to leap, and to spin as she did.
On the seventh day, she brought with her a small bag that jingled as she walked.
WHAT DO YOU HAVE THERE, LITTLE DANCING MOUSE?
THE FINAL PART OF YOUR TRAINING.
THE FINAL PART? BUT WE'VE HARDLY BEGUN!
I'VE TAUGHT YOU ALL THAT I CAN TEACH, O WEASEL.
BUT NEVER FEAR – BY DAY'S END, I'LL HAVE YOU TRANSFORMED.

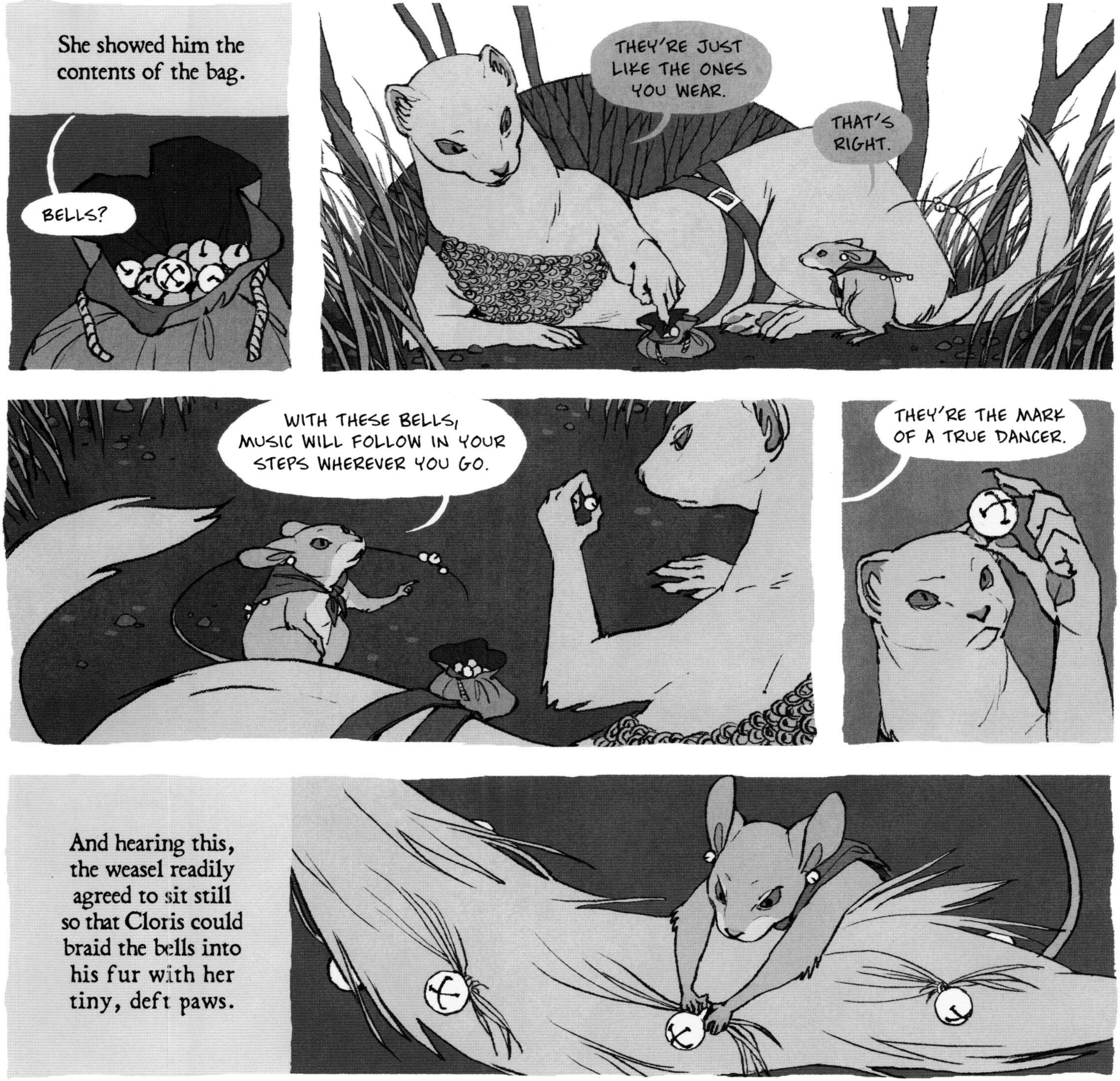
She showed him the contents of the bag.
BELLS?
THEY'RE JUST LIKE THE ONES YOU WEAR.
THAT'S RIGHT.
WITH THESE BELLS, MUSIC WILL FOLLOW IN YOUR STEPS WHEREVER YOU GO.
THEY'RE THE MARK OF A TRUE DANCER.
And hearing this, the weasel readily agreed to sit still so that Cloris could braid the bells into his fur with her tiny, deft paws.

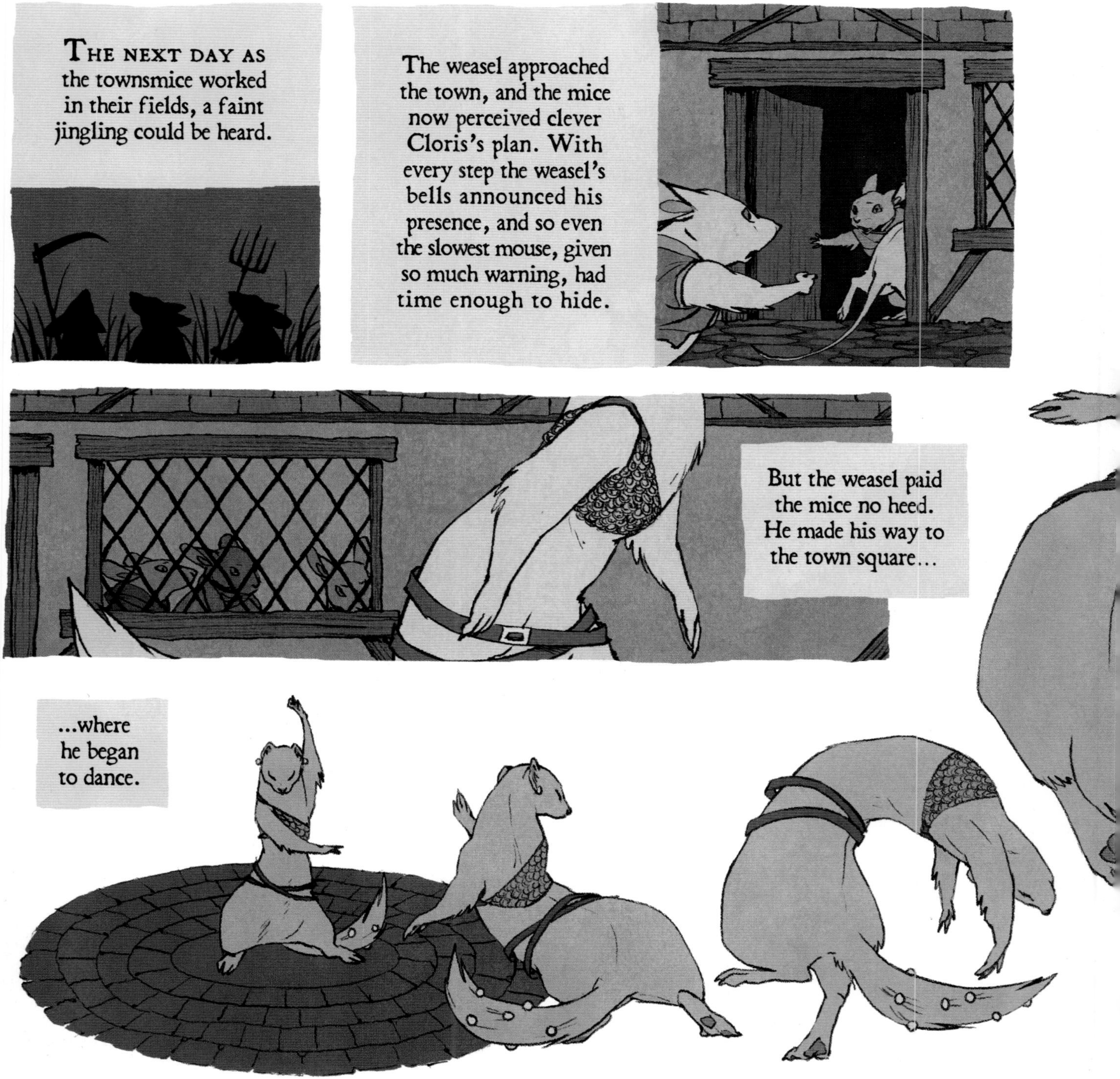
THE NEXT DAY AS the townsmice worked in their fields, a faint jingling could be heard.
The weasel approached the town, and the mice now perceived clever Cloris's plan. With every step the weasel's bells announced his presence, and so even the slowest mouse, given so much warning, had time enough to hide.
But the weasel paid the mice no heed. He made his way to the town square...
...where he began to dance.

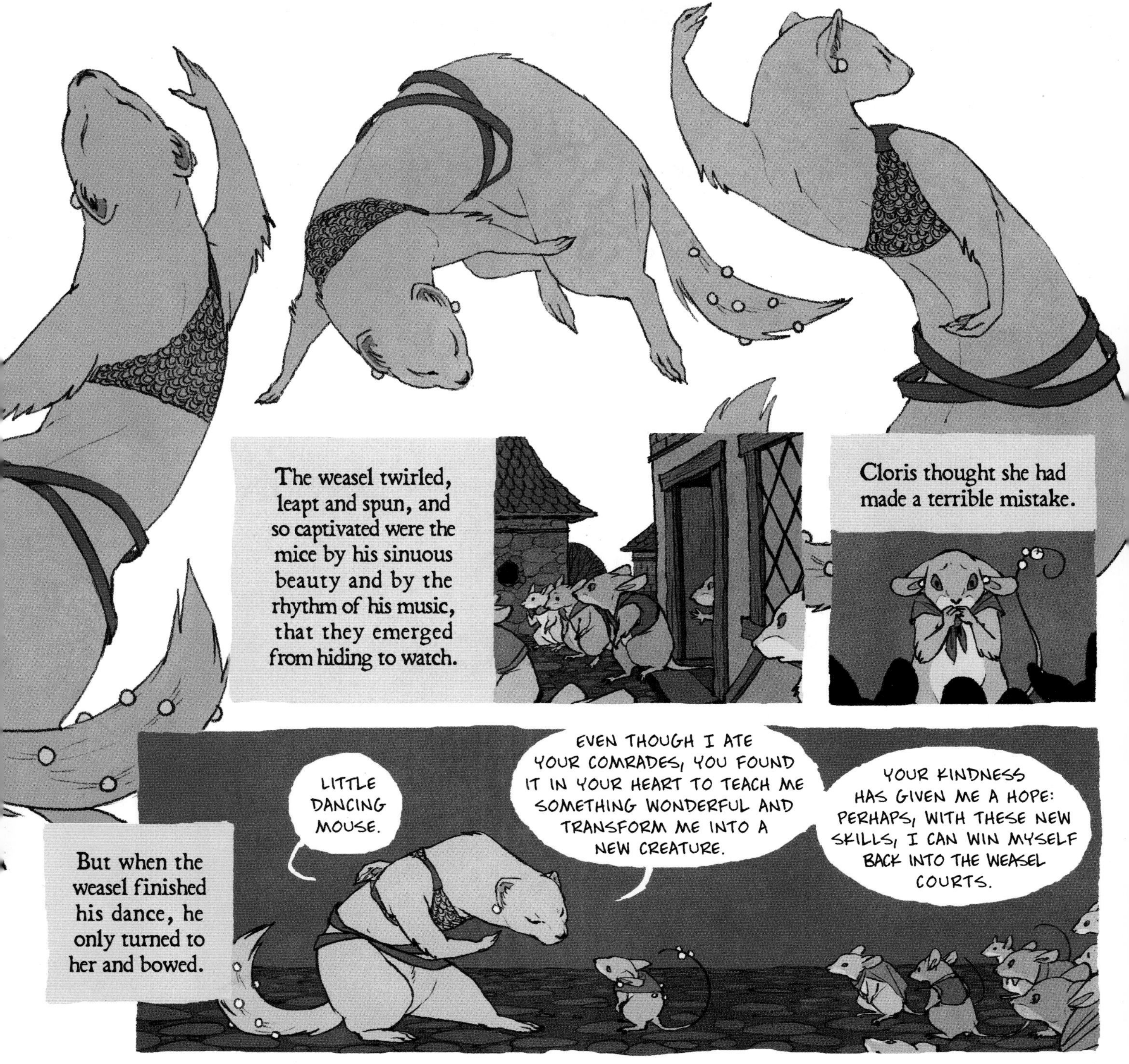
The weasel twirled, leapt and spun, and so captivated were the mice by his sinuous beauty and by the rhythm of his music, that they emerged from hiding to watch.
Cloris thought she had made a terrible mistake.
But when the weasel finished his dance, he only turned to her and bowed.
LITTLE DANCING MOUSE.
EVEN THOUGH I ATE YOUR COMRADES, YOU FOUND IT IN YOUR HEART TO TEACH ME SOMETHING WONDERFUL AND TRANSFORM ME INTO A NEW CREATURE.
YOUR KINDNESS HAS GIVEN ME A HOPE: PERHAPS, WITH THESE NEW SKILLS, I CAN WIN MYSELF BACK INTO THE WEASEL COURTS.

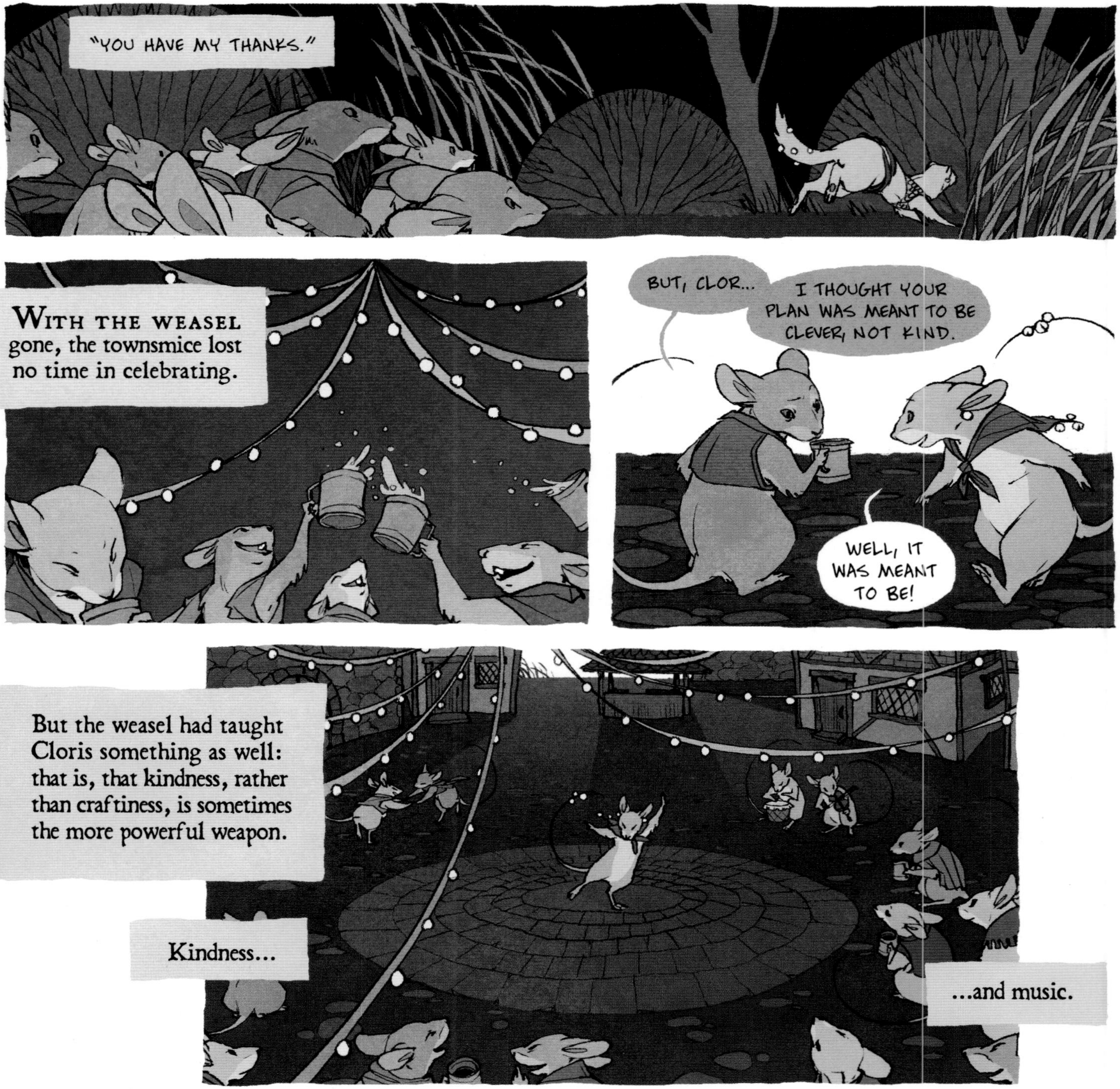
"YOU HAVE MY THANKS."
WITH THE WEASEL gone, the townsmice lost no time in celebrating.
BUT, CLOR...
I THOUGHT YOUR PLAN WAS MEANT TO BE CLEVER, NOT KIND.
WELL, IT WAS MEANT TO BE!
But the weasel had taught Cloris something as well: that is, that kindness, rather than craftiness, is sometimes the more powerful weapon.
Kindness...
...and music.

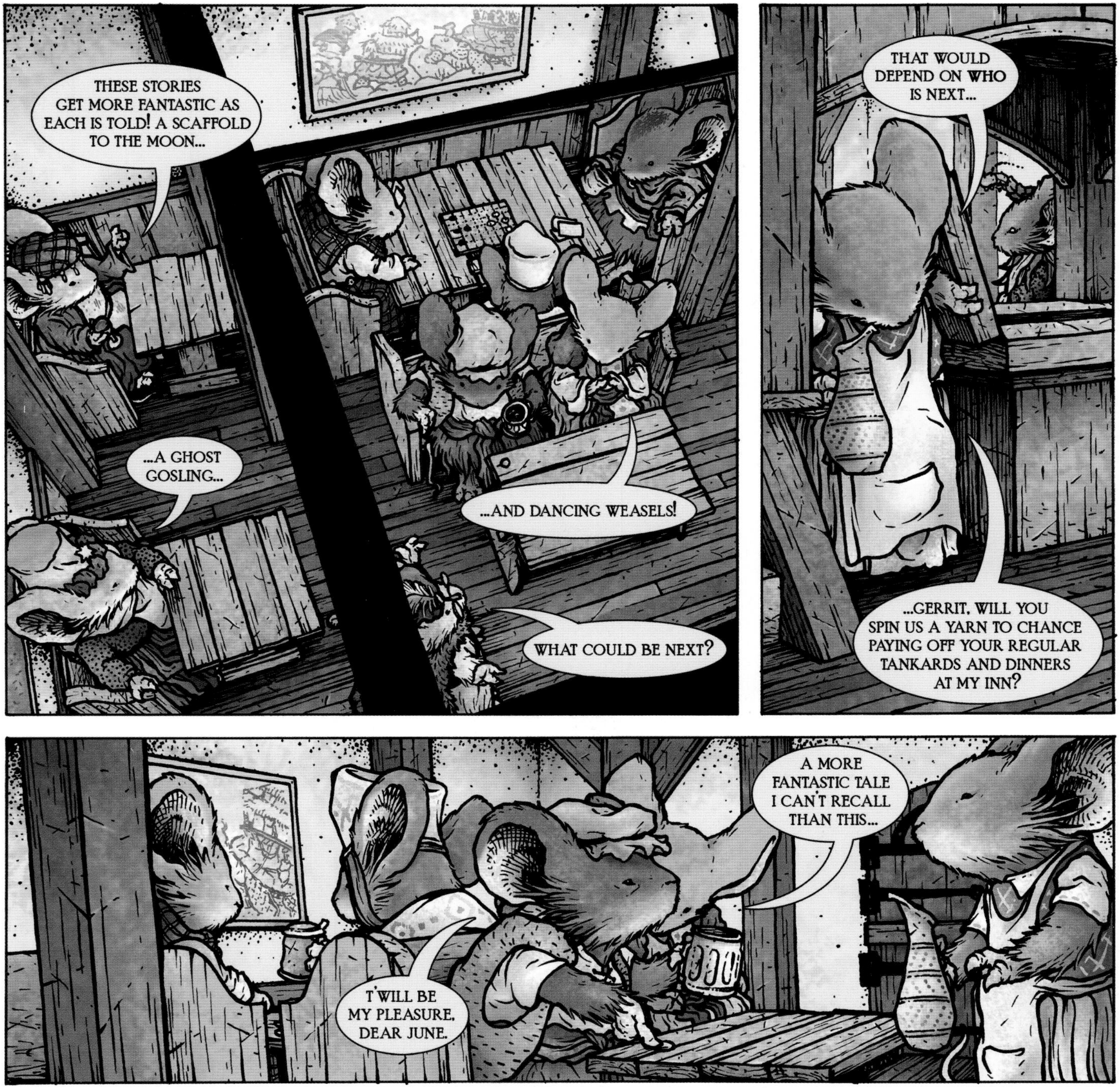
THESE STORIES GET MORE FANTASTIC AS EACH IS TOLD! A SCAFFOLD TO THE MOON...
...A GHOST GOSLING...
...AND DANCING WEASELS!
WHAT COULD BE NEXT?
THAT WOULD DEPEND ON WHO IS NEXT...
...GERRIT, WILL YOU SPIN US A YARN TO CHANCE PAYING OFF YOUR REGULAR TANKARDS AND DINNERS AT MY INN?
A MORE FANTASTIC TALE I CAN'T RECALL THAN THIS...
T'WILL BE MY PLEASURE, DEAR JUNE.

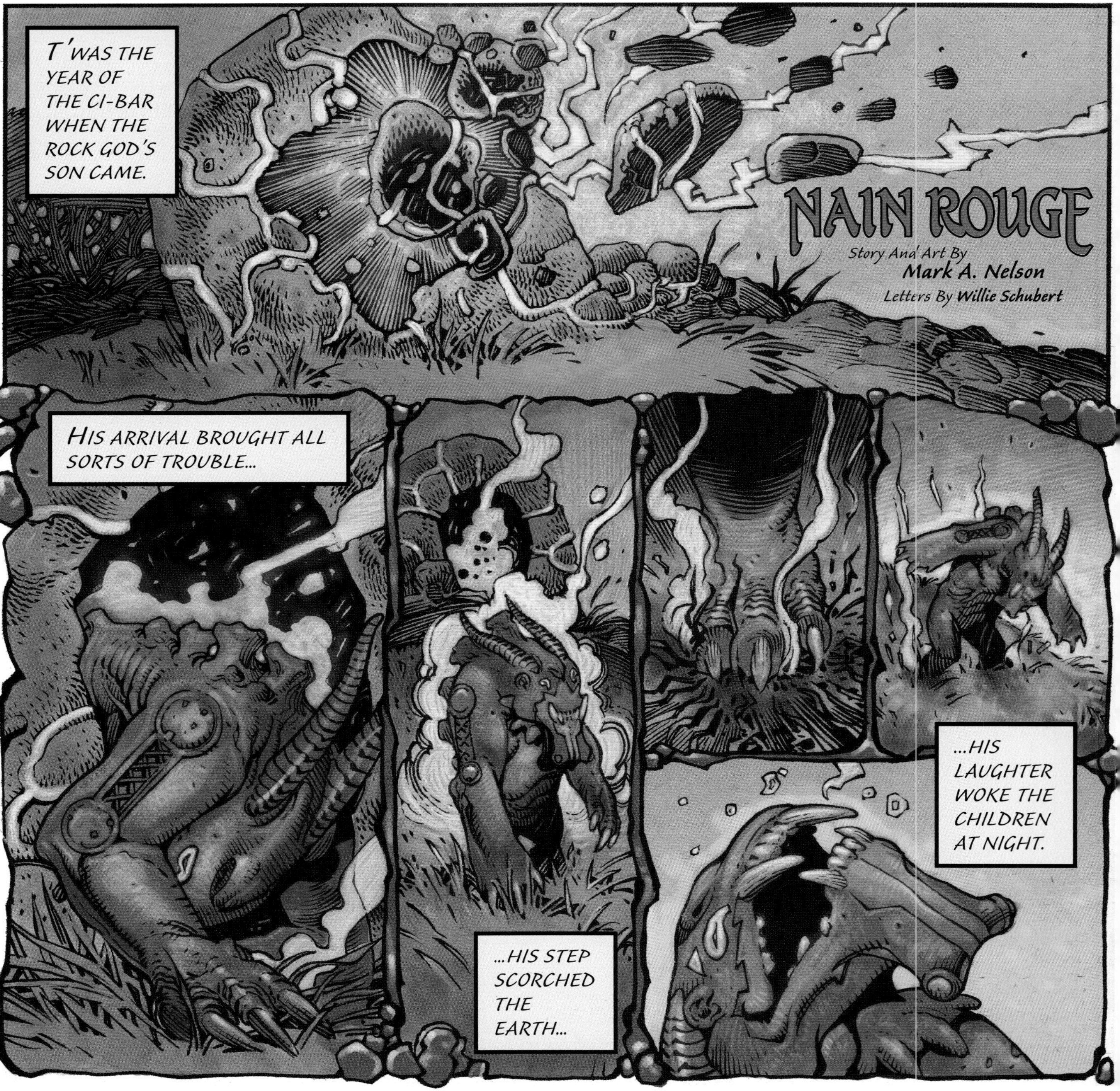

T'WAS THE YEAR OF THE CI-BAR WHEN THE ROCK GOD'S SON CAME.
NAIN ROUGE
Story And Art By
Mark A. Nelson
Letters By Willie Schubert
HIS ARRIVAL BROUGHT ALL SORTS OF TROUBLE...
...HIS STEP SCORCHED THE EARTH...
...HIS LAUGHTER WOKE THE CHILDREN AT NIGHT.

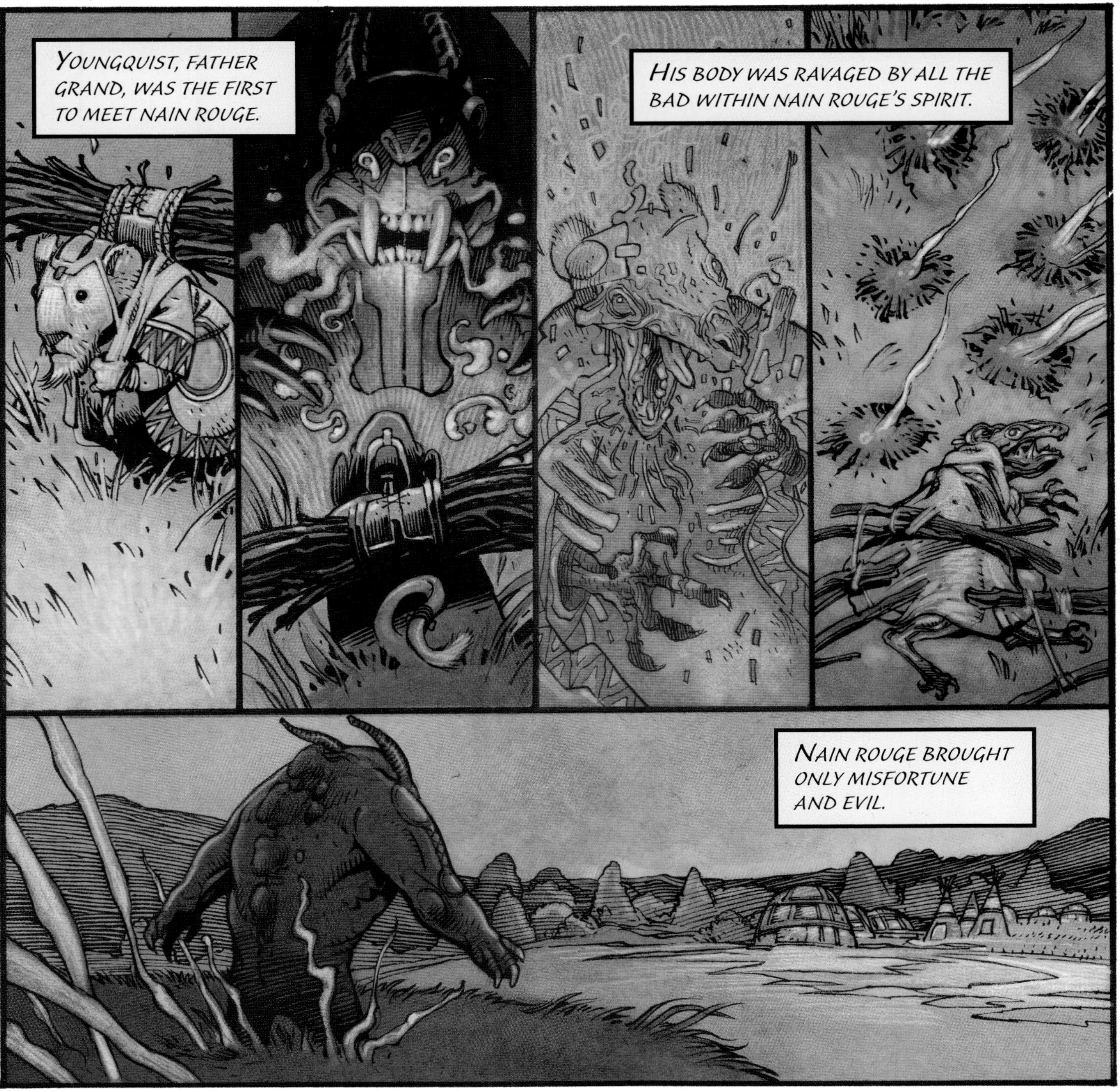
YOUNGQUIST, FATHER GRAND, WAS THE FIRST TO MEET NAIN ROUGE.
HIS BODY WAS RAVAGED BY ALL THE BAD WITHIN NAIN ROUGE'S SPIRIT.
NAIN ROUGE BROUGHT ONLY MISFORTUNE AND EVIL.

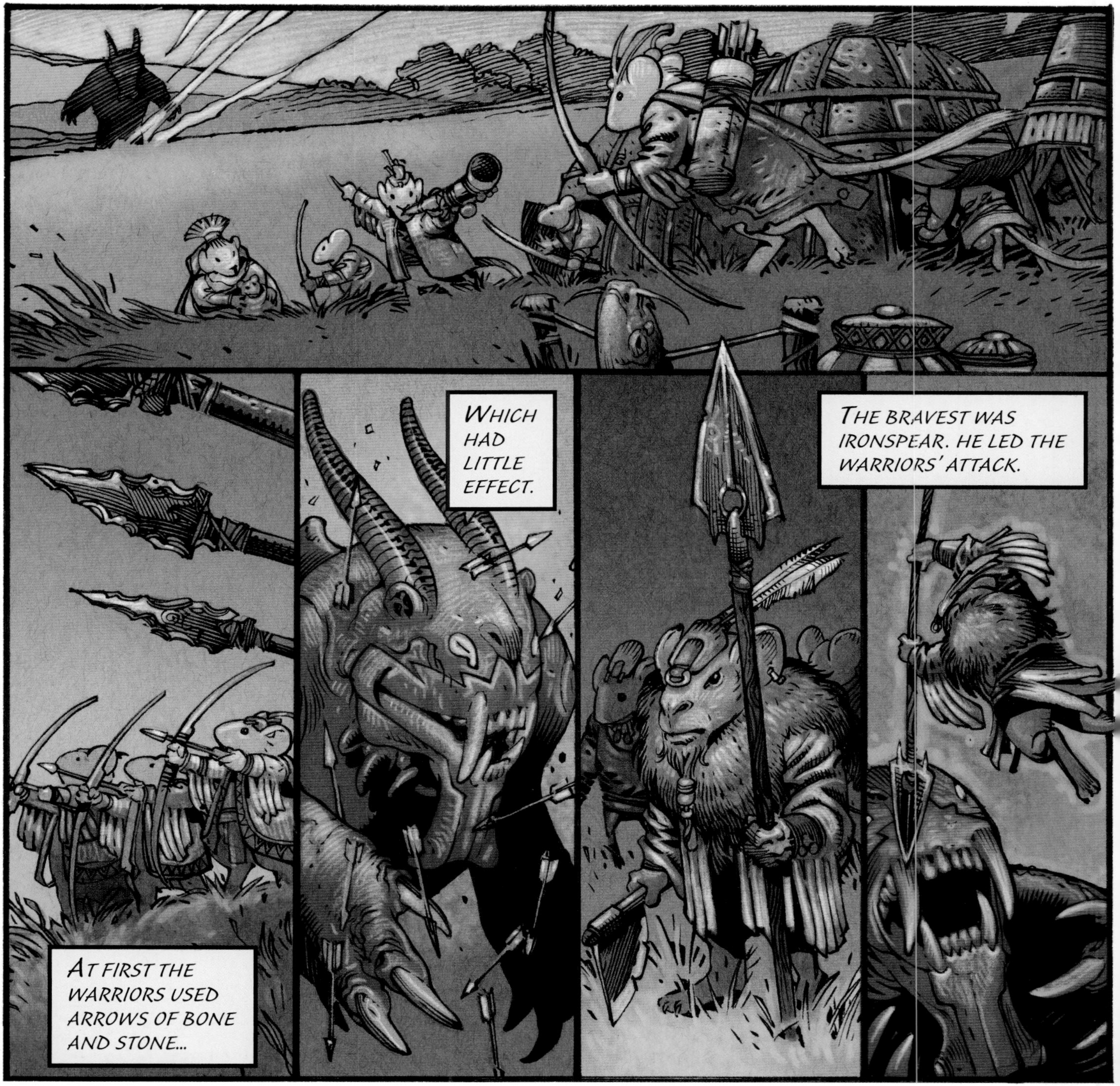

AT FIRST THE WARRIORS USED ARROWS OF BONE AND STONE...
WHICH HAD LITTLE EFFECT.
THE BRAVEST WAS IRONSPEAR. HE LED THE WARRIORS' ATTACK.

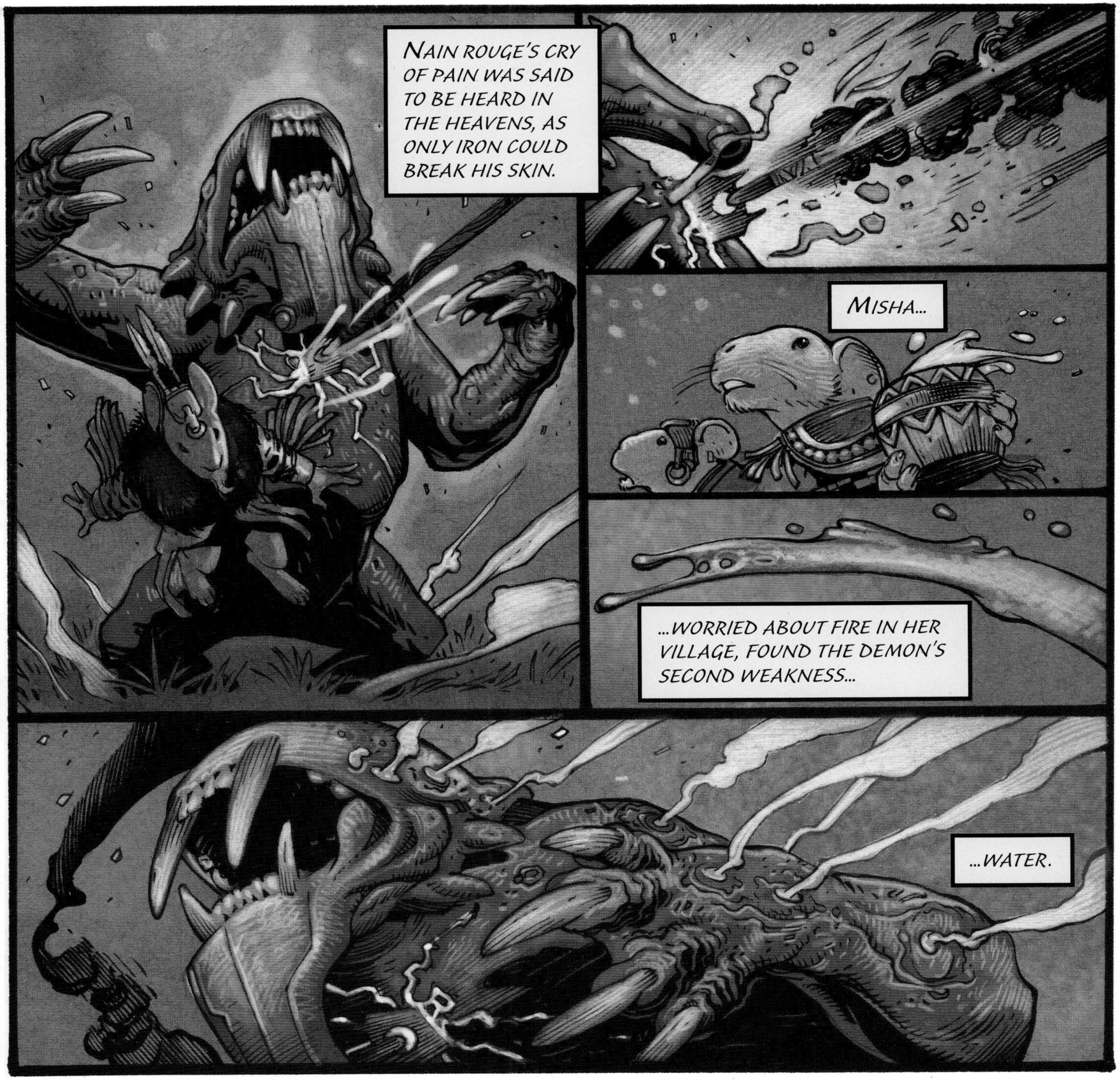
NAIN ROUGE'S CRY OF PAIN WAS SAID TO BE HEARD IN THE HEAVENS, AS ONLY IRON COULD BREAK HIS SKIN.
MISHA...
...WORRIED ABOUT FIRE IN HER VILLAGE, FOUND THE DEMON'S SECOND WEAKNESS...
...WATER.

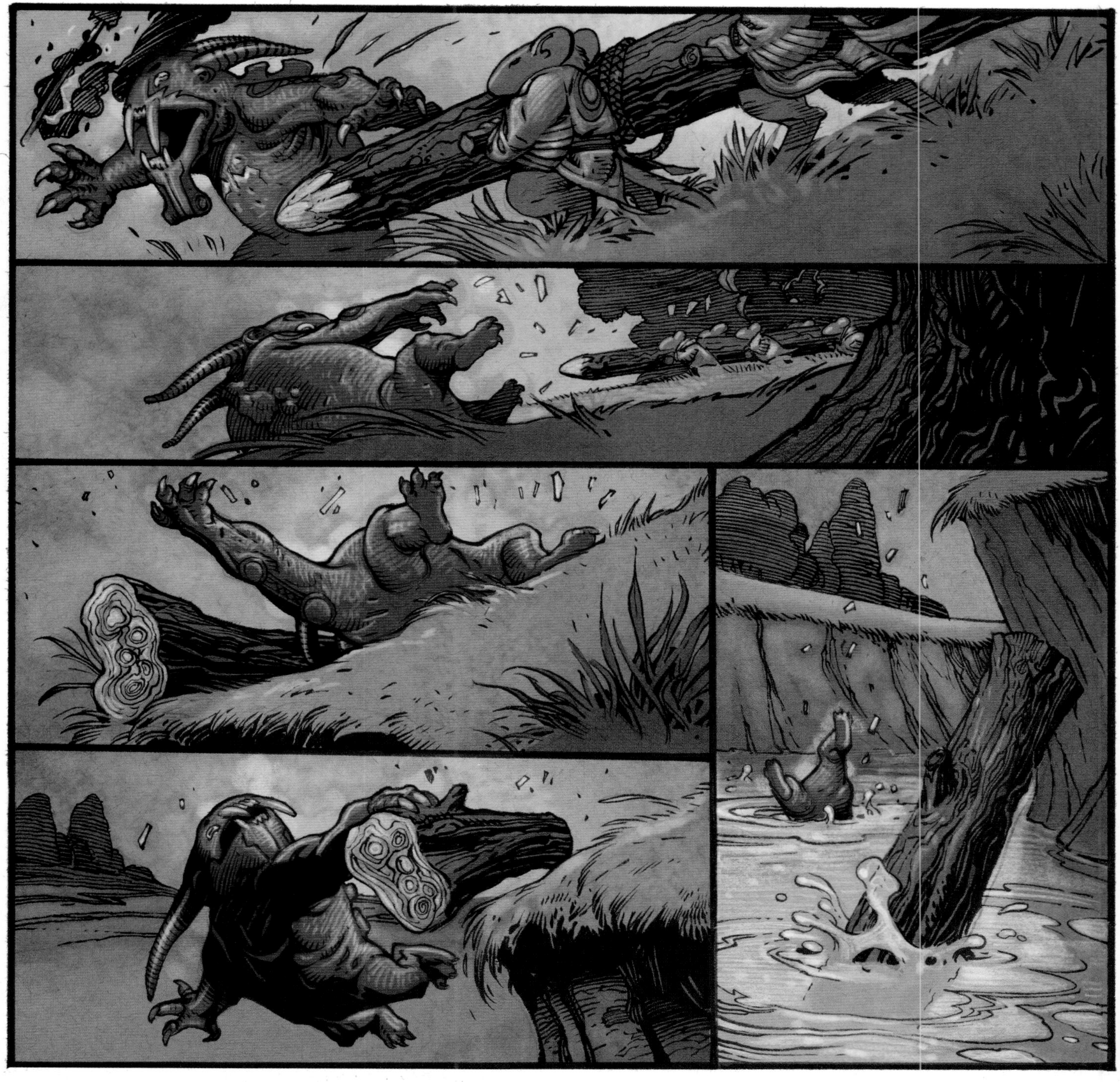

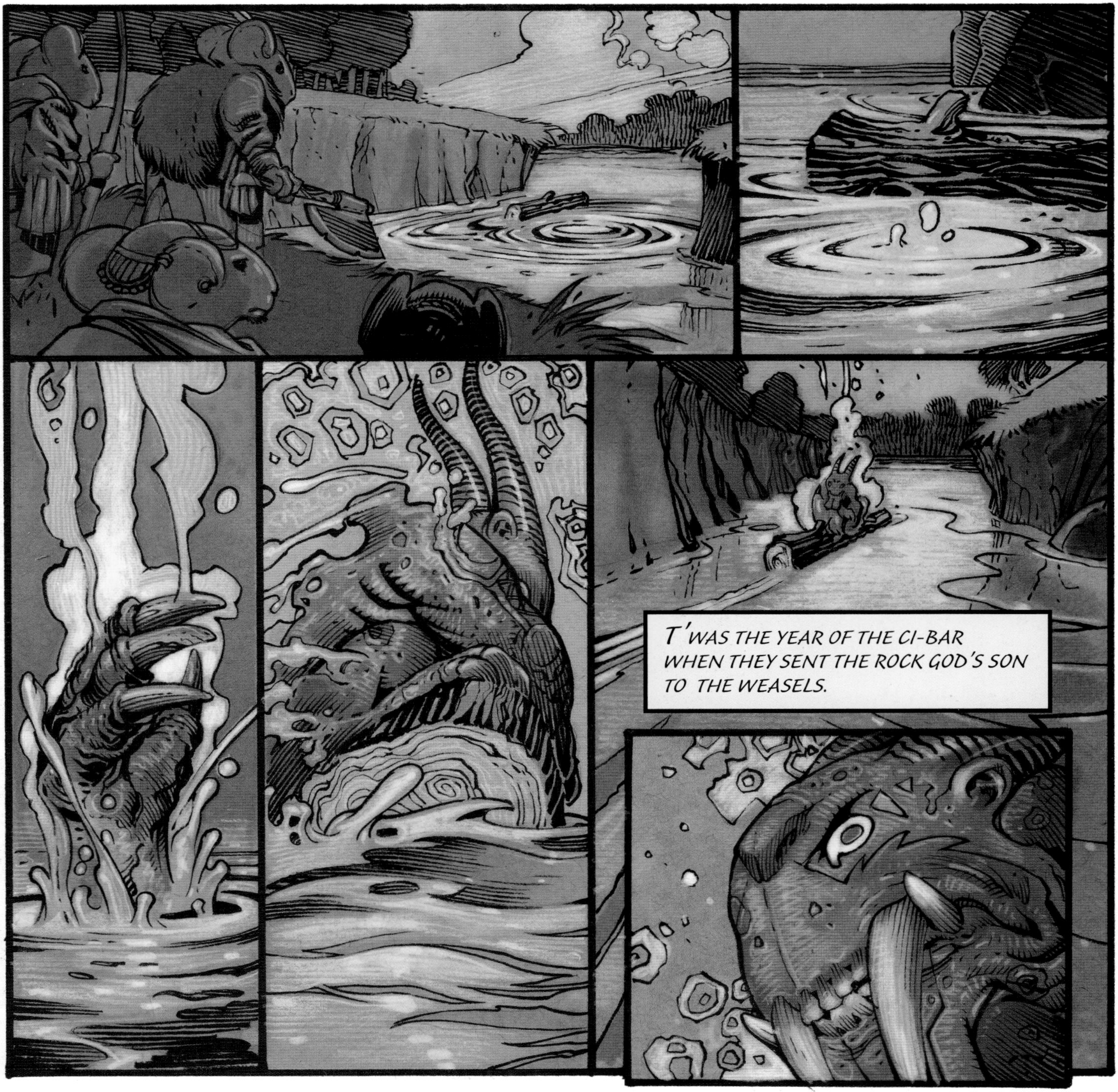
T'WAS THE YEAR OF THE CI-BAR
WHEN THEY SENT THE ROCK GOD'S SON
TO THE WEASELS.

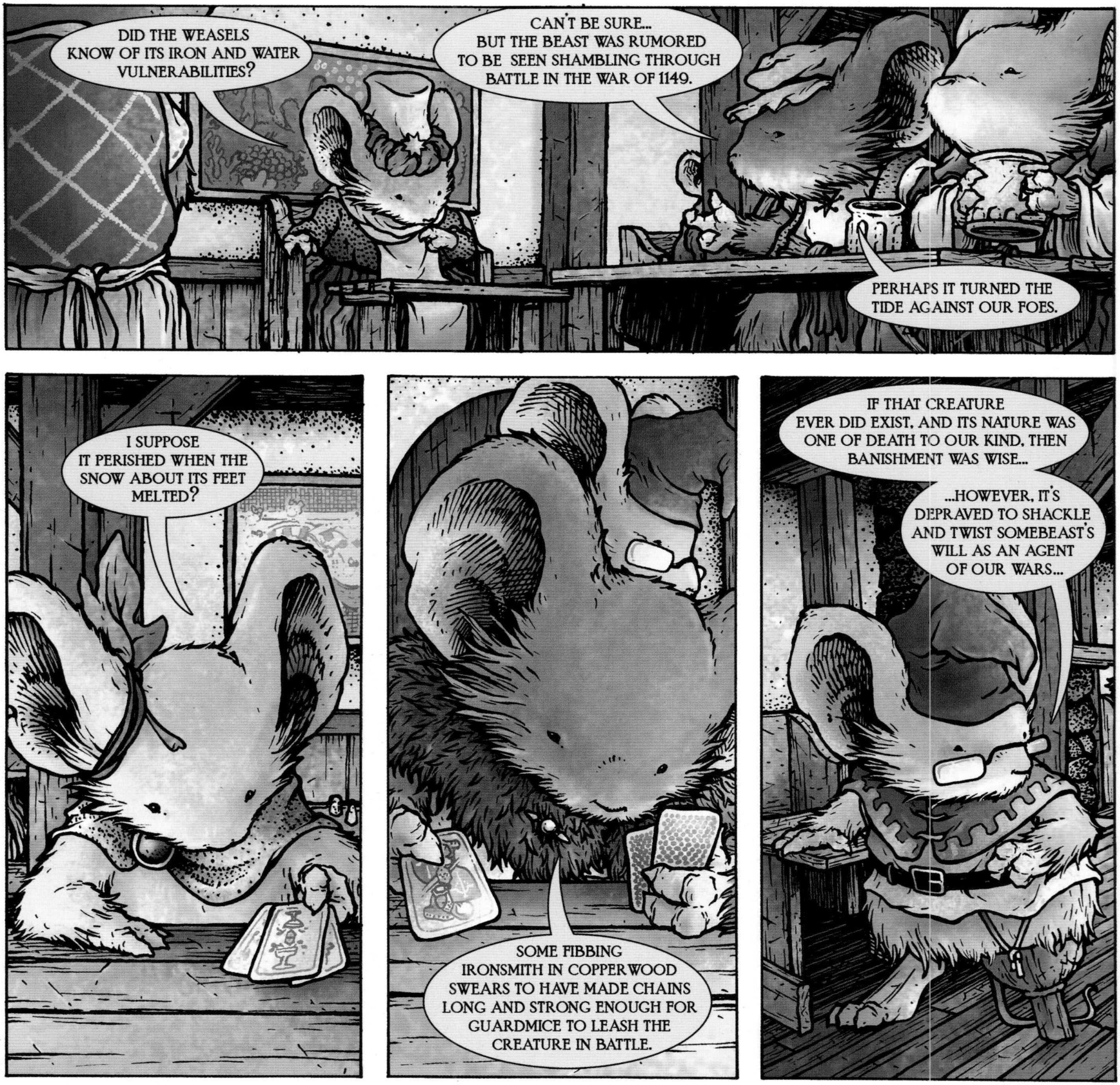
DID THE WEASELS KNOW OF ITS IRON AND WATER VULNERABILITIES?
CAN'T BE SURE... BUT THE BEAST WAS RUMORED TO BE SEEN SHAMBLING THROUGH BATTLE IN THE WAR OF 1149.
PERHAPS IT TURNED THE TIDE AGAINST OUR FOES.
I SUPPOSE IT PERISHED WHEN THE SNOW ABOUT ITS FEET MELTED?
SOME FIBBING IRONSMITH IN COPPERWOOD SWEARS TO HAVE MADE CHAINS LONG AND STRONG ENOUGH FOR GUARDMICE TO LEASH THE CREATURE IN BATTLE.
IF THAT CREATURE EVER DID EXIST, AND ITS NATURE WAS ONE OF DEATH TO OUR KIND, THEN BANISHMENT WAS WISE...
...HOWEVER, IT'S DEPRAVED TO SHACKLE AND TWIST SOMEBEAST'S WILL AS AN AGENT OF OUR WARS...

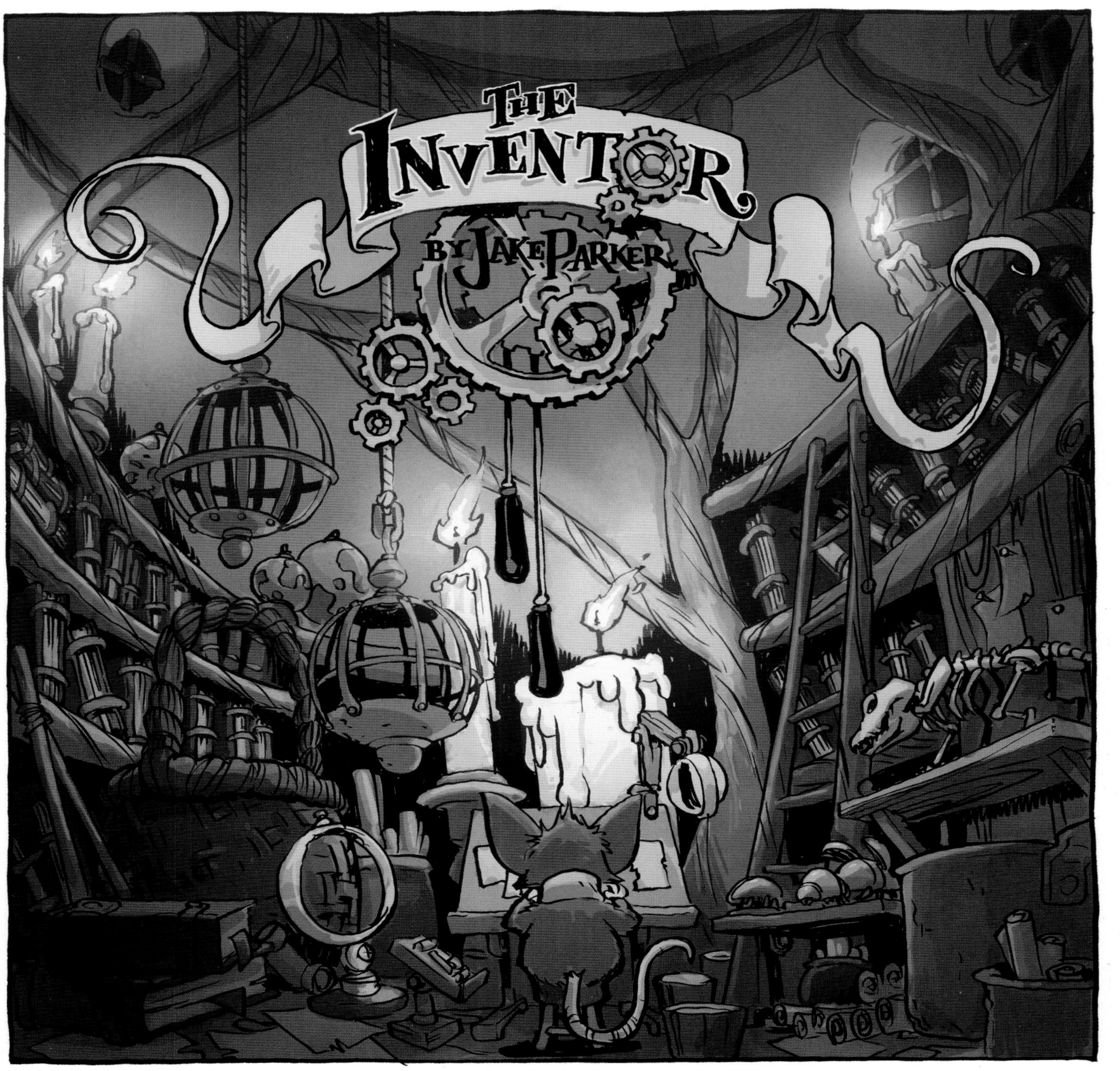
THE INVENTOR
BY JAKE PARKER

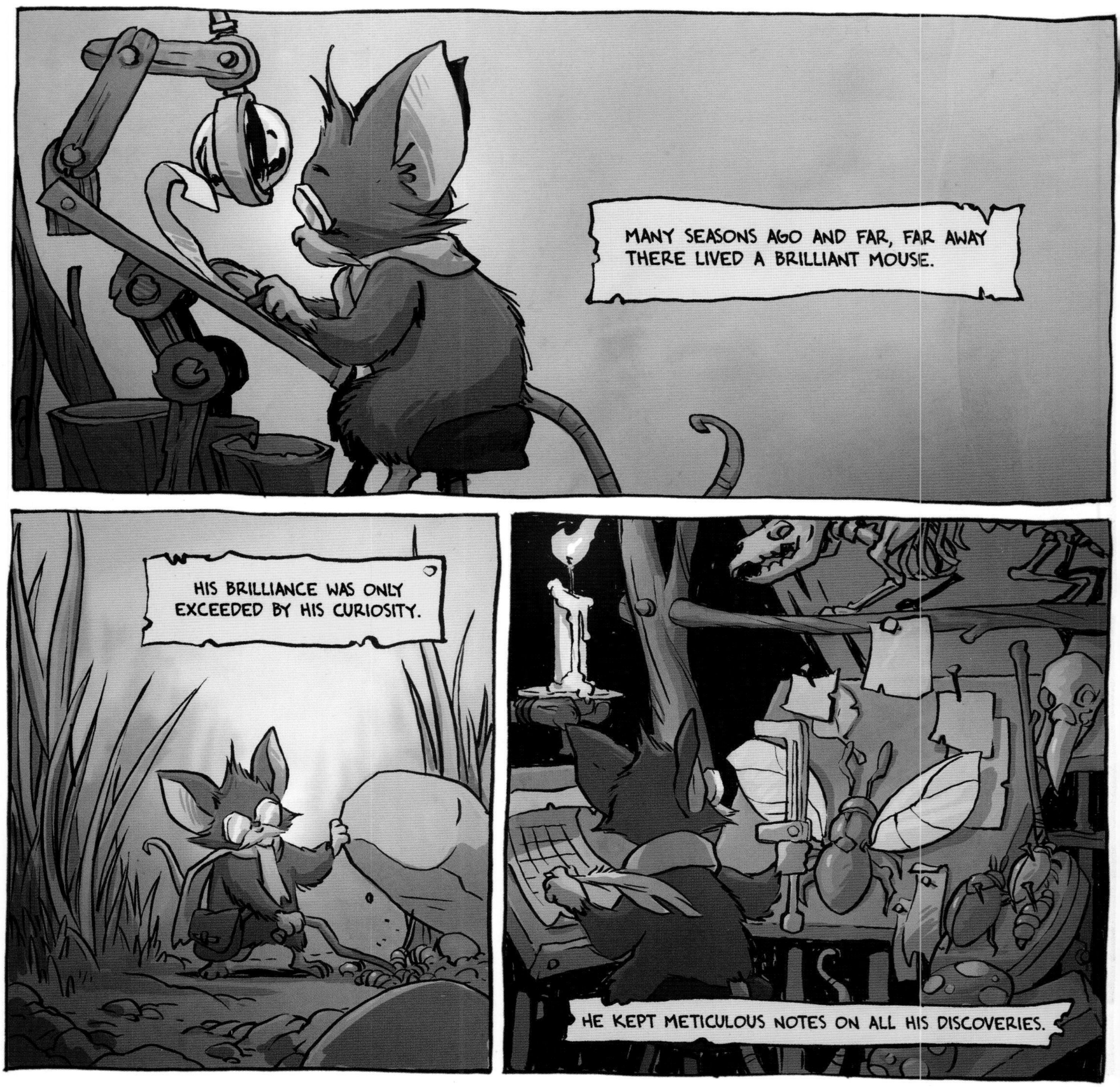
MANY SEASONS AGO AND FAR, FAR AWAY THERE LIVED A BRILLIANT MOUSE.
HIS BRILLIANCE WAS ONLY EXCEEDED BY HIS CURIOSITY.
HE KEPT METICULOUS NOTES ON ALL HIS DISCOVERIES.

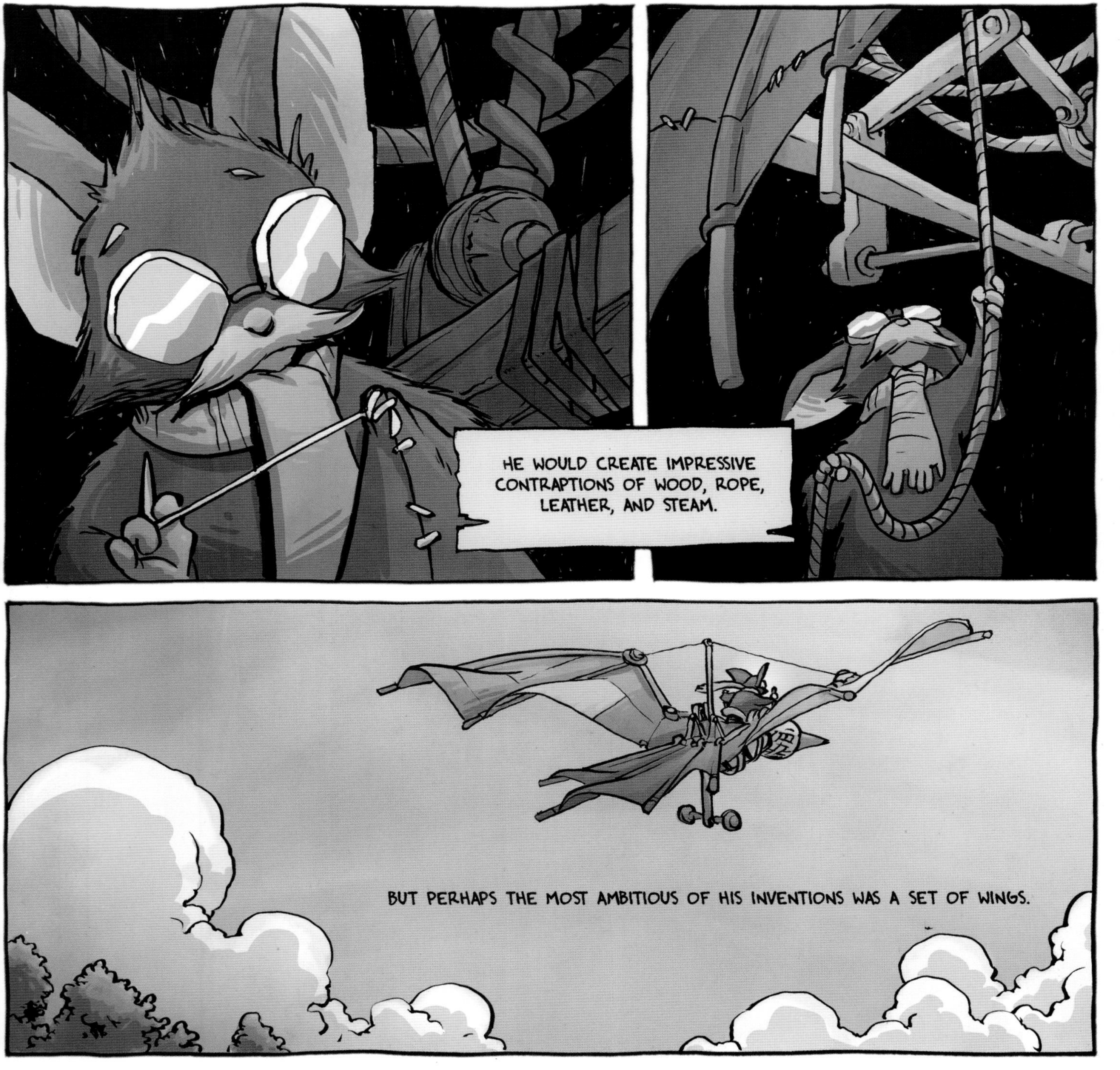
HE WOULD CREATE IMPRESSIVE CONTRAPTIONS OF WOOD, ROPE, LEATHER, AND STEAM.
BUT PERHAPS THE MOST AMBITIOUS OF HIS INVENTIONS WAS A SET OF WINGS.

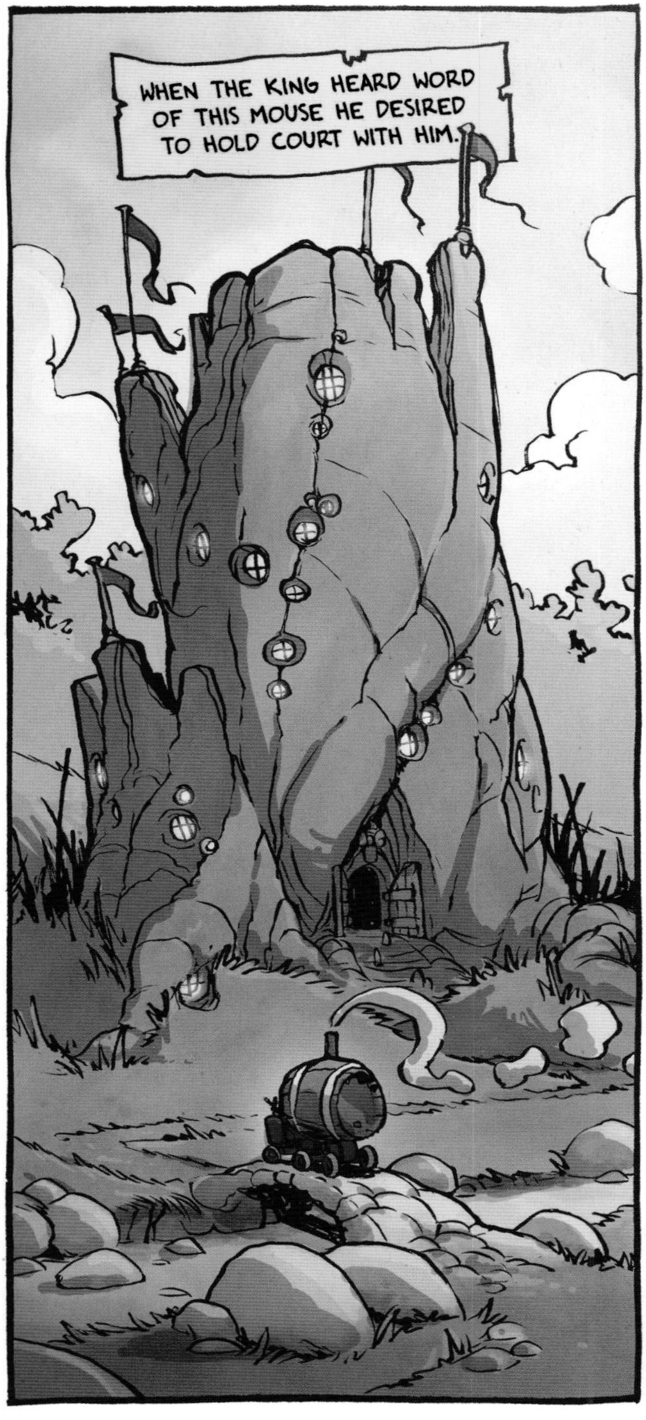
WHEN THE KING HEARD WORD OF THIS MOUSE HE DESIRED TO HOLD COURT WITH HIM.
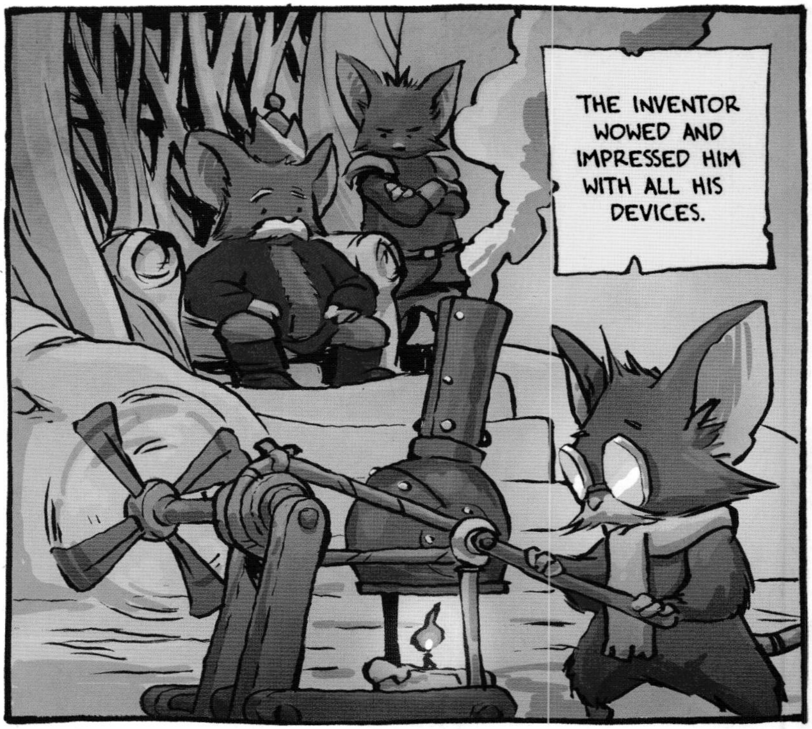
THE INVENTOR WOWED AND IMPRESSED HIM WITH ALL HIS DEVICES.
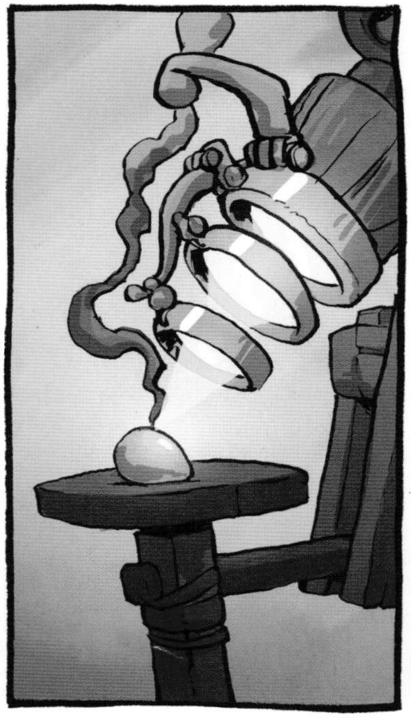
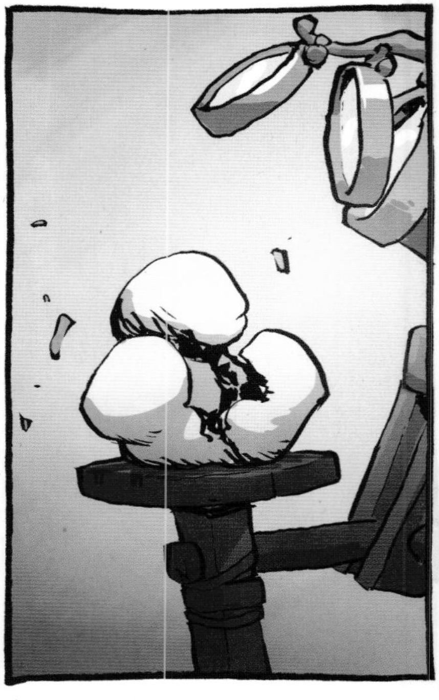

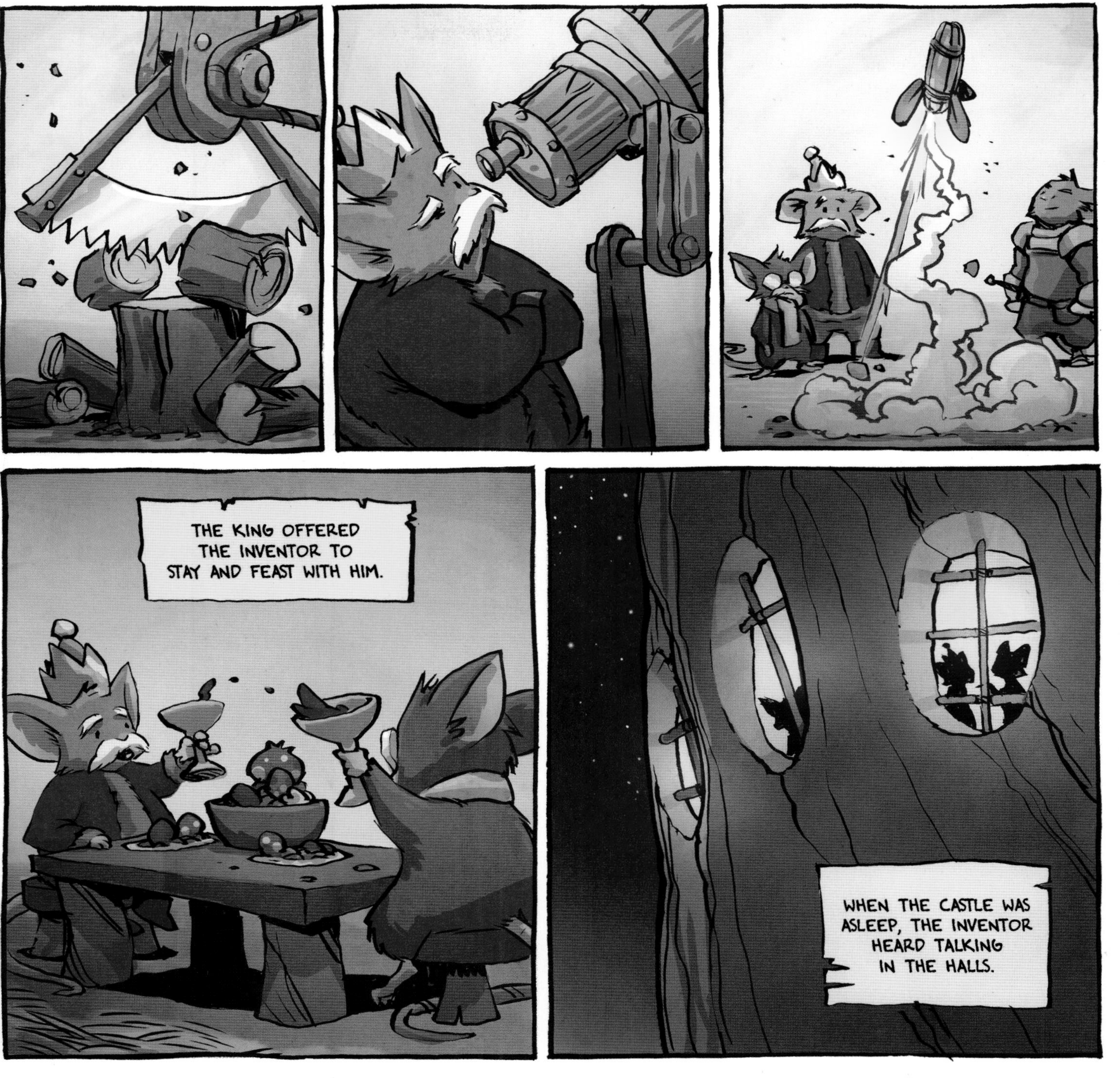
THE KING OFFERED THE INVENTOR TO STAY AND FEAST WITH HIM.
WHEN THE CASTLE WAS ASLEEP, THE INVENTOR HEARD TALKING IN THE HALLS.

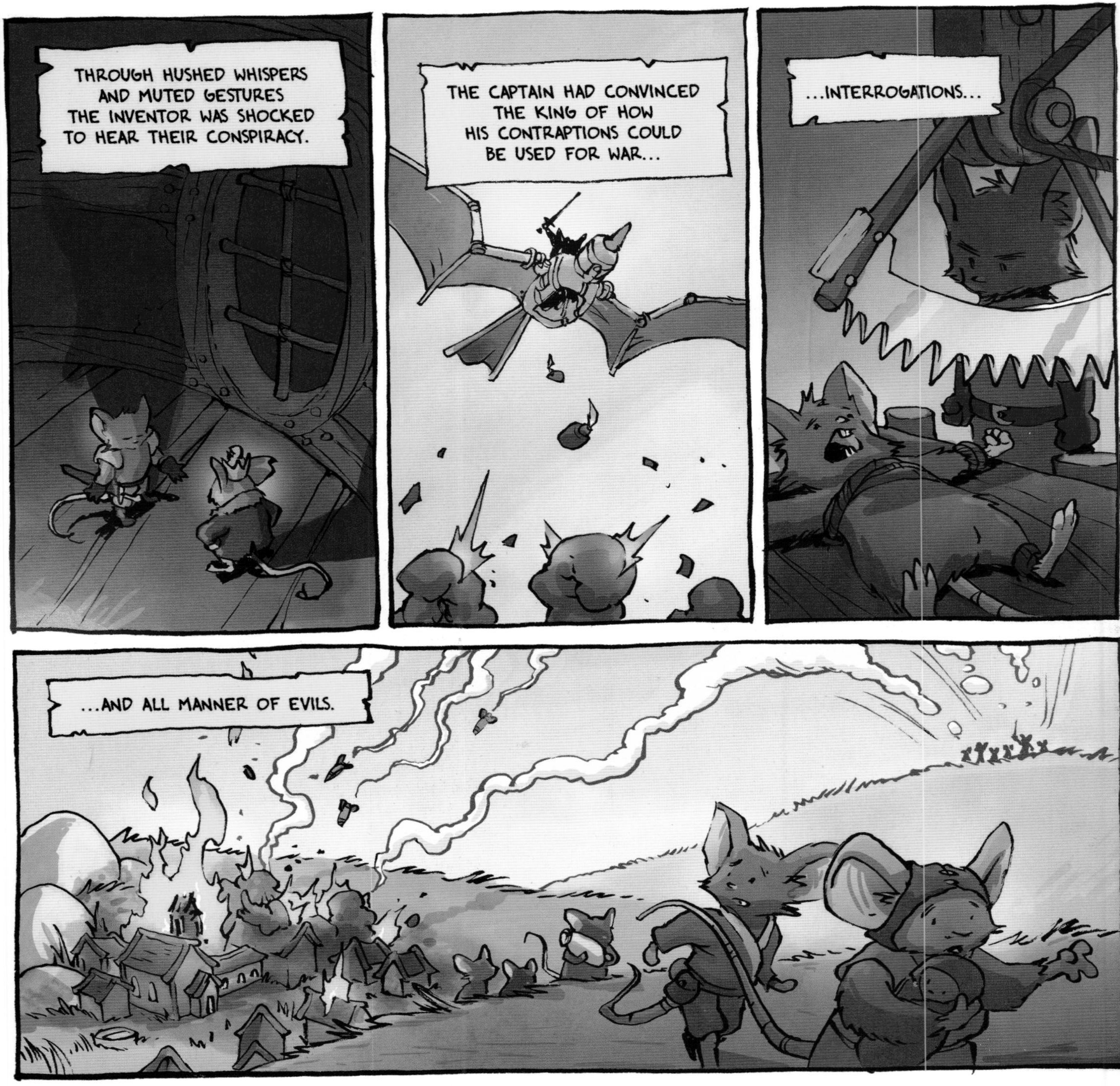
THROUGH HUSHED WHISPERS AND MUTED GESTURES THE INVENTOR WAS SHOCKED TO HEAR THEIR CONSPIRACY.
THE CAPTAIN HAD CONVINCED THE KING OF HOW HIS CONTRAPTIONS COULD BE USED FOR WAR...
...INTERROGATIONS...
...AND ALL MANNER OF EVILS.

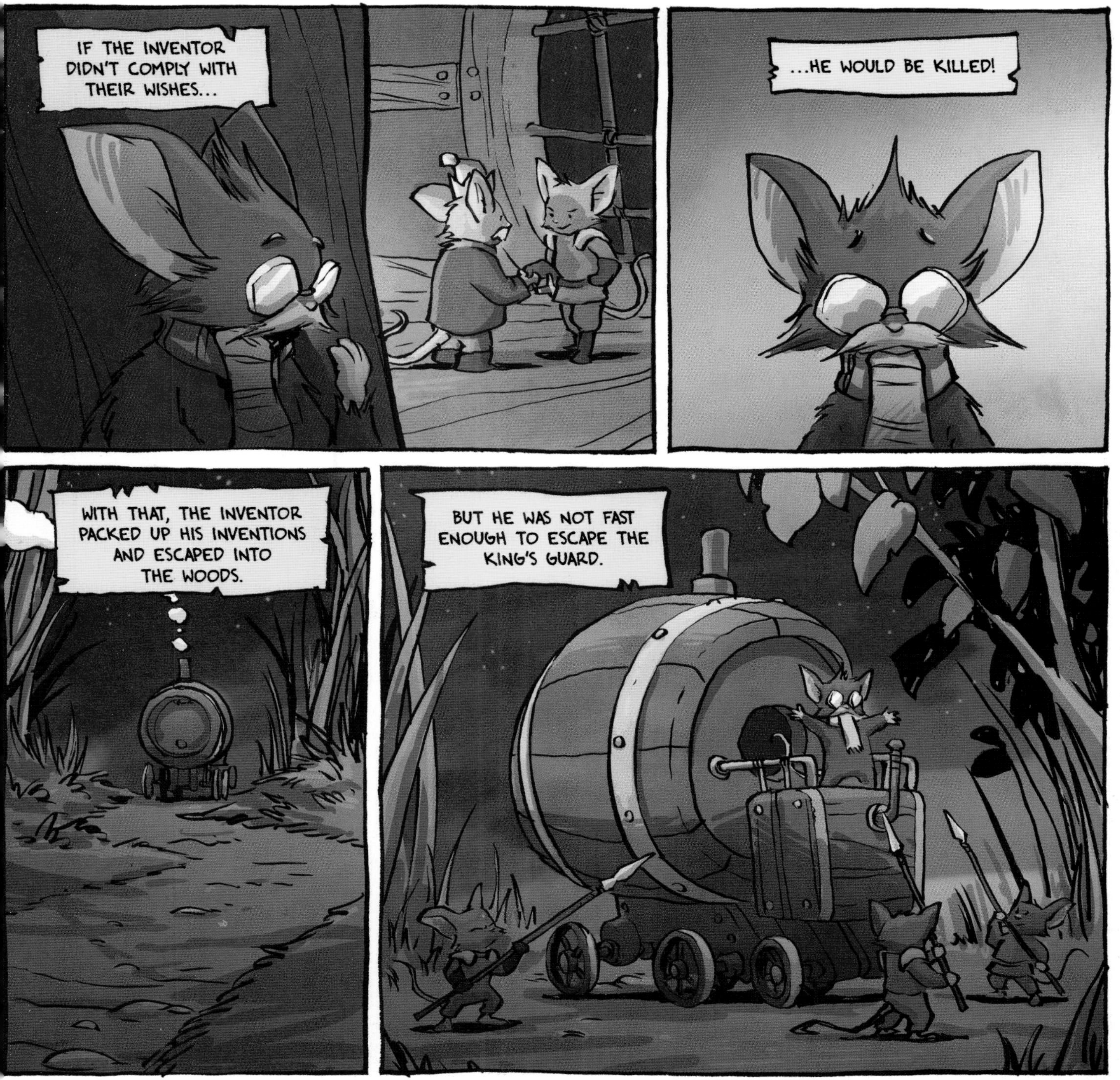
IF THE INVENTOR DIDN'T COMPLY WITH THEIR WISHES...
...HE WOULD BE KILLED!
WITH THAT, THE INVENTOR PACKED UP HIS INVENTIONS AND ESCAPED INTO THE WOODS.
BUT HE WAS NOT FAST ENOUGH TO ESCAPE THE KING'S GUARD.

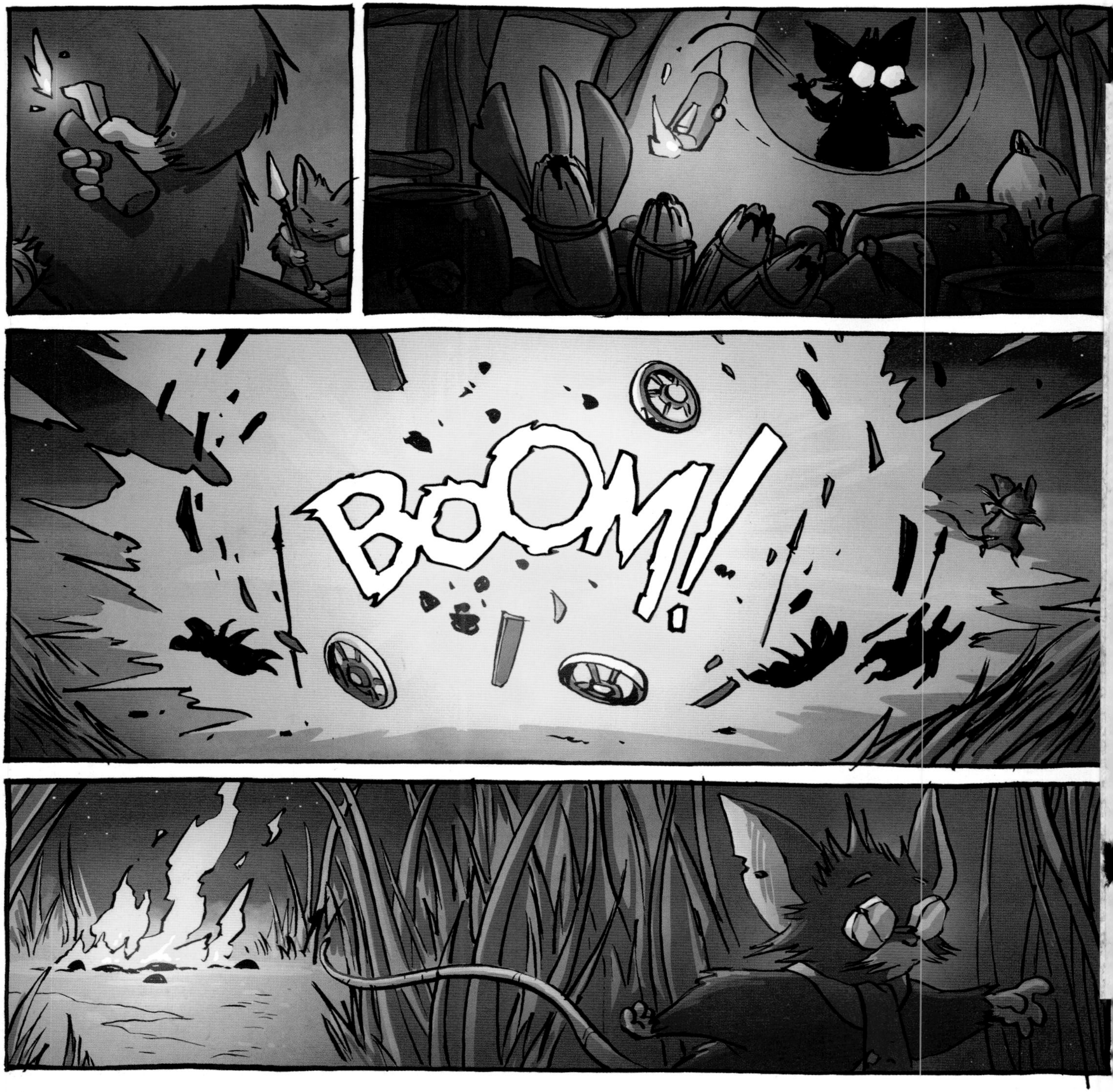
BOOM!!

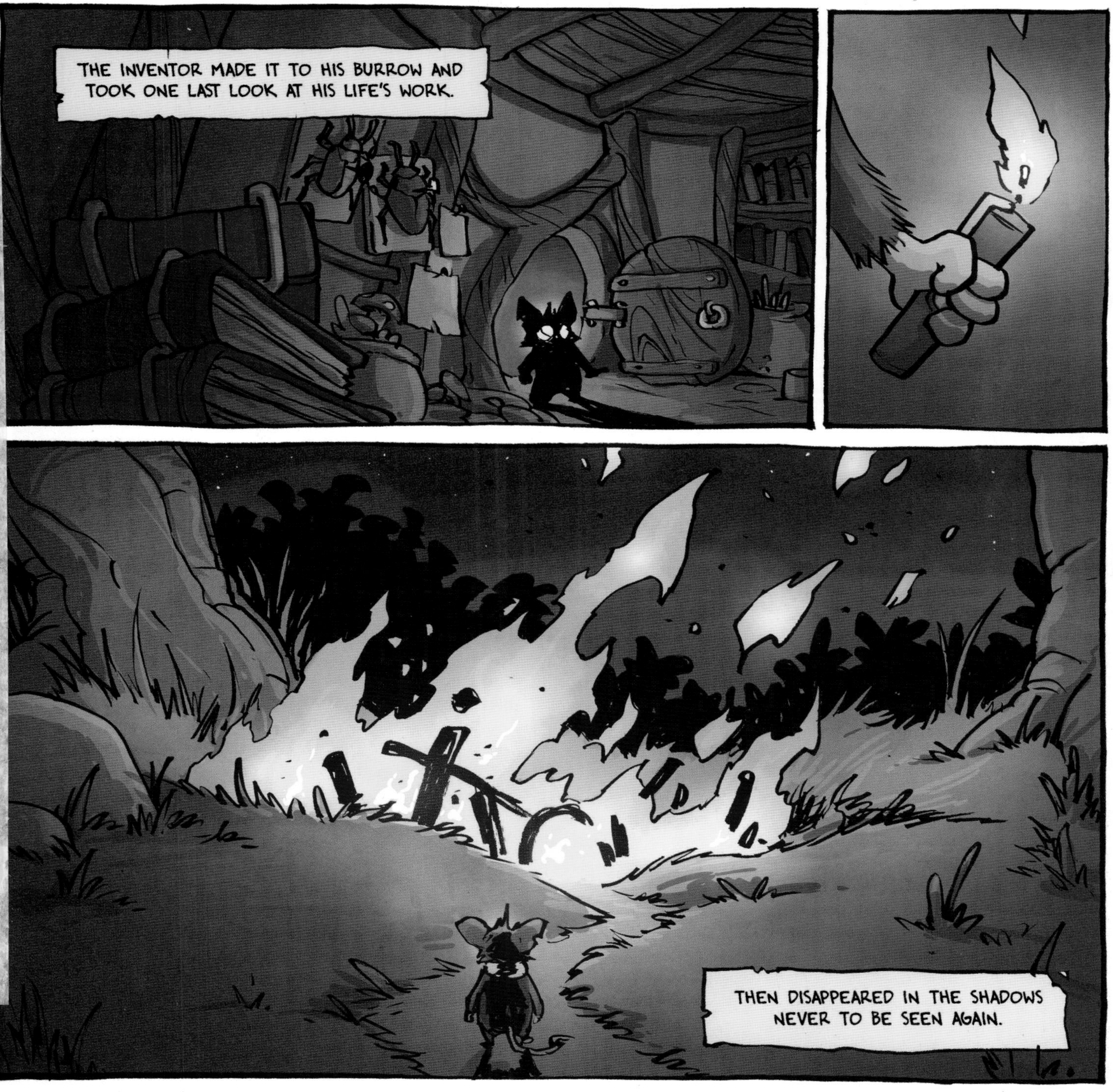
THE INVENTOR MADE IT TO HIS BURROW AND TOOK ONE LAST LOOK AT HIS LIFE'S WORK.
THEN DISAPPEARED IN THE SHADOWS NEVER TO BE SEEN AGAIN.

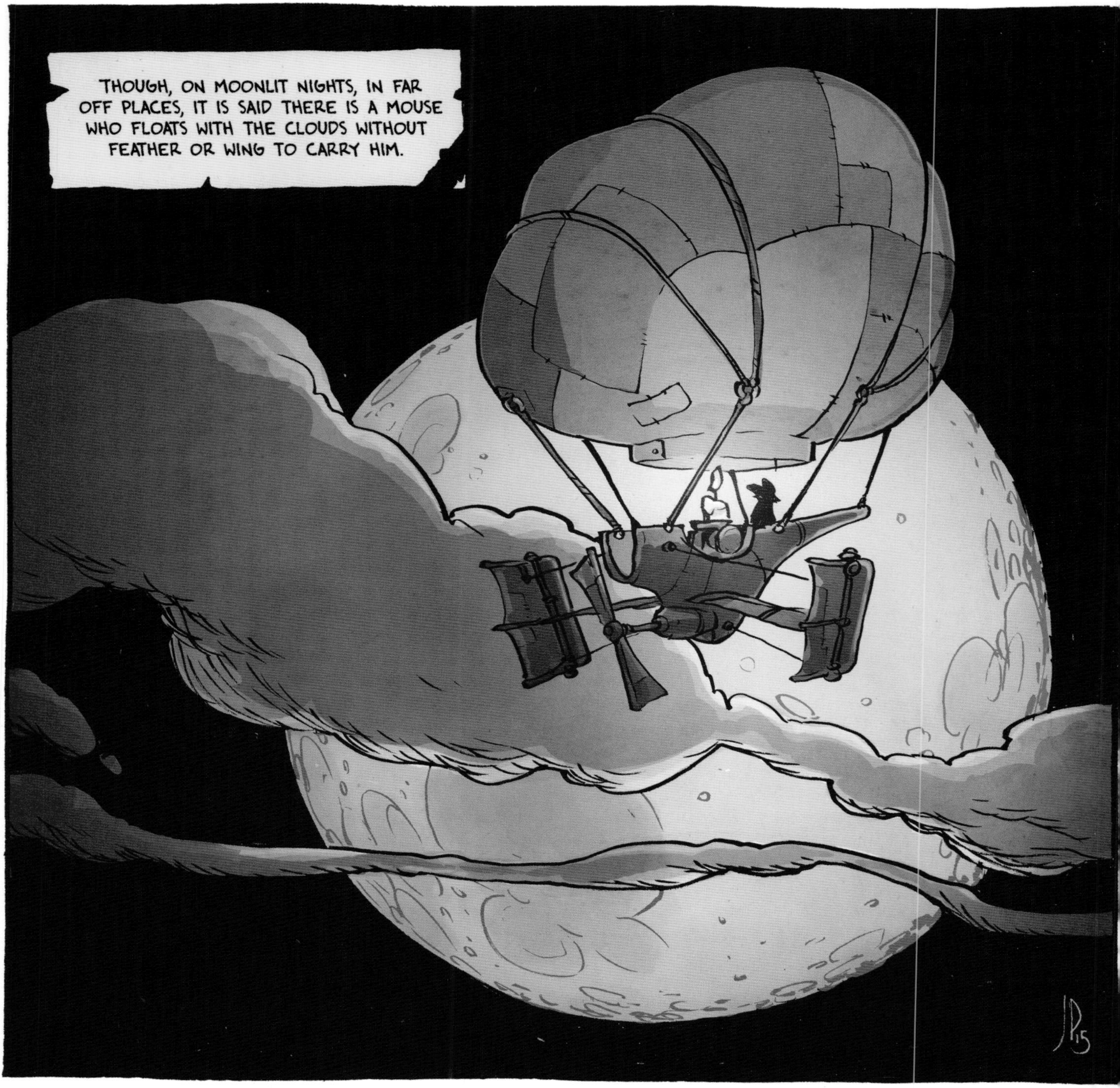
THOUGH, ON MOONLIT NIGHTS, IN FAR OFF PLACES, IT IS SAID THERE IS A MOUSE WHO FLOATS WITH THE CLOUDS WITHOUT FEATHER OR WING TO CARRY HIM.

A SAD, SAD THOUGHT THAT HIS TYPE OF BRILLIANCE MAY NEVER BE SEEN AGAIN.

A MOUSE AMONGST THE CLOUDS?

HOW WONDERFUL IT WOULD BE TO SOAR AS THE BIRDS DO.

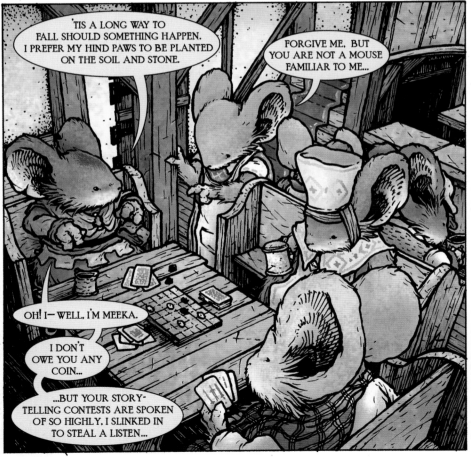

'TIS A LONG WAY TO FALL SHOULD SOMETHING HAPPEN. I PREFER MY HIND PAWS TO BE PLANTED ON THE SOIL AND STONE.

FORGIVE ME, BUT YOU ARE NOT A MOUSE FAMILIAR TO ME...

OH! I— WELL, I'M MEEKA.

I DON'T OWE YOU ANY COIN...

...BUT YOUR STORY-TELLING CONTESTS ARE SPOKEN OF SO HIGHLY, I SLINKED IN TO STEAL A LISTEN...

BE CAREFUL WITH YOUR THIEVING.

EVEN THE MOST INNOCENT OWNERS OF LIGHT FINGERED PAWS, OR EARS, CAN GET CAUGHT UP IN THEIR OWN UNSEEN GREED...

Imprisoned in the blackened spire by her overzealous father, Abdiel sits atop her throne, a lover forlorn.

THE TALE OF ABDIEL'S HEART
words & pictures | ramon k perez.

For a time untold she wept, tears falling as diamonds, till her heart beat no more, crystallized into a wealth unknown.

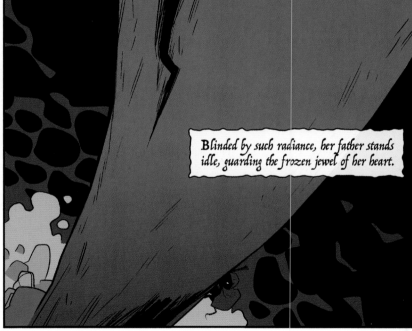

Blinded by such radiance, her father stands idle, guarding the frozen jewel of her heart.

But legend foretells of a true love setting her free.

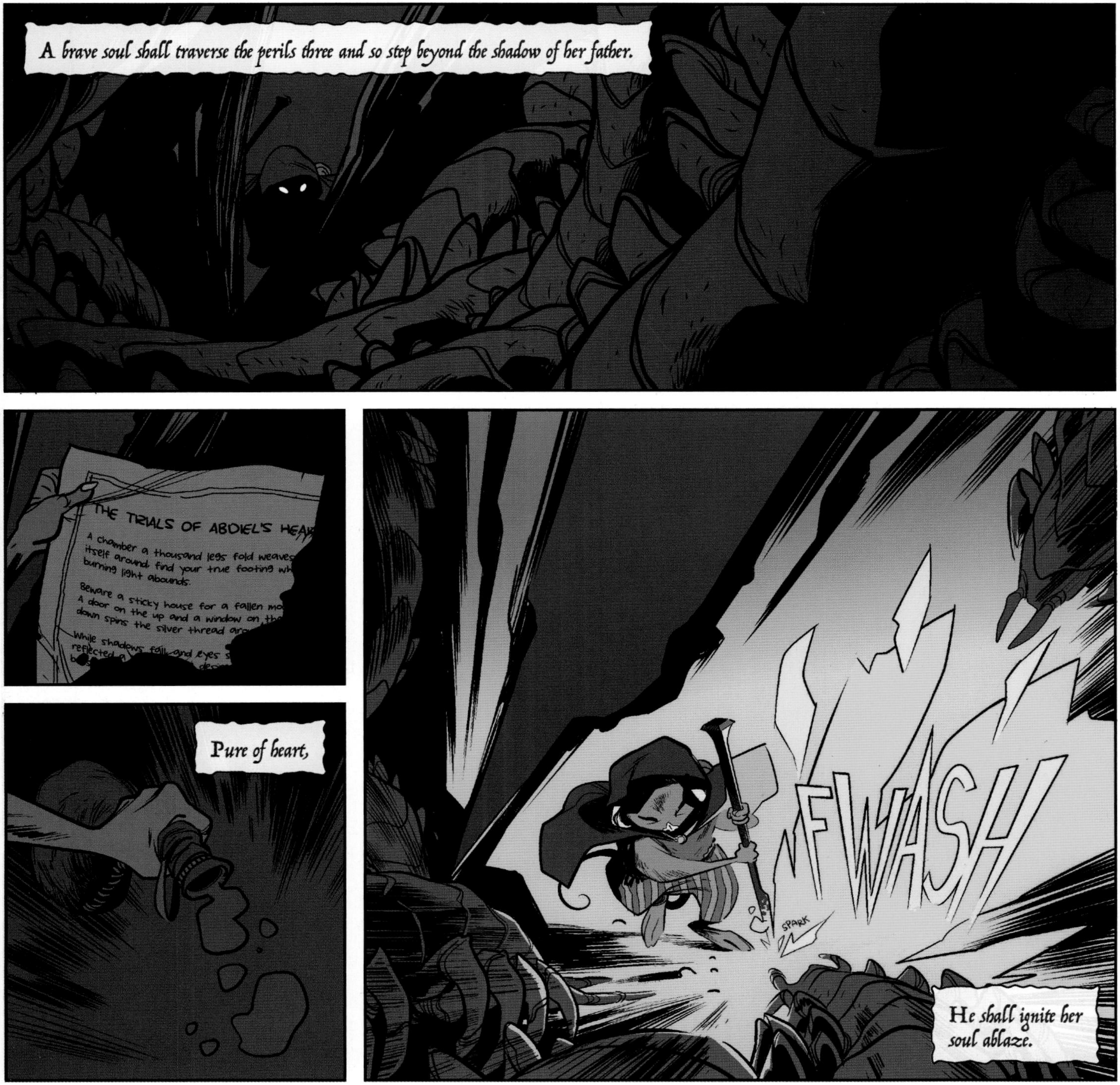
A brave soul shall traverse the perils three and so step beyond the shadow of her father.
THE TRIALS OF ABDIEL'S
A chamber a thousand legs fold
itself around, find your true footing
burning light abounds.
Beware a sticky house for a fallen
A door on the up and a window on
down spins the silver thread
While shadows fall and eyes
reflected
Pure of heart,
FWASH
SPARK
He shall ignite her soul ablaze.

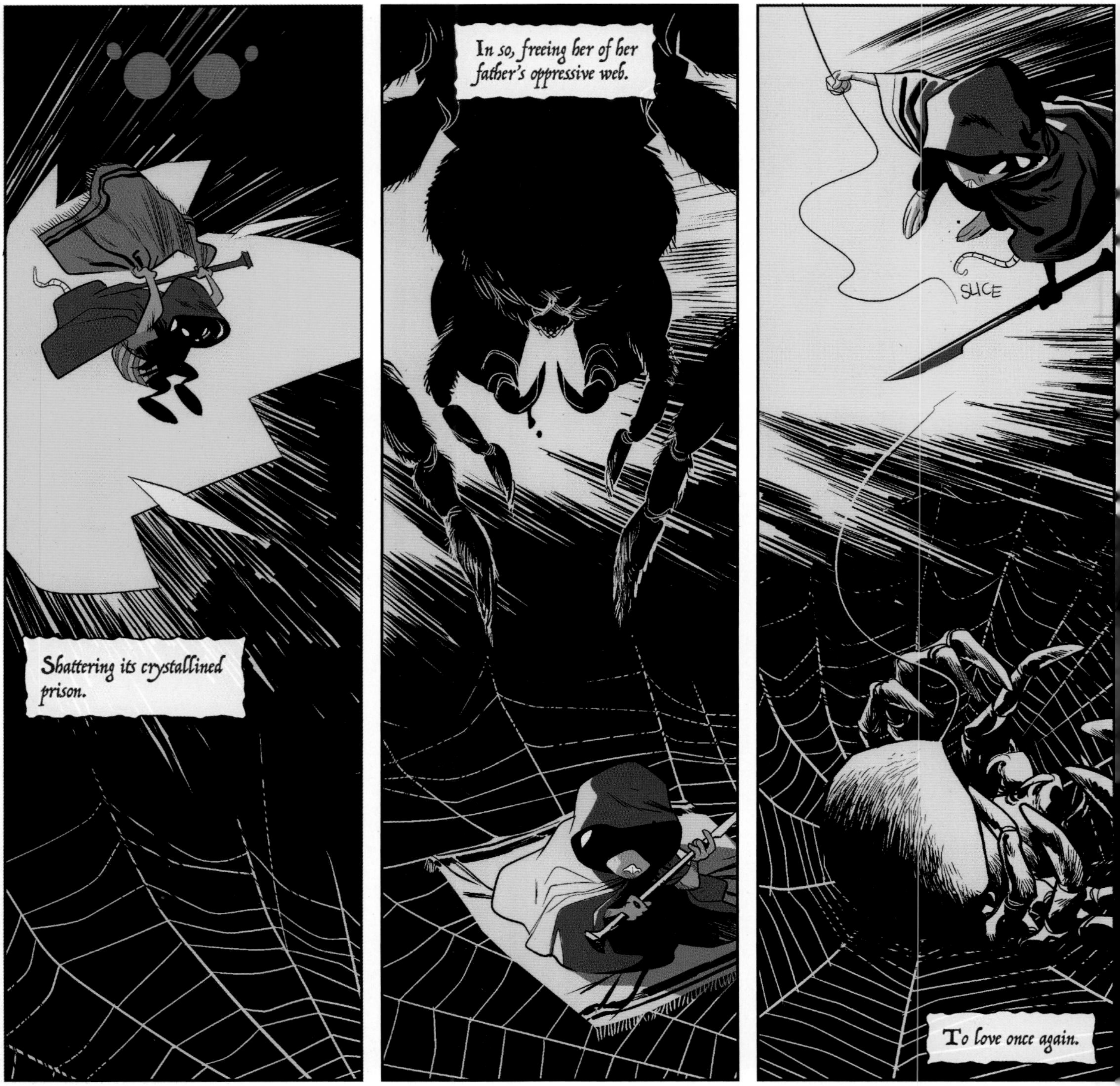
Shattering its crystallined prison.
In so, freeing her of her father's oppressive web.
SLICE
To love once again.

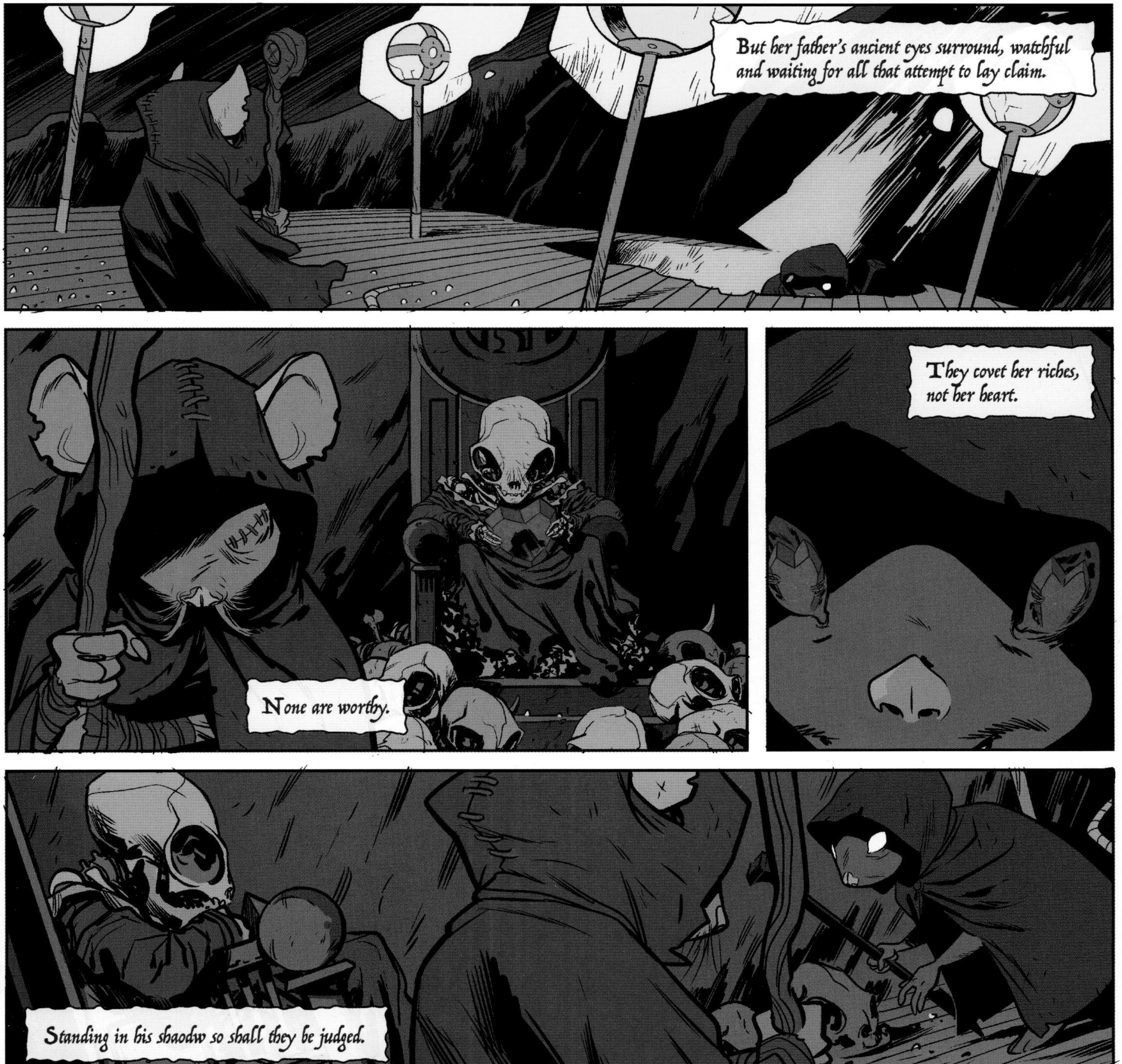
But her father's ancient eyes surround, watchful and waiting for all that attempt to lay claim.
None are worthy.
They covet her riches, not her heart.
Standing in his shadow so shall they be judged.

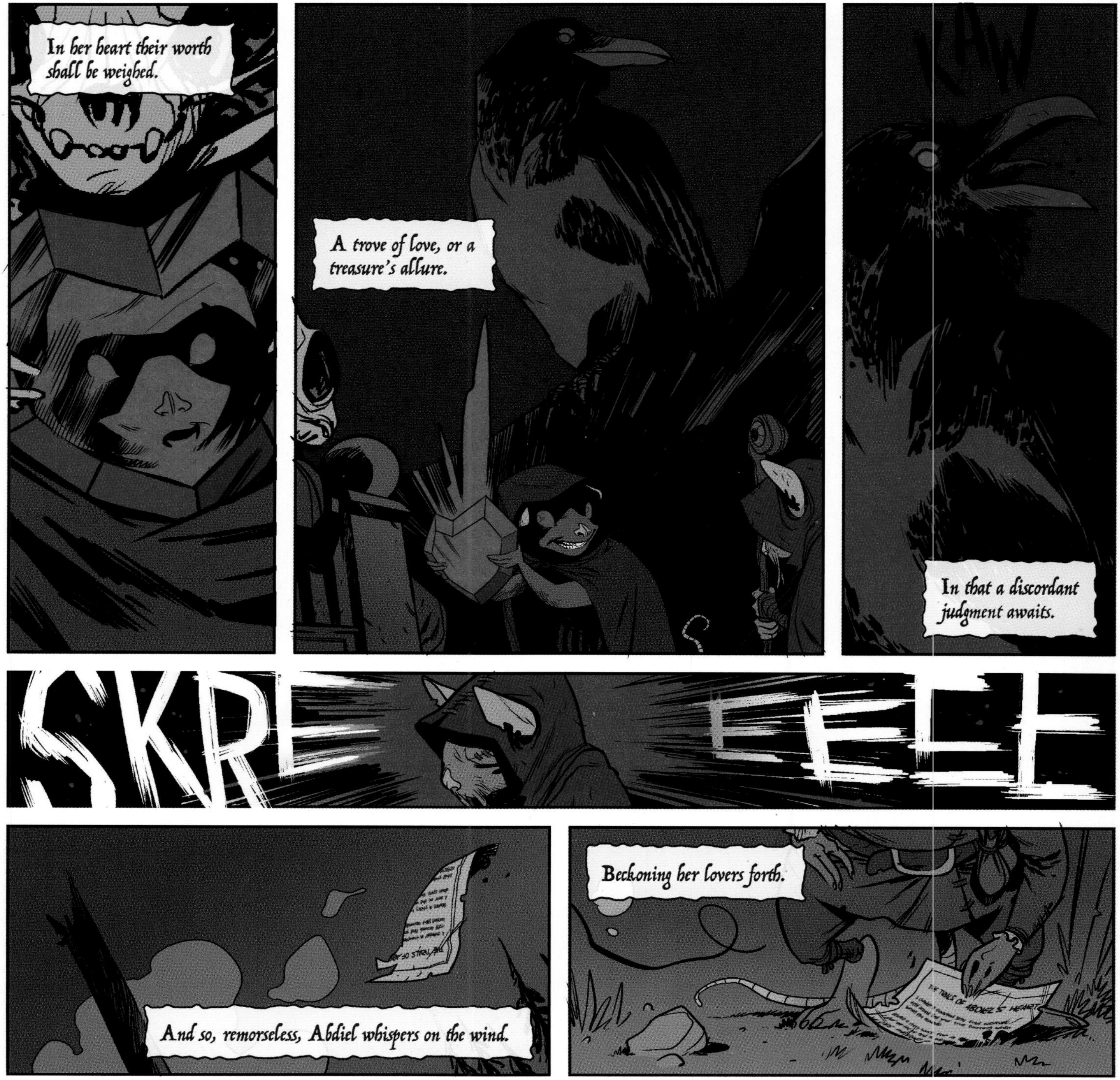
In her heart their worth shall be weighed.
A trove of love, or a treasure's allure.
KAW
In that a discordant judgment awaits.
SKREEEEE
And so, remorseless, Abdiel whispers on the wind.
Beckoning her lovers forth.

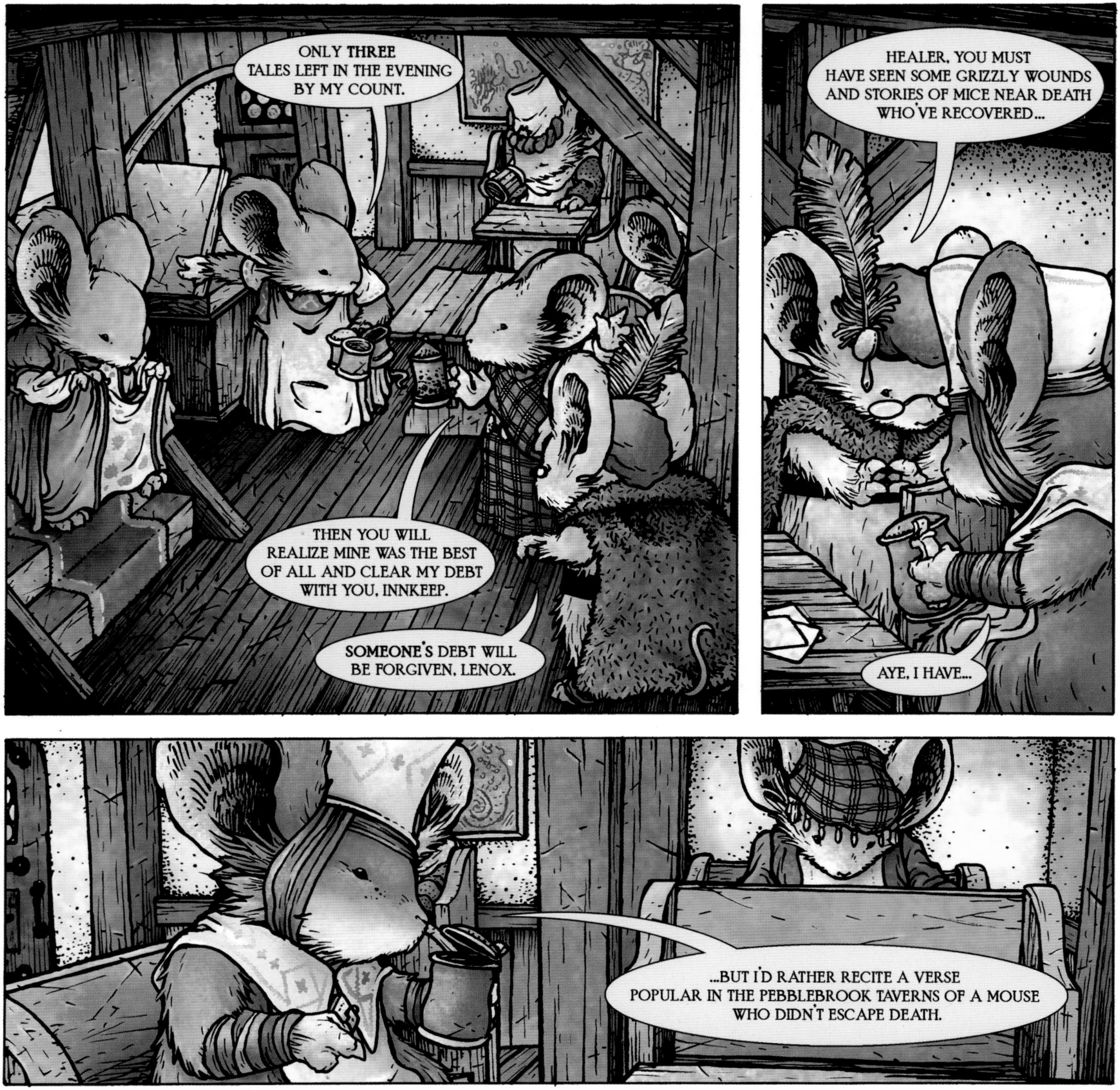
ONLY THREE TALES LEFT IN THE EVENING BY MY COUNT.
THEN YOU WILL REALIZE MINE WAS THE BEST OF ALL AND CLEAR MY DEBT WITH YOU, INNKEEP.
SOMEONE'S DEBT WILL BE FORGIVEN, LENOX.
HEALER, YOU MUST HAVE SEEN SOME GRIZZLY WOUNDS AND STORIES OF MICE NEAR DEATH WHO'VE RECOVERED...
AYE, I HAVE...
...BUT I'D RATHER RECITE A VERSE POPULAR IN THE PEBBLEBROOK TAVERNS OF A MOUSE WHO DIDN'T ESCAPE DEATH.

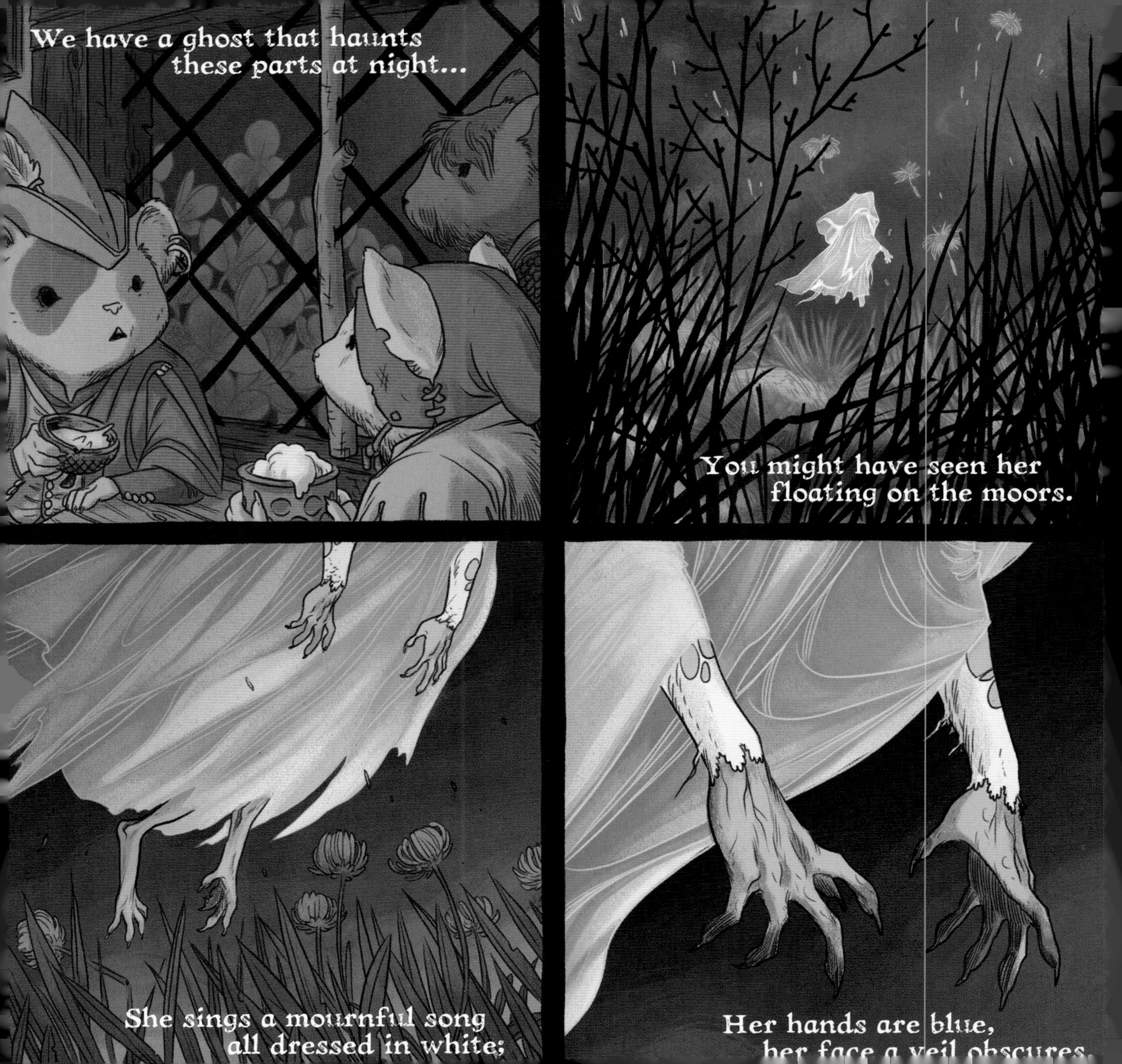
We have a ghost that haunts these parts at night...
You might have seen her floating on the moors.
She sings a mournful song all dressed in white;
Her hands are blue, her face a veil obscures.

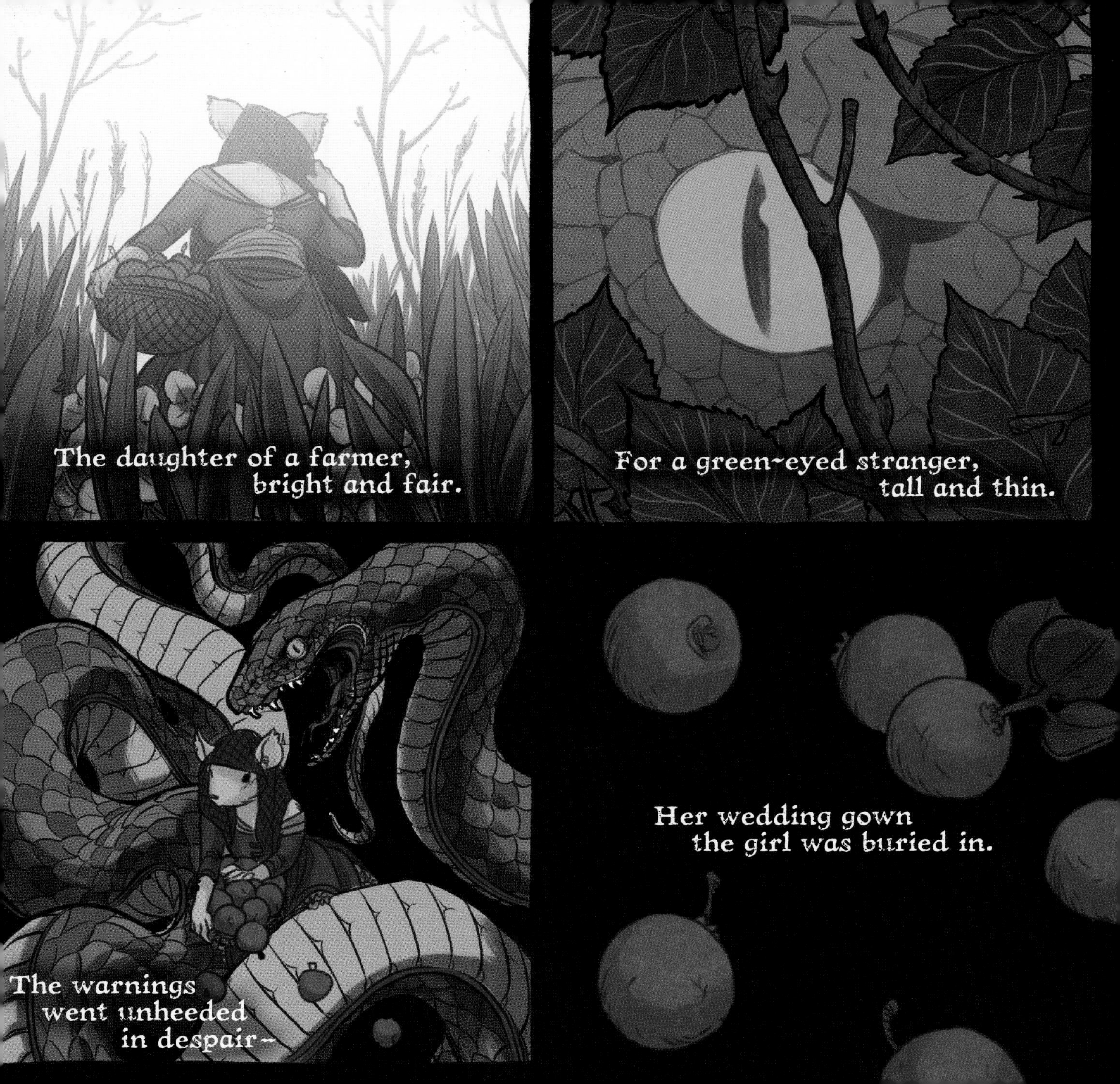
The daughter of a farmer, bright and fair.
For a green-eyed stranger, tall and thin.
The warnings went unheeded in despair~
Her wedding gown the girl was buried in.

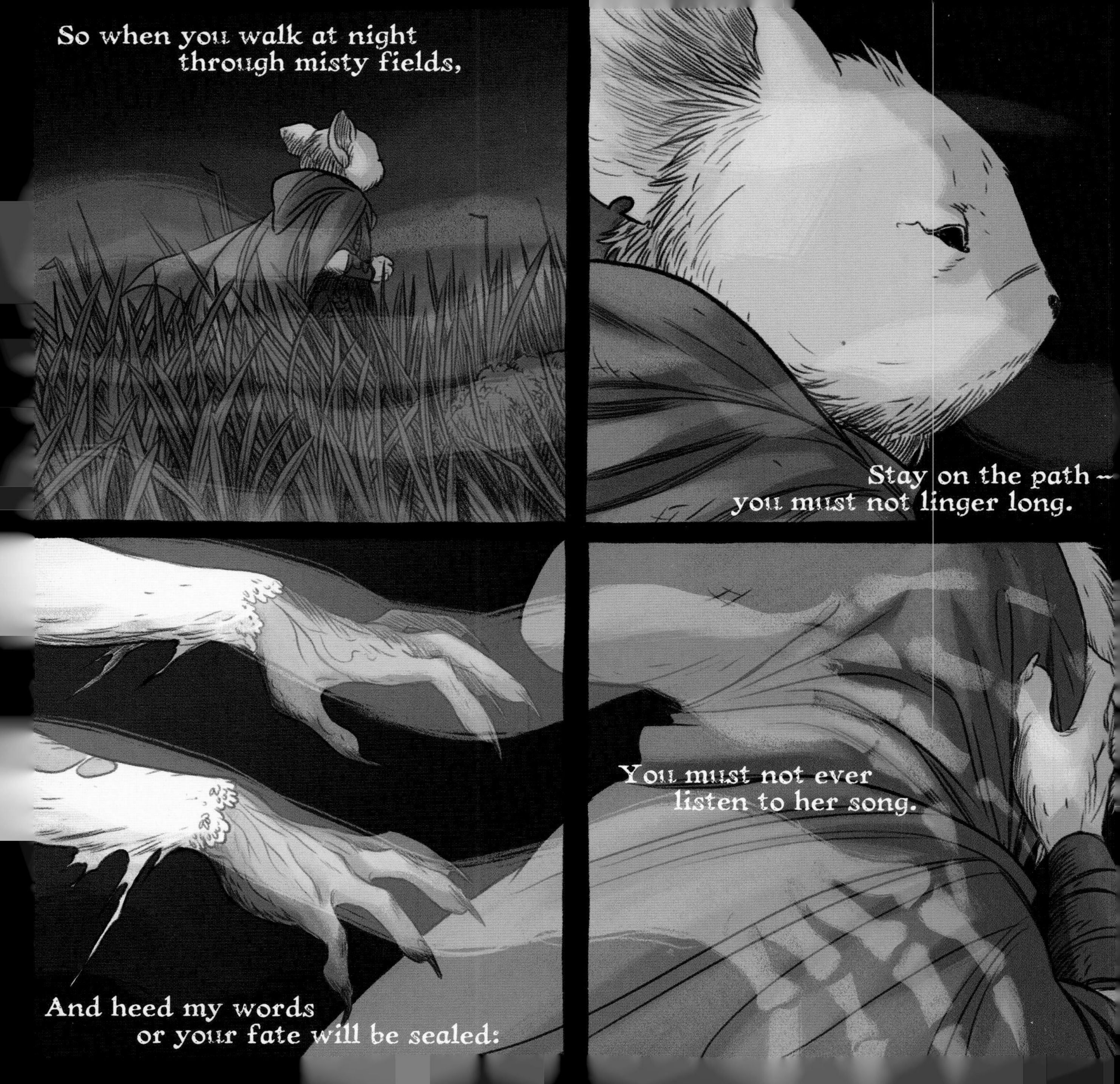
So when you walk at night through misty fields,
Stay on the path – you must not linger long.
And heed my words or your fate will be sealed:
You must not ever listen to her song.

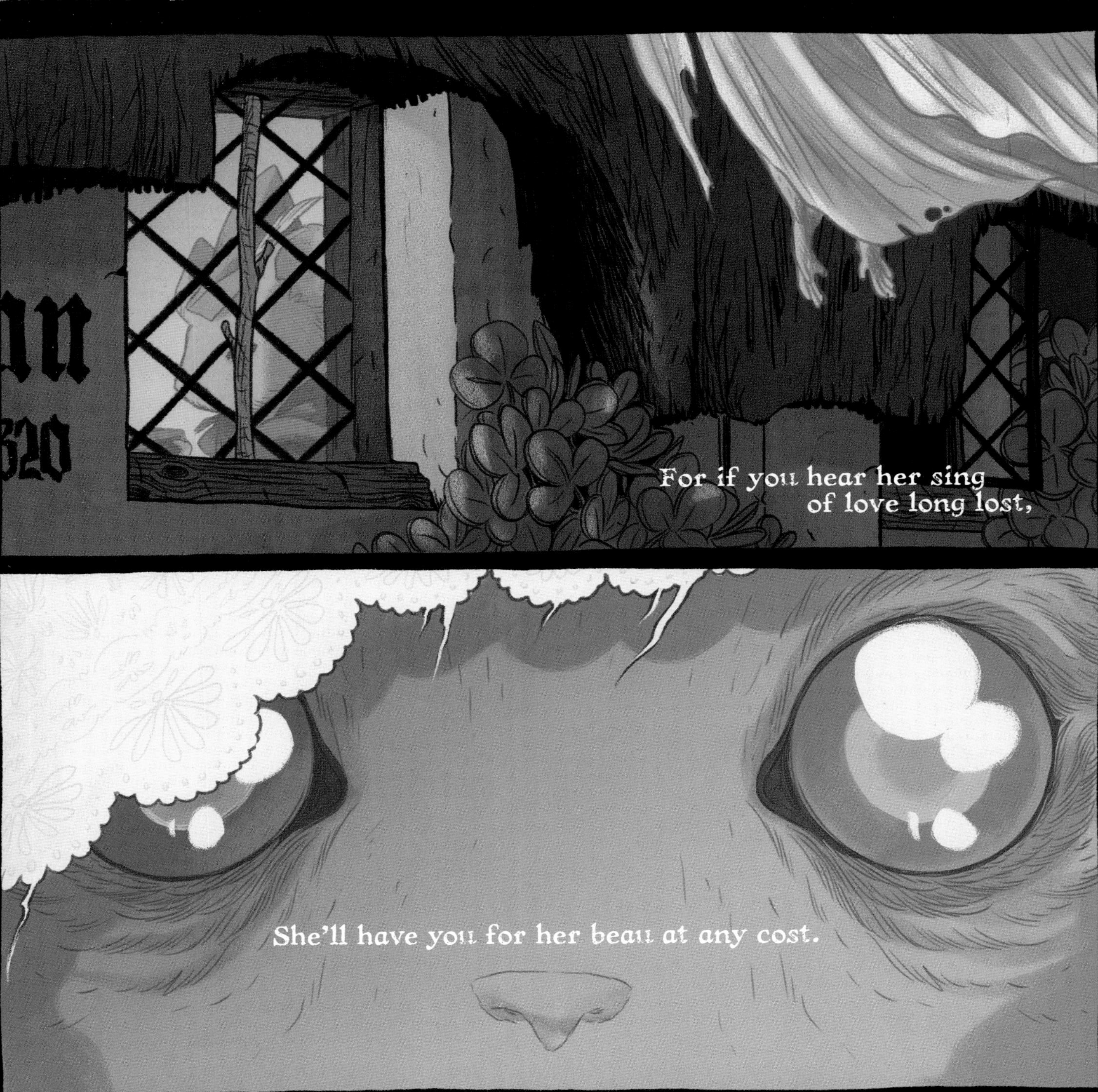
For if you hear her sing
of love long lost,
She'll have you for her beau at any cost.

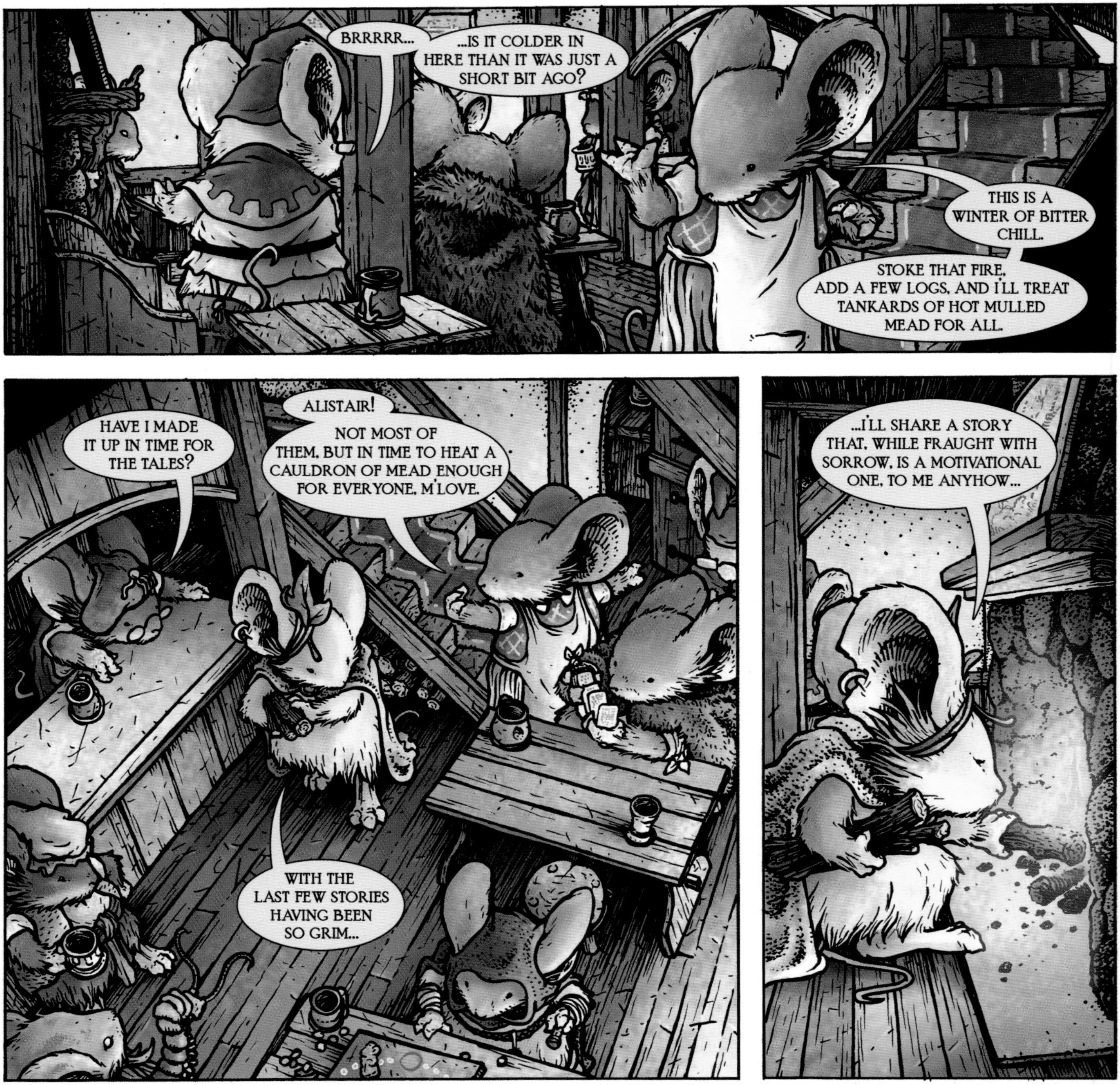
BRRRRR...
...IS IT COLDER IN HERE THAN IT WAS JUST A SHORT BIT AGO?
THIS IS A WINTER OF BITTER CHILL.
STOKE THAT FIRE, ADD A FEW LOGS, AND I'LL TREAT TANKARDS OF HOT MULLED MEAD FOR ALL.
HAVE I MADE IT UP IN TIME FOR THE TALES?
ALISTAIR!
NOT MOST OF THEM, BUT IN TIME TO HEAT A CAULDRON OF MEAD ENOUGH FOR EVERYONE, M'LOVE.
WITH THE LAST FEW STORIES HAVING BEEN SO GRIM...
...I'LL SHARE A STORY THAT, WHILE FRAUGHT WITH SORROW, IS A MOTIVATIONAL ONE, TO ME ANYHOW...

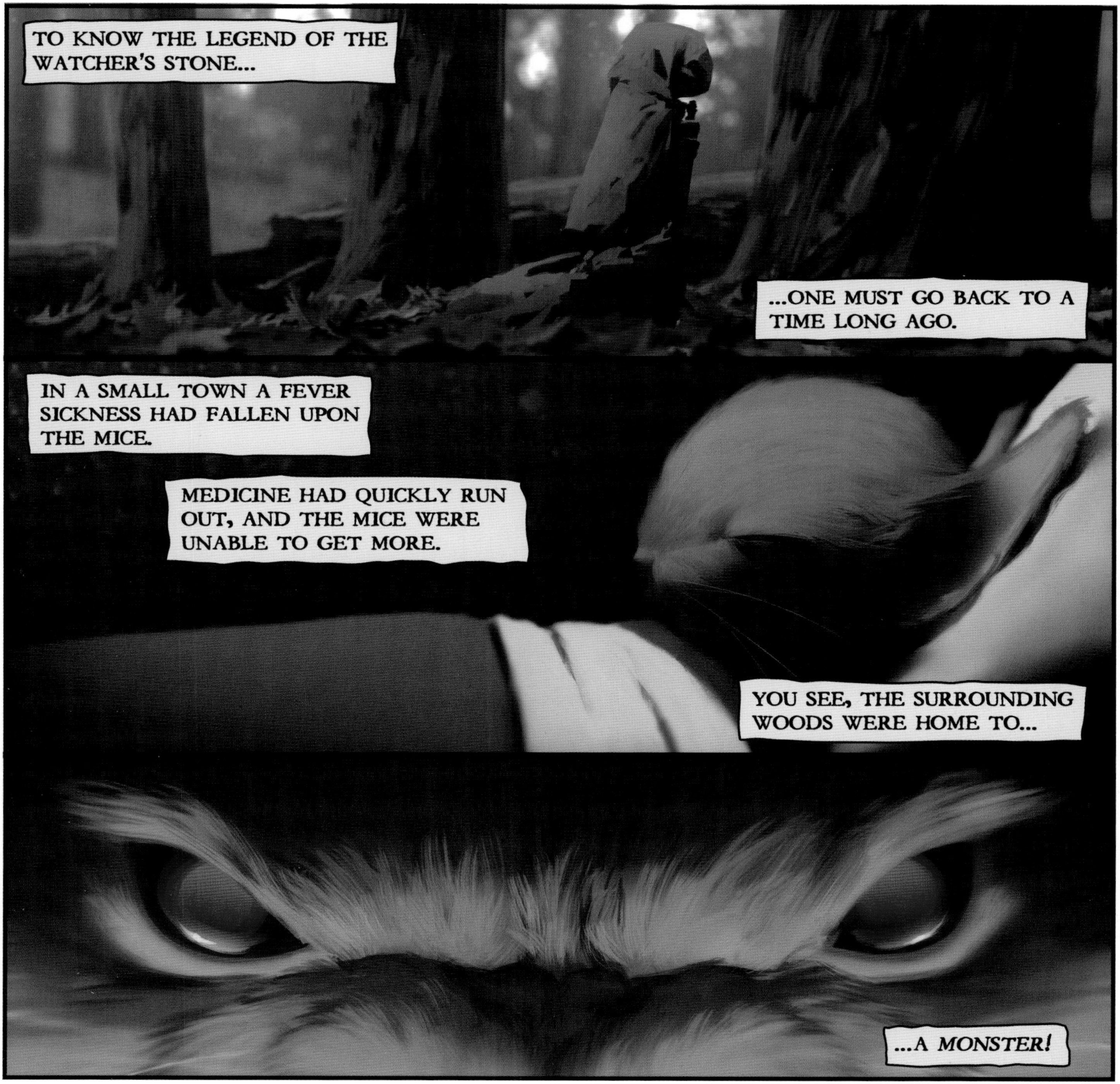
TO KNOW THE LEGEND OF THE WATCHER'S STONE...
...ONE MUST GO BACK TO A TIME LONG AGO.
IN A SMALL TOWN A FEVER SICKNESS HAD FALLEN UPON THE MICE.
MEDICINE HAD QUICKLY RUN OUT, AND THE MICE WERE UNABLE TO GET MORE.
YOU SEE, THE SURROUNDING WOODS WERE HOME TO...
...A *MONSTER!*

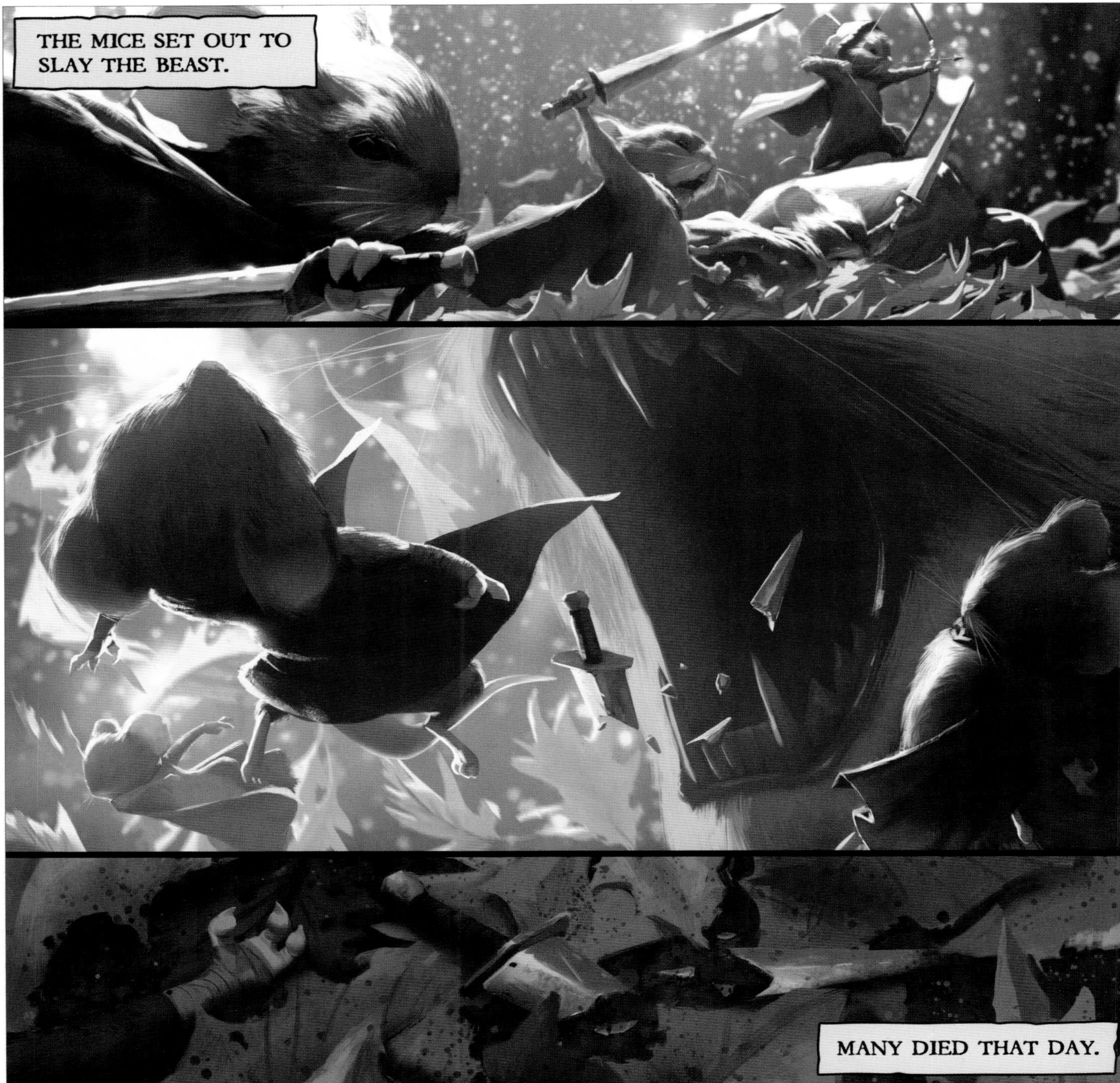
THE MICE SET OUT TO SLAY THE BEAST.
MANY DIED THAT DAY.

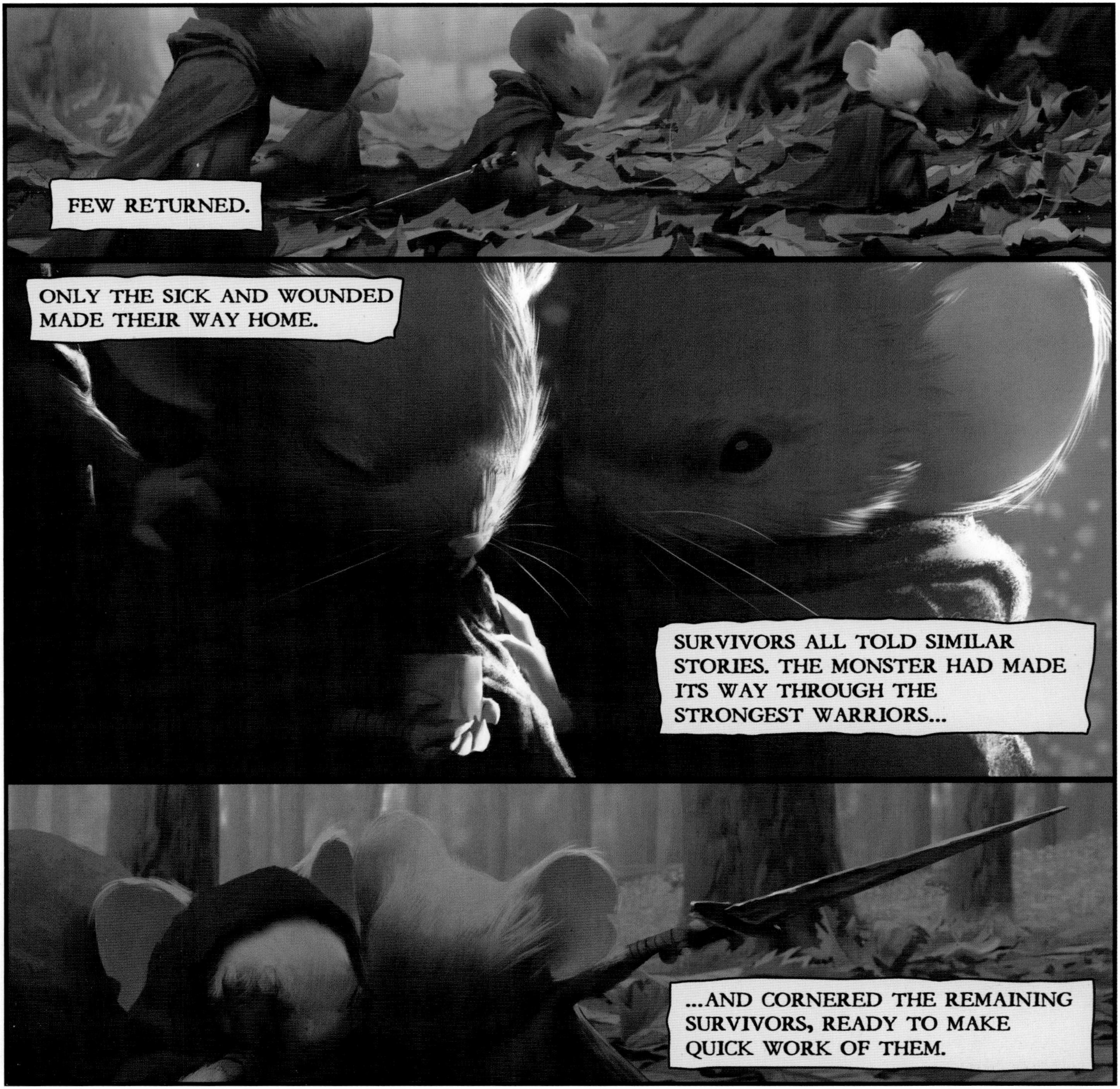
FEW RETURNED.
ONLY THE SICK AND WOUNDED MADE THEIR WAY HOME.
SURVIVORS ALL TOLD SIMILAR STORIES. THE MONSTER HAD MADE ITS WAY THROUGH THE STRONGEST WARRIORS...
...AND CORNERED THE REMAINING SURVIVORS, READY TO MAKE QUICK WORK OF THEM.

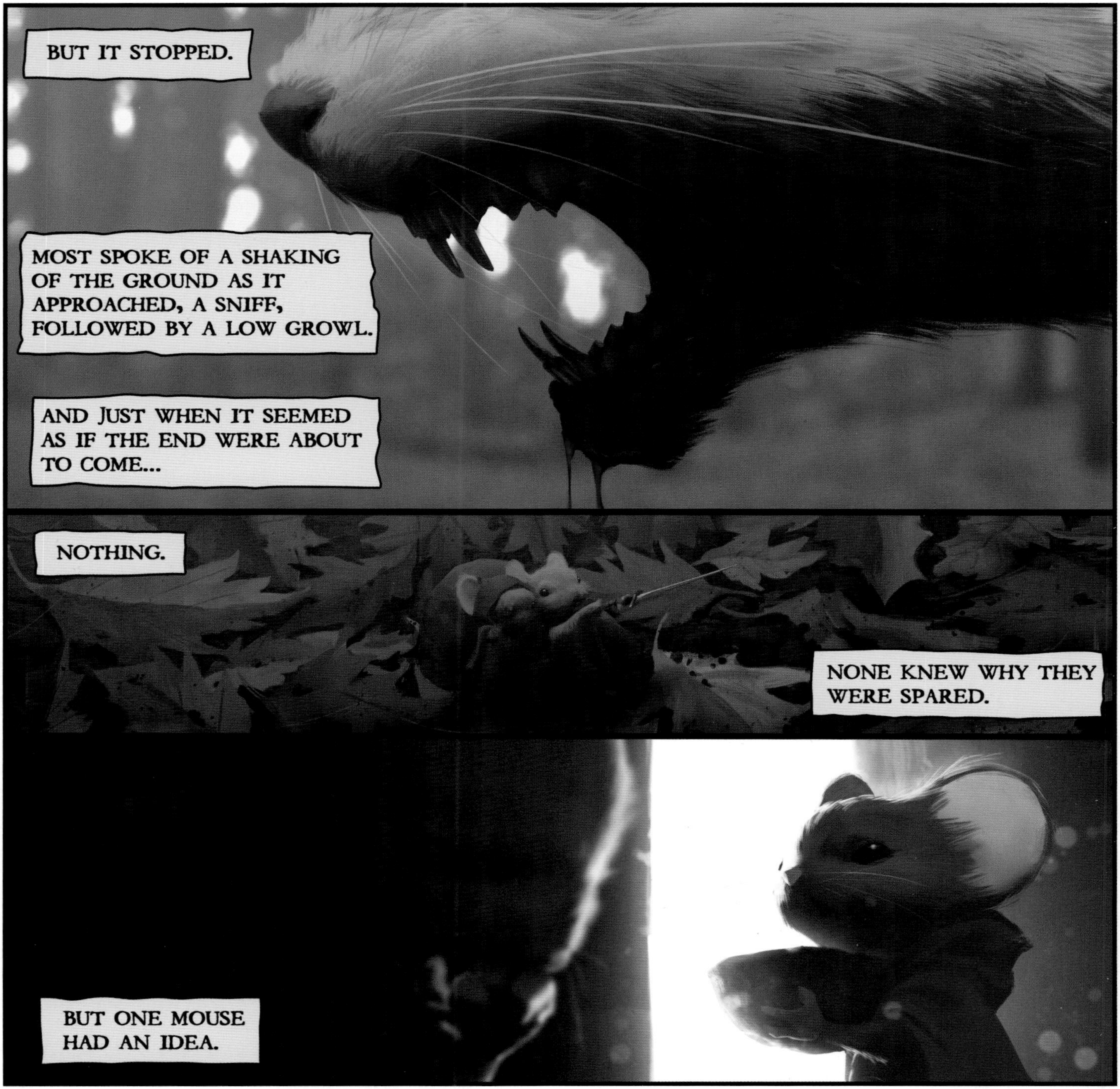
BUT IT STOPPED.
MOST SPOKE OF A SHAKING OF THE GROUND AS IT APPROACHED, A SNIFF, FOLLOWED BY A LOW GROWL.
AND JUST WHEN IT SEEMED AS IF THE END WERE ABOUT TO COME...
NOTHING.
NONE KNEW WHY THEY WERE SPARED.
BUT ONE MOUSE HAD AN IDEA.

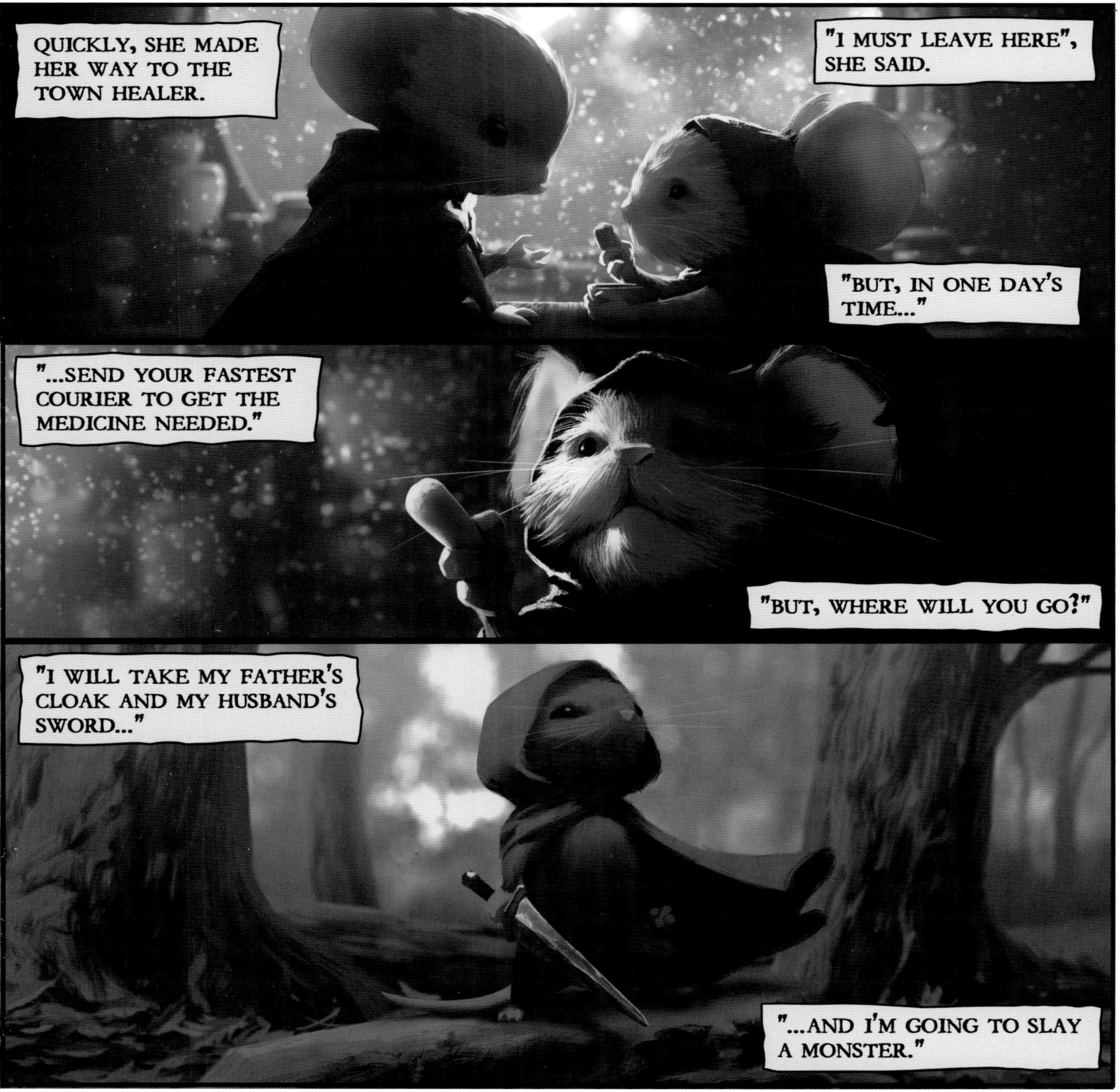
QUICKLY, SHE MADE HER WAY TO THE TOWN HEALER.
"I MUST LEAVE HERE", SHE SAID.
"BUT, IN ONE DAY'S TIME..."
"...SEND YOUR FASTEST COURIER TO GET THE MEDICINE NEEDED."
"BUT, WHERE WILL YOU GO?"
"I WILL TAKE MY FATHER'S CLOAK AND MY HUSBAND'S SWORD..."
"...AND I'M GOING TO SLAY A MONSTER."

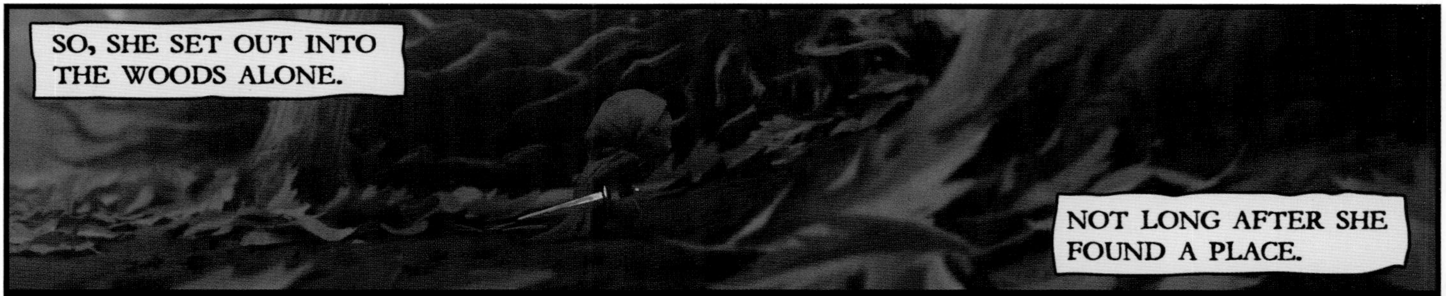
SO, SHE SET OUT INTO THE WOODS ALONE.
NOT LONG AFTER SHE FOUND A PLACE.

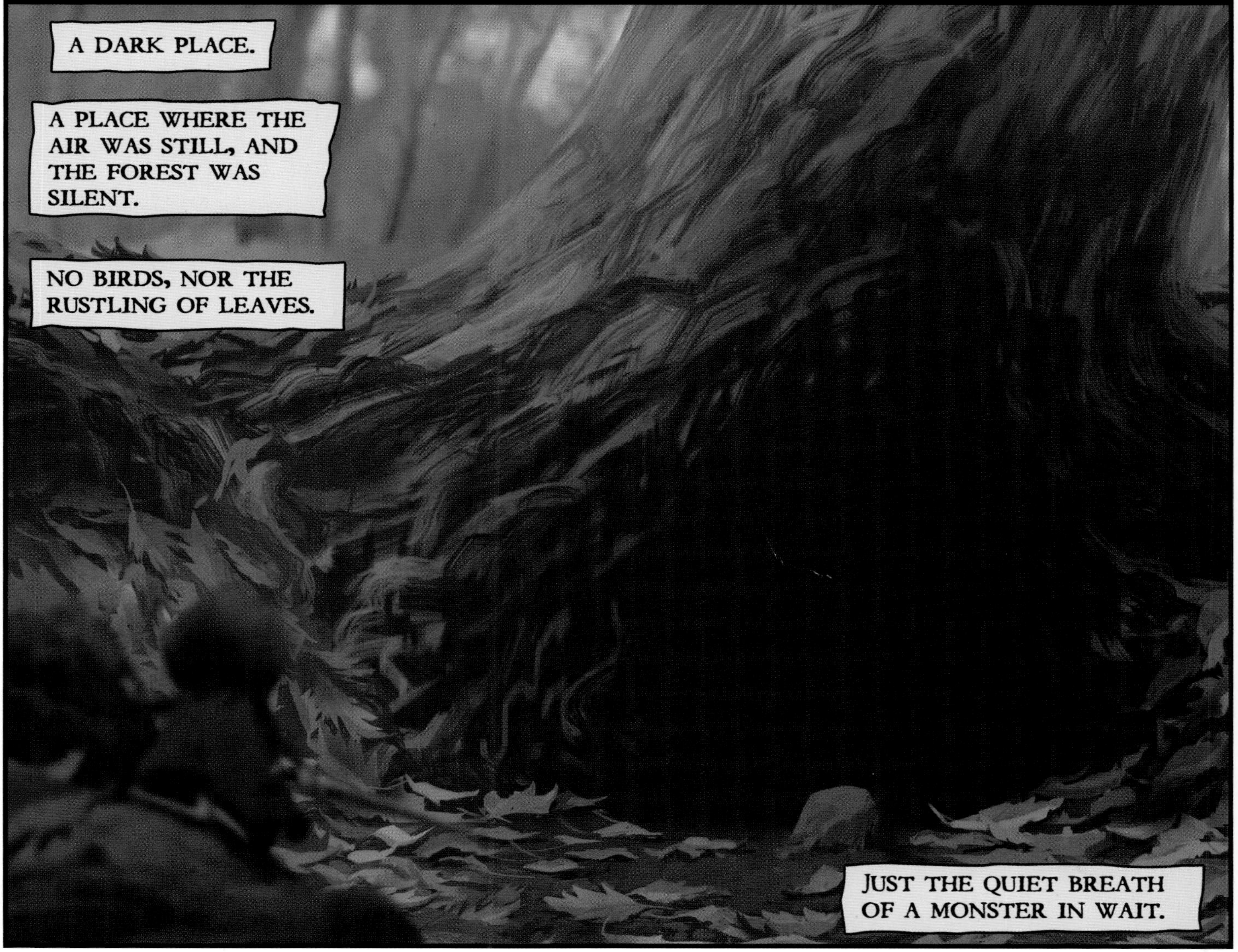
A DARK PLACE.
A PLACE WHERE THE AIR WAS STILL, AND THE FOREST WAS SILENT.
NO BIRDS, NOR THE RUSTLING OF LEAVES.
JUST THE QUIET BREATH OF A MONSTER IN WAIT.

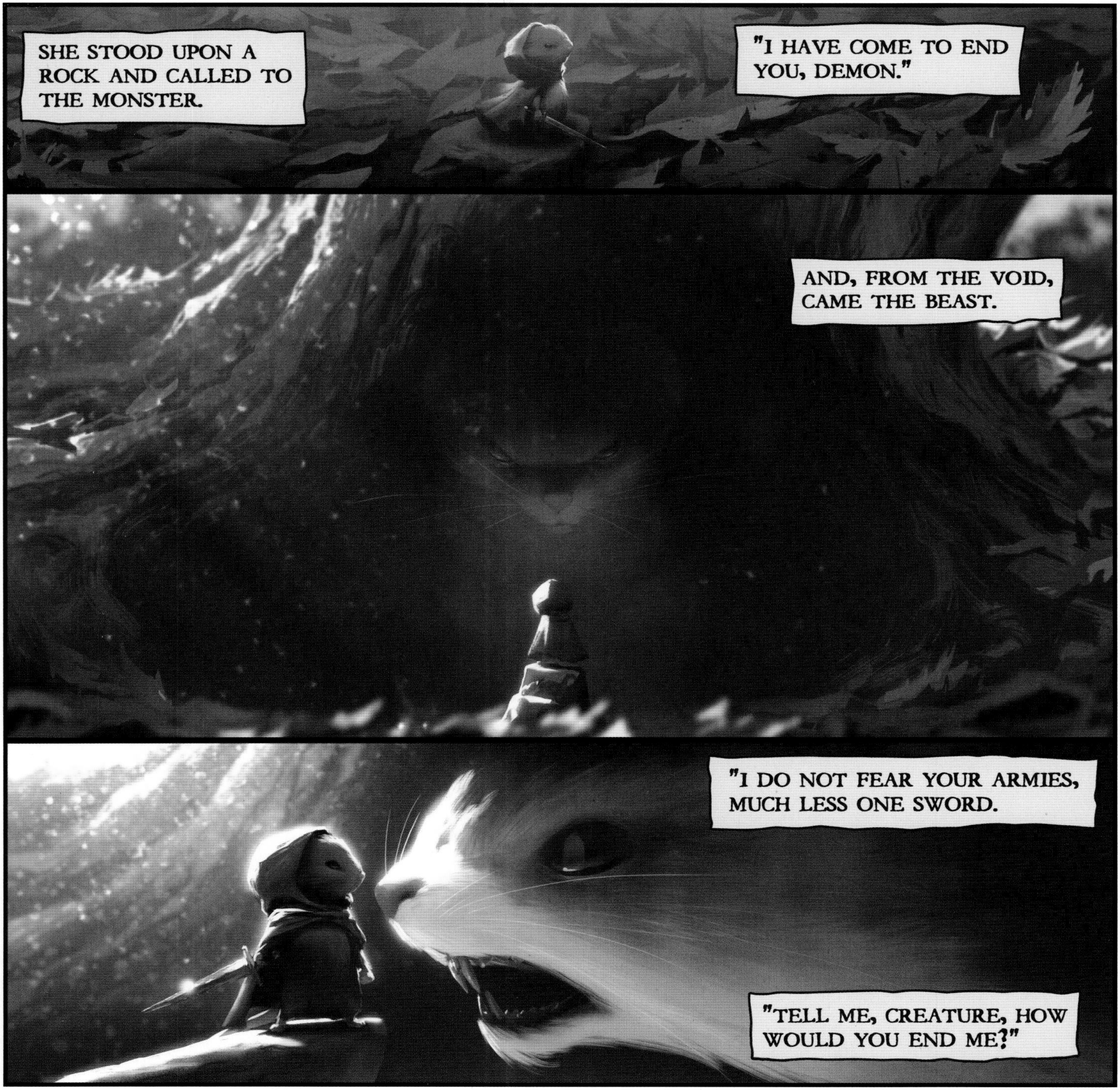
SHE STOOD UPON A ROCK AND CALLED TO THE MONSTER.
"I HAVE COME TO END YOU, DEMON."
AND, FROM THE VOID, CAME THE BEAST.
"I DO NOT FEAR YOUR ARMIES, MUCH LESS ONE SWORD.
"TELL ME, CREATURE, HOW WOULD YOU END ME?"

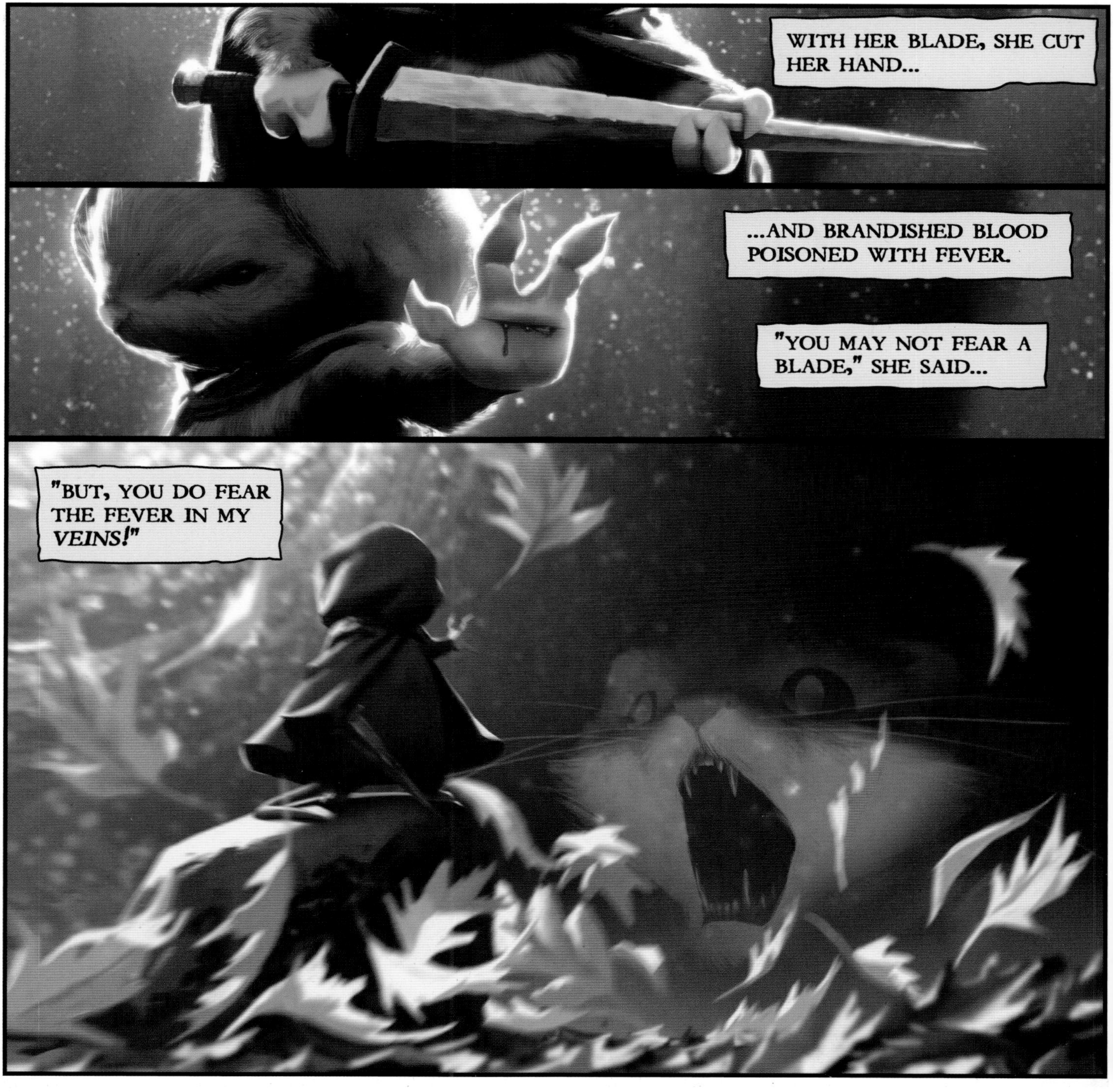
WITH HER BLADE, SHE CUT HER HAND...
...AND BRANDISHED BLOOD POISONED WITH FEVER.
"YOU MAY NOT FEAR A BLADE," SHE SAID...
"BUT, YOU DO FEAR THE FEVER IN MY *VEINS!*"

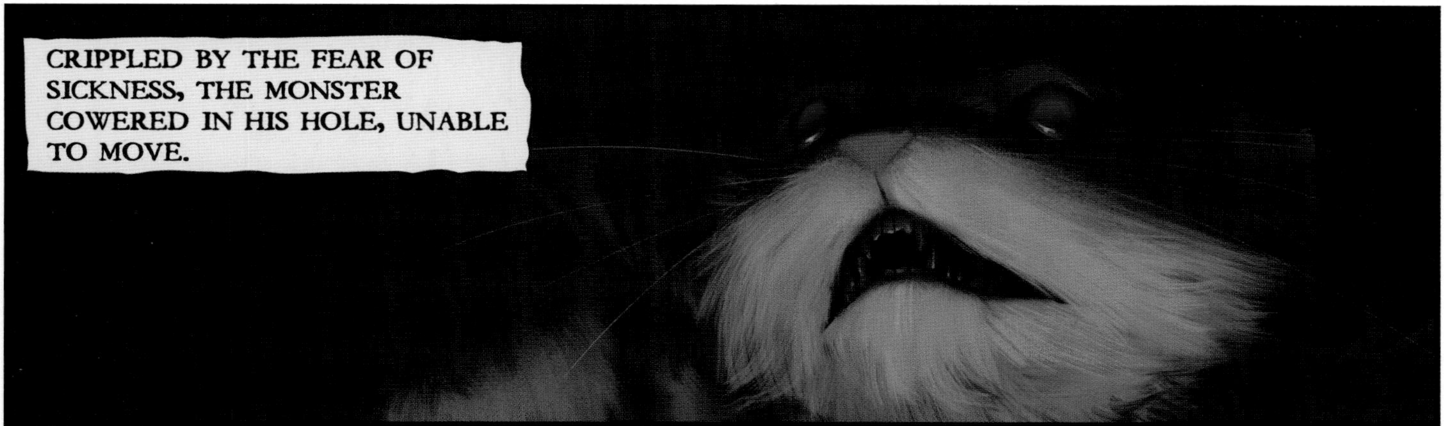
CRIPPLED BY THE FEAR OF SICKNESS, THE MONSTER COWERED IN HIS HOLE, UNABLE TO MOVE.

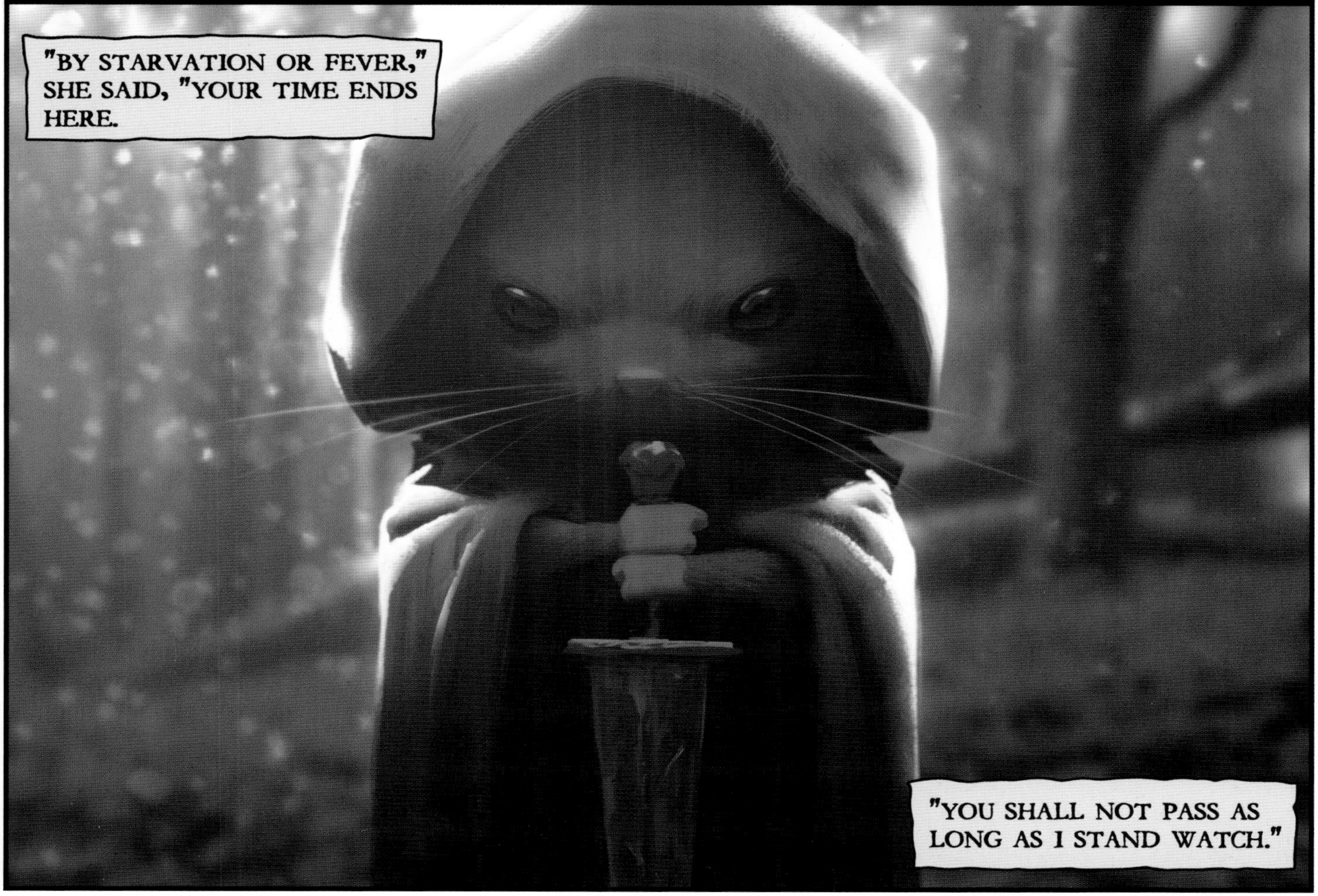
"BY STARVATION OR FEVER," SHE SAID, "YOUR TIME ENDS HERE.
"YOU SHALL NOT PASS AS LONG AS I STAND WATCH."

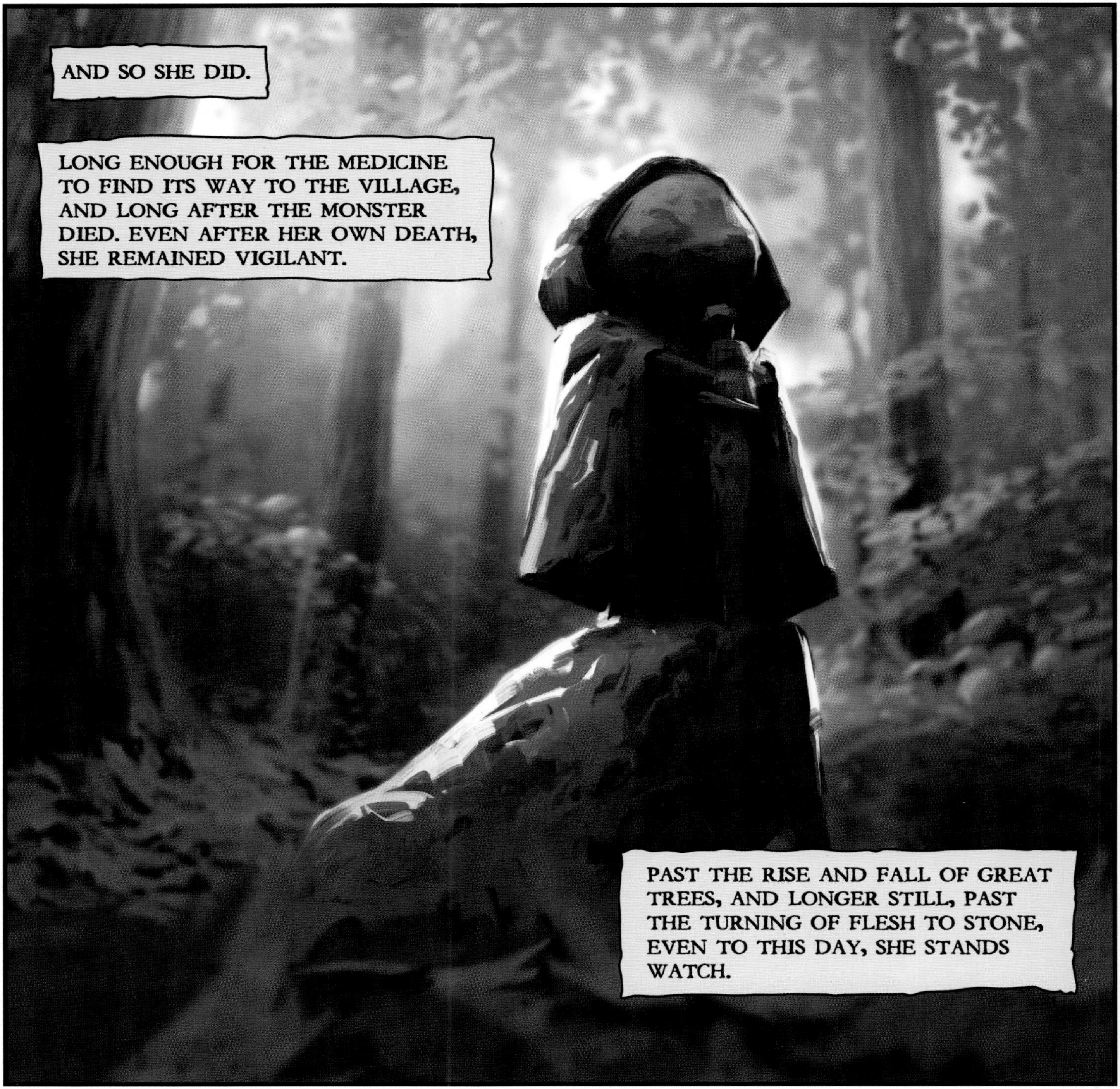
AND SO SHE DID.
LONG ENOUGH FOR THE MEDICINE TO FIND ITS WAY TO THE VILLAGE, AND LONG AFTER THE MONSTER DIED. EVEN AFTER HER OWN DEATH, SHE REMAINED VIGILANT.
PAST THE RISE AND FALL OF GREAT TREES, AND LONGER STILL, PAST THE TURNING OF FLESH TO STONE, EVEN TO THIS DAY, SHE STANDS WATCH.

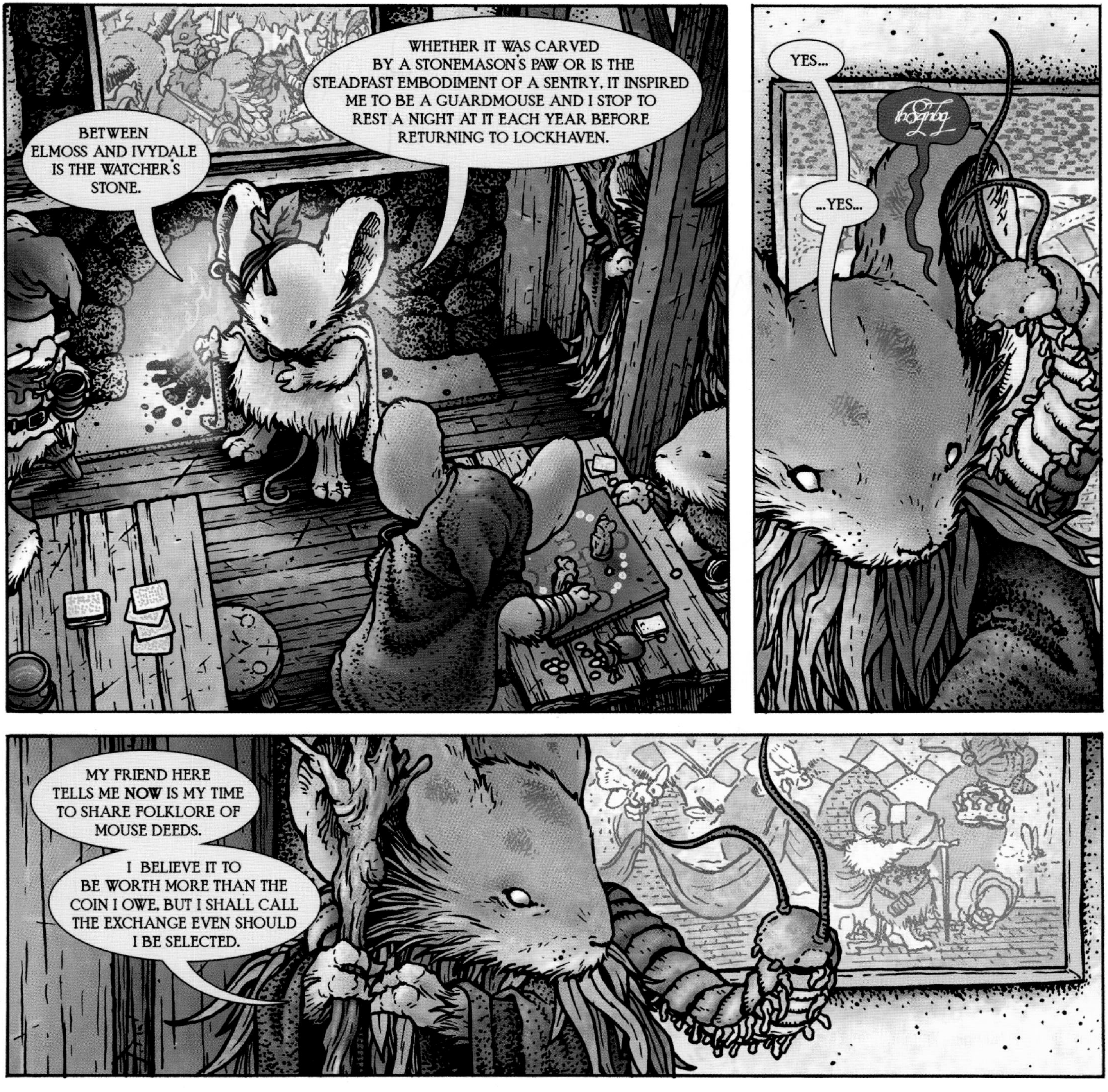
BETWEEN ELMOSS AND IVYDALE IS THE WATCHER'S STONE.
WHETHER IT WAS CARVED BY A STONEMASON'S PAW OR IS THE STEADFAST EMBODIMENT OF A SENTRY, IT INSPIRED ME TO BE A GUARDMOUSE AND I STOP TO REST A NIGHT AT IT EACH YEAR BEFORE RETURNING TO LOCKHAVEN.
YES...
...YES...
MY FRIEND HERE TELLS ME **NOW** IS MY TIME TO SHARE FOLKLORE OF MOUSE DEEDS.
I BELIEVE IT TO BE WORTH MORE THAN THE COIN I OWE, BUT I SHALL CALL THE EXCHANGE EVEN SHOULD I BE SELECTED.

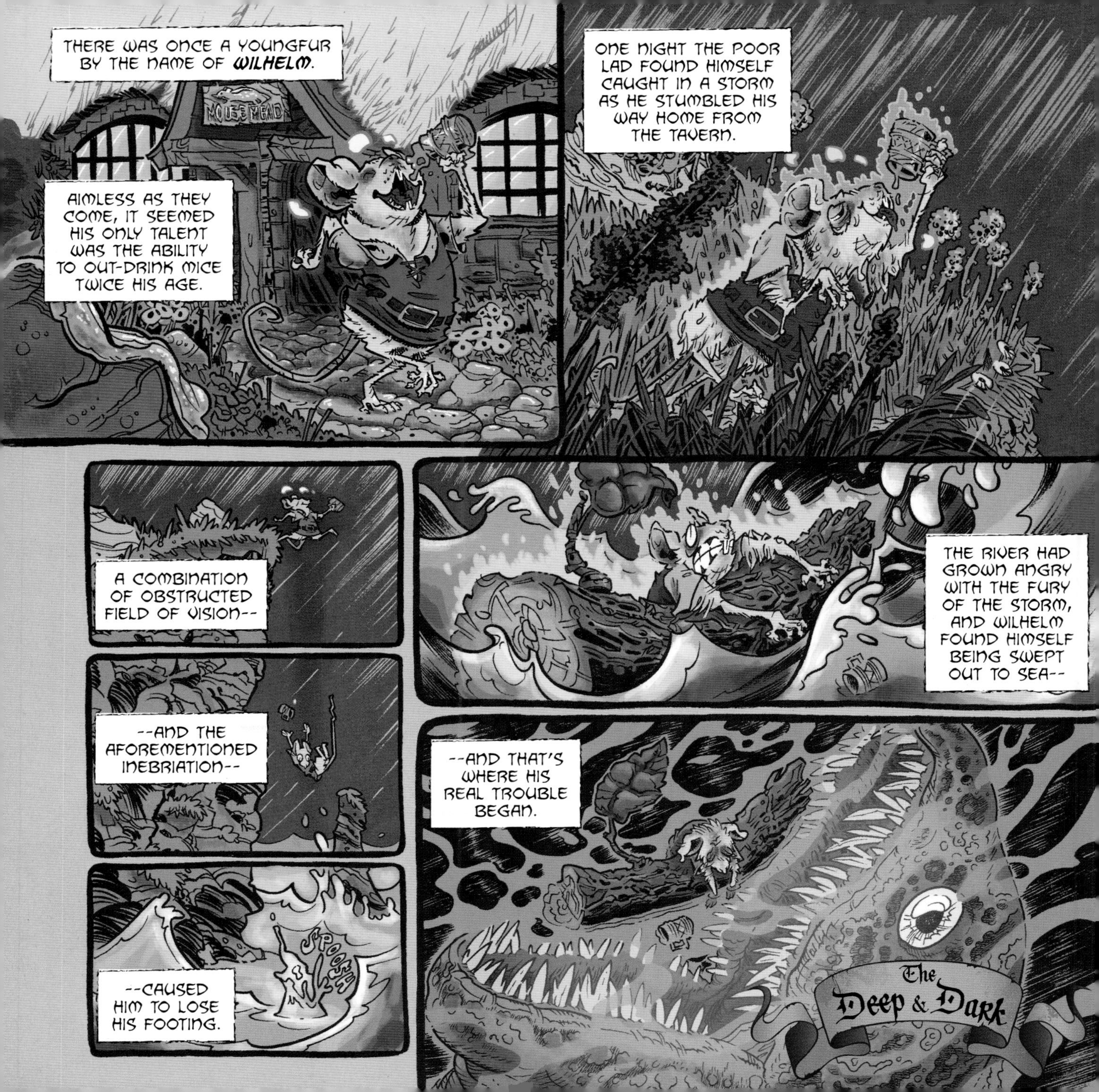
THERE WAS ONCE A YOUNGFUR BY THE NAME OF WILHELM.
MOUSE MEAD
AIMLESS AS THEY COME, IT SEEMED HIS ONLY TALENT WAS THE ABILITY TO OUT-DRINK MICE TWICE HIS AGE.
ONE NIGHT THE POOR LAD FOUND HIMSELF CAUGHT IN A STORM AS HE STUMBLED HIS WAY HOME FROM THE TAVERN.
A COMBINATION OF OBSTRUCTED FIELD OF VISION--
--AND THE AFOREMENTIONED INEBRIATION--
--CAUSED HIM TO LOSE HIS FOOTING.
SPOOSH
THE RIVER HAD GROWN ANGRY WITH THE FURY OF THE STORM, AND WILHELM FOUND HIMSELF BEING SWEPT OUT TO SEA--
--AND THAT'S WHERE HIS REAL TROUBLE BEGAN.
The Deep & Dark

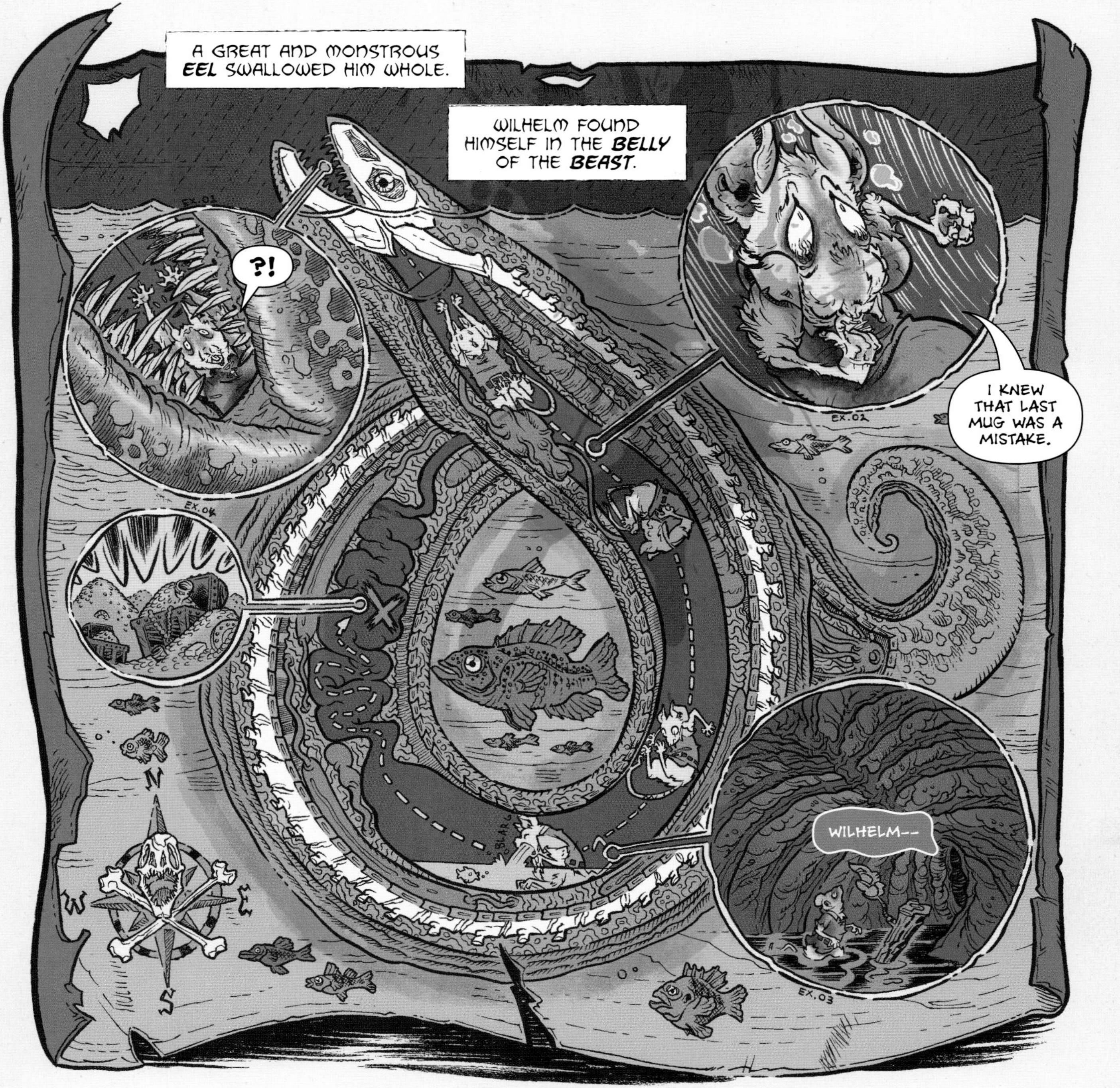
A GREAT AND MONSTROUS EEL SWALLOWED HIM WHOLE.
WILHELM FOUND HIMSELF IN THE BELLY OF THE BEAST.
EX.01
?!
EX.02
I KNEW THAT LAST MUG WAS A MISTAKE.
EX.04
BLARG
WILHELM--
EX.03
N
W
E
S

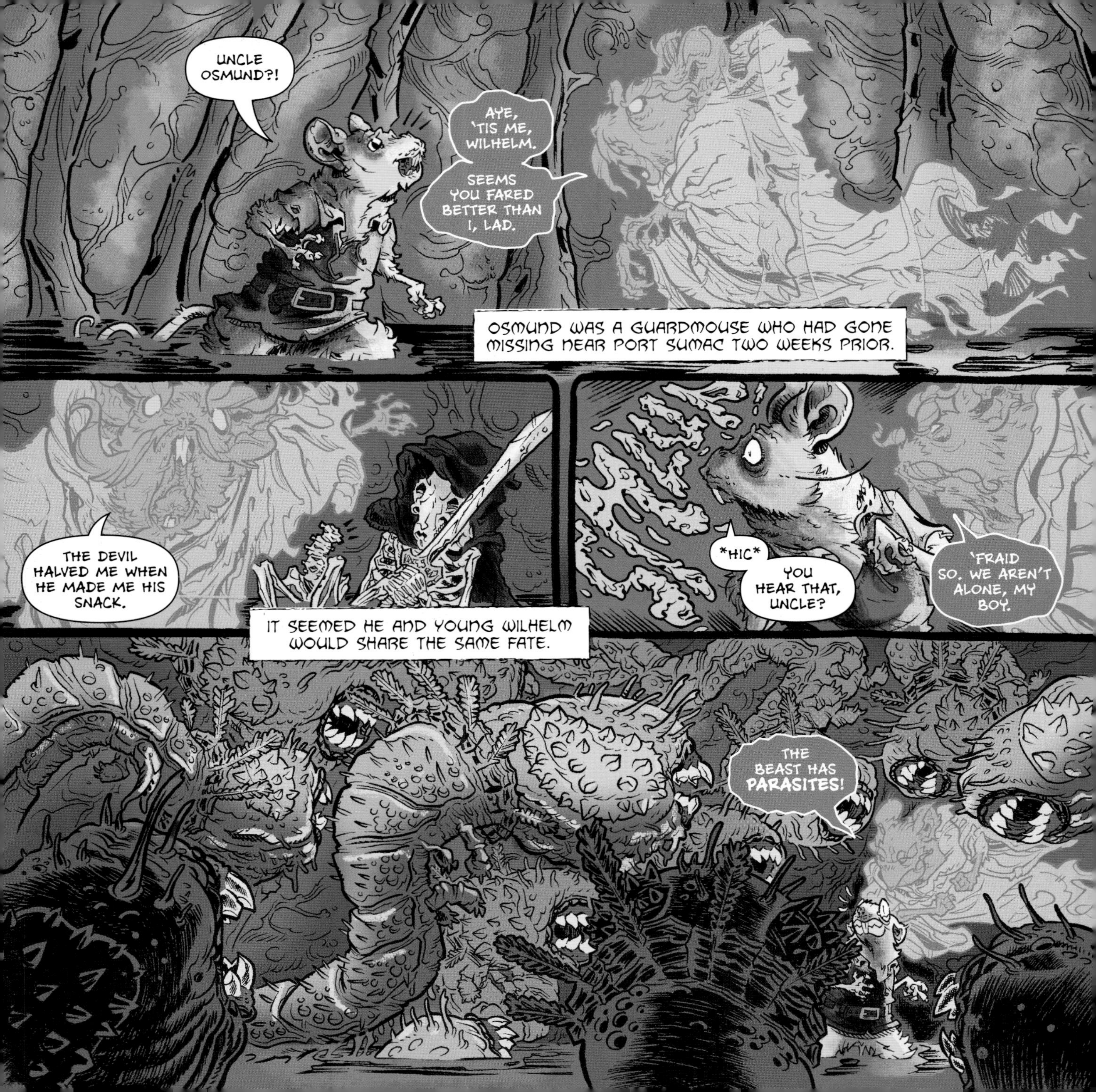
UNCLE OSMUND?!
AYE, 'TIS ME, WILHELM.
SEEMS YOU FARED BETTER THAN I, LAD.
OSMUND WAS A GUARDMOUSE WHO HAD GONE MISSING NEAR PORT SUMAC TWO WEEKS PRIOR.
THE DEVIL HALVED ME WHEN HE MADE ME HIS SNACK.
HIC
YOU HEAR THAT, UNCLE?
'FRAID SO. WE AREN'T ALONE, MY BOY.
IT SEEMED HE AND YOUNG WILHELM WOULD SHARE THE SAME FATE.
THE BEAST HAS **PARASITES!**

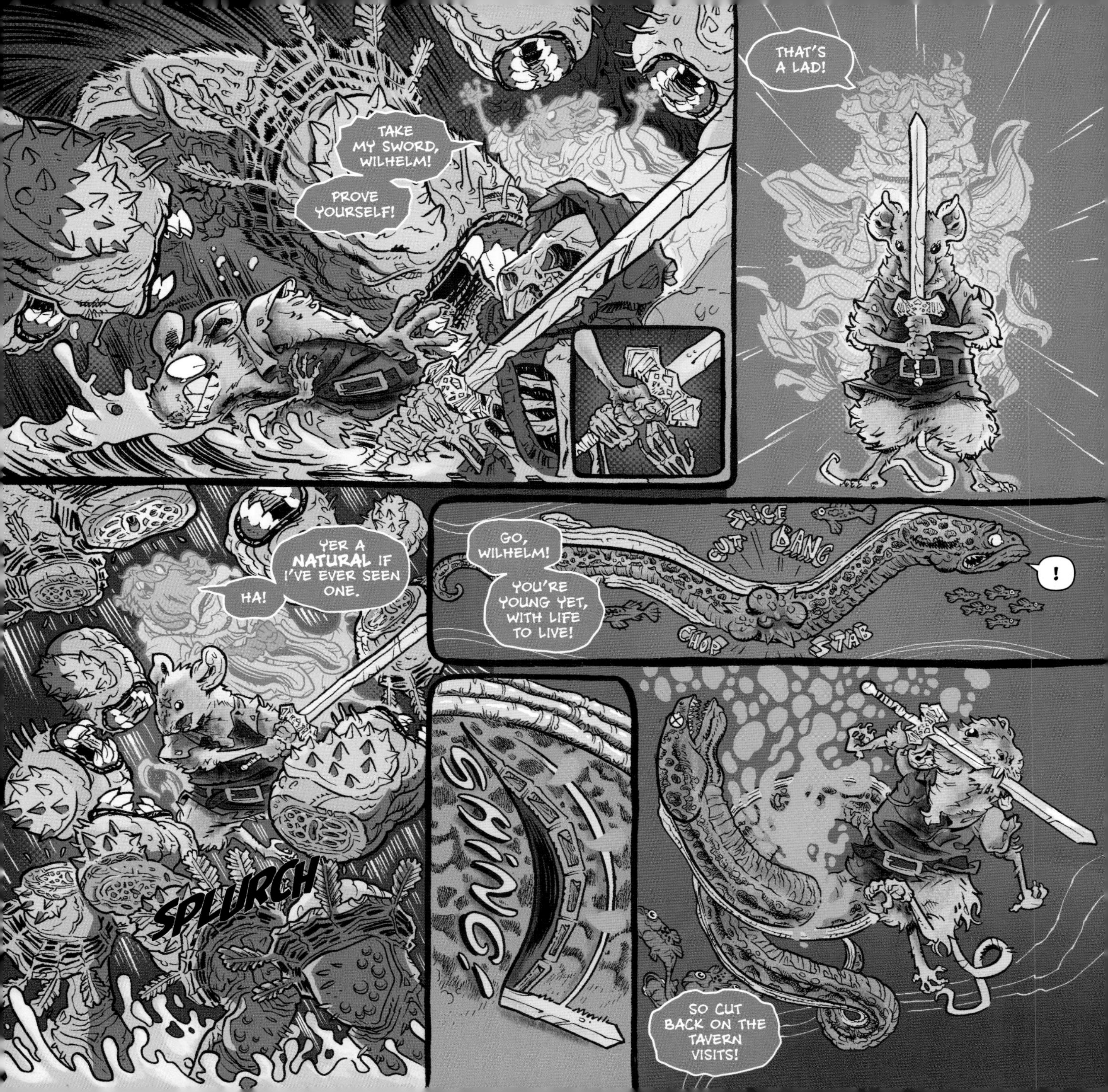
TAKE MY SWORD, WILHELM!
PROVE YOURSELF!
THAT'S A LAD!
HA!
YER A **NATURAL** IF I'VE EVER SEEN ONE.
GO, WILHELM!
YOU'RE YOUNG YET, WITH LIFE TO LIVE!
SLICE
CUT
BANG
CHOP
STAB
!
SPLURCH
SHING!
SO CUT BACK ON THE TAVERN VISITS!

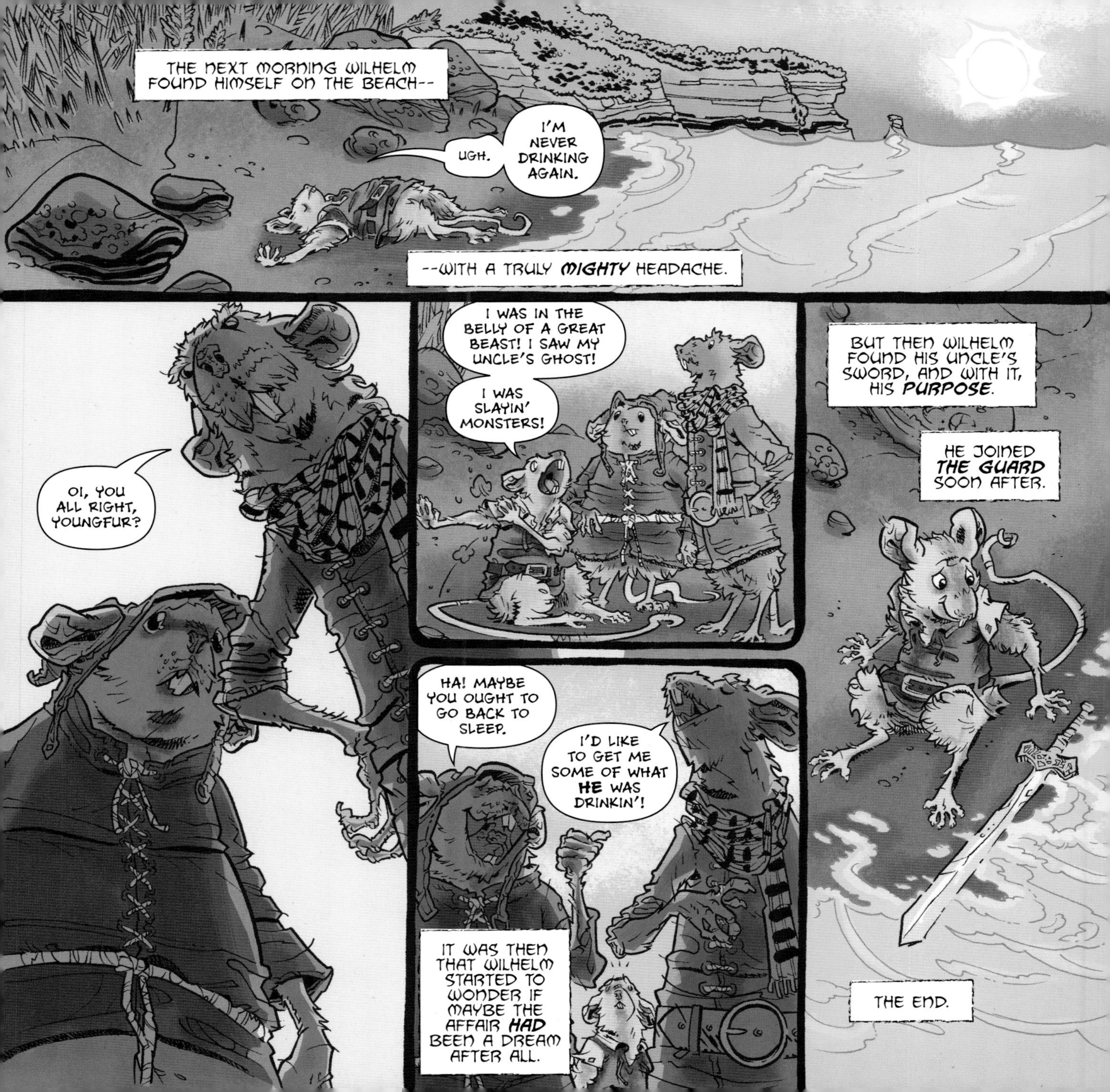
THE NEXT MORNING WILHELM FOUND HIMSELF ON THE BEACH--
UGH.
I'M NEVER DRINKING AGAIN.
--WITH A TRULY MIGHTY HEADACHE.
OI, YOU ALL RIGHT, YOUNGFUR?
I WAS IN THE BELLY OF A GREAT BEAST! I SAW MY UNCLE'S GHOST!
I WAS SLAYIN' MONSTERS!
HA! MAYBE YOU OUGHT TO GO BACK TO SLEEP.
I'D LIKE TO GET ME SOME OF WHAT HE WAS DRINKIN'!
IT WAS THEN THAT WILHELM STARTED TO WONDER IF MAYBE THE AFFAIR HAD BEEN A DREAM AFTER ALL.
BUT THEN WILHELM FOUND HIS UNCLE'S SWORD, AND WITH IT, HIS PURPOSE.
HE JOINED THE GUARD SOON AFTER.
THE END.

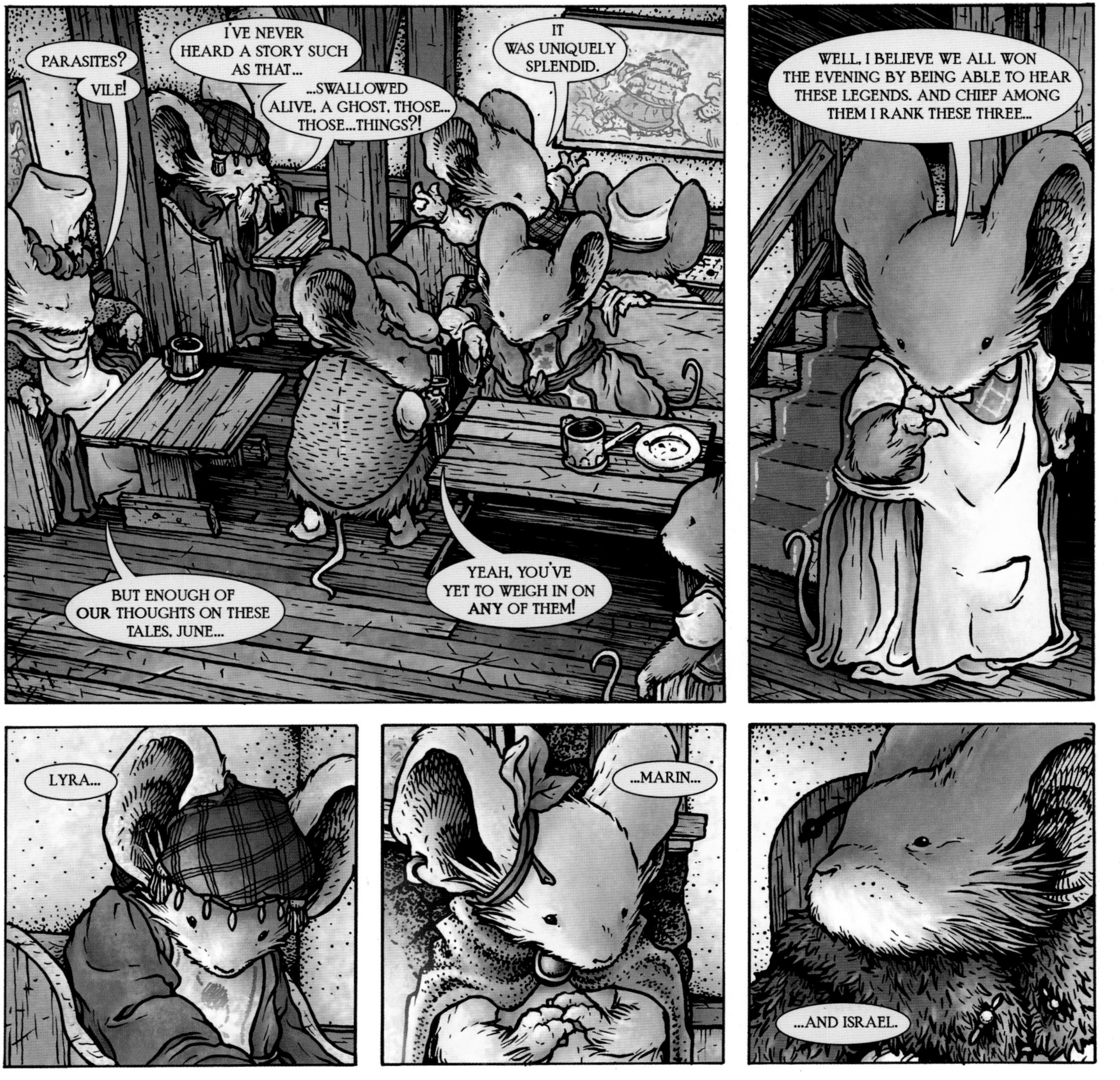
PARASITES?
VILE!
I'VE NEVER HEARD A STORY SUCH AS THAT...
...SWALLOWED ALIVE, A GHOST, THOSE... THOSE...THINGS?!
IT WAS UNIQUELY SPLENDID.
BUT ENOUGH OF OUR THOUGHTS ON THESE TALES, JUNE...
YEAH, YOU'VE YET TO WEIGH IN ON ANY OF THEM!
WELL, I BELIEVE WE ALL WON THE EVENING BY BEING ABLE TO HEAR THESE LEGENDS. AND CHIEF AMONG THEM I RANK THESE THREE...
LYRA...
...MARIN...
...AND ISRAEL.

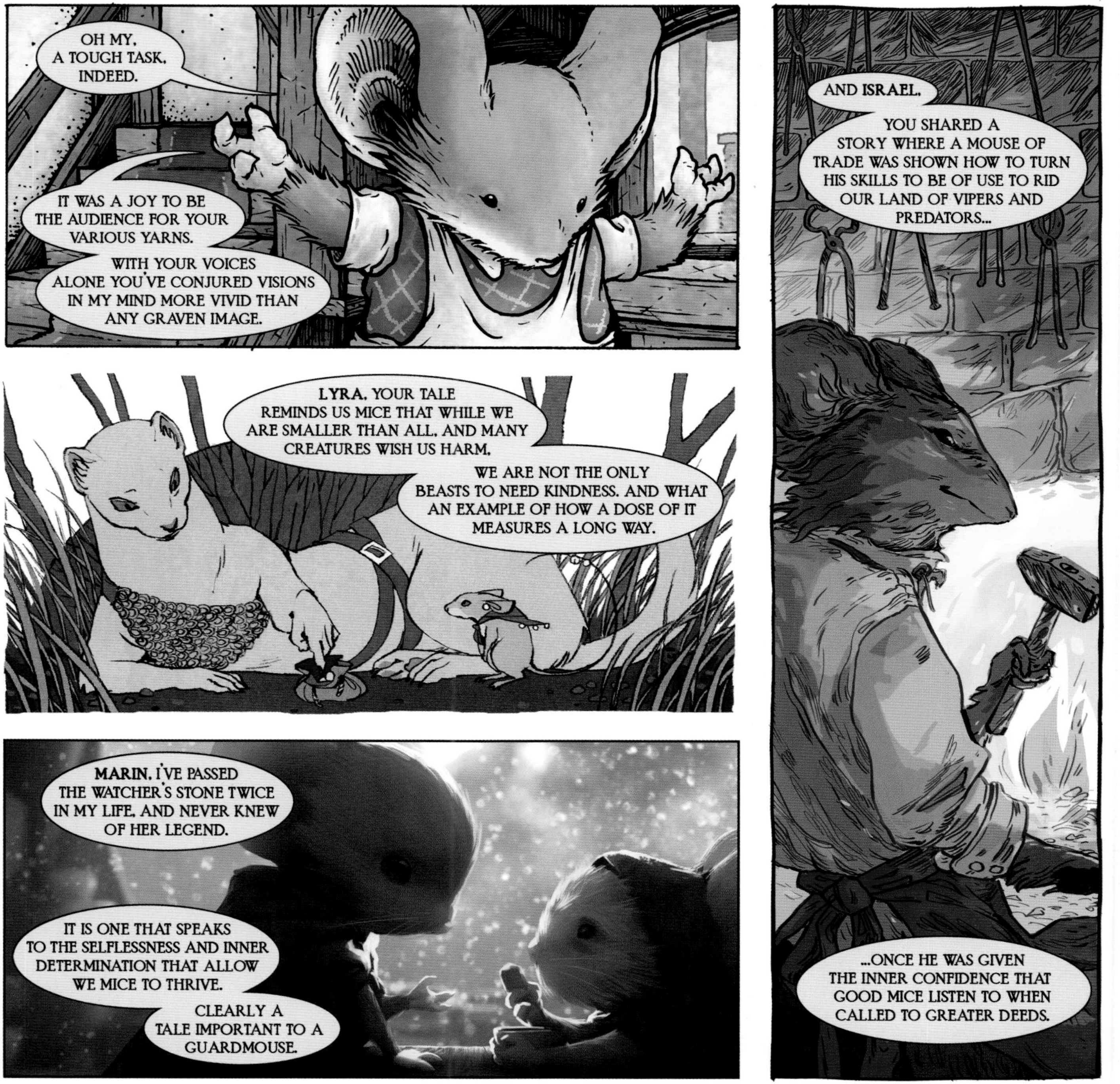
OH MY, A TOUGH TASK, INDEED.
IT WAS A JOY TO BE THE AUDIENCE FOR YOUR VARIOUS YARNS.
WITH YOUR VOICES ALONE YOU'VE CONJURED VISIONS IN MY MIND MORE VIVID THAN ANY GRAVEN IMAGE.
LYRA, YOUR TALE REMINDS US MICE THAT WHILE WE ARE SMALLER THAN ALL, AND MANY CREATURES WISH US HARM,
WE ARE NOT THE ONLY BEASTS TO NEED KINDNESS. AND WHAT AN EXAMPLE OF HOW A DOSE OF IT MEASURES A LONG WAY.
MARIN, I'VE PASSED THE WATCHER'S STONE TWICE IN MY LIFE, AND NEVER KNEW OF HER LEGEND.
IT IS ONE THAT SPEAKS TO THE SELFLESSNESS AND INNER DETERMINATION THAT ALLOW WE MICE TO THRIVE.
CLEARLY A TALE IMPORTANT TO A GUARDMOUSE.
AND ISRAEL,
YOU SHARED A STORY WHERE A MOUSE OF TRADE WAS SHOWN HOW TO TURN HIS SKILLS TO BE OF USE TO RID OUR LAND OF VIPERS AND PREDATORS...
...ONCE HE WAS GIVEN THE INNER CONFIDENCE THAT GOOD MICE LISTEN TO WHEN CALLED TO GREATER DEEDS.

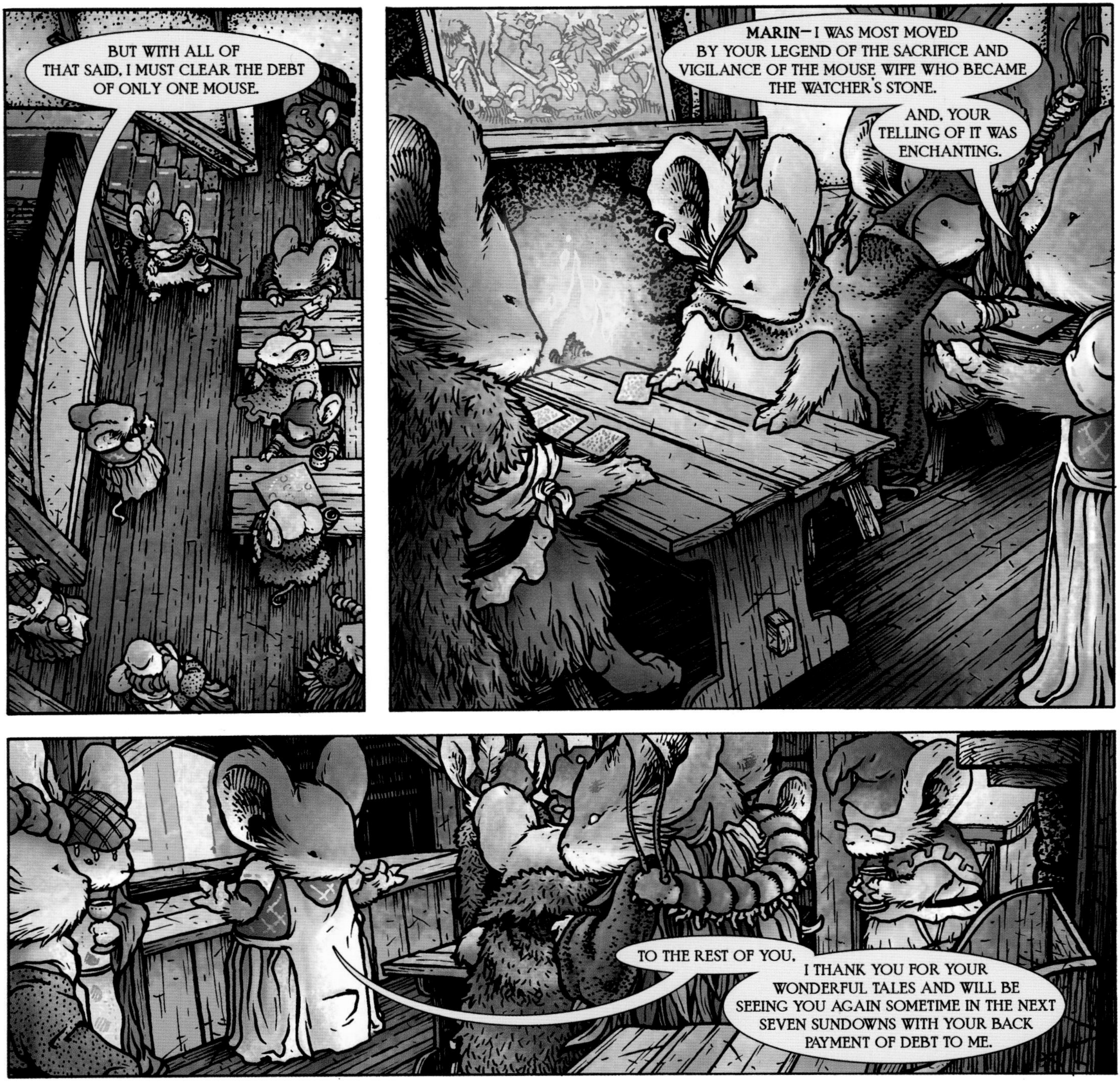
BUT WITH ALL OF THAT SAID, I MUST CLEAR THE DEBT OF ONLY ONE MOUSE.
MARIN— I WAS MOST MOVED BY YOUR LEGEND OF THE SACRIFICE AND VIGILANCE OF THE MOUSE WIFE WHO BECAME THE WATCHER'S STONE.
AND, YOUR TELLING OF IT WAS ENCHANTING.
TO THE REST OF YOU,
I THANK YOU FOR YOUR WONDERFUL TALES AND WILL BE SEEING YOU AGAIN SOMETIME IN THE NEXT SEVEN SUNDOWNS WITH YOUR BACK PAYMENT OF DEBT TO ME.

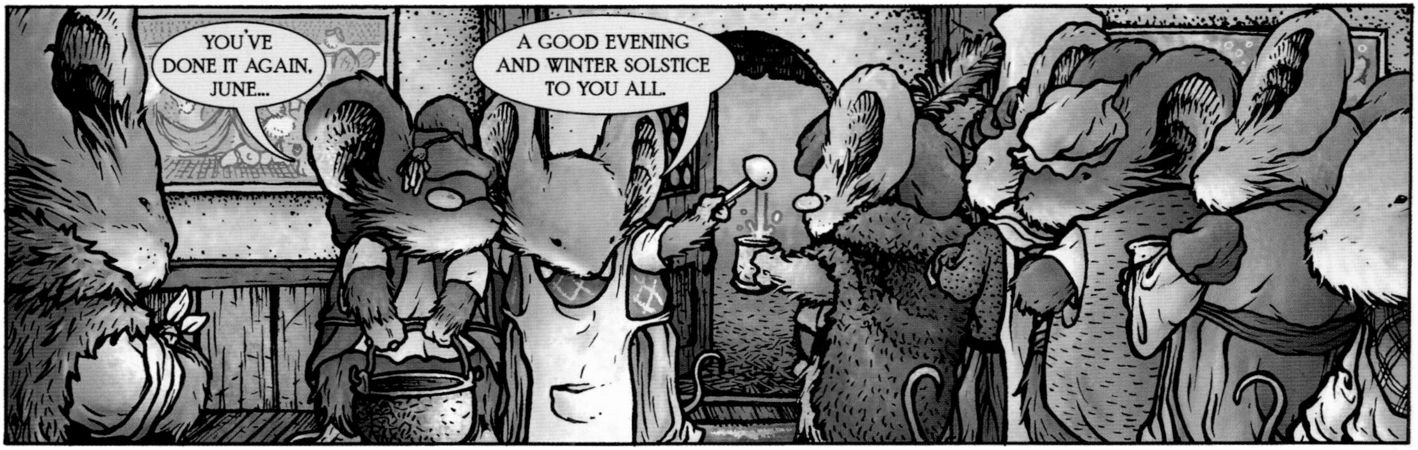
YOU'VE DONE IT AGAIN, JUNE...
A GOOD EVENING AND WINTER SOLSTICE TO YOU ALL.

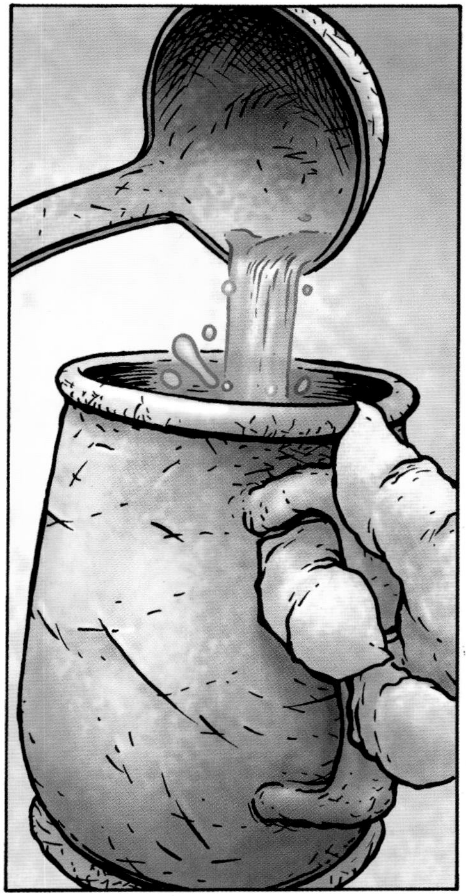

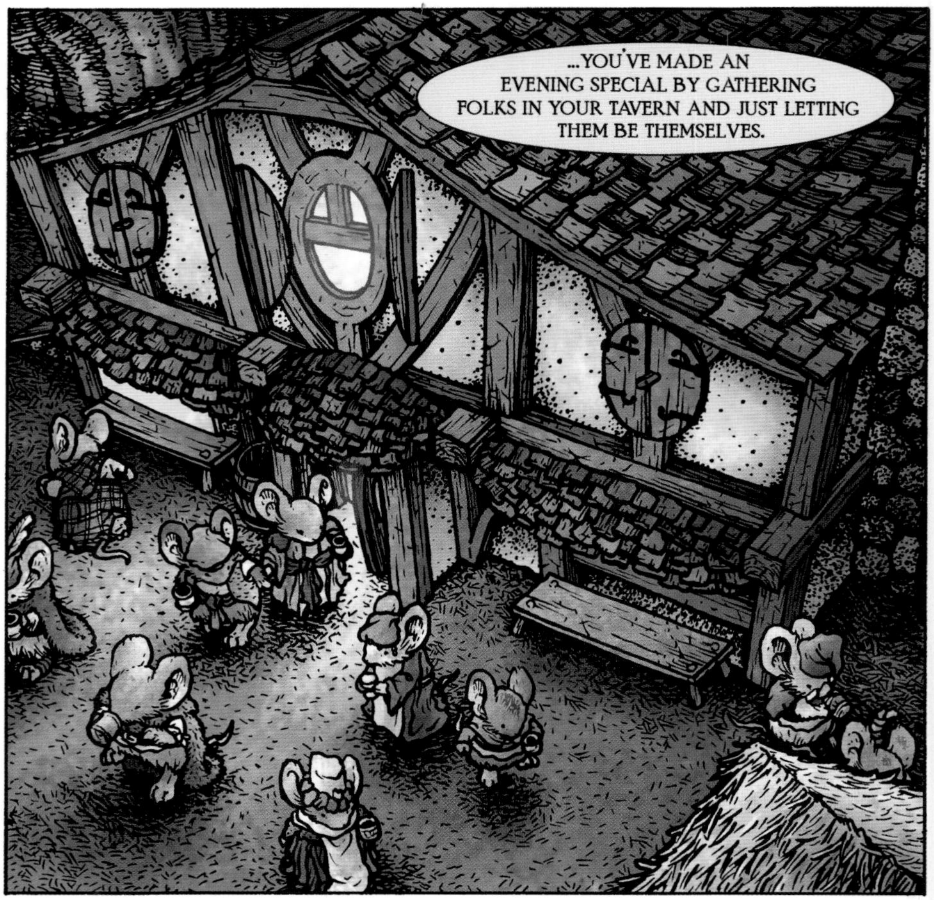
...YOU'VE MADE AN EVENING SPECIAL BY GATHERING FOLKS IN YOUR TAVERN AND JUST LETTING THEM BE THEMSELVES.

END

EPILOGUE

ART & STORY: LAUREN PETTAPIECE
& DAVID PETERSEN

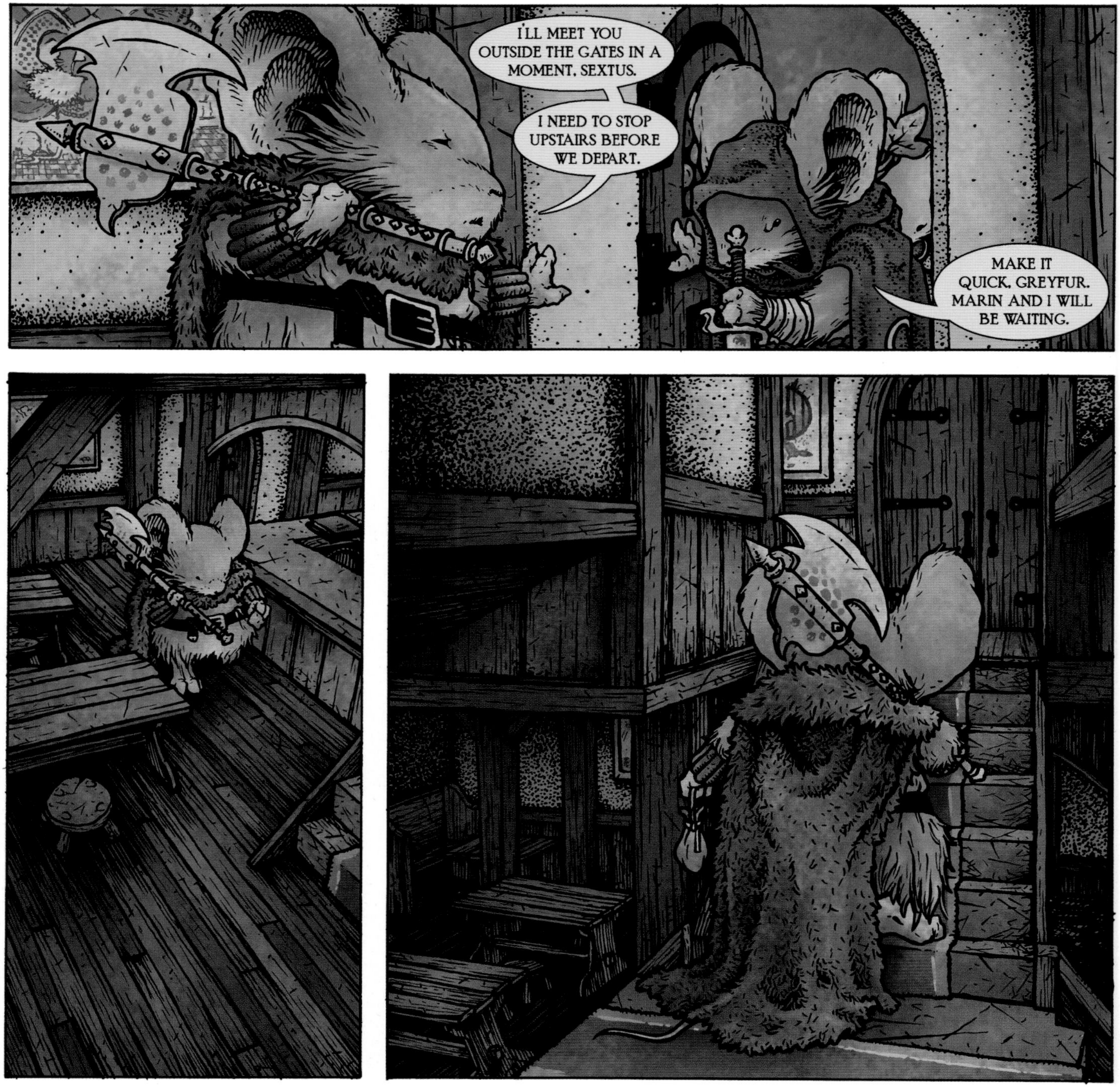
I'LL MEET YOU OUTSIDE THE GATES IN A MOMENT, SEXTUS.
I NEED TO STOP UPSTAIRS BEFORE WE DEPART.
MAKE IT QUICK, GREYFUR. MARIN AND I WILL BE WAITING.

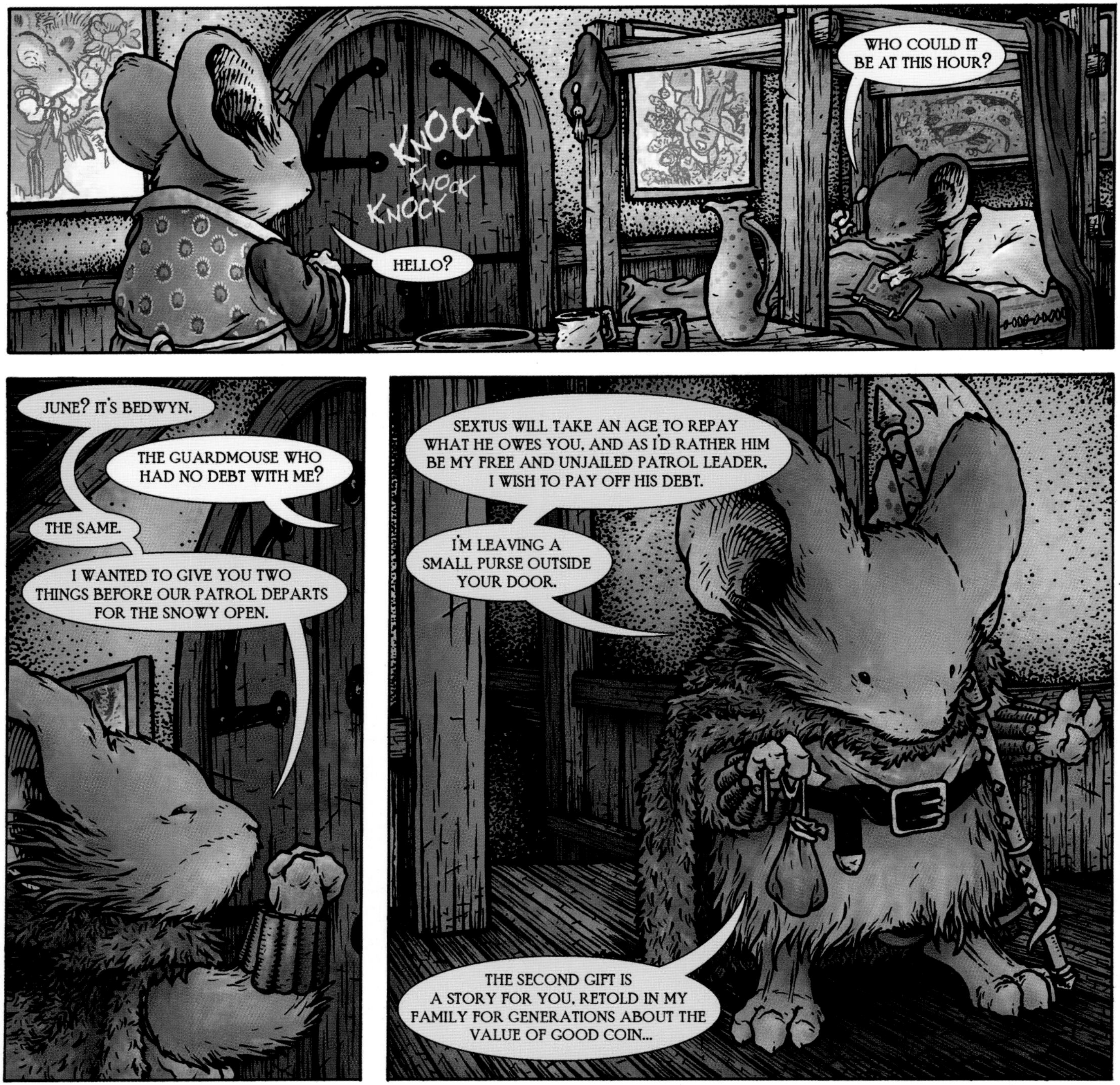
KNOCK KNOCK KNOCK
HELLO?
WHO COULD IT BE AT THIS HOUR?
JUNE? IT'S BEDWYN.
THE GUARDMOUSE WHO HAD NO DEBT WITH ME?
THE SAME.
I WANTED TO GIVE YOU TWO THINGS BEFORE OUR PATROL DEPARTS FOR THE SNOWY OPEN.
SEXTUS WILL TAKE AN AGE TO REPAY WHAT HE OWES YOU, AND AS I'D RATHER HIM BE MY FREE AND UNJAILED PATROL LEADER, I WISH TO PAY OFF HIS DEBT.
I'M LEAVING A SMALL PURSE OUTSIDE YOUR DOOR.
THE SECOND GIFT IS A STORY FOR YOU, RETOLD IN MY FAMILY FOR GENERATIONS ABOUT THE VALUE OF GOOD COIN...

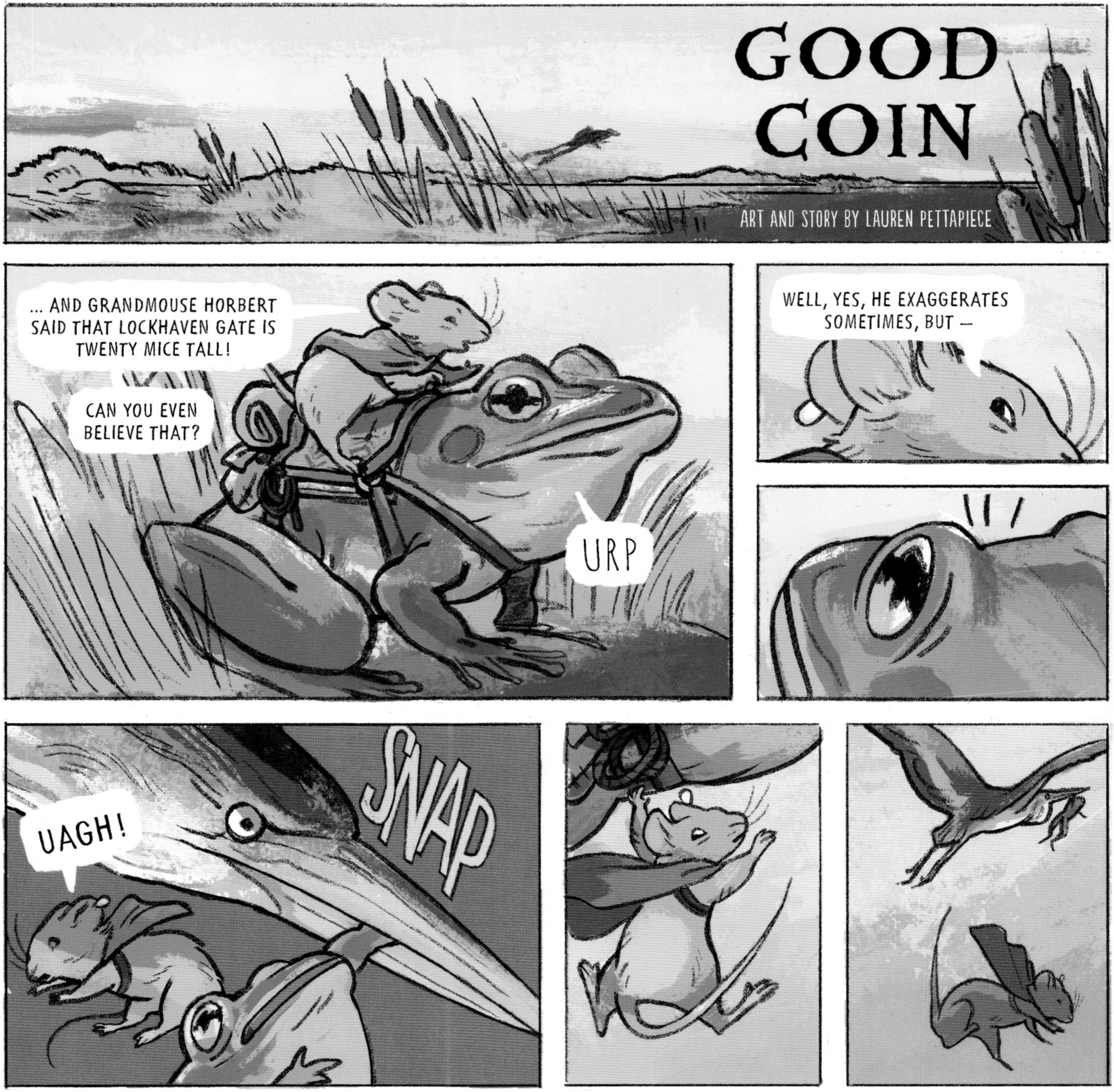
GOOD COIN
ART AND STORY BY LAUREN PETTAPIECE
... AND GRANDMOUSE HORBERT SAID THAT LOCKHAVEN GATE IS TWENTY MICE TALL!
CAN YOU EVEN BELIEVE THAT?
URP
WELL, YES, HE EXAGGERATES SOMETIMES, BUT —
SNAP
UAGH!

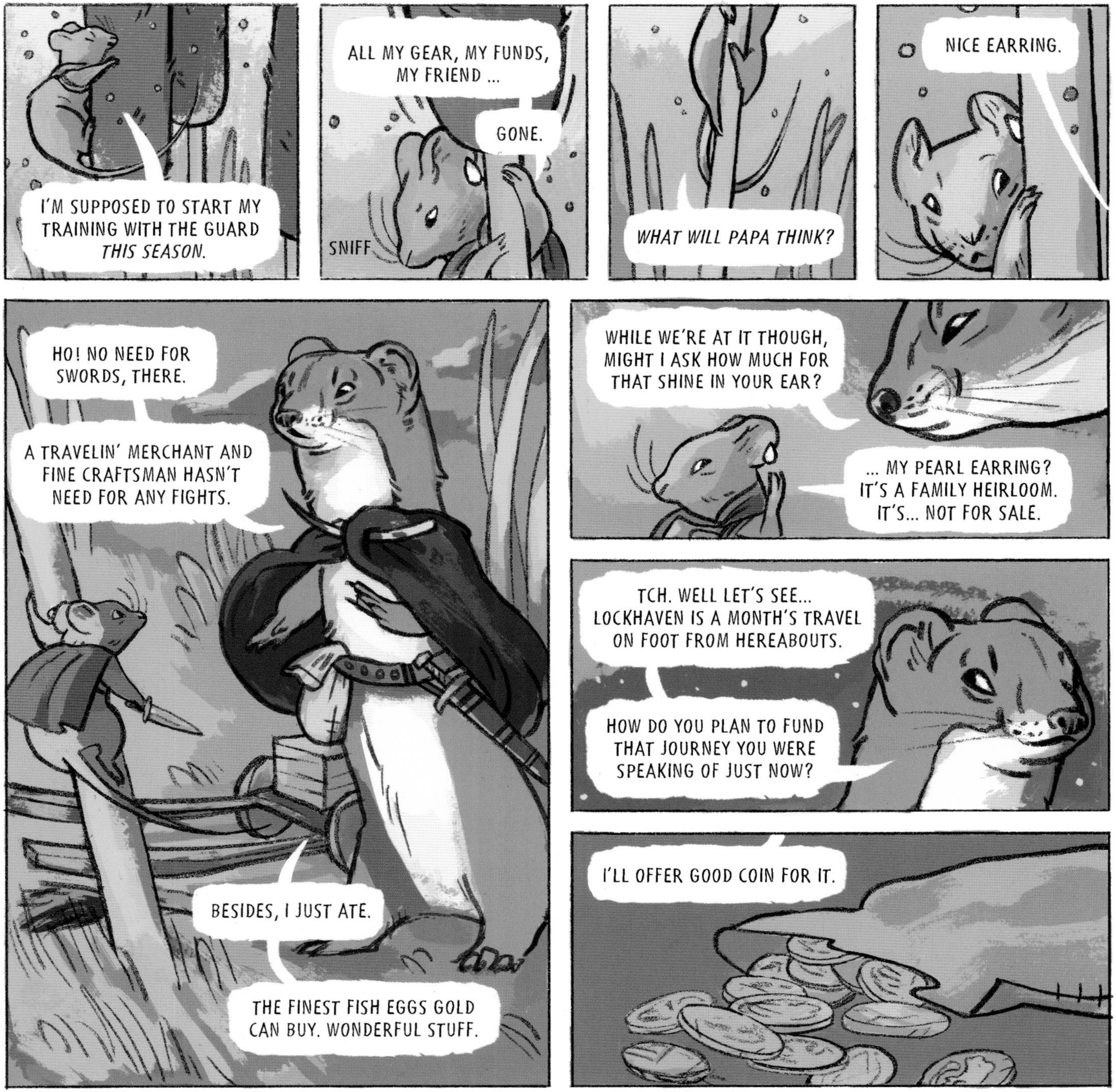
I'M SUPPOSED TO START MY TRAINING WITH THE GUARD *THIS SEASON*.
ALL MY GEAR, MY FUNDS, MY FRIEND ...
GONE.
SNIFF
WHAT WILL PAPA THINK?
NICE EARRING.
HO! NO NEED FOR SWORDS, THERE.
A TRAVELIN' MERCHANT AND FINE CRAFTSMAN HASN'T NEED FOR ANY FIGHTS.
BESIDES, I JUST ATE.
THE FINEST FISH EGGS GOLD CAN BUY. WONDERFUL STUFF.
WHILE WE'RE AT IT THOUGH, MIGHT I ASK HOW MUCH FOR THAT SHINE IN YOUR EAR?
... MY PEARL EARRING? IT'S A FAMILY HEIRLOOM. IT'S... NOT FOR SALE.
TCH. WELL LET'S SEE... LOCKHAVEN IS A MONTH'S TRAVEL ON FOOT FROM HEREABOUTS.
HOW DO YOU PLAN TO FUND THAT JOURNEY YOU WERE SPEAKING OF JUST NOW?
I'LL OFFER GOOD COIN FOR IT.

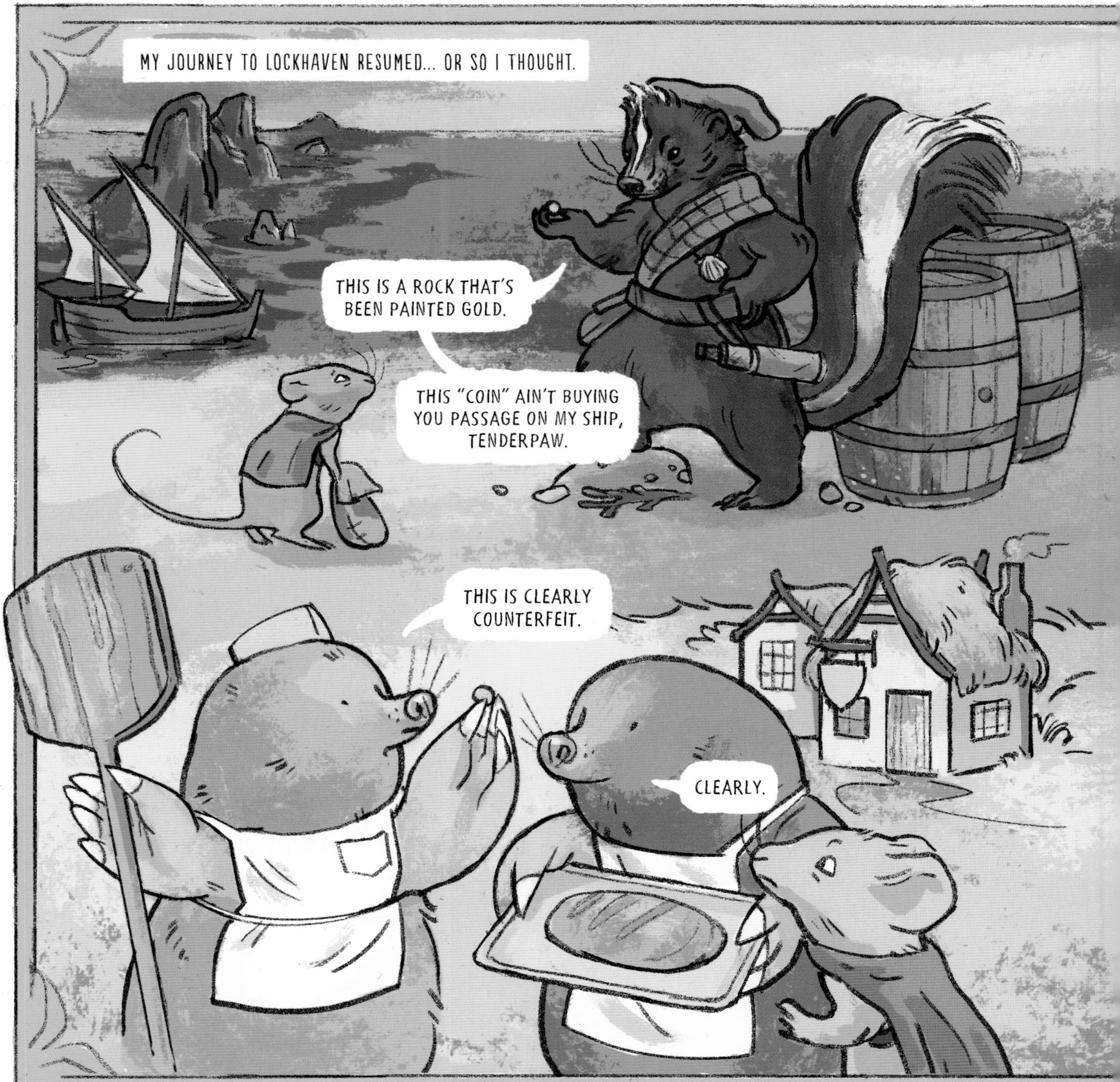
MY JOURNEY TO LOCKHAVEN RESUMED... OR SO I THOUGHT.
THIS IS A ROCK THAT'S BEEN PAINTED GOLD.
THIS "COIN" AIN'T BUYING YOU PASSAGE ON MY SHIP, TENDERPAW.
THIS IS CLEARLY COUNTERFEIT.
CLEARLY.

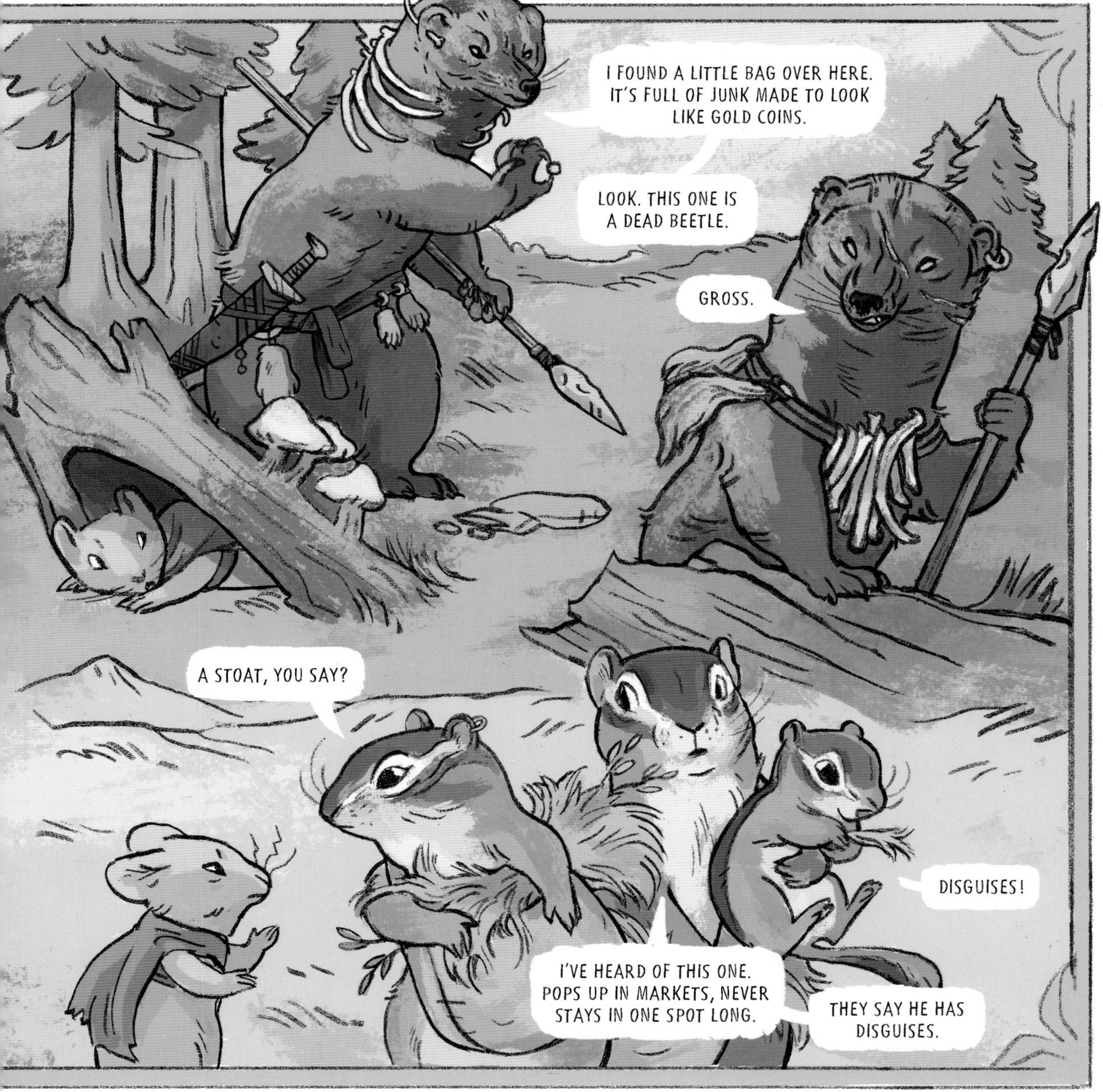
I FOUND A LITTLE BAG OVER HERE. IT'S FULL OF JUNK MADE TO LOOK LIKE GOLD COINS.
LOOK. THIS ONE IS A DEAD BEETLE.
GROSS.
A STOAT, YOU SAY?
I'VE HEARD OF THIS ONE. POPS UP IN MARKETS, NEVER STAYS IN ONE SPOT LONG.
THEY SAY HE HAS DISGUISES.
DISGUISES!

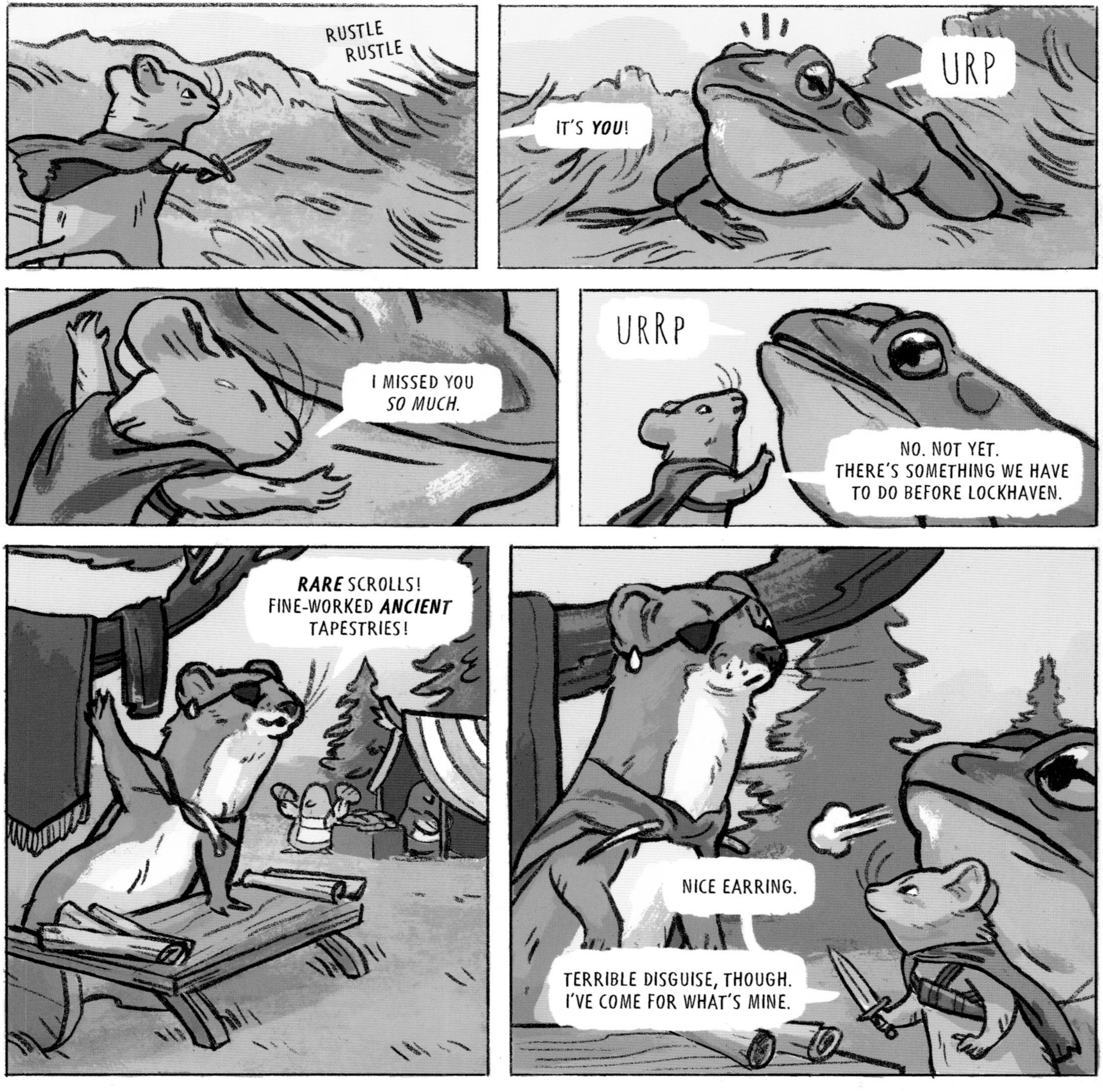

RUSTLE RUSTLE
URP
IT'S ***YOU***!
I MISSED YOU *SO MUCH.*
URRP
NO. NOT YET. THERE'S SOMETHING WE HAVE TO DO BEFORE LOCKHAVEN.
RARE SCROLLS! FINE-WORKED ***ANCIENT*** TAPESTRIES!
NICE EARRING.
TERRIBLE DISGUISE, THOUGH. I'VE COME FOR WHAT'S MINE.

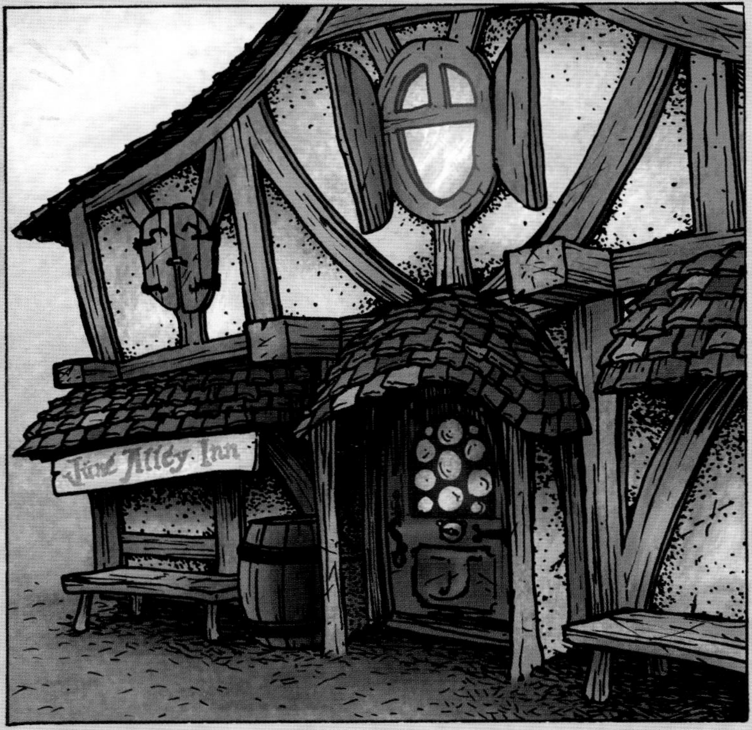
Fine Alley Inn

Legend Cover Gallery

Legend of the Lost Calogero Caravan:
After a nasty swarming infestation of Fishflies in the spring of 921, the residents of the seaside village of Calogero lashed their homes onto cooperative box turtles and began a slow plodding westward pilgrimage to relocate. The caravan was unfortunately never seen again. The only remaining structure still in Calogero, now a Guardmouse outpost, belonged to a stubborn mouse who decided not to uproot his home & stayed put.

Legend of Bernarr & the Maple War:
For the summer and fall of 892 the tree canopy near Mapleharbor echoed with the battle between a clan of chipmunks and the grey squirrels of the region. They shed each other's blood for ownership of the oldest and largest maple and its plentiful samaras produced each fall. The Guardmouse Bernarr raised his axe to turn the tide in favor of the chipmunks & rightful heirs of the tree and drove the squirrels into the Wild Country.

Legend of Barron Finbarr Murough:
Far below the surface of the cresting waves atop the Northern Sea is the kingdom of Havkoral. The rightful ruler, a many legged beast, Queen Ottena has long been missing. In her absence the undersea mouse Finbarr Murough, merely a Barron in that place's royal court, usurped the power from the three next in line for the throne and commands creatures of the wet with cruel brutality for any who cross him.

Legend of the Moth Potentate Coronation:
It is fabled that in the abandoned northern mink tunnels of Darkheather, a daring mouse hunting for raw textile silk came upon a rather welcoming covey of moths. Enchanted by the fireflies he'd brought along for light in those dark passages, the moths and their kin coronated him as their potentate and gave him royal command throughout those echoing tiled halls.

Legend of Lucien's Incarceration Melody:
As depicted by Ramón K. Pérez

The wandering balladeer Lucien was said to be so good at spinning a tale with song, the sovereign of Oakwood locked him away in the tallest tower of that city so his music could be heard by every mouse living in Oakwood. The key to that tower room was lost, and though several lifetimes have passed since Lucien's incarceration, the townsfolk can still faintly hear melody and verse of epic deeds drifting from the window.

Legend of Oskar of Rosestone's Grave:
As depicted by Eric Muller, with colors by Scott Keating

Oskar, a royal mouse sentry of Rosestone, was slain on the grounds of the kingdom of Cedarloch in one of the many past feuds between the now long fallen cities. One of his fellow mouse-in-arms summoned Oskar's wife Wyra and the pair laid him to rest with a stone burial mound on enemy soil instead of returning him to his native land to symbolize Oskar never retreating or surrendering his ground.

Legend of the Warden Claw Patrol:
As depicted by Humberto Ramos, with colors by Edgar Delgado

No group of Guardmice have more tales of their deeds together than the patrol known as "Warden Claw": Led by the armored swordmouse Henley, his military tactics won them many an outnumbered battle. Norward, wielder of a massive peaked axe, was also the party's cook & baker. Moving targets could not outmanuver the pathfinder Errol's arrows. And the animal lore studied by Ansel was as sharp as that mouse's blade.

Legend of the Cloverdale Snake Tamer:
When clearing the territory surrounding the town of Cloverdale, a guardmouse came upon a clutch of snake eggs. All but one had been broken. The mouse carefully hatched the egg itself, with a plan to raise the offsping as his own mount for patrolling the cloverfields and ridding them of predators. And while this was famed to have briefly worked, some beast's nature is rumored not to be swayed, and the guardmouse and town all fell victim to the scaled predator's fang.

The Lost Calogero Caravan

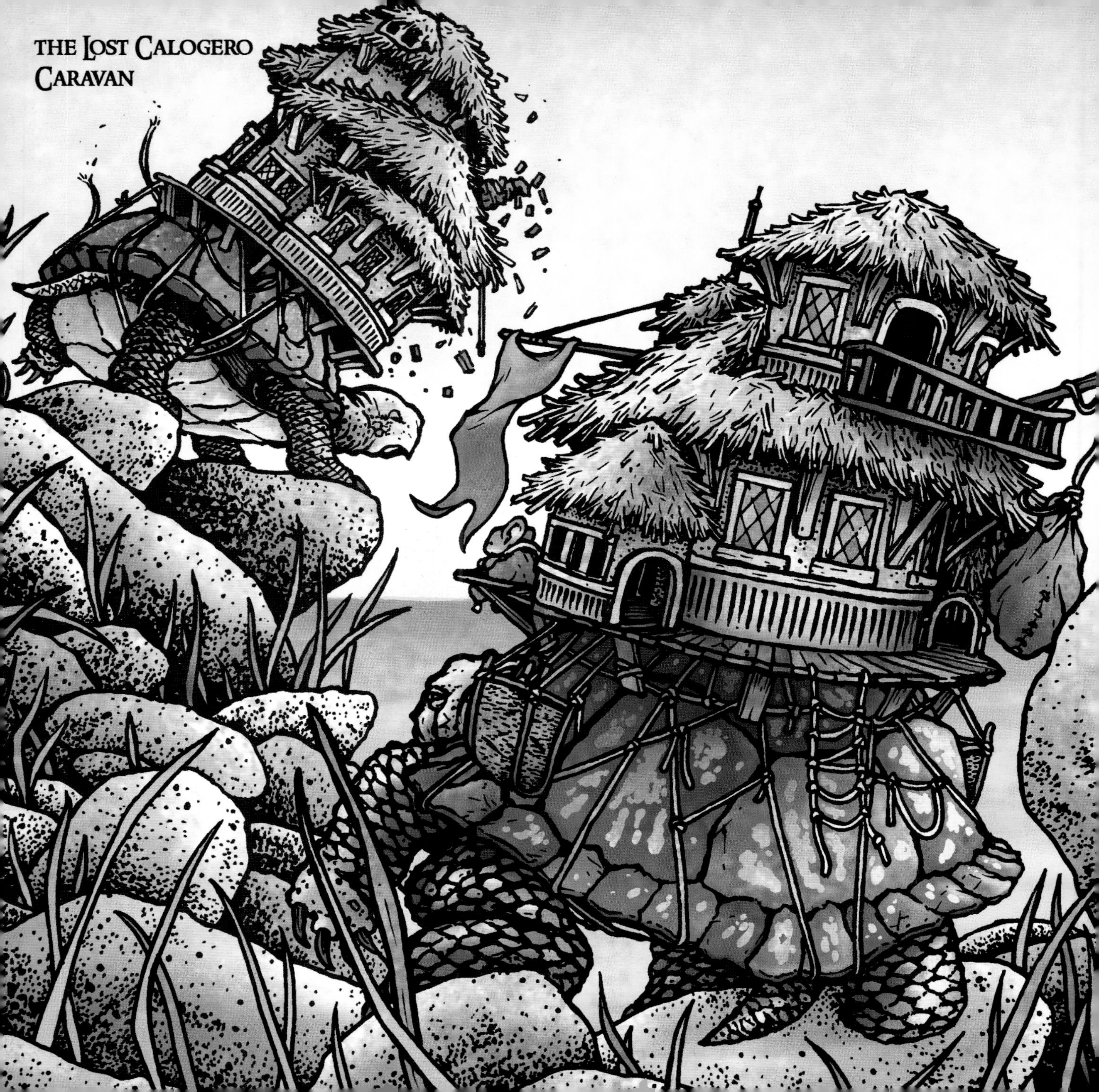

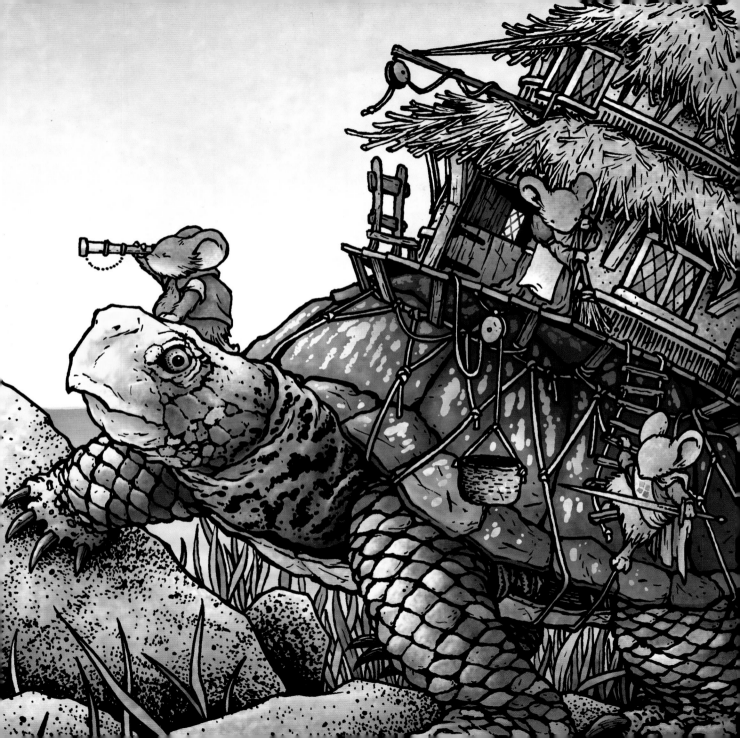

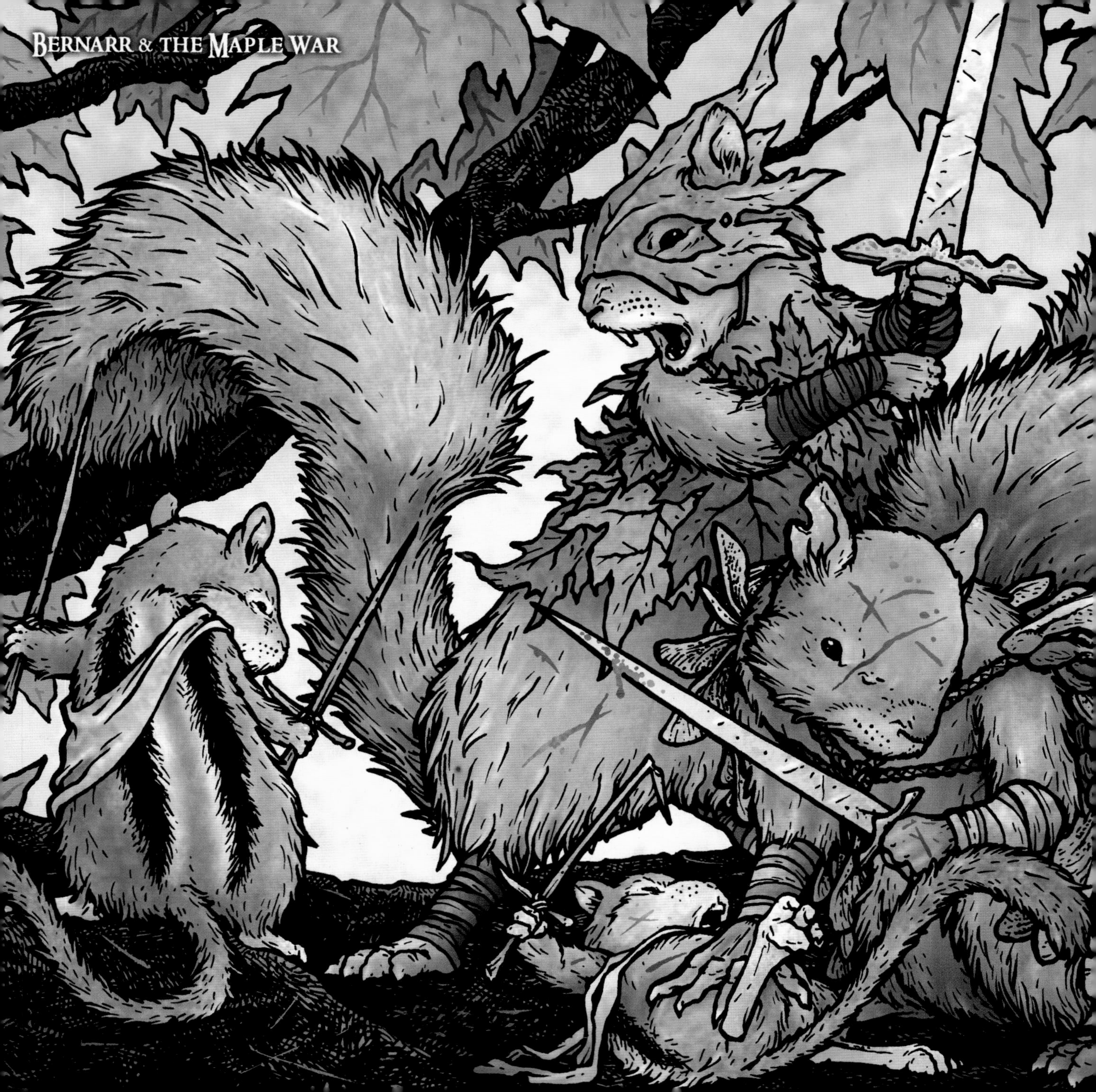

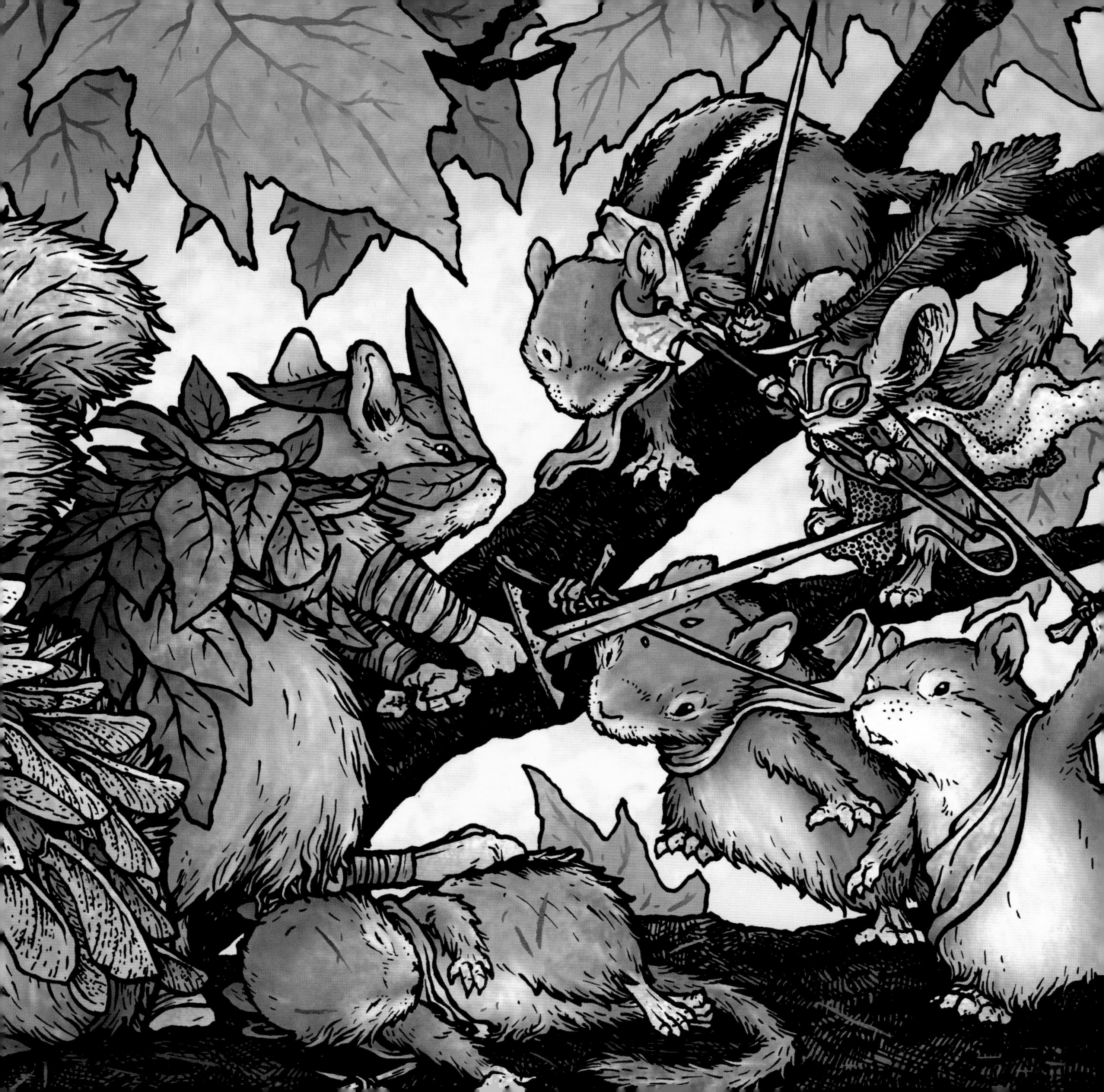

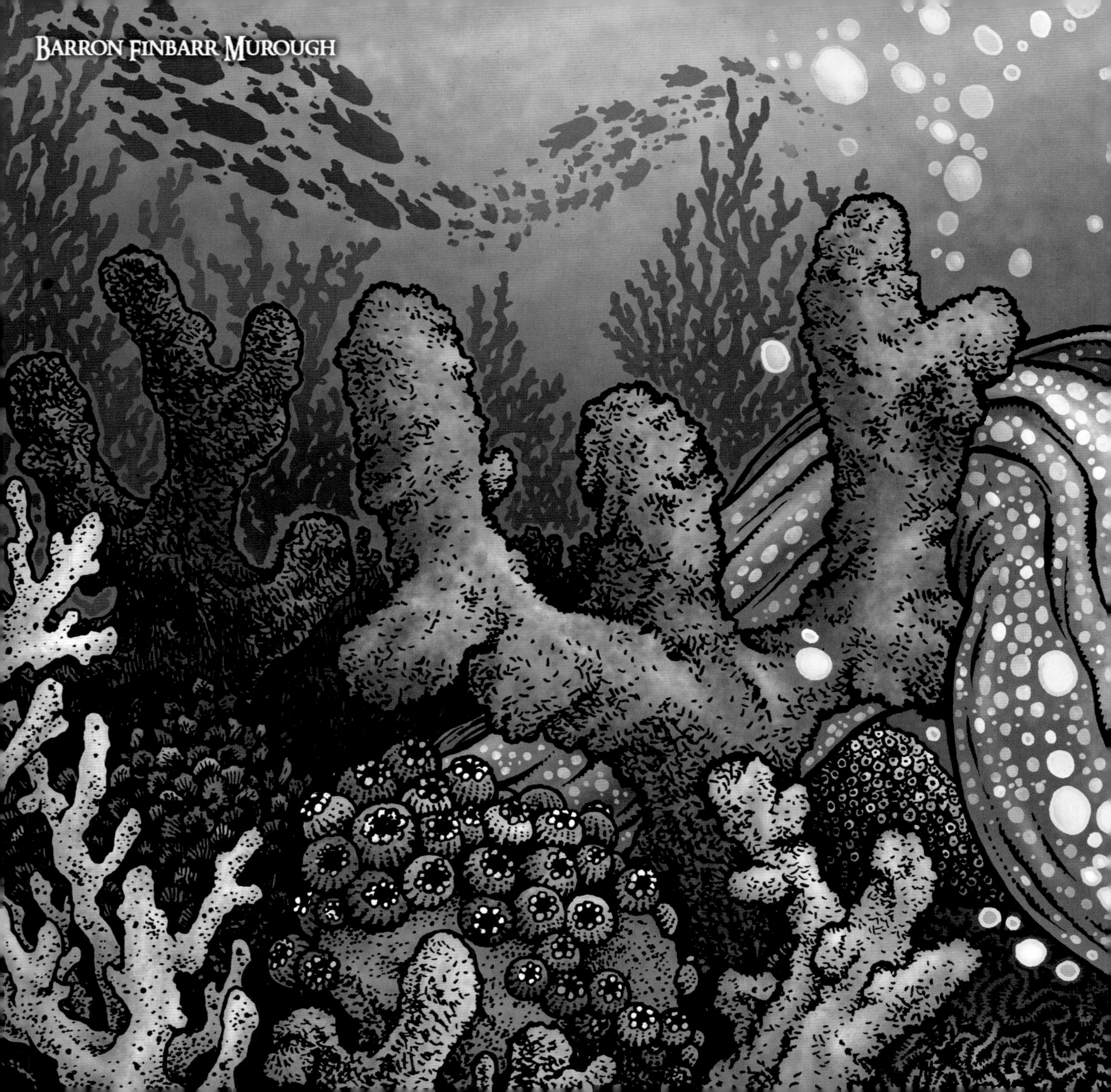
BARRON FINBARR MUROUGH

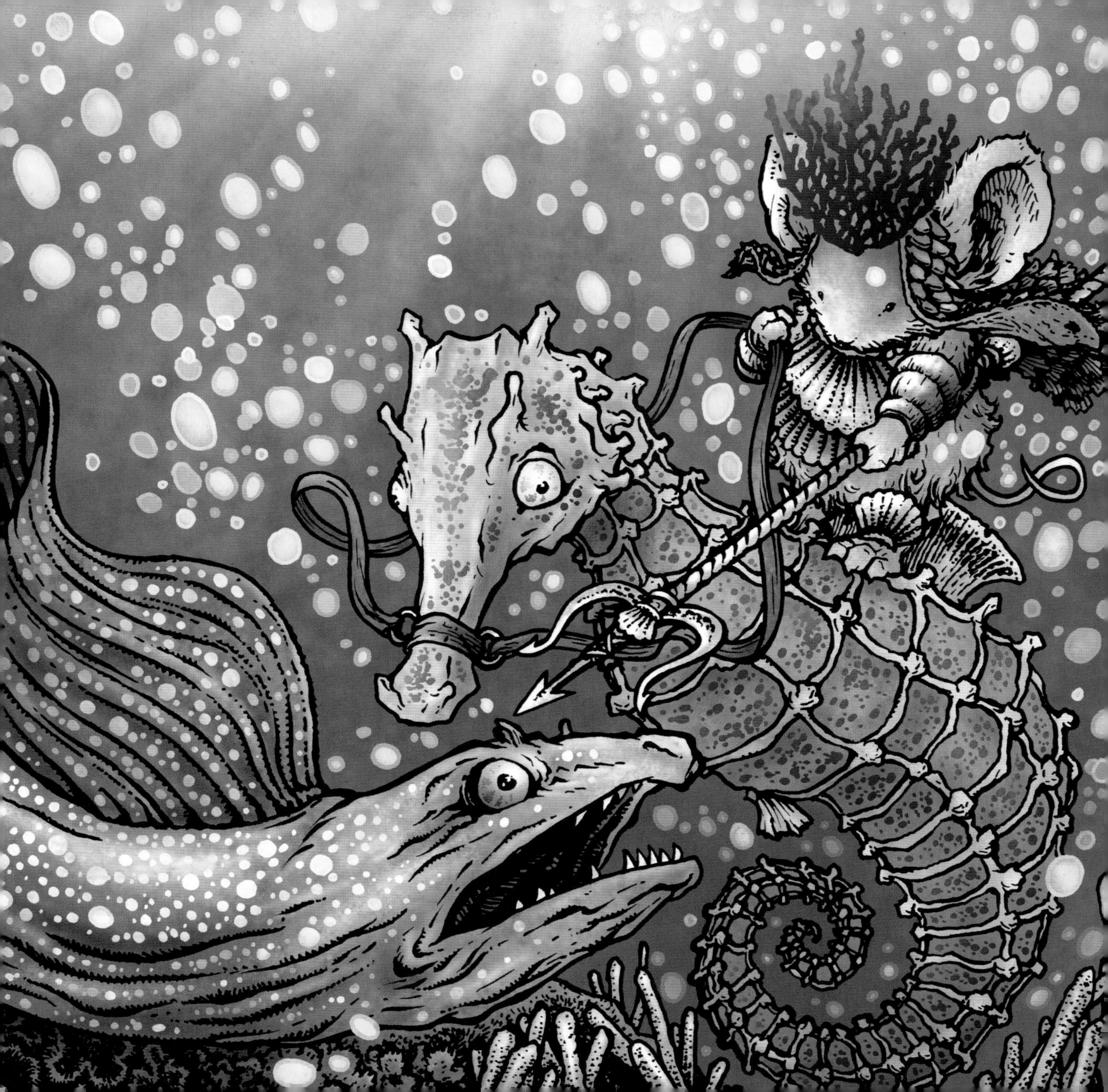

THE MOTH POTENTATE CORONATION

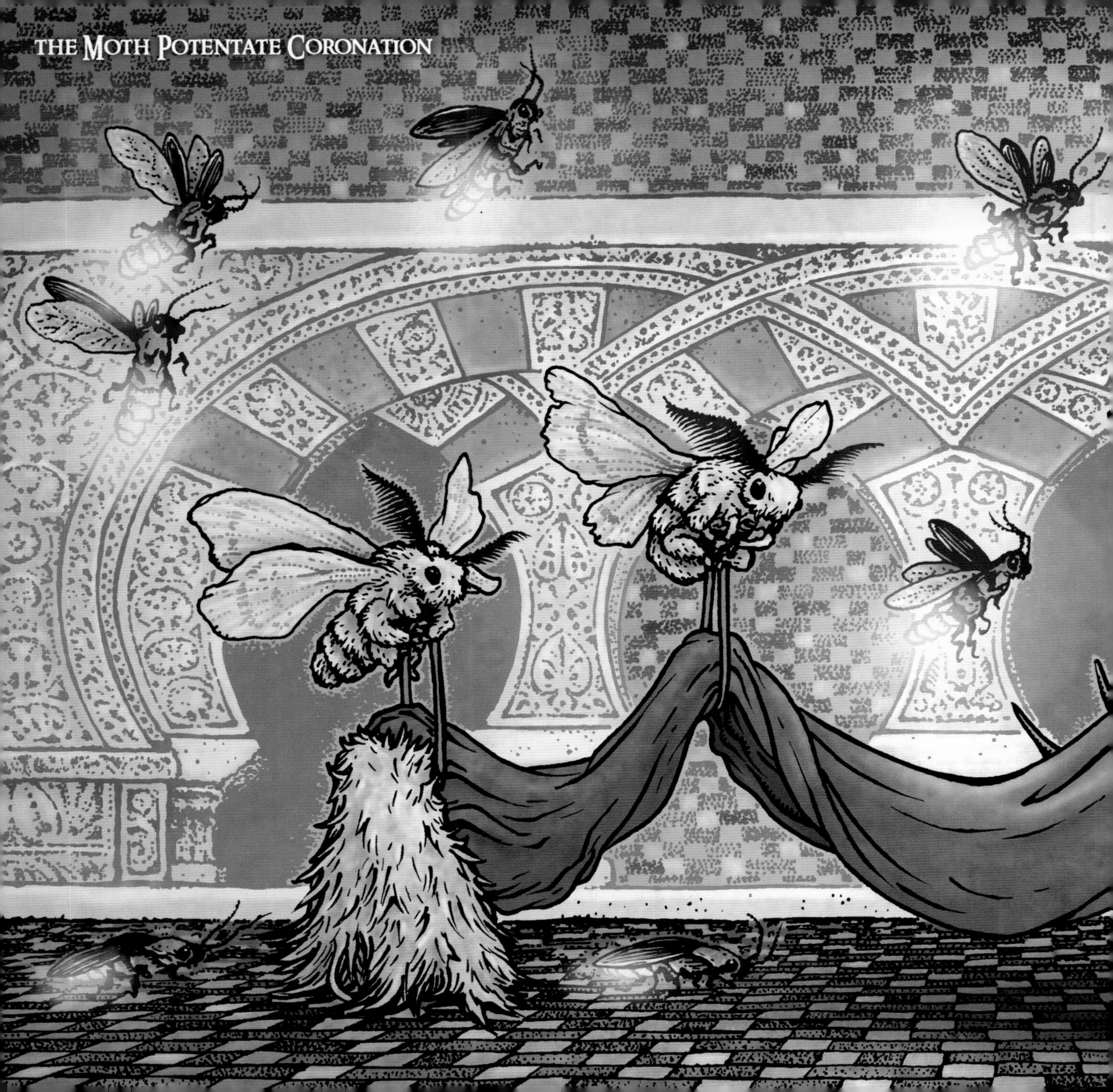

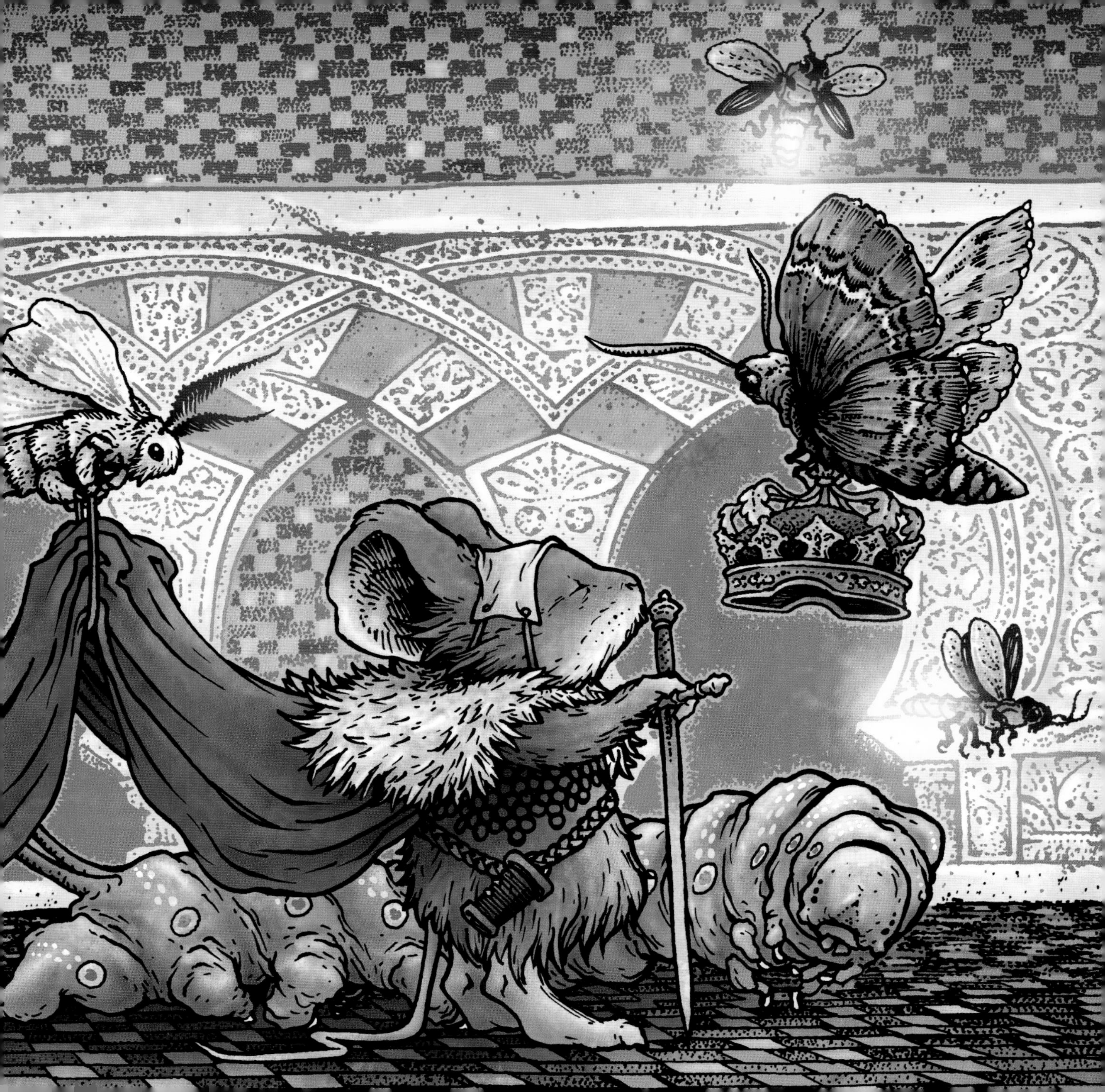

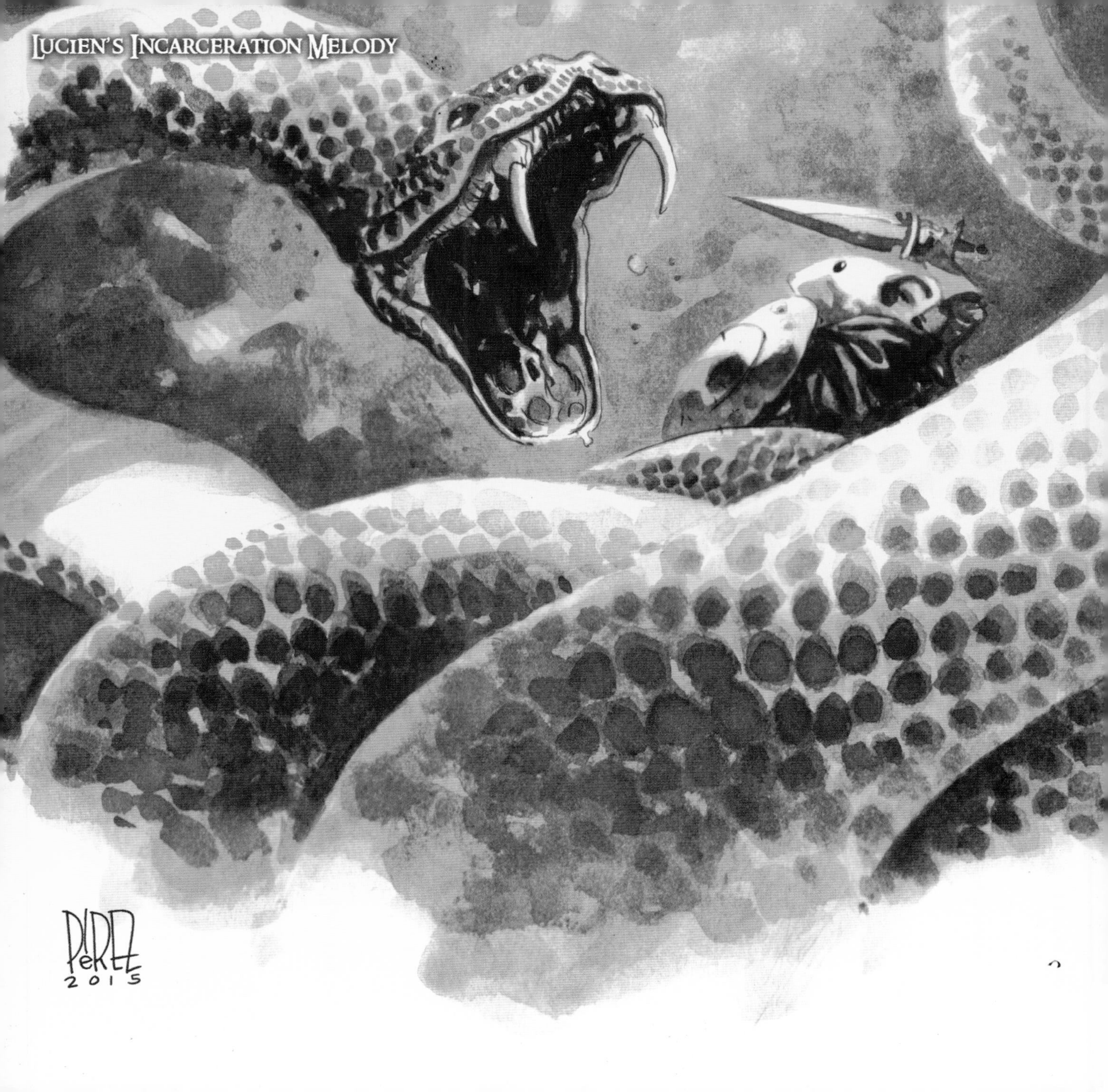
LUCIEN'S INCARCERATION MELODY
PEREZ
2015

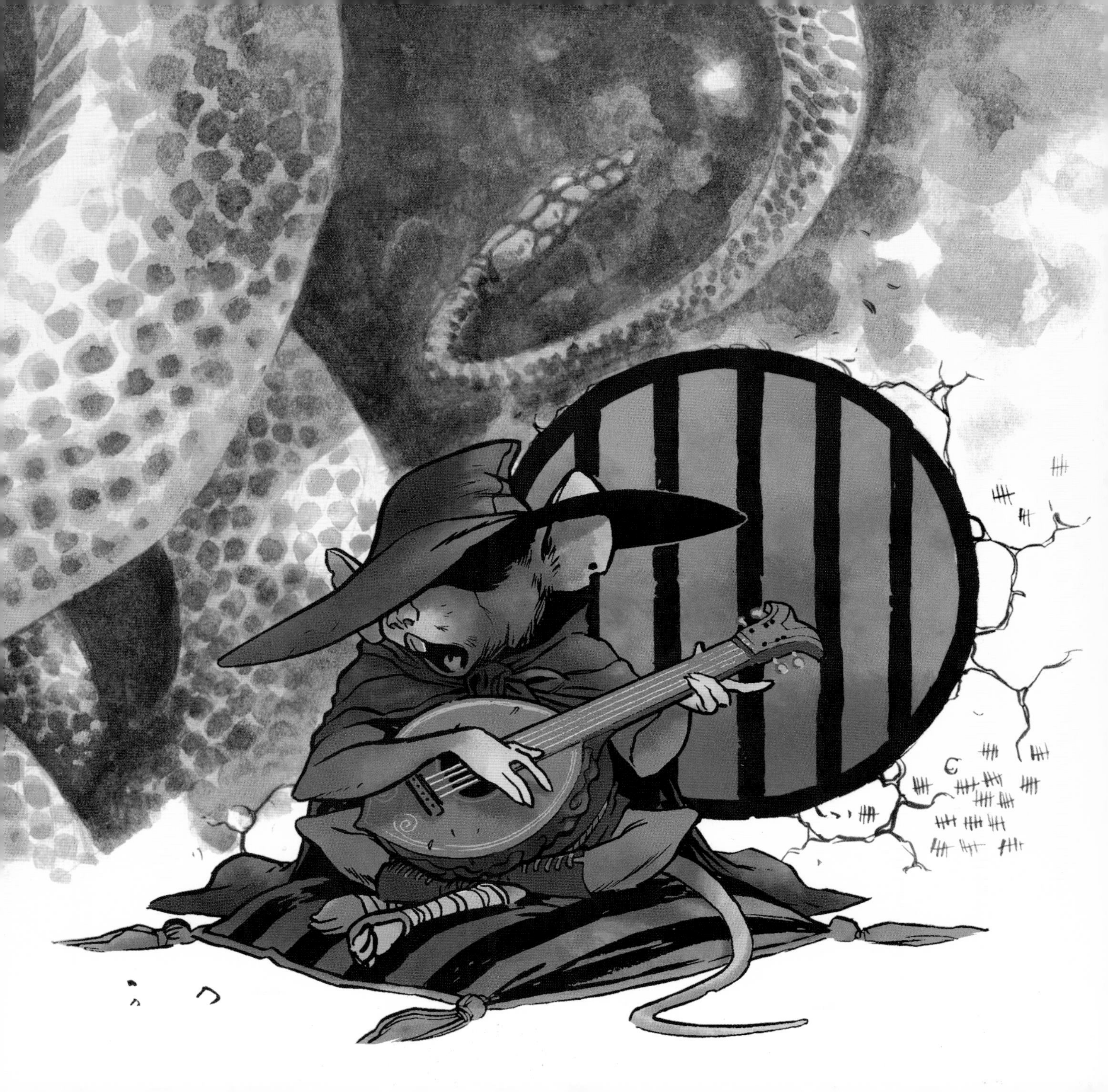

Oskar of Rosestone's Grave

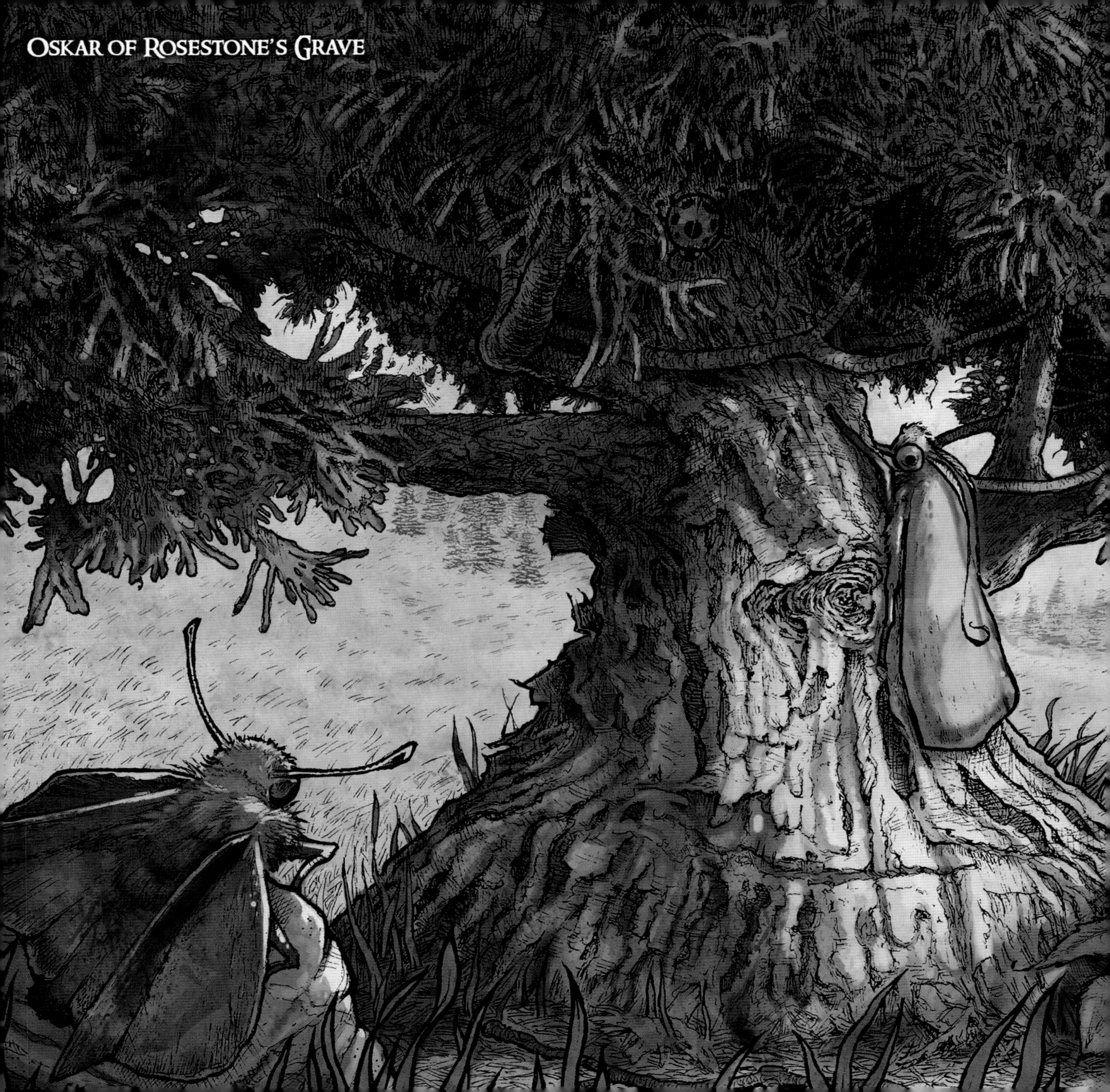

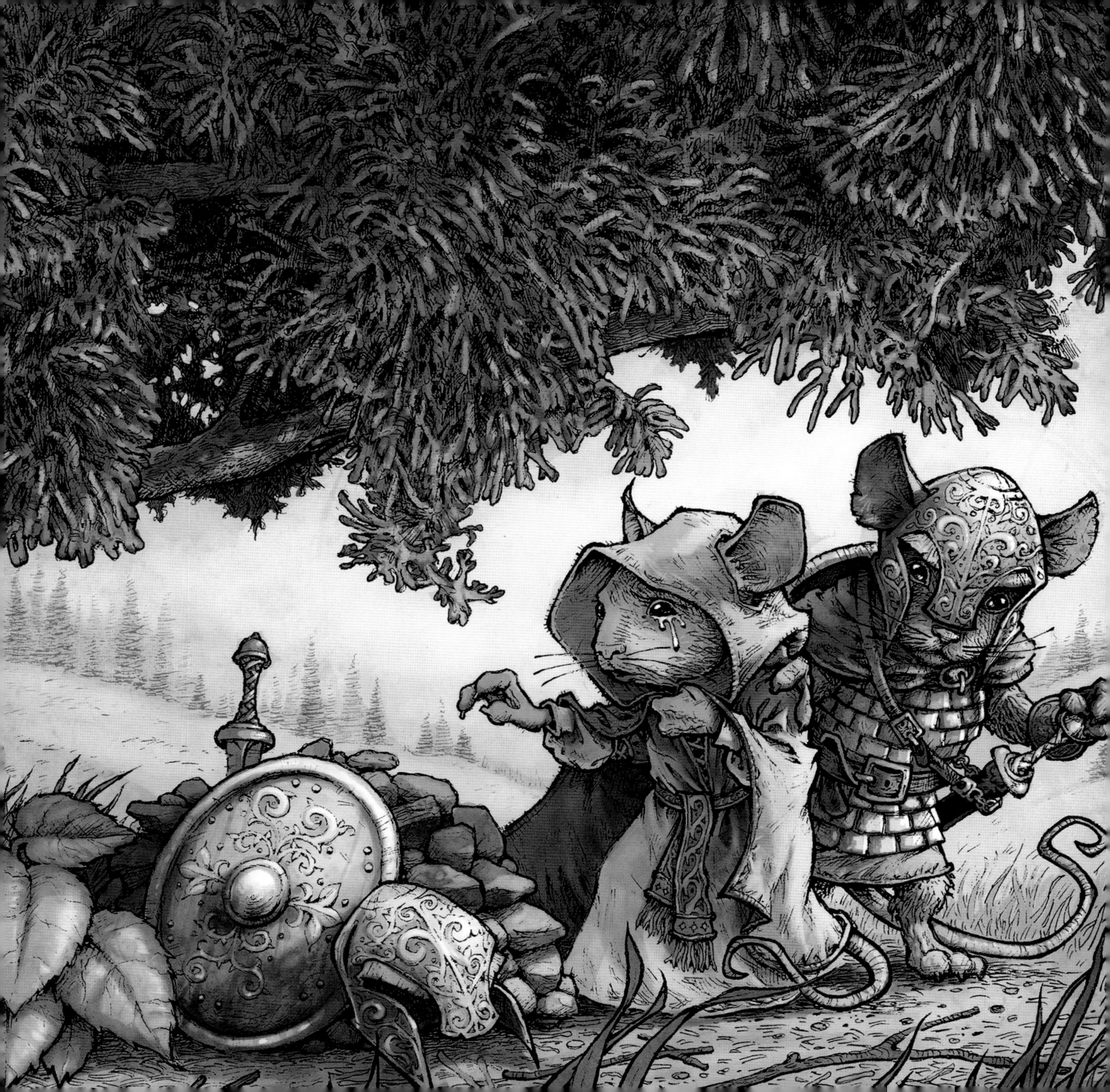

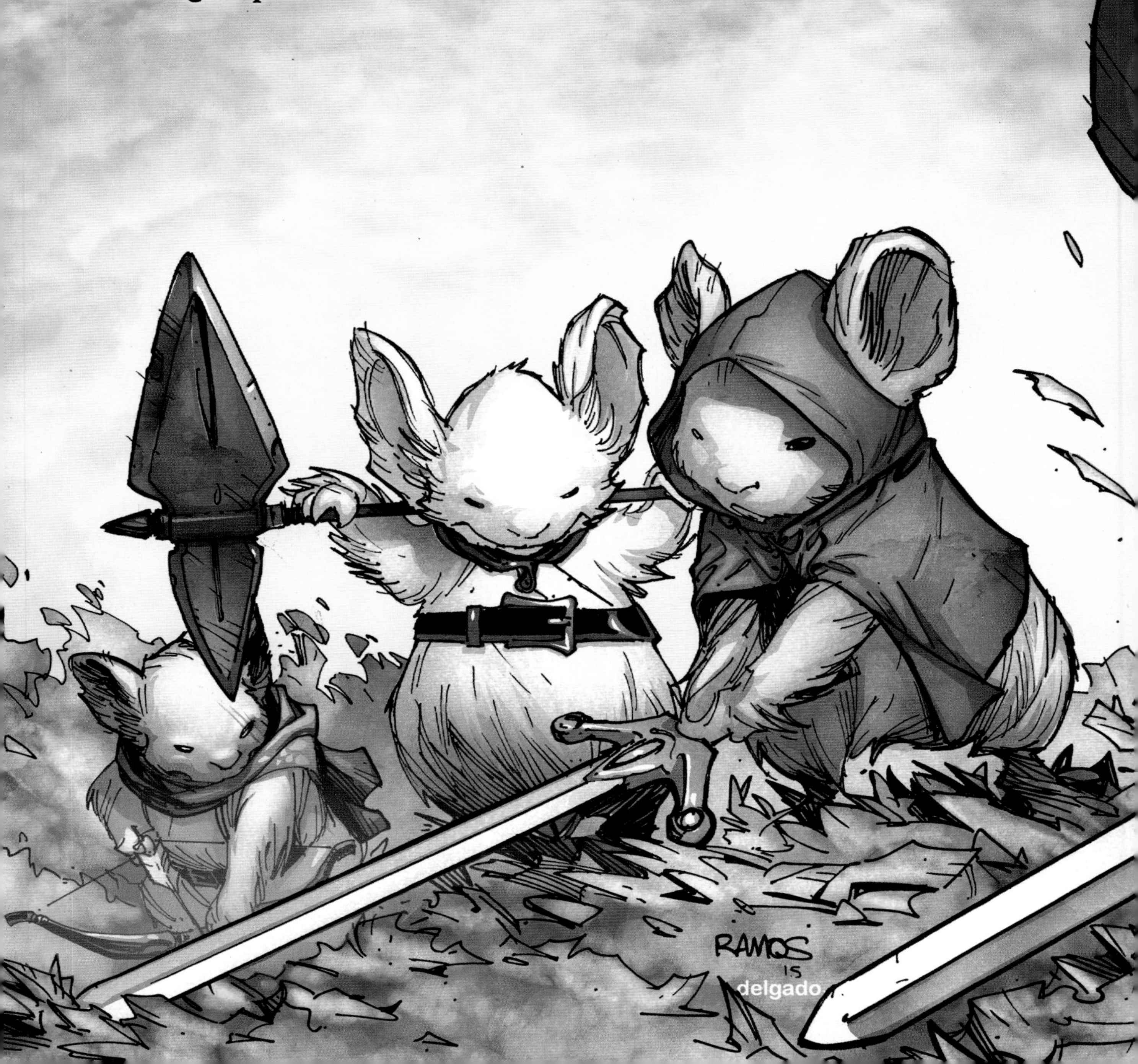
RAMOS
15
delgado

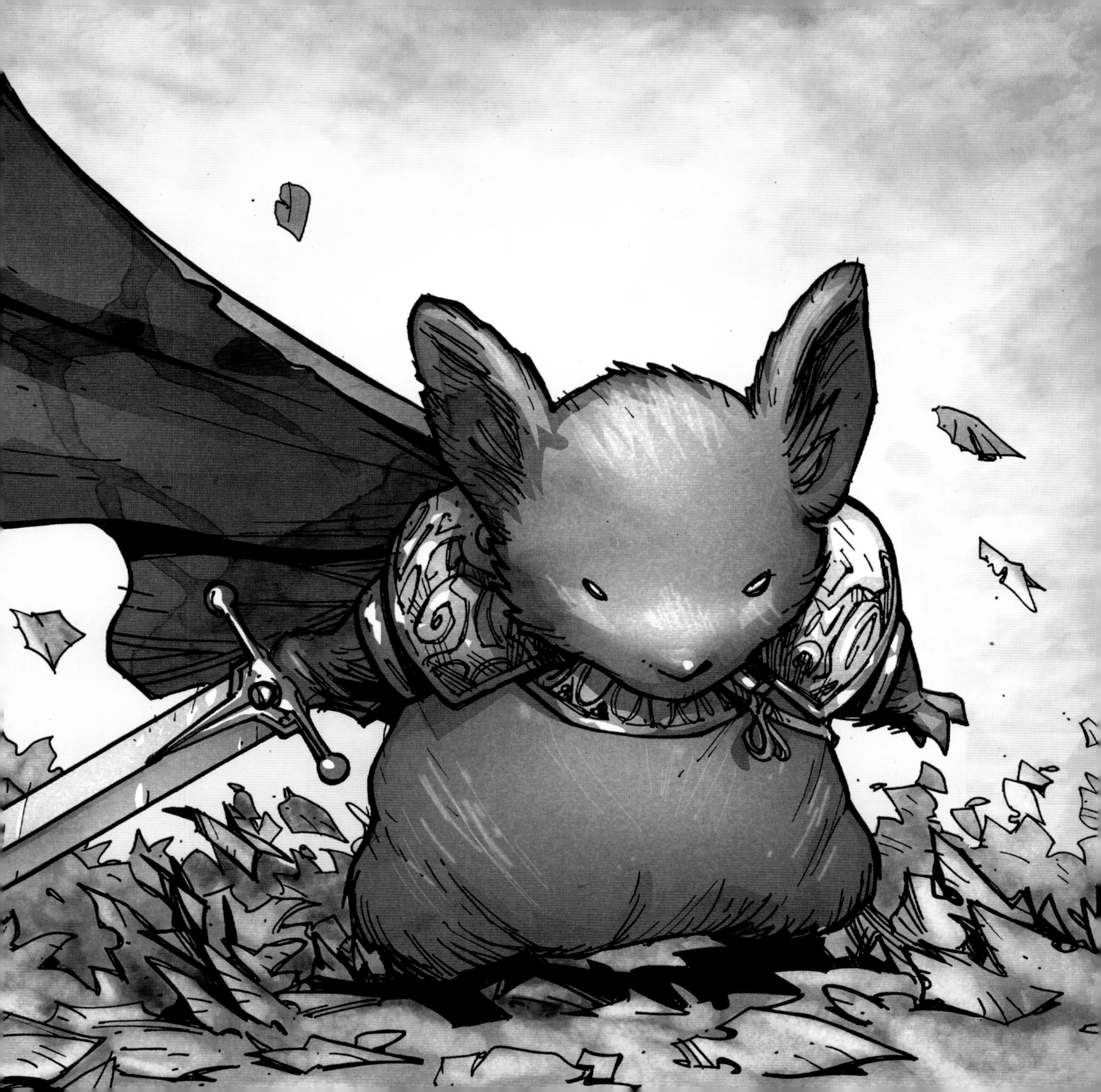

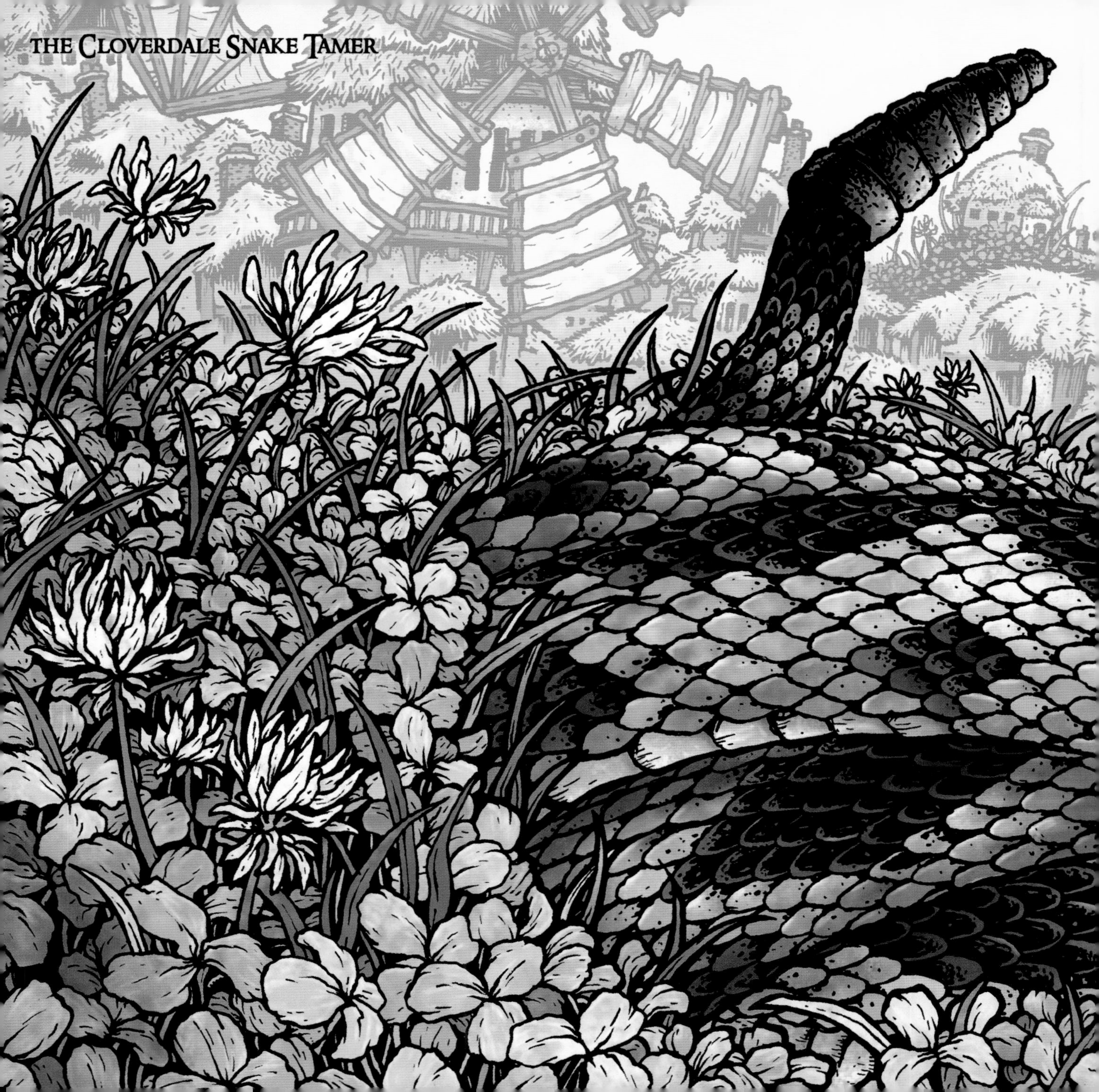

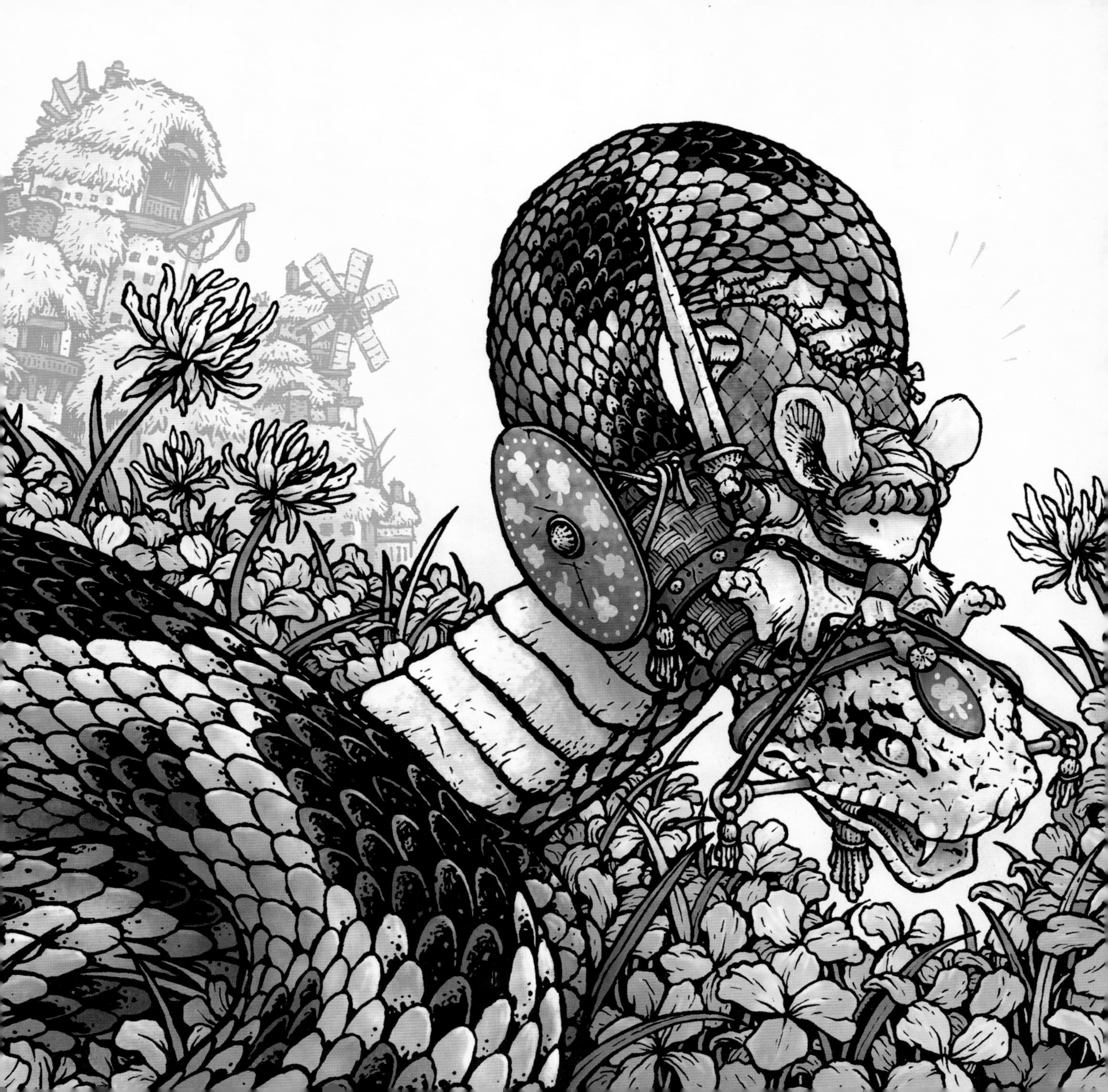

THE INN'S PATRONS:

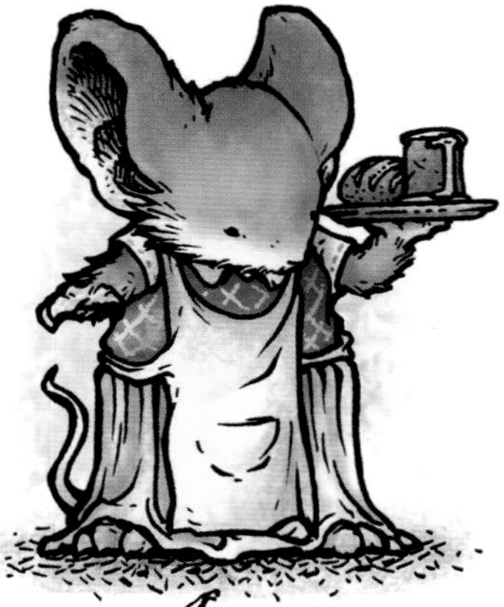

June

Owner and operator of the June Alley Inn, which is known as the most hospitable inn on the west end of the Mouse Territories.

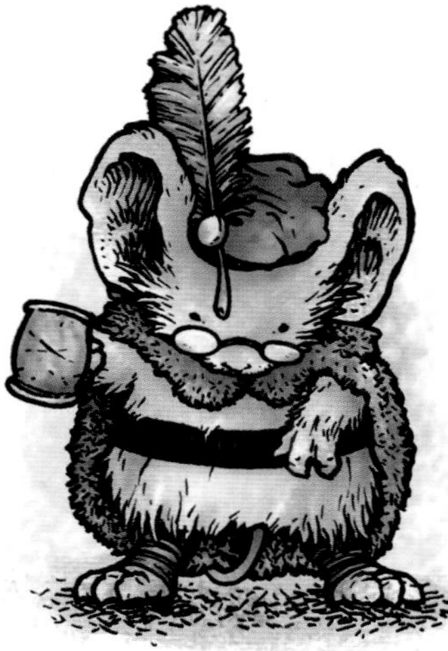

Fyodor

Studies and trains owls in the wild to be used as mounts for mice for travel and message delivery.

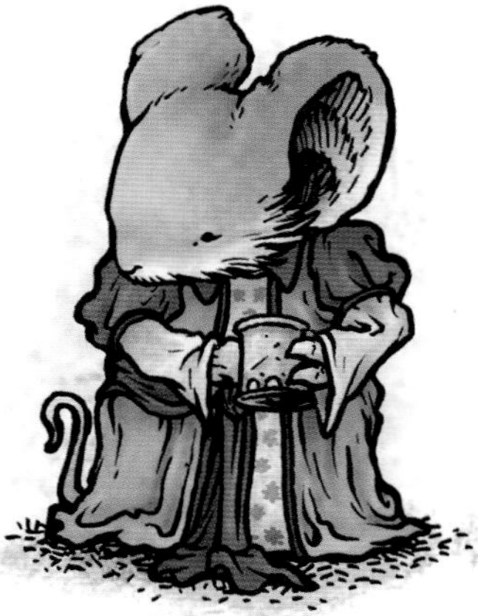

Quinn

A textile master in Barkstone who's dyed, woven, & embroidered garments are of the higest quality.

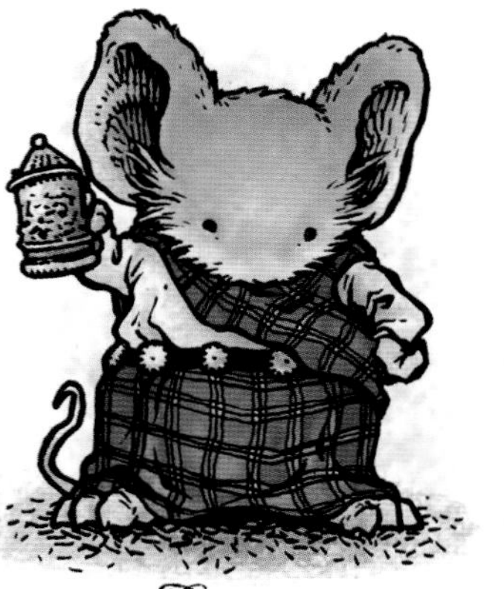

Lenox

The leading trade merchant in Rustleaf who ventures accross the territories for goods to sell.

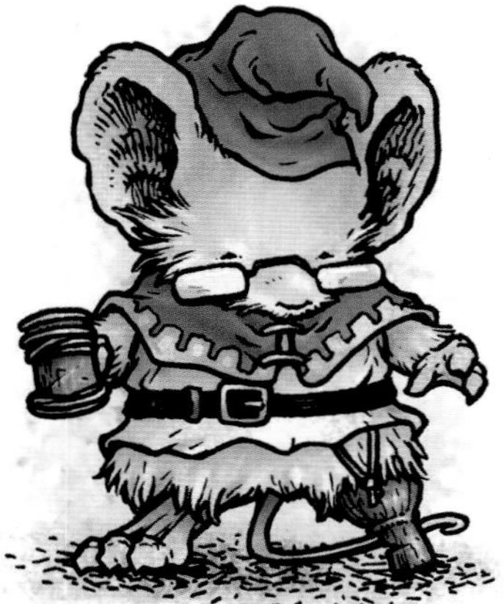

Oswynn

A Mathematician who belongs to every builder's discipline guild.

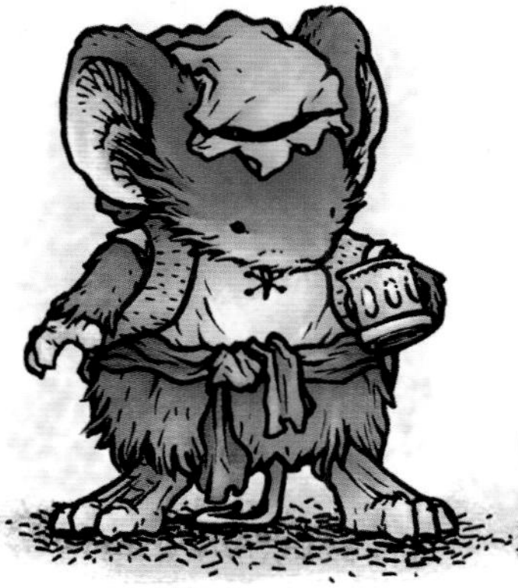

Gerrit

Shapes molten glass into decorative and usable objects as one of Barkstone's glassblowers.

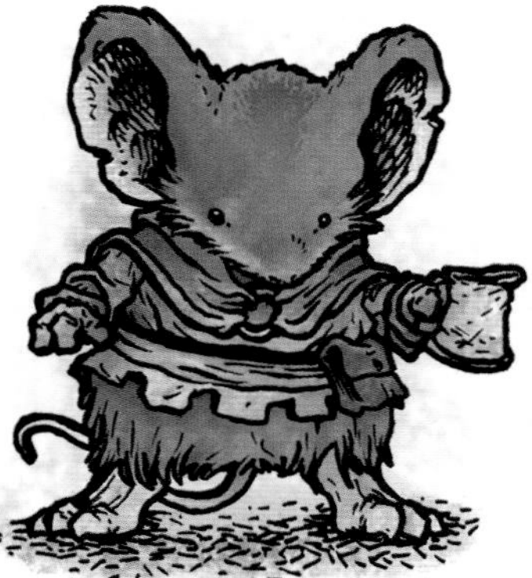

Meeka

Harvests berries, grasses, and minerals to be ground into dyes and pigments.

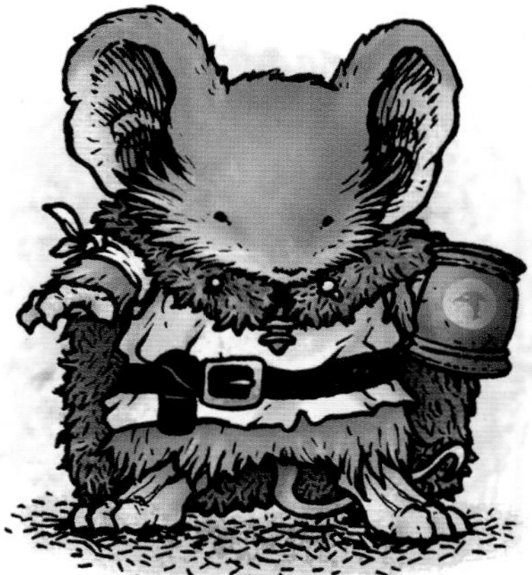

Israel

The master smithy of Lockhaven who retired as a patrol mouse and took up the post after Midnight's treason.

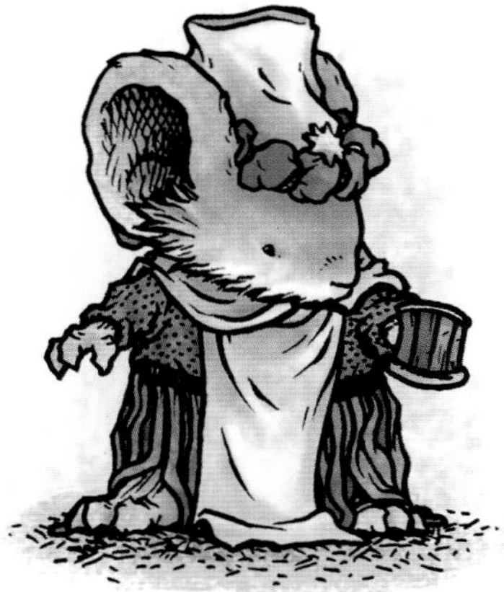

Mercer

The stargazer of Barkstone. He watches, charts, and tracks the movements of the night skies.

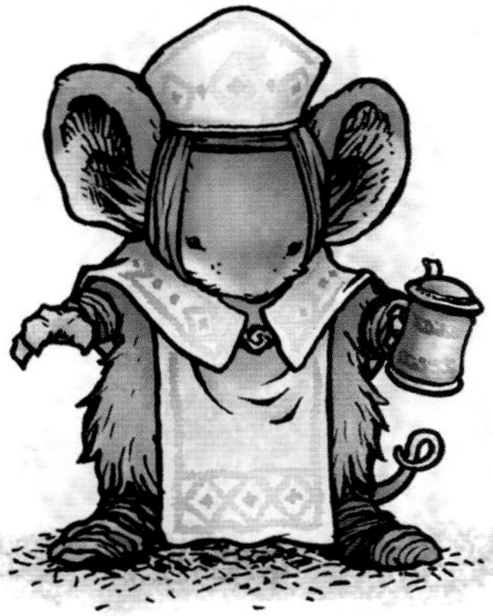

Asa

A mouse healer from Pebblebrook known for her successful & tender care of the ill.

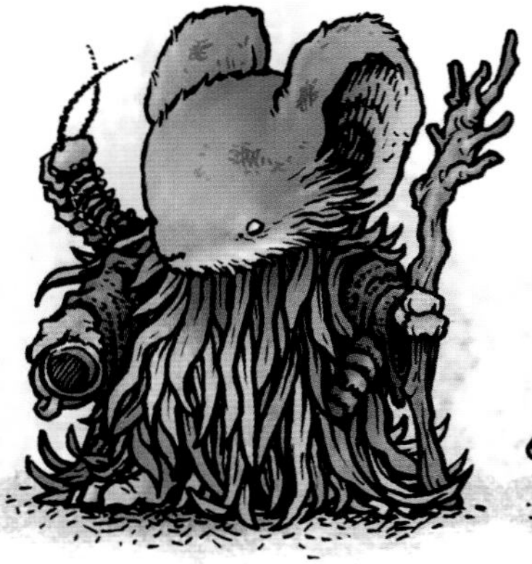

Silas

A blind hermit mouse who lives in the open country between mouse settlements as an insectrist.

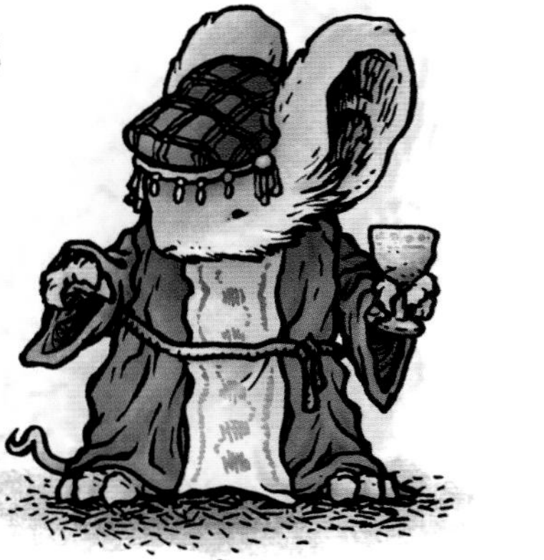

Lyra

A naturalist who wanders the Southern Territories as a pathfinder.

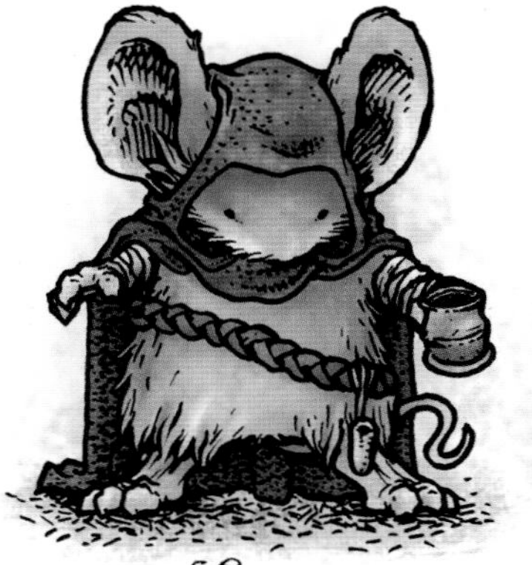

Sextus

A Guardmouse patrol leader stationed to protect Barkstone, Pebblebrook, & Windselm.

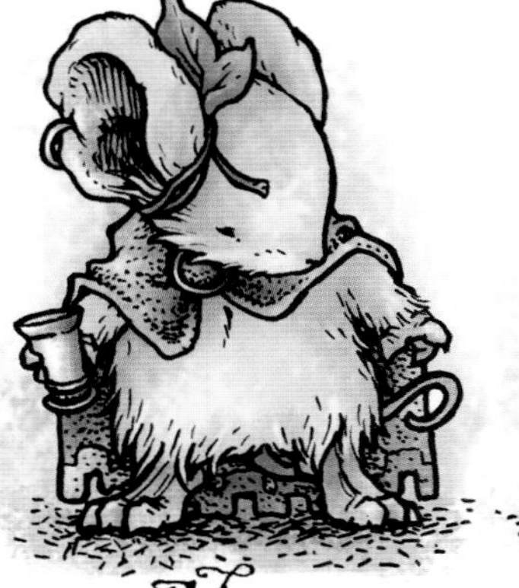

Marin

A Guardmouse in Sextus' patrol who is deadly accurate with arrows fired from her bow.

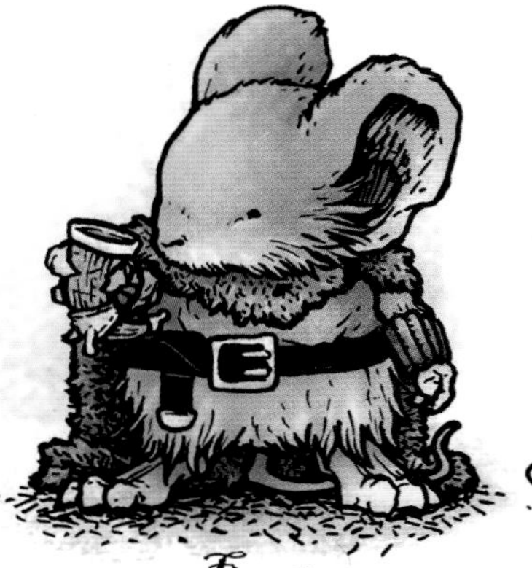

Bedwyn

An axe wielding Guardmouse in Sextus' patrol of the Northeast Territories.

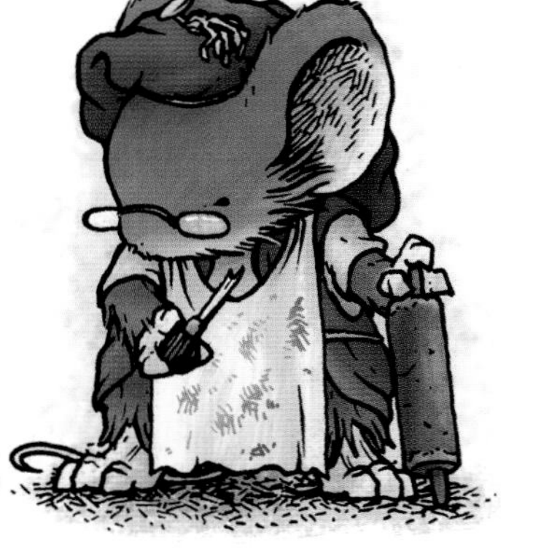

Alistair

June's husband & a printmaker who uses his craft to mass-produce images for greater mousekind.

THE JUNE ALLEY INN
MAIN FLOOR

a: Entrance

b: June's Ledger

c: Stairs to Rooms

d: Back Bar Access

e: Doors to Kitchen

f: Firewood Storage

g: Stone Hearth

h: The Legend of Bernarr & the Maple War

i: The Legend of the Moth Potentate Coronation

j: The Legend of Barron Finbarr Murough

k: The Legend of the Lost Calogero Caravan

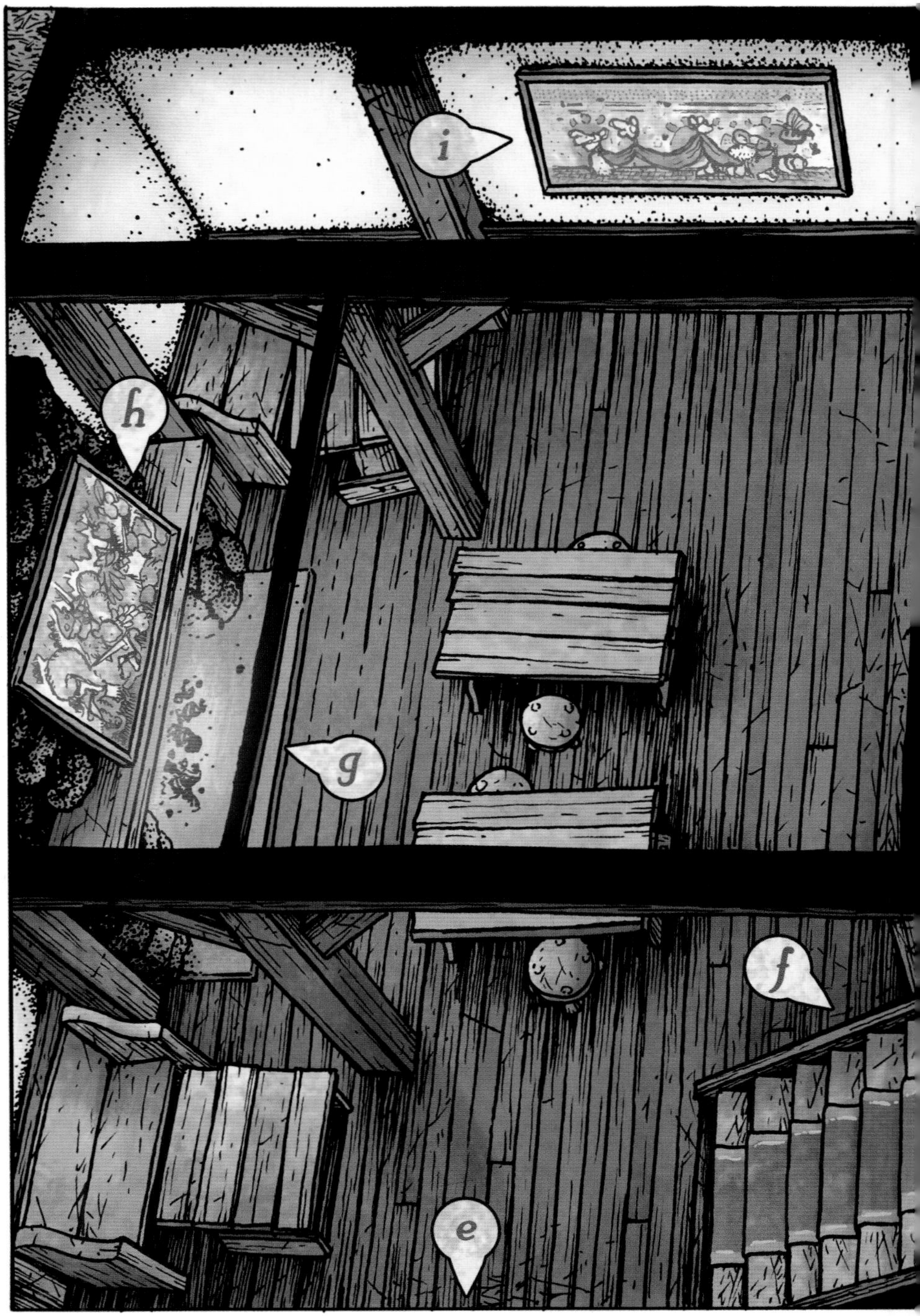
i
h
g
f
e

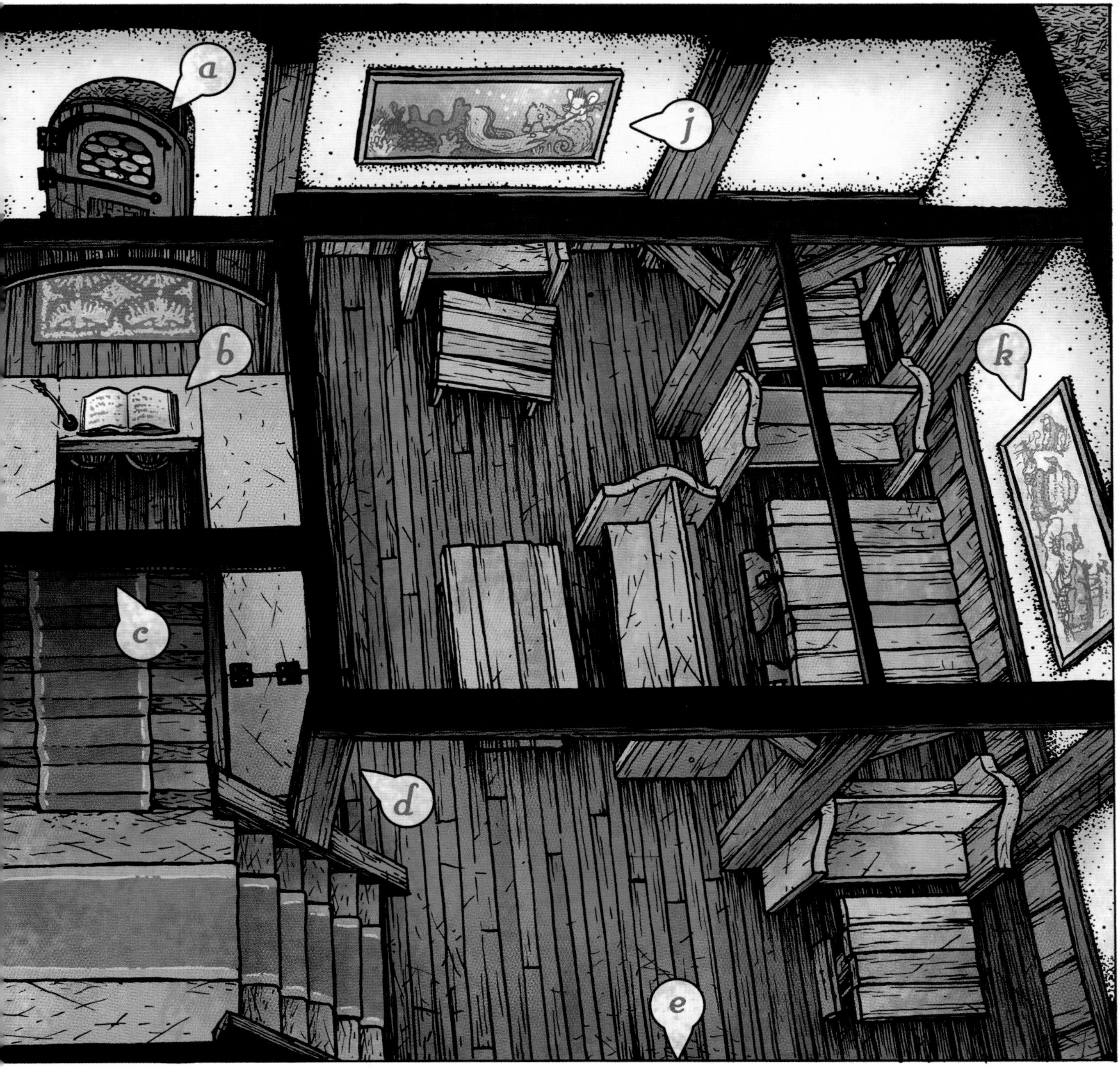
a
j
b
k
c
d
e

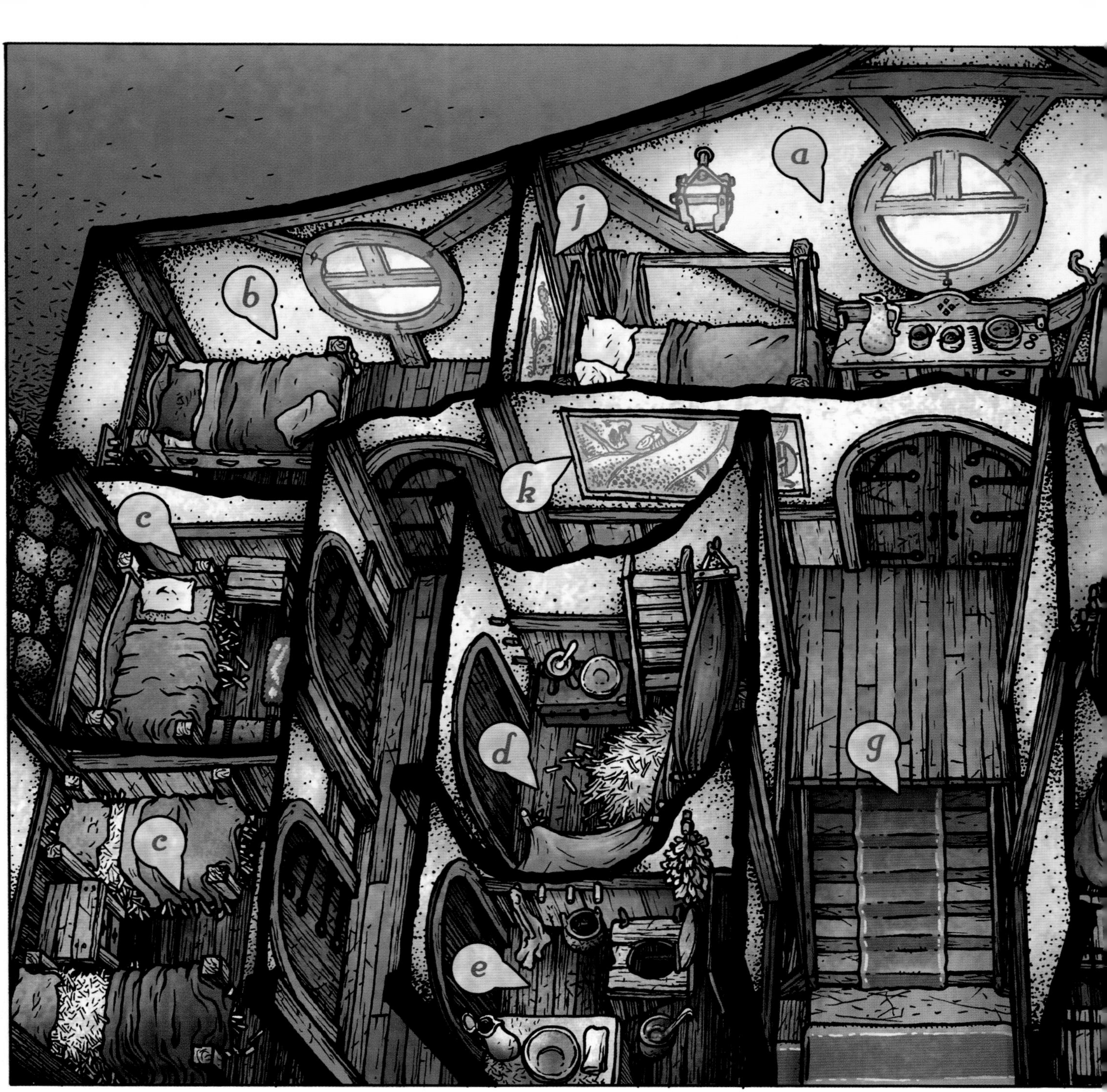
a
b
j
k
c
c
d
g
e

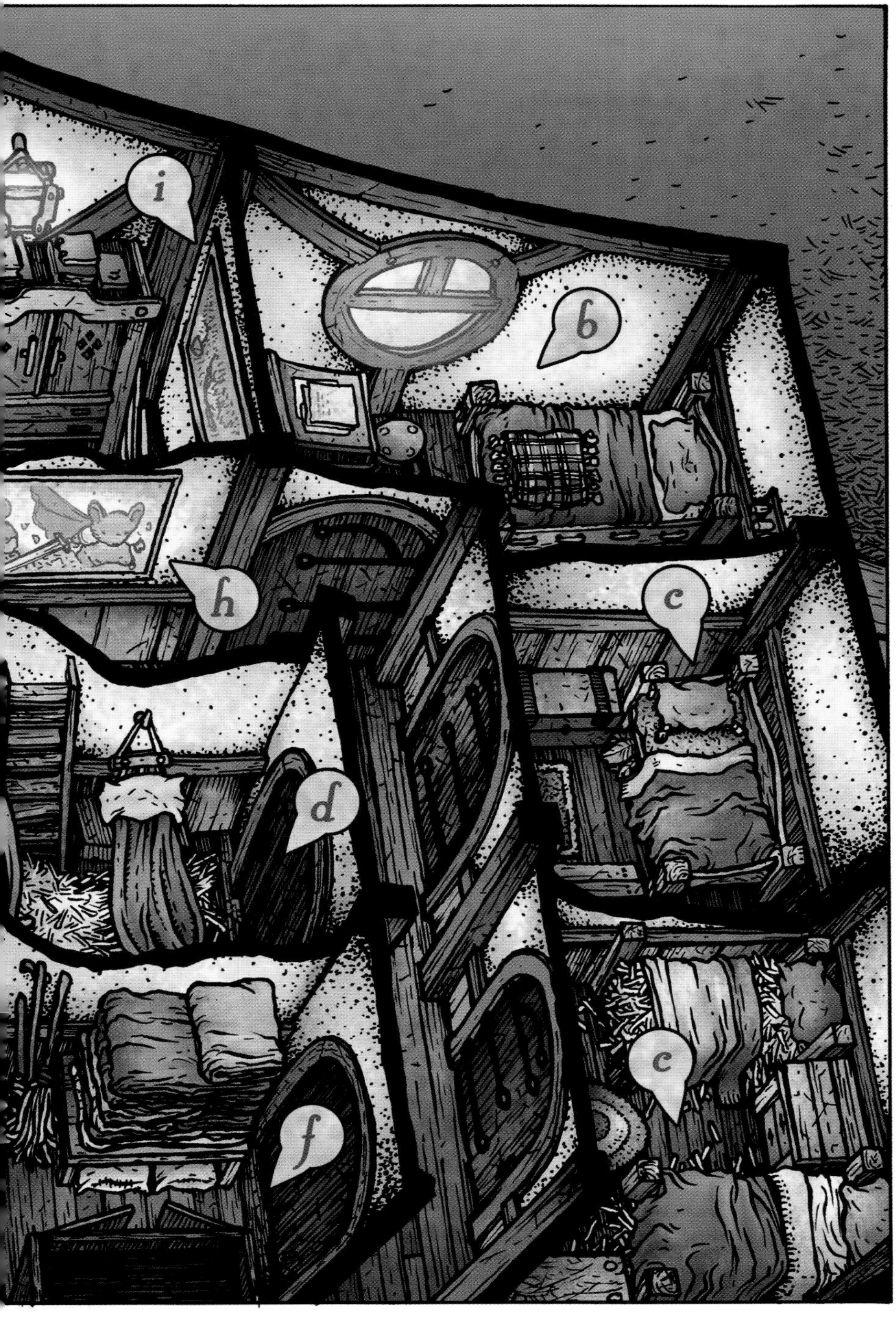
i
b
h
c
d
c
f

THE
JUNE ALLEY INN
UPPER FLOOR

a: June & Alistair's room

b: Premium Rooms

c: Standard Rooms

d: Common Bunk Rooms

e: Lavatory

f: Linen/Storage Closet

g: Stairs to the Tavern

h: The Legend of the Warden Claw Patrol

i: The Legend of Oskar of Rosestone's Grave

j: The Legend of the Cloverdale Snake Tamer

k: The Legend of Lucien's Incarceration Melody

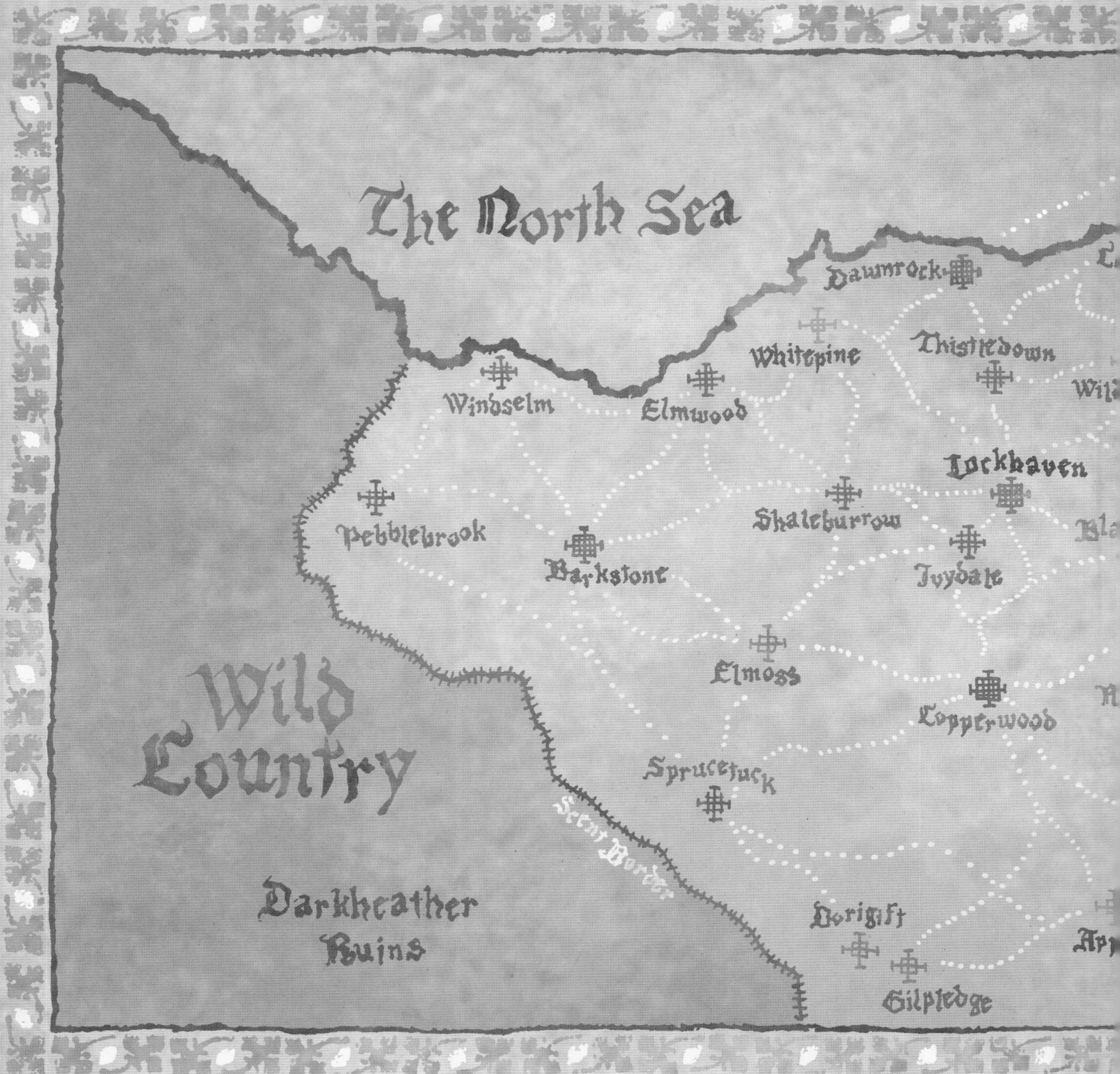
The North Sea
Dawnrock
Whitepine
Thistledown
Windselm
Elmwood
Lockhaven
Pebblebrook
Shaleburrow
Barkstone
Ivydale
Elmoss
Copperwood
Wild Country
Sprucetuck
Scent Border
Darkheather Ruins
Dorigift
Gilpledge

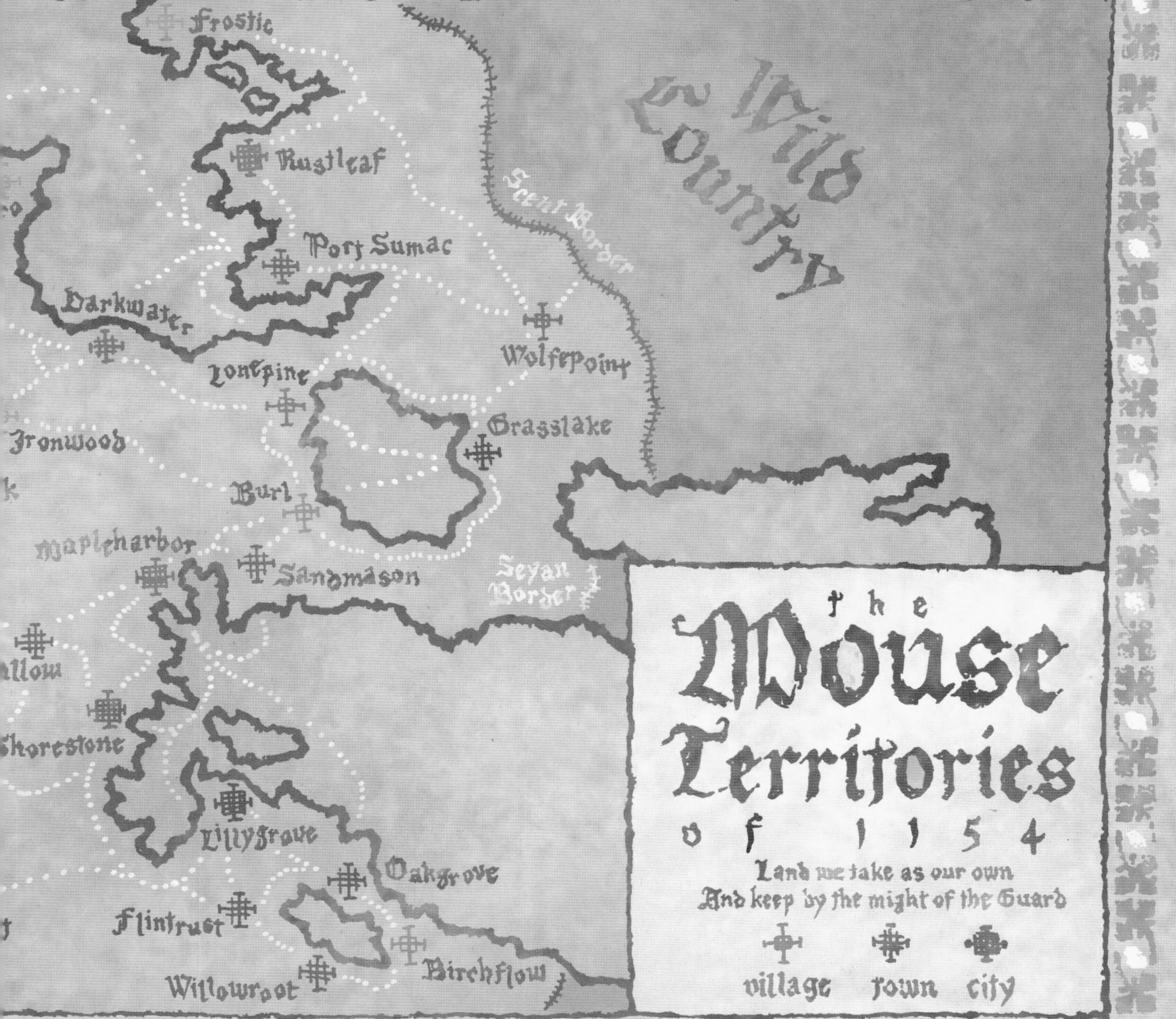

Frostic
Rustleaf
Port Sumac
Darkwater
Lonepine
Wolfepoint
Wild Country
Scent Border
Grasslake
Ironwood
Burl
Mapleharbor
Sandmason
Seyan Border
allow
Shorestone
Lillygrove
Oakgrove
Flintrust
Birchflow
Willowroot
the Mouse Territories of 1154
Land we take as our own
And keep by the might of the Guard
village
town
city

ABOUT THE AUTHORS

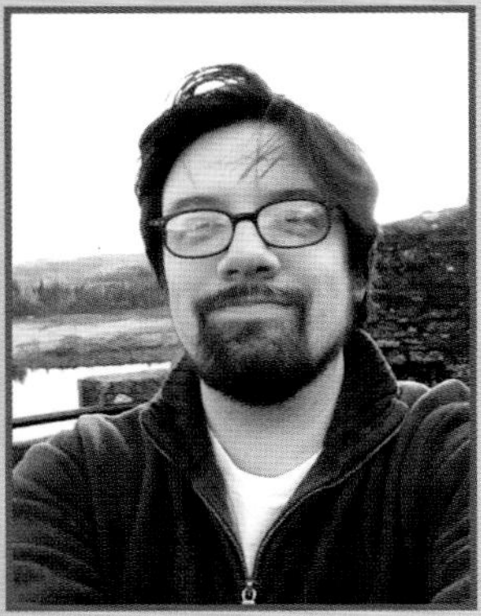

David Petersen was born in 1977. His artistic career soon followed. A steady diet of cartoons, comics, and tree climbing fed his imagination and is what still inspires his work today. He is a three time Eisner Award winner and recipient of a Harvey Award for his continued work on the *Mouse Guard* series. David received his BFA in Printmaking from Eastern Michigan University where he met his wife Julia. They continue to reside in Michigan with their dogs Autumn & Bronwyn.

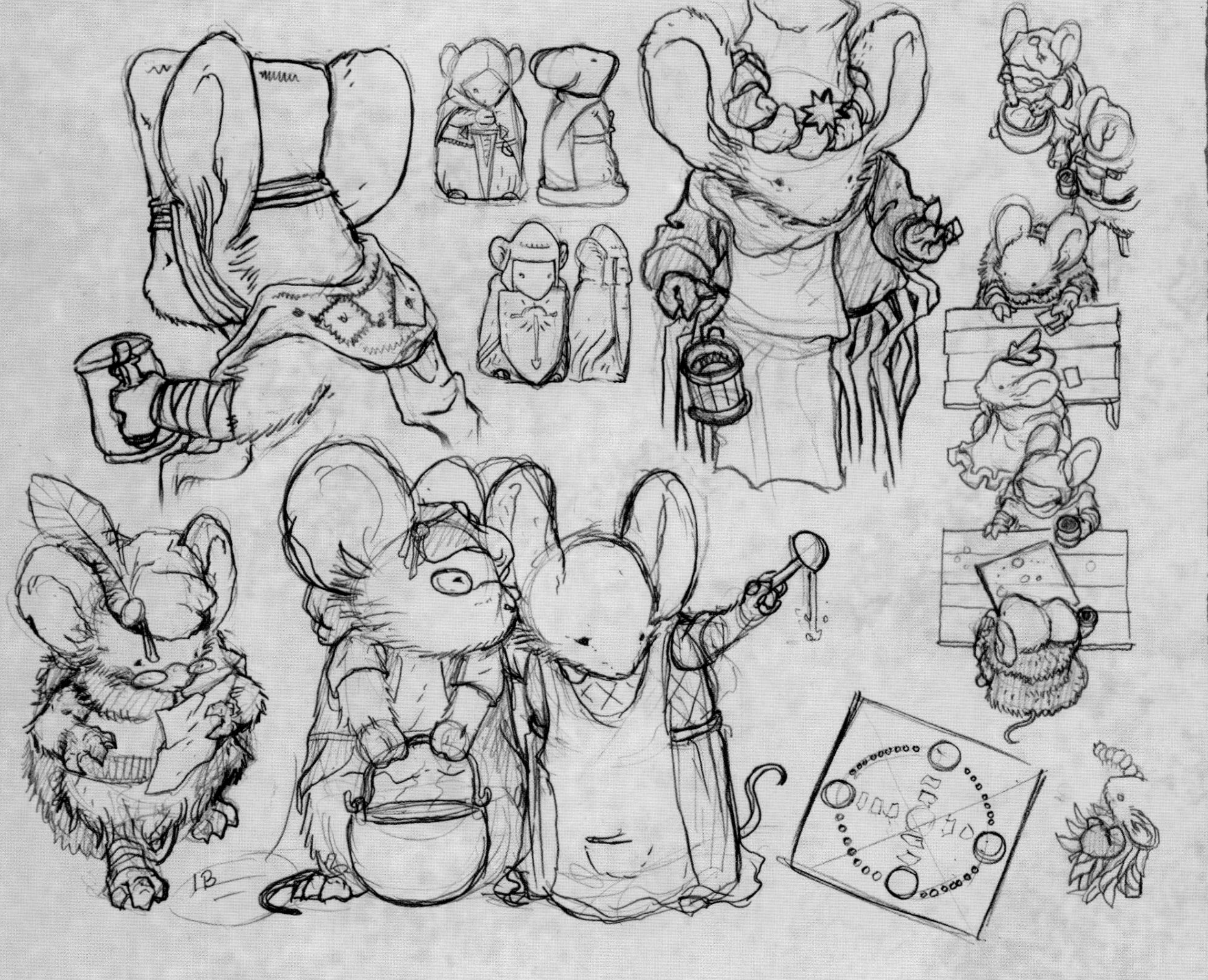

PHOTO CREDIT: ALLAN AMATO

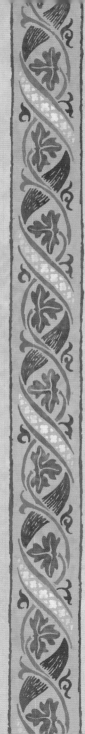

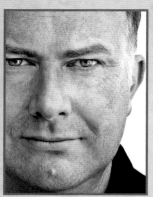

MARK BUCKINGHAM HAS BEEN WORKING IN COMICS FOR OVER 28 YEARS, BUILDING A REPUTATION FOR DESIGN, STORYTELLING AND A CHAMELEON LIKE DIVERSITY OF ART STYLES. HE IS KNOWN FOR HIS WORK ON NUMEROUS COMICS INCLUDING *MIRACLEMAN (MARVELMAN)*, *HELLBLAZER*, *SANDMAN*, *DEATH*, *BATMAN: SHADOW OF THE BAT*, AND *PETER PARKER: SPIDER-MAN*. SINCE 2002 MARK HAS BEEN THE REGULAR ARTIST ON *FABLES* FOR VERTIGO/DC COMICS, WORKING WITH ITS WRITER AND CREATOR BILL WILLINGHAM, FOR WHICH THEY HAVE EARNED NUMEROUS COMIC INDUSTRY AWARDS. HE HAS JUST COMPLETED WORK ON ITS FINAL EPISODE, ENDING WITH THE ONE HUNDRED AND FIFTY PAGE *FABLES* #150, RELEASED JULY 2015. MARK RECENTLY WROTE "THE CLAMOUR FOR GLAMOUR," THE FINAL STORY ARC OF *FAIREST*, THE COMPANION TITLE TO *FABLES*. IN ADDITION MARK HAS ALSO BEEN THE REGULAR COVER ARTIST, CO-PLOTTER AND PENCILLER/LAYOUT ARTIST ON *DEAD BOY DETECTIVES*, SPINNING NEIL GAIMAN'S CHARACTERS FROM *SANDMAN* #25 INTO THEIR OWN MONTHLY COMIC WITH NOVELIST TOBY LITT. IN THE SUMMER OF 2015 MARK REUNITED WITH NEIL GAIMAN AS THEY RETURNED TO WORK, AFTER A TWENTY-TWO YEAR WAIT, ON *MIRACLEMAN* FOR MARVEL COMICS.

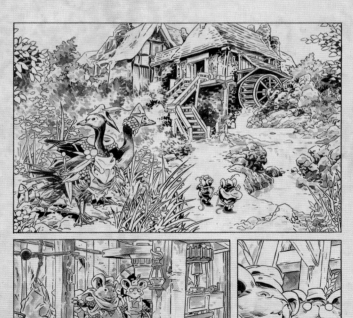

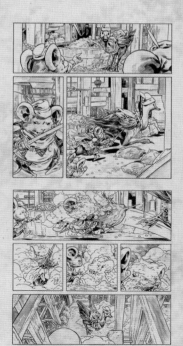

SKOTTIE YOUNG HAS BEEN CARTOONING HIS WAY THRU COMICS SINCE 2001. GETTING HIS START AT MARVEL ON TITLES LIKE *SPIDER-MAN: LEGEND OF THE SPIDER CLAN*, *HUMAN TORCH*, AND *VENOM*, HE SOON MOVED ONTO RELAUNCHING *NEW WARRIORS* WITH ZEB WELLS AND A RUN ON *NEW X-MEN*. IN 2008 SKOTTIE, ALONG WITH ERIC SHANOWER, BEGAN ADAPTING THE L. FRANK BAUM *OZ* NOVELS AT MARVEL. OVER SIX VOLUMES, THE *OZ GRAPHIC NOVELS* BECAME *NEW YORK TIMES* BEST SELLERS AND WON MULTIPLE EISNER AWARDS. HE IS CURRENTLY BEST KNOWN FOR WRITING AND DRAWING THE HIT SERIES *ROCKET RACCOON*, ILLUSTRATING THE CHILDREN'S BOOK *FORTUNATELY, THE MILK* BY NEIL GAIMAN, AND THE YOUNG MARVEL VARIANT COVERS. SKOTTIE LIVES IN ILLINOIS WITH HIS WIFE CASEY, THEIR SON, THEIR SAINT BERNARD AND GOLDEN DOODLE.

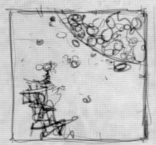

HANNAH CHRISTENSON CREATES ILLUSTRATIONS FOR BOOKS, COMICS, AND GAMES. HER WORK HAS BEEN RECOGNIZED BY A VARIETY OF PUBLICATIONS INCLUDING THE SOCIETY OF ILLUSTRATORS AND SPECTRUM. WHEN SHE'S NOT WORKING, HANNAH CAN BE FOUND ADVENTURING ON SOME SIDE-QUEST IN SEARCH OF TREASURES WITH HER TRUSTY ST. BERNARD COMPANION, LUCCA.

NICOLE GUSTAFSSON IS AN ARTIST AND ILLUSTRATOR LIVING IN THE PACIFIC NORTHWEST. ORIGINALLY FROM NEBRASKA, SHE LOVES THE OUTDOORS AND CONTINUES TO BE INSPIRED BY THE NATURAL WORLD. SHE SPECIALIZES IN TRADITIONAL MEDIA PAINTINGS FEATURING THEMES OF ADVENTURE AND EXPLORATION IN THE FANTASTICAL ENVIRONMENTS. NICOLE RESIDES IN WASHINGTON STATE WITH HER HUSBAND AND FELLOW CREATIVE C.M. GALDRE. TO VIEW NICOLE'S LATEST VENTURE, VISIT NIMASPROUT.COM.

C.M. GALDRE IS A WRITER, CRAFTSMAN, AND GAME DESIGNER LIVING IN THE PACIFIC NORTHWEST. HE SPECIALIZES IN WORKS OF FANTASY AND HORROR, OFTEN ON A GRAND SCALE. HE IS PART OF THE COLLECTIVE WRITING GROUP SWORD AND PORTENT (SWORDANDPORTENT.COM) AND IS THE VENERATED DUNGEON MASTER FOR THE MIGHTY STRONG LADIES (STRONGLADYDND.COM). ONE MIGHT CALL HIM AN ESCAPIST, BUT IF YOU GREW UP IN THE MIDWESTERN UNITED STATES YOU WOULDN'T HOLD IT AGAINST HIM. HE LIVES WITH A MENAGERIE OF STRANGE CREATURES INCLUDING TWO MASSIVE CATS, A PRINCELING DOG, AND A RESIDENT ARTIST. MORE OF C.M. GALDRE'S WORK CAN BE FOUND AT CMGALDRE.COM.

The Fall of Brierwall

PAGE 1
Panel 1: Full Page Panel Depicts thriving market scene in the heart of Brierwall. Brier branches weave throughout the city. (also contains title and author info).
"Brierwall stood upon the edge of the wild north, a bastion against the cold and the creatures that dwelled there. A center for trade and industry for all who lived near the edge of the great cold plains."

PAGE 2
Panel 1: Wide panel showing the city of Brierwall
"The great bramble wall had stood for an age. The city growing ever in its shadow"

Panel 2: A close up view of Lord Rond
"The Fortress Keep ruled by benevolent Lord Rond the Bulwark"

Panel 3: A close up view of Ivytha looking over the city
"and his beloved daughter Ivytha."

PAGE 3
Panel 1: View of Lord Rond pans out and you see he is in a trophy room. Feathers, mounts, bones, and relics of his hunts clutter the room.
"The King was a foe hunter, a warrior mouse who excelled at finding and defeating the enemies of Brierwall before they could prove a danger to the city.

Panel 2: King packing a bag for traveling
"A dangerous hobby"

Panel 3: King leaving the city into the northern wilds
" which eventually brought him to the cold lands beyond

the wall."

Panel 4: A wolf pack on a hill overlooking the expedition
"And that is how the trouble began."

PAGE 4
Panel 1: Large white wolf faces down smaller dark wolves
"For in that year a Winter Wolf had found his way among the northern packs"

Panel 2: Detail view of white wolf muzzle chewing bones
"His cruelty and hunger turned his cold eye south to the wall and the warm lands beyond."

Panel 3: King Rond in his adventuring gear wondering the snowy wild

Panel 4: Aerial view of King Rond surrounded by wolf pack.
"So strode King Rond into the Winter Wolfs domain"

PAGE 5
Panel 1: King Rond bristling for battle in the shadow of a wolf
"Now King Rond was a mighty warrior, a Guardmouse through and through."

Panel 2: Detail view of King Rond. His glaive breaks in the fight.

Panel 3: Broken Glaive (King Ronds weapon), with broken shield in snowy wolf prints
"But age, experience, and valor were no match for the wolf of winter."

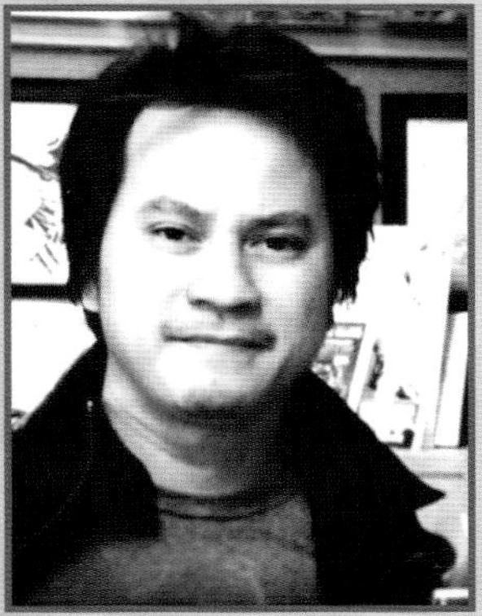

DUSTIN NGUYEN IS BEST KNOWN FOR HIS MANY INTERPRETATIONS OF BATMAN FOR DC COMICS, INCLUDING THE CO-CREATION OF DC'S ALL AGES SERIES *BATMAN: LIL GOTHAM* WRITTEN BY HIMSELF AND DEREK FRIDOLFS. CURRENTLY, HE ILLUSTRATES LOTS AND LOTS OF ROBOTS AND ALIENS ON *DESCENDER*, A MONTHLY COMIC PUBLISHED THROUGH IMAGE COMICS WHICH HE IS ALSO CO-CREATOR OF, ALONGSIDE ARTIST/WRITER JEFF LEMIRE. OUTSIDE OF COMICS, DUSTIN ALSO MOONLIGHTS AS A CONCEPTUAL ARTIST FOR TOYS AND CONSUMER PRODUCTS, GAMES, AND ANIMATION. HE ENJOYS SLEEPING, DRIVING, AND SKETCHING THINGS HE CARES ABOUT.

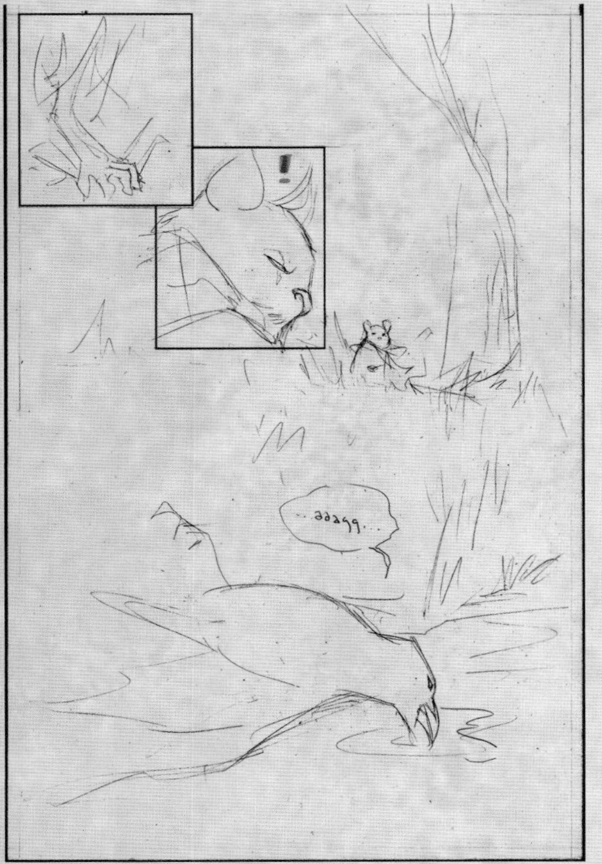
...aaagg...

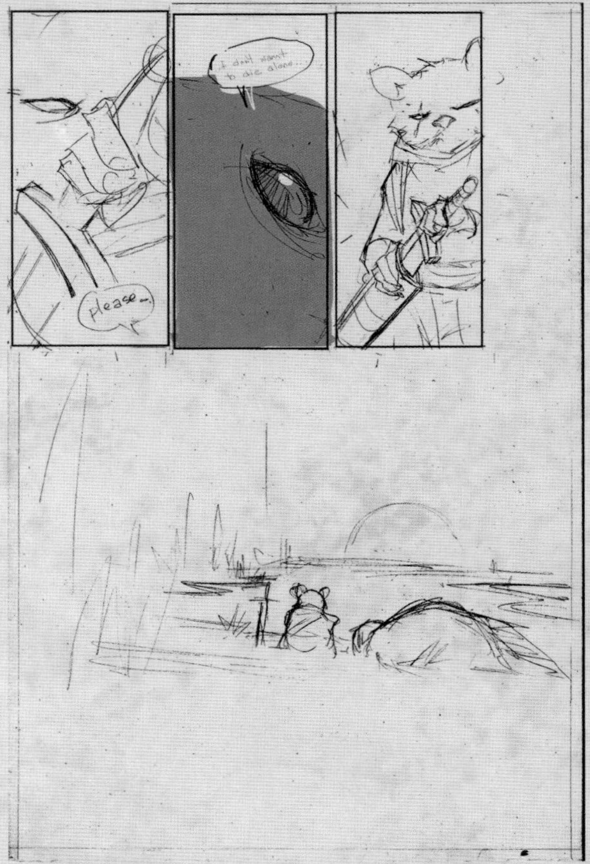
Please...
I don't want to die alone...

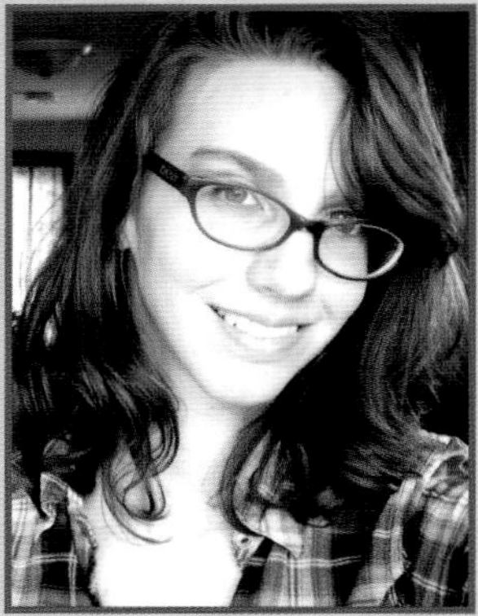

KYLA VANDERKLUGT WAS BORN, RAISED, EDUCATED AND PARTIALLY CIVILISED IN TORONTO BEFORE SHE MOVED TO RURAL ONTARIO TO WORK AS A FREELANCE ILLUSTRATOR IN THE COUNTRYSIDE AND FORGET ALL HER MANNERS. HER COMICS WORK INCLUDES CONTRIBUTIONS TO THE *FLIGHT* AND *NOBROW* ANTHOLOGIES, *SPERA*, *JIM HENSON'S THE STORYTELLER: WITCHES*, AND VARIOUS SELF-PUBLISHED SHORTS. THIS IS HER FIRST TIME DRAWING WARRIOR MICE, BUT SHE WAGES BATTLE AGAINST THEM IN HER DAILY LIFE AS THEY ENCROACH ON THE TERRITORIES OF HER PANTRY AND SOCK DRAWER.

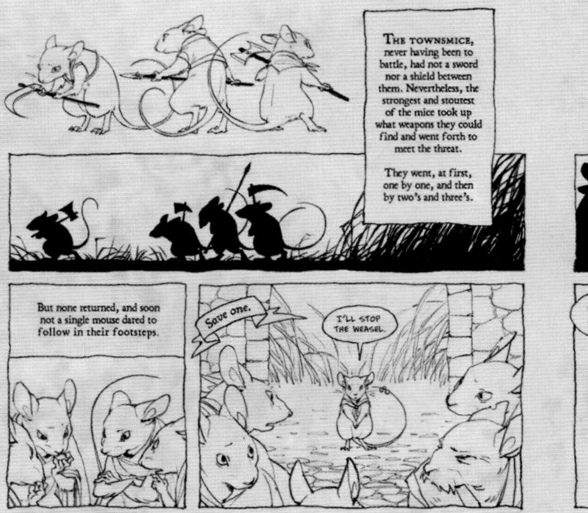
THE TOWNSMICE, never having been to battle, had not a sword nor a shield between them. Nevertheless, the strongest and stoutest of the mice took up what weapons they could find and went forth to meet the threat.
They went, at first, one by one, and then by two's and three's.
But none returned, and soon not a single mouse dared to follow in their footsteps.
Save one.
I'LL STOP THE WEASEL.

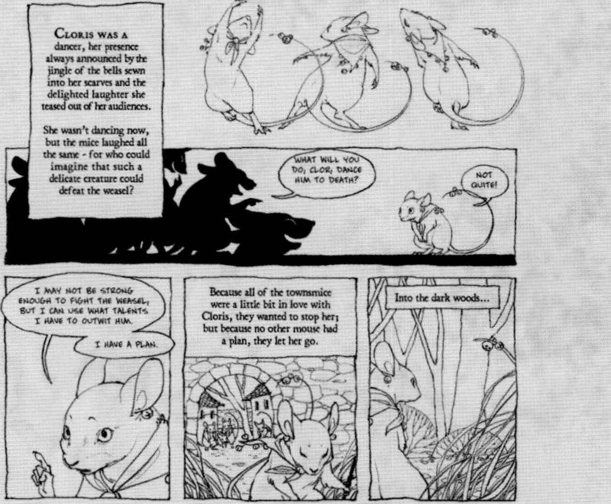
CLORIS WAS A dancer, her presence always announced by the jingle of the bells sewn into her scarves and the delighted laughter she teased out of her audiences.
She wasn't dancing now, but the mice laughed all the same - for who could imagine that such a delicate creature could defeat the weasel?
WHAT WILL YOU DO, CLOR, DANCE HIM TO DEATH?
NOT QUITE!
I MAY NOT BE STRONG ENOUGH TO FIGHT THE WEASEL, BUT I CAN USE WHAT TALENTS I HAVE TO OUTWIT HIM.
I HAVE A PLAN.
Because all of the townsmice were a little bit in love with Cloris, they wanted to stop her; but because no other mouse had a plan, they let her go.
Into the dark woods...

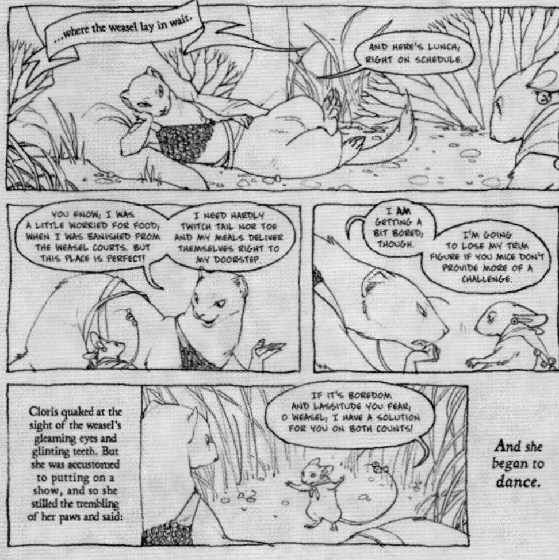
...where the weasel lay in wait.
AND HERE'S LUNCH, RIGHT ON SCHEDULE.
YOU KNOW, I WAS A LITTLE WORRIED FOR FOOD, WHEN I WAS BANISHED FROM THE WEASEL COURTS. BUT THIS PLACE IS PERFECT!
I NEED HARDLY TWITCH TAIL NOR TOE AND MY MEALS DELIVER THEMSELVES RIGHT TO MY DOORSTEP.
I AM GETTING A BIT BORED, THOUGH.
I'M GOING TO LOSE MY TRIM FIGURE IF YOU MICE DON'T PROVIDE MORE OF A CHALLENGE.
Cloris quaked at the sight of the weasel's gleaming eyes and glinting teeth. But she was accustomed to putting on a show, and so she stilled the trembling of her paws and said:
IF IT'S BOREDOM AND LASSITUDE YOU FEAR, O WEASEL, I HAVE A SOLUTION FOR YOU ON BOTH COUNTS!
And she began to dance.

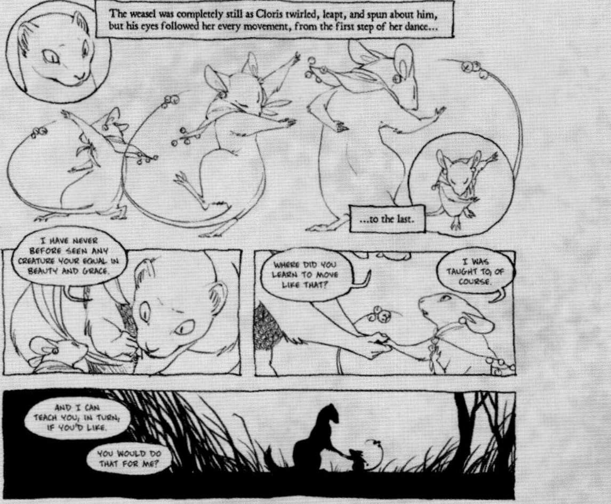
The weasel was completely still as Cloris twirled, leapt, and spun about him, but his eyes followed her every movement, from the first step of her dance...
...to the last.
I HAVE NEVER BEFORE SEEN ANY CREATURE YOUR EQUAL IN BEAUTY AND GRACE.
WHERE DID YOU LEARN TO MOVE LIKE THAT?
I WAS TAUGHT TO, OF COURSE.
AND I CAN TEACH YOU, IN TURN, IF YOU'D LIKE.
YOU WOULD DO THAT FOR ME?

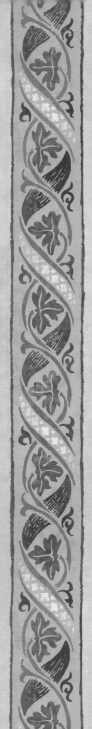

MARK A. NELSON IS CURRENTLY A FREELANCE ARTIST AT GRAZING DINOSAUR PRESS. HIS CURRENT PROJECT IS *THUNDER HUNTERS*, THE STORY OF AN ARTIST ON A FOREIGN PLANET. HIS PREVIOUS WORK INCLUDES: ARTWORK FOR THE HARVEY NOMINATED *ALIENS* COMIC WITH MARK VERHEIDEN FOR DARK HORSE; *BLOOD AND SHADOWS*, A CREATOR OWNED COMIC FOR DC COMICS CO-CREATED WITH JOE R. LANSDALE; *FEUD*, A CREATOR OWNED COMIC FOR MARVEL CO-CREATED WITH MIKE BARON; *HELLRAISER*, *NIGHTBREED*, *HEAVY METAL*, *DHP*, *TSR*, AND MORE. MARK HAS ALSO BEEN A PROFESSOR OF ART AT NORTHERN ILLINOIS UNIVERSITY, LEAD TEACHER IN THE ANIMATION AREA AT MADISON AREA TECHNICAL COLLEGE, PROFESSOR AT SCAD IN THE SEQA DEPARTMENT, AND WORKING IN VIDEO GAMES AS THE ART DIRECTOR AT PI STUDIOS AND SENIOR ARTIST AT RAVEN SOFTWARE.

WWW.GRAZINGDINOSAURPRESS.COM
WWW.FACEBOOK.COM/GRAZINGDINOSAURPRESS
WWW.MANSYC.DEVIANTART.COM

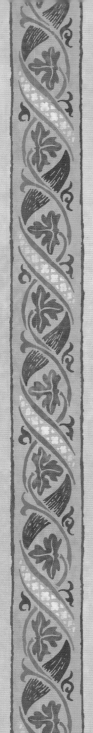

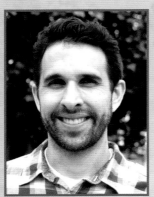

JAKE PARKER HAS WORKED ON EVERYTHING FROM ANIMATED FILMS TO COMICS TO PICTURE BOOKS FOR THE LAST 15 YEARS. HIS COMIC CREDITS INCLUDE *ROCKET RACCOON* FOR MARVEL COMICS, *MISSILE MOUSE* FOR GRAPHIX, AND THE SELF-PUBLISHED ANTHOLOGY *THE ANTLER BOY AND OTHER STORIES*. HE WORKS OUT OF HIS HOME STUDIO IN UTAH.

THE INVENTOR
BY JAKE PARKER

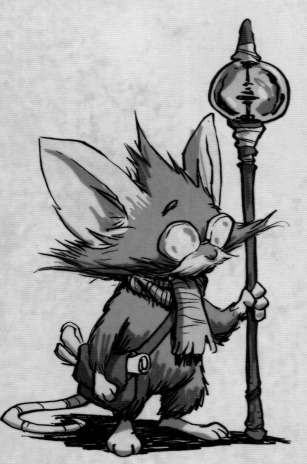

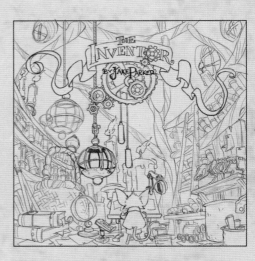

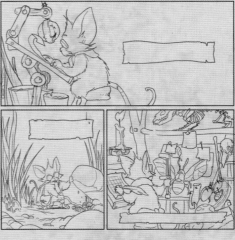

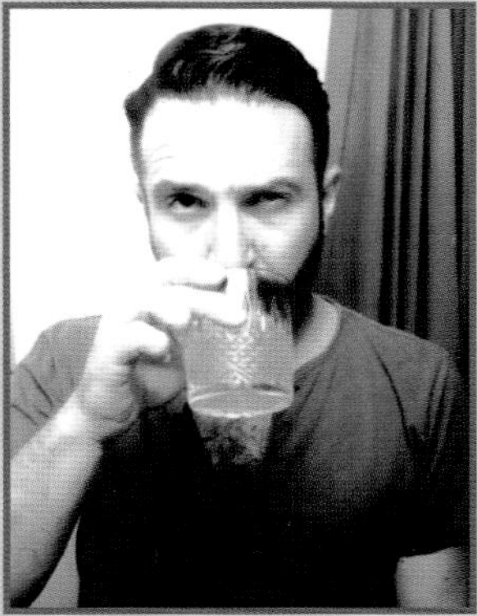

RAMÓN K. PÉREZ IS THE MULTIPLE EISNER AND HARVEY AWARD WINNING CARTOONIST BEST KNOWN FOR HIS GRAPHIC NOVEL ADAPTATION OF *JIM HENSON'S TALE OF SAND* FOR PUBLISHER ARCHAIA ENTERTAINMENT. OTHER LAUDED SEQUENTIAL WORKS INCLUDE *ALL-NEW HAWKEYE*, *THE AMAZING SPIDER-MAN: LEARNING TO CRAWL*, *JOHN CARTER: THE GODS OF MARS*, *WOLVERINE & THE X-MEN*, AND CREATOR OWNED ENDEAVOURS *BUTTERNUTSQUASH* AND *KUKUBURI*. OUTSIDE OF COMICS, RAMÓN'S WORK CAN BE FOUND IN CLASSIC RPG'S AND CCG'S, AND IN VARIOUS EDITORIAL, BOOK, AND ADVERTISING ILLUSTRATION. RAMÓN RESIDES IN TORONTO, IN A HORSE HOUSE, WITH HIS THREE PLANTS AND BOBA FETT.

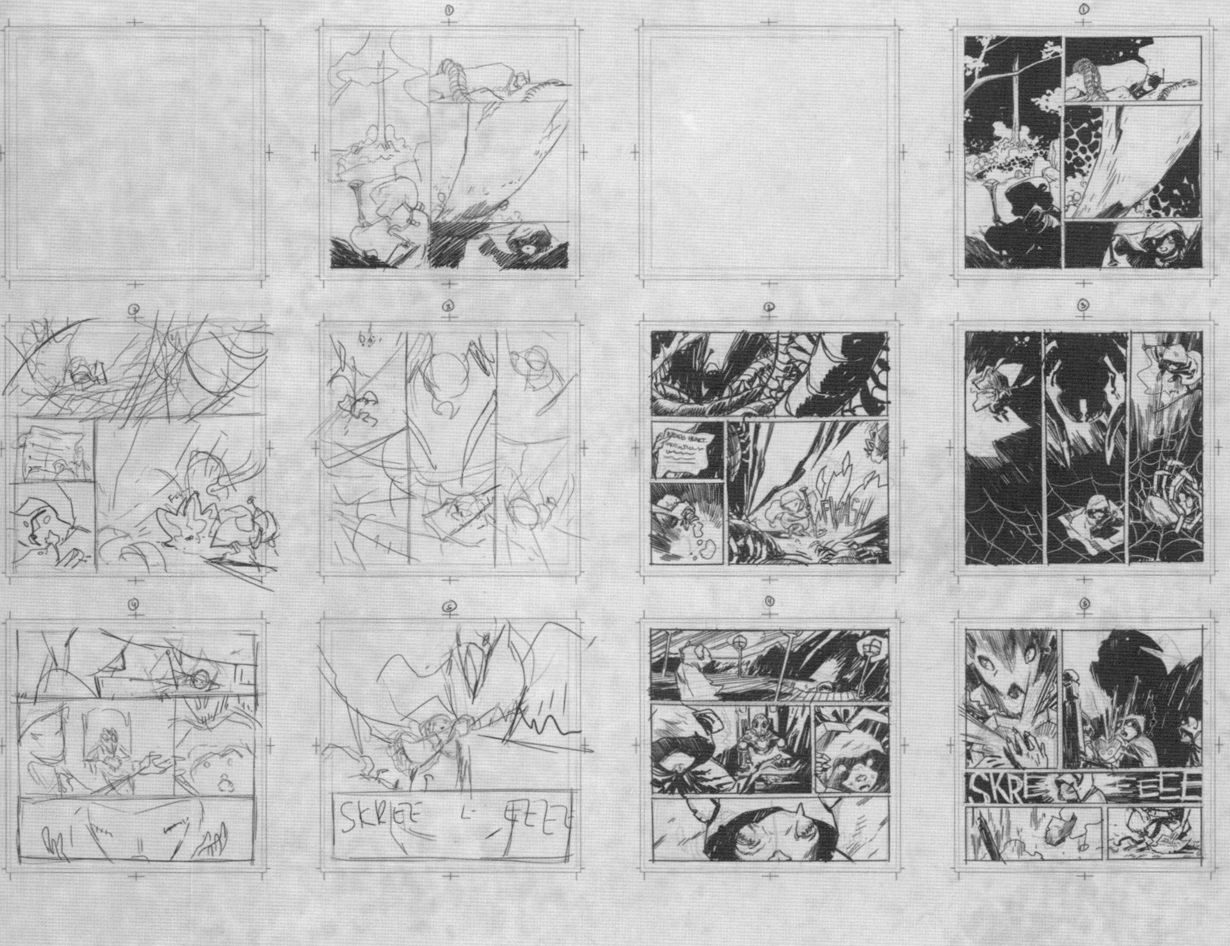

PHOTO CREDIT: SETH KUSHNER

BECKY CLOONAN IS BEST KNOWN AS A CARTOONIST, DOING WORK FOR DC, VERTIGO, DARK HORSE, HARPER COLLINS, AND IMAGE, WINNING A FEW EISNER AWARDS ALONG THE WAY, BOTH FOR HER CRITICALLY ACCLAIMED SELF-PUBLISHED COMICS. IN 2012 SHE BROKE A GLASS CEILING, BECOMING THE FIRST WOMAN TO ILLUSTRATE AN ISSUE OF *BATMAN*. BESIDES COMICS, CLOONAN ALSO DOES ILLUSTRATION WORK FOR BANDS, MOVIES AND FUN. SHE ENJOYS ADVENTURE.

```
The Lament of Poor Lenora


We have a ghost that haunts these parts at night,

You might have seen her floating on the moors.

She sings a mournful song all dressed in white;

Her hands are blue, her face a veil obscures.


The daughter of a farmer, bright and fair,

Fell for a green-eyed stranger, tall and thin.

The warnings went unheeded in despair--

Her wedding gown the girl was buried in.


So when you walk at night through misty fields,

Stay on the path-- you must not linger long.

And heed my words or your fate will be sealed:

You must not ever listen to her song.


For if you hear her song of love long lost,

She'll have you for her beau at any cost.
```

AARON CONLEY IS THE WINNER OF THE 2014 RUSS MANNING AWARD FOR MOST OUTSTANDING NEWCOMER. HE IS THE CO-CREATOR AND ARTIST OF THE DARK HORSE GRAPHIC NOVEL *SABERTOOTH SWORDSMAN* AND ABOUT TO BEGIN WORK ON THE FOLLOW UP DUE OUT SOMETIME IN 2016. HIS FAVORITE MOUSE-RELATED THINGS (BESIDES *MOUSE GUARD* THAT IS) ARE THE *SECRET OF NIMH*, ROALD DAHL'S *THE WITCHES*, AND THE BAND MOUSE RAT. YOU CAN USUALLY FIND HIM SWEATING AWAY IN A TINY ART ROOM IN FLORIDA LISTENING TO PODCASTS WITH A BOSTON TERRIER ASLEEP NEARBY.

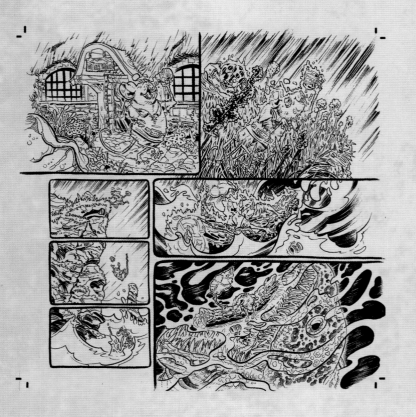

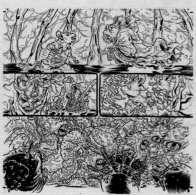

FABIAN RANGEL JR. HAS BEEN WRITING AND SELF PUBLISHING COMICS SINCE 2010. HE'S RUN FOUR SUCCESSFUL KICKSTARTER CAMPAIGNS THROUGH HIS BELIEVE IN COMICS IMPRINT, MOST NOTABLY, FOR HIS SUPERNATURAL PULP SERIES *DOC UNKNOWN* WITH RYAN CODY. FABIAN IS ALSO THE WRITER AND CO-CREATOR OF *SPACE RIDERS* WITH ALEXIS ZIRITT THROUGH BLACK MASK STUDIOS, AND *BLACK PAST* WITH PABLO CLARK IN THE PAGES OF *DARK HORSE PRESENTS*. FABIAN LIVES IN CORPUS CHRISTI, TEXAS WITH HIS AMAZING FAMILY AND SOME BATS.

The Deep and the Dark

PAGE ONE (FIVE PANELS)

PANEL ONE
Tall panel: Night. Here we see our main character WILHELM. He's a young mouse, early 20's (not sure if you'll be able to tell anyway). He's exiting a tavern, he's drunk, shaky, not walking in a straight line.
1 CAP: There was once a youngfur by the name of WILHELM.
2 CAP (2): Aimless as they come, it seemed his only talent was the ability to out-drink mice twice his age.

PANEL TWO
Small panel ABOVE Panel Three: WILHELM is now getting pelted by rain; he's having a hard time walking. Not sure if there will be room, but maybe put a glimpse of the river beside him.
3 CAP: One night the poor lad found himself caught in a storm as he stumbled his way home from the tavern.

PANEL THREE
Small panel UNDER Panel Two: I was thinking it would be cool to have two figures of Wilhelm, to show the action: 1. WILHELM has lost his footing, and is in mid-air as he topples over about to land in the rover. 2. Another WILHELM is falling into the river, with a splash.
4 CAP: A combination of obstructed field of vision and the aforementioned inebriation caused him to lose his footing.

PANEL FOUR
Wide panel: WILHEM is clinging to a twig (or leaf), being rained on, and holding on for dear life in the rapids of the river. His eyes are wide with fear.
5 CAP: The river had grown angry with the fury of the storm, and Wilhelm found himself being swept out to sea--

PANEL FIVE
Wide panel: WILHEM and the leaf are small on the surface of the water; underneath the water we can see the giant and ghastly head of THE EEL, looking up at him, its mouth wide open as it propels itself upward to swallow the mouse.
6 CAP: --and that's where his REAL trouble began.

PAGE TWO (THREE PANELS)

PANEL ONE
Half splash: Side profile shot of THE EEL, we can see inside of it, like an X-Ray, we can see it's bones, and the outline of its flesh/body. We can see WILHELM tumbling through its body towards its stomach. I like the idea of having this panel look like it's a page from an old zoological text book, or pirate map, yellow and stained coloring, an old diagram looking thing. Up to you, though.
1 CAP: A great and monstrous EEL swallowed him whole.
2 CAP (2): Wilhelm found himself--

PANEL TWO
Small panel: We are behind WILHELM, he is looking at a black and bone lined tunnel. It's way bigger than it should be, like a cave or tavern. Dark.
3 CAP: --in the BELLY of the BEAST.
4 WILHELM: ?!

PANEL THREE
Small panel: Close on WILHELM looking worried (still drunk).

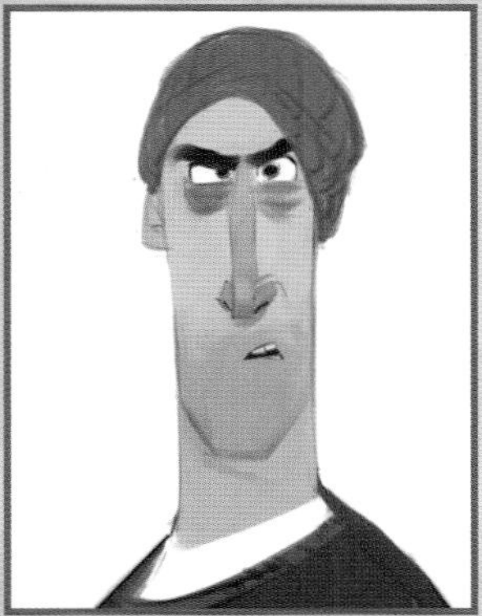

PORTRAIT CREDIT: CORY LOFTIS

RYAN LANG WAS BORN AND RAISED IN HAWAII, AND STARTED OUT AS A 3D MODELER AT A SMALL GAME COMPANY. AFTER RETURNING TO SCHOOL TO PURSUE AN ILLUSTRATION CAREER, HE BECAME A VISUAL DEVELOPMENT ARTIST AT WALT DISNEY ANIMATION STUDIOS WHERE HE WORKED ON *WRECK-IT RALPH* AND *BIG HERO 6*. CURRENTLY, HE IS A FREELANCE CONCEPT ARTIST WORKING IN FILM. CORY LOFTIS' CARICATURE OF HIM IS AN ACCURATE REPRESENTATION OF RYAN IN THE WILD.

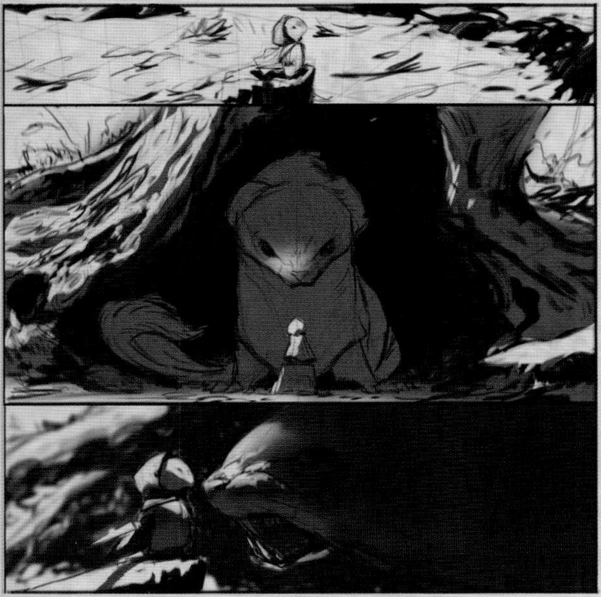

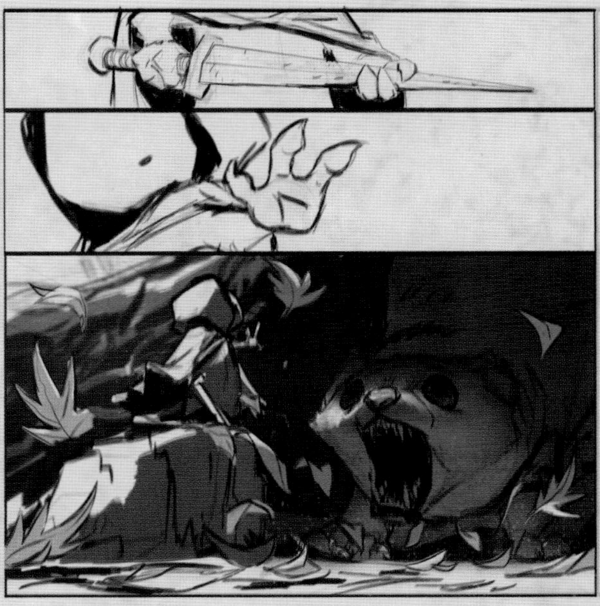

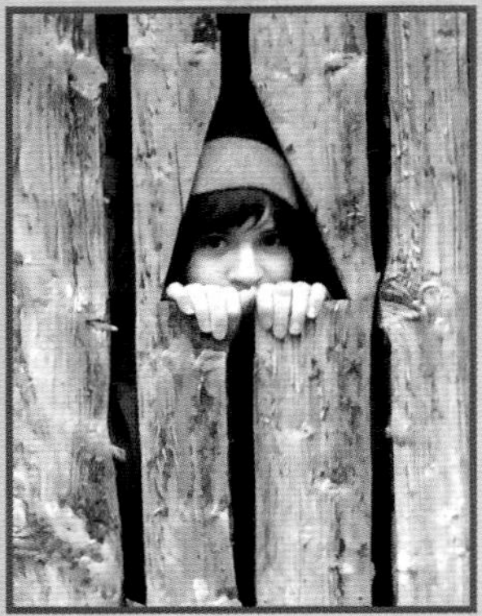

LAUREN PETTAPIECE IS A FREELANCE ILLUSTRATOR LIVING IN BOSTON. ORIGINALLY FROM PITTSBURGH, SHE GRADUATED FROM SYRACUSE UNIVERSITY WITH A BFA IN ILLUSTRATION. IN COLLEGE, A TEACHER USED THE TERM "IMPISH" TO DESCRIBE HER IN THE MARGIN OF A CLASS ROSTER. SHE CURRENTLY WORKS AS A CHILDREN'S BOOK DESIGNER MAKING BOOKS FOR YOUNG READERS. SHE CAN USUALLY BE FOUND HIKING OR BUYING TOO MANY USED BOOKS.

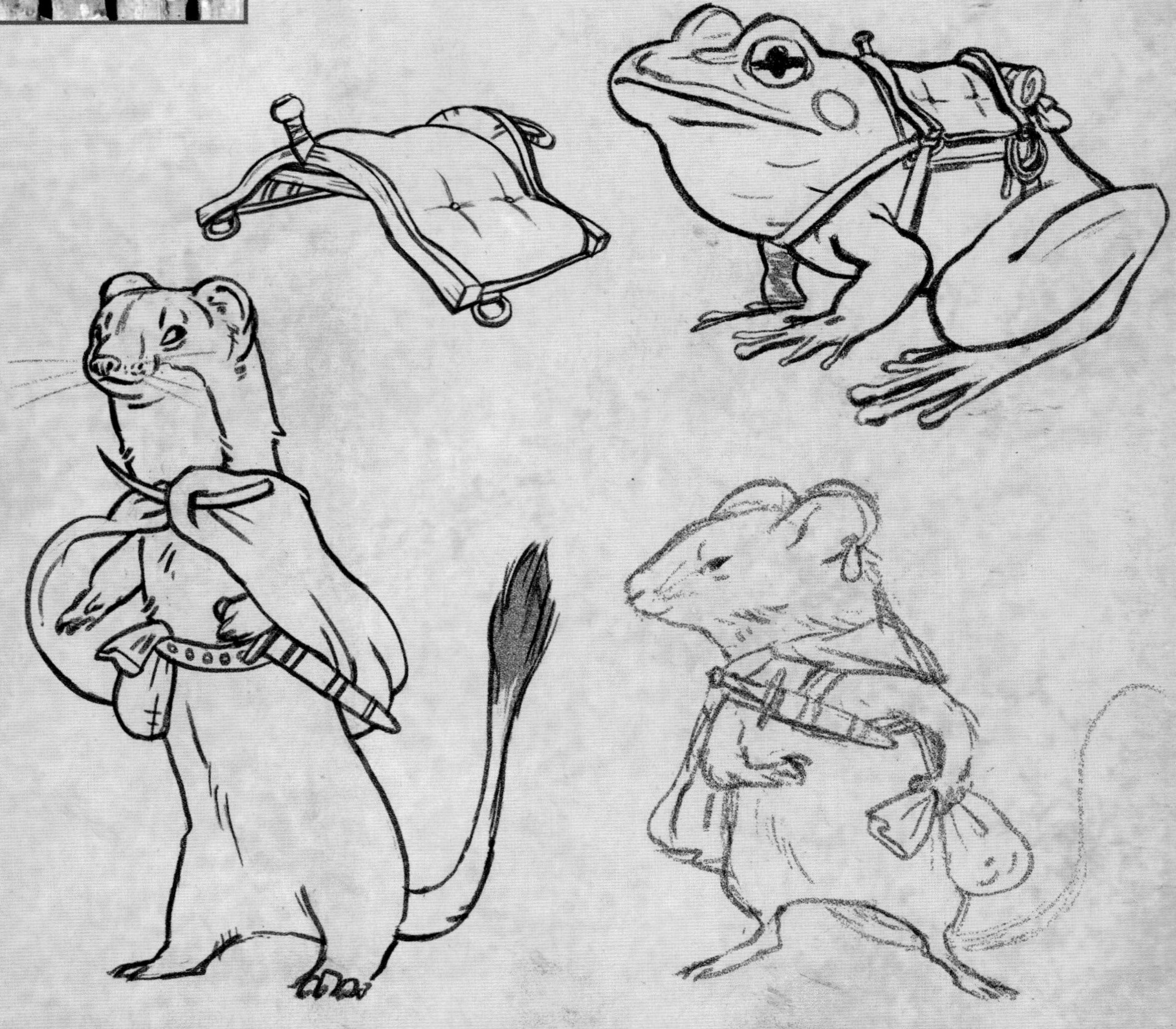

ERIC MULLER IS A PORTRAITIST AND ILLUSTRATOR. SPECIALIZING IN THE MONOCHROMATIC MEDIA, HIS TOOLS OF CHOICE ARE PEN AND INK AND PENCIL. HE ALSO ENJOYS MAKING SILHOUETTES AND PYROGRAPHY, OR WOODBURNED DRAWINGS ON UNFINISHED WOOD. HIS BUSINESS, HAND IN HAND ARTWORKS, IS LOCATED IN EASTERN PA WHERE HE IS A HUSBAND, A FATHER, AND HE OWES EVERYTHING TO OUR LORD AND SAVIOR.

HUMBERTO RAMOS WAS BORN IN MEXICO, AND WAS DISCOVERED BY LEGENDARY ARTIST WALT SIMONSON AND JON BOGDANOVE DURING THE 1993 SAN DIEGO COMIC-CON. HE GOT HIS FIRST ASSIGNMENT AT MILESTONE MEDIA, AND HAS CONTINUED TO WORK ON ICONIC TITLES WITH THE TOP PUBLISHERS IN THE UNITED STATES, TRULY MAKING HIS MARK AND BECOMING A WORLD-RENOWNED COMIC BOOK ARTIST. HE CURRENTLY STILL LIVES IN MEXICO, AND WE SUSPECT HE IS CREATING NEW STORIES AS YOU READ THIS.

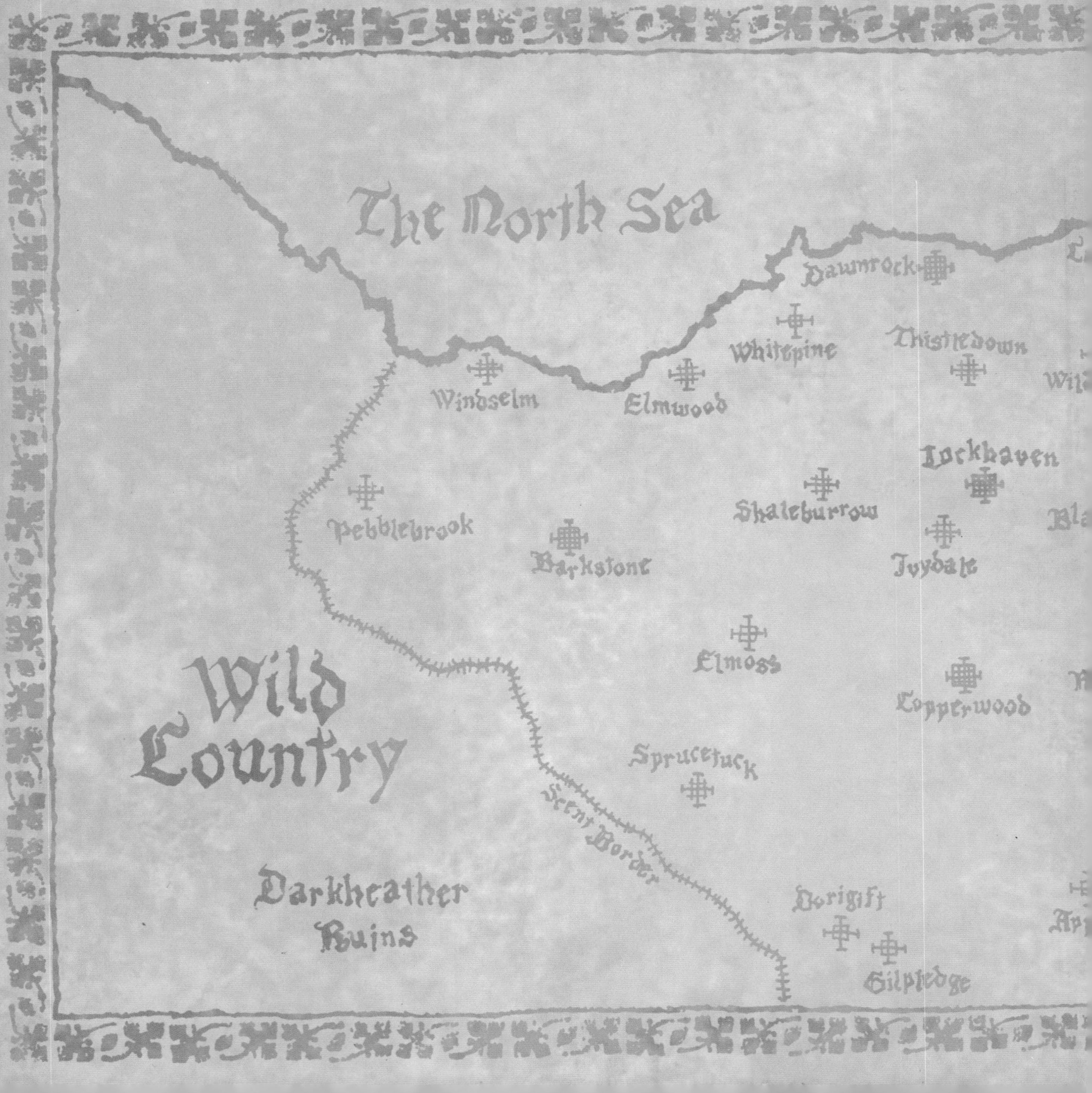

The North Sea
Dawnrock
Whitepine
Thistledown
Windselm
Elmwood
Lockhaven
Shaleburrow
Pebblebrook
Barkstone
Ivydale
Elmoss
Copperwood
Wild Country
Sprucetuck
Scent Border
Darkheather Ruins
Dorigift
Gilpledge